Teacher chool! Vol. 1

Maì Tanaka

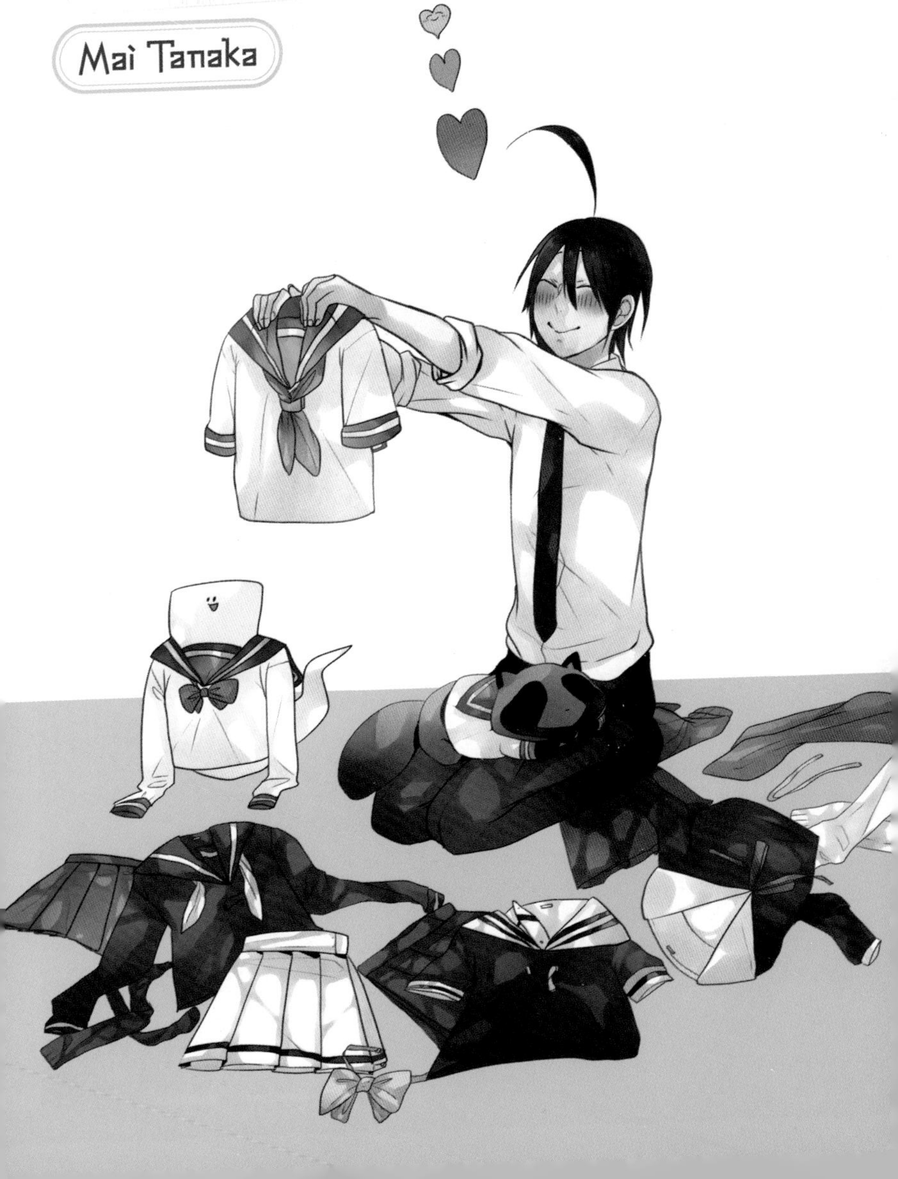

CONTENTS

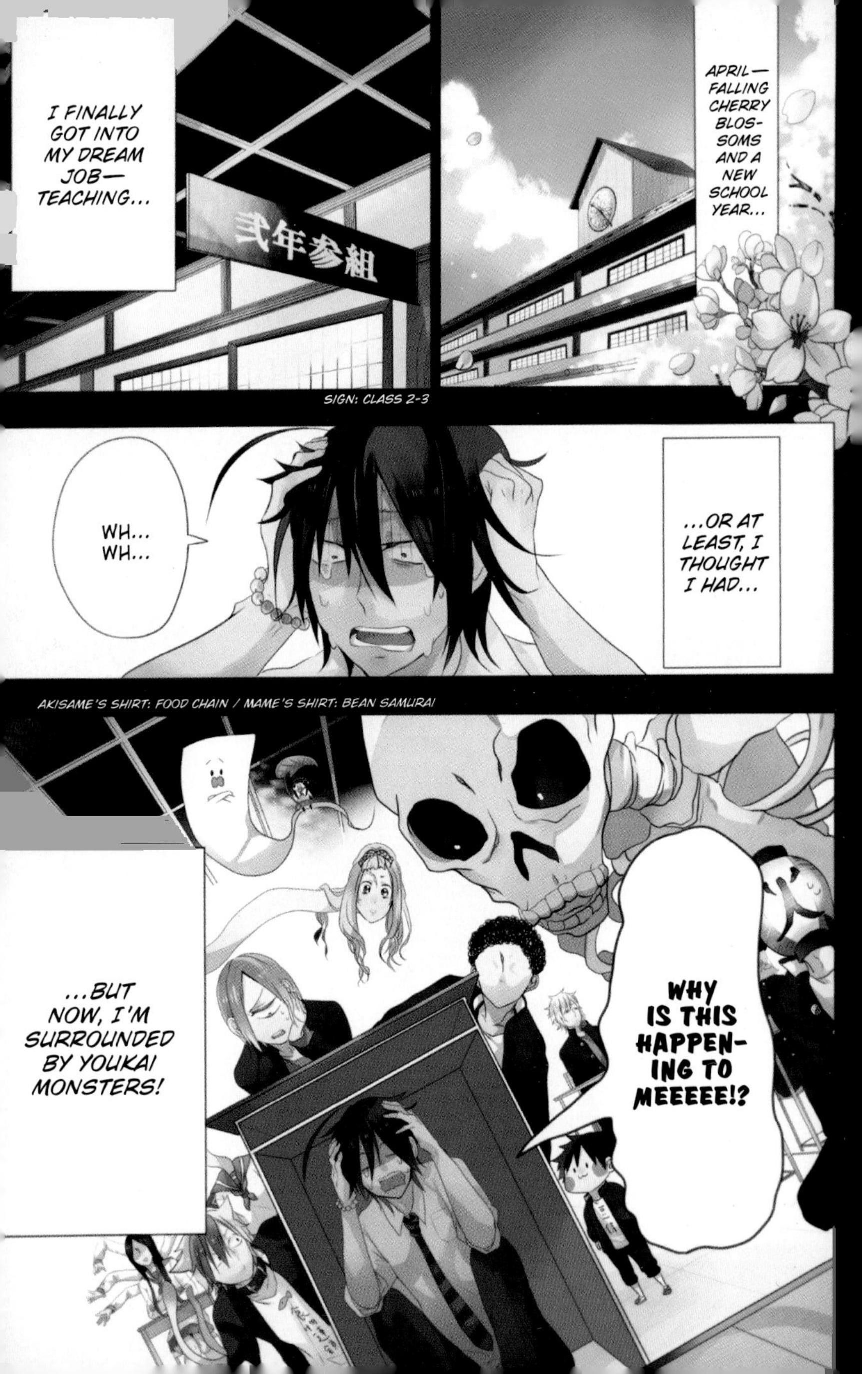
APRIL—FALLING CHERRY BLOSSOMS AND A NEW SCHOOL YEAR...
I FINALLY GOT INTO MY DREAM JOB—TEACHING...
弐年参組
SIGN: CLASS 2-3
...OR AT LEAST, I THOUGHT I HAD...
WH... WH...
AKISAME'S SHIRT: FOOD CHAIN / MAME'S SHIRT: BEAN SAMURAI
...BUT NOW, I'M SURROUNDED BY YOUKAI MONSTERS!
WHY IS THIS HAPPENING TO MEEEEE!?

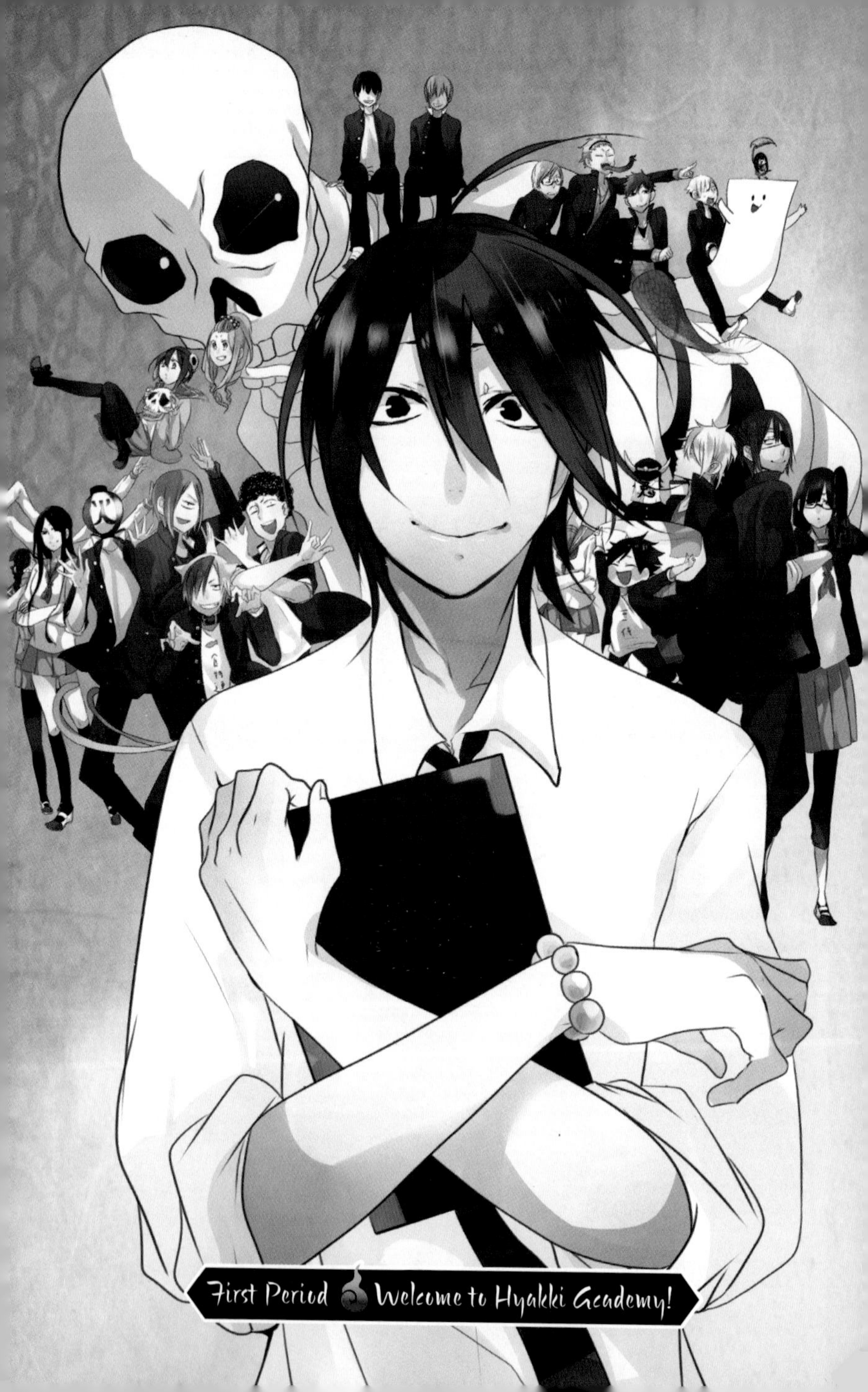
First Period Welcome to Hyakki Academy!

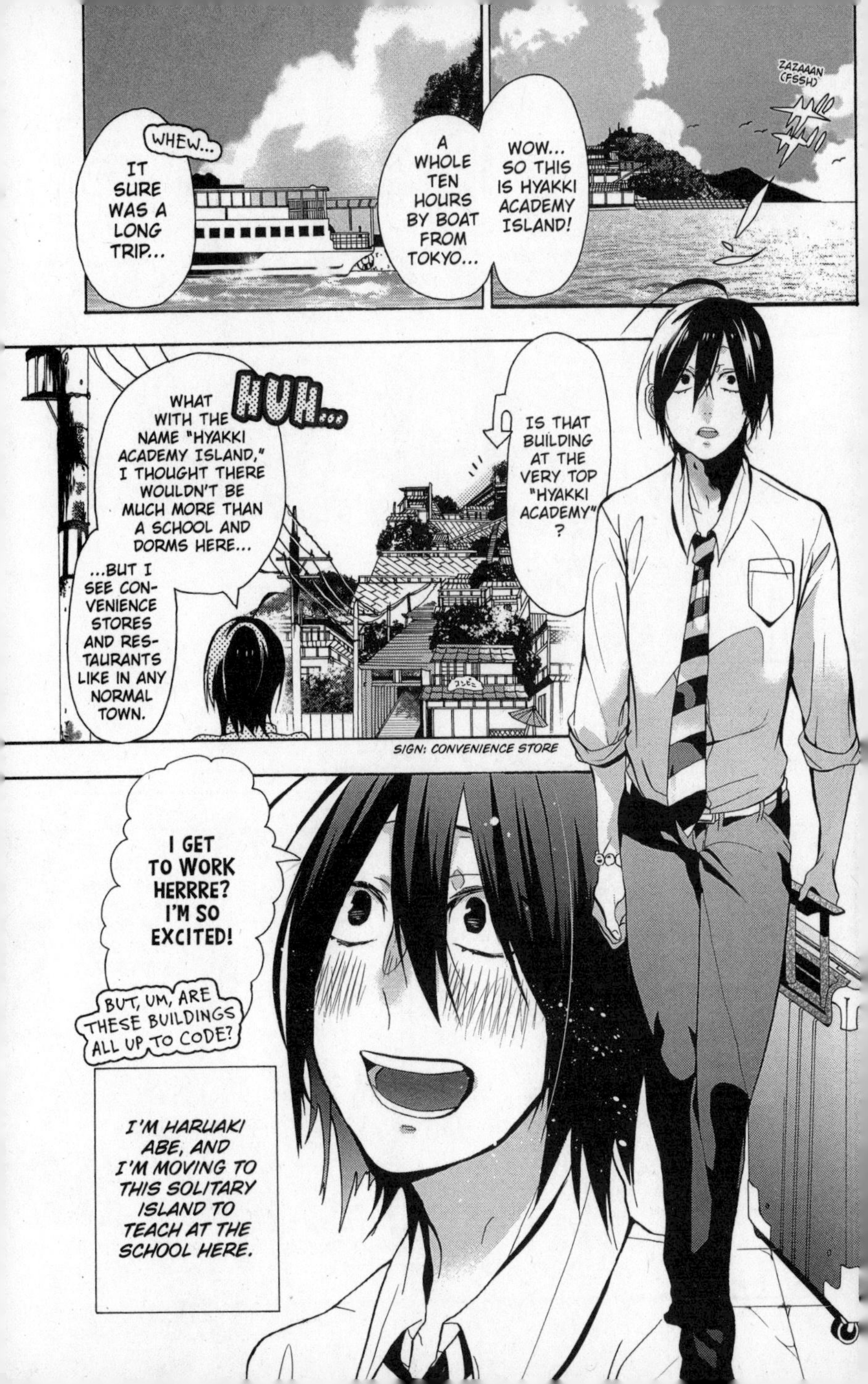
ZAZAAAN (FSSH)
WOW... SO THIS IS HYAKKI ACADEMY ISLAND!
A WHOLE TEN HOURS BY BOAT FROM TOKYO...
WHEW...
IT SURE WAS A LONG TRIP...
IS THAT BUILDING AT THE VERY TOP "HYAKKI ACADEMY"?
HUH...
WHAT WITH THE NAME "HYAKKI ACADEMY ISLAND," I THOUGHT THERE WOULDN'T BE MUCH MORE THAN A SCHOOL AND DORMS HERE...
...BUT I SEE CON-VENIENCE STORES AND RES-TAURANTS LIKE IN ANY NORMAL TOWN.
SIGN: CONVENIENCE STORE
I GET TO WORK HERRRE? I'M SO EXCITED!
BUT, UM, ARE THESE BUILDINGS ALL UP TO CODE?
I'M HARUAKI ABE, AND I'M MOVING TO THIS SOLITARY ISLAND TO TEACH AT THE SCHOOL HERE.

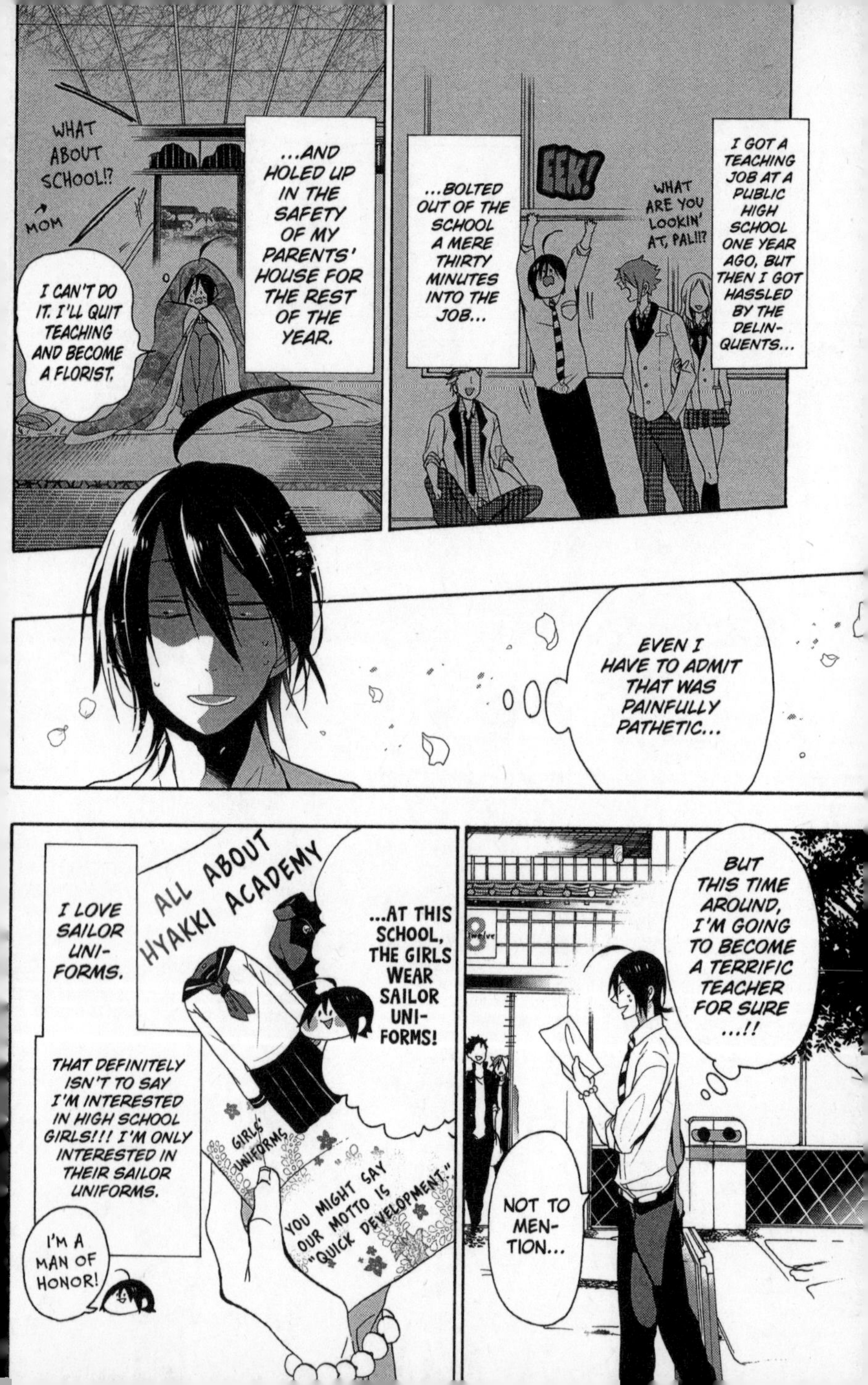
I GOT A TEACHING JOB AT A PUBLIC HIGH SCHOOL ONE YEAR AGO, BUT THEN I GOT HASSLED BY THE DELIN-QUENTS...
WHAT ARE YOU LOOKIN' AT, PAL!?
EEK!
...BOLTED OUT OF THE SCHOOL A MERE THIRTY MINUTES INTO THE JOB...
...AND HOLED UP IN THE SAFETY OF MY PARENTS' HOUSE FOR THE REST OF THE YEAR.
WHAT ABOUT SCHOOL!?
MOM
I CAN'T DO IT. I'LL QUIT TEACHING AND BECOME A FLORIST.
EVEN I HAVE TO ADMIT THAT WAS PAINFULLY PATHETIC...
BUT THIS TIME AROUND, I'M GOING TO BECOME A TERRIFIC TEACHER FOR SURE...!!
NOT TO MEN-TION...
ALL ABOUT HYAKKI ACADEMY
...AT THIS SCHOOL, THE GIRLS WEAR SAILOR UNI-FORMS!
GIRLS' UNIFORMS
YOU MIGHT SAY OUR MOTTO IS "QUICK DEVELOPMENT."
I LOVE SAILOR UNI-FORMS.
THAT DEFINITELY ISN'T TO SAY I'M INTERESTED IN HIGH SCHOOL GIRLS!!! I'M ONLY INTERESTED IN THEIR SAILOR UNIFORMS.
I'M A MAN OF HONOR!

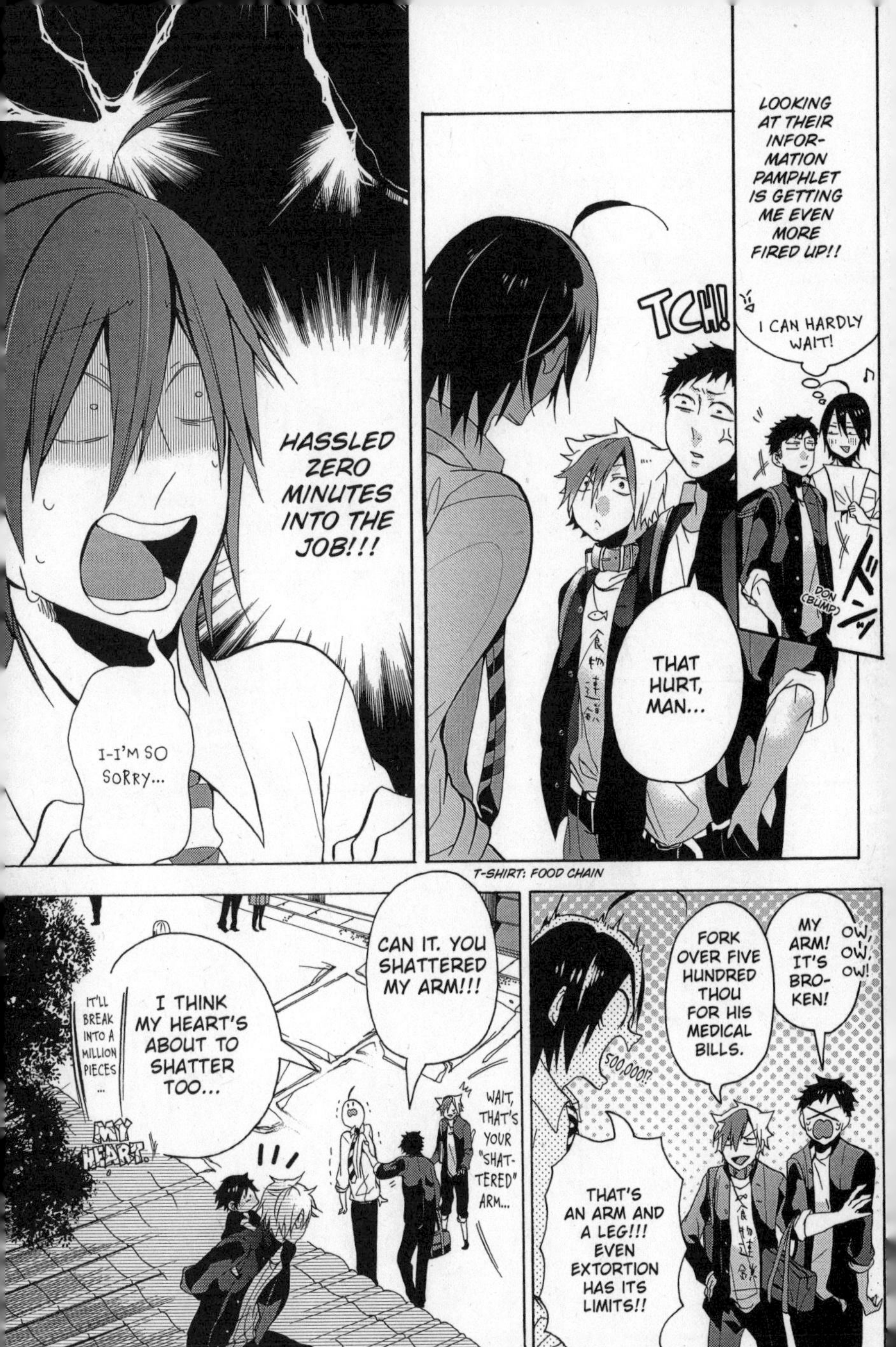
LOOKING AT THEIR INFORMATION PAMPHLET IS GETTING ME EVEN MORE FIRED UP!!
I CAN HARDLY WAIT!
DON (BUMP)
TCH!
THAT HURT, MAN...
HASSLED ZERO MINUTES INTO THE JOB!!!
I-I'M SO SORRY...
T-SHIRT: FOOD CHAIN
MY ARM! IT'S BRO-KEN!
OW, OW, OW!
FORK OVER FIVE HUNDRED THOU FOR HIS MEDICAL BILLS.
500,000!?
THAT'S AN ARM AND A LEG!!! EVEN EXTORTION HAS ITS LIMITS!!
CAN IT. YOU SHATTERED MY ARM!!!
WAIT, THAT'S YOUR "SHAT-TERED" ARM...
I THINK MY HEART'S ABOUT TO SHATTER TOO...
IT'LL BREAK INTO A MILLION PIECES...
MY HEART.

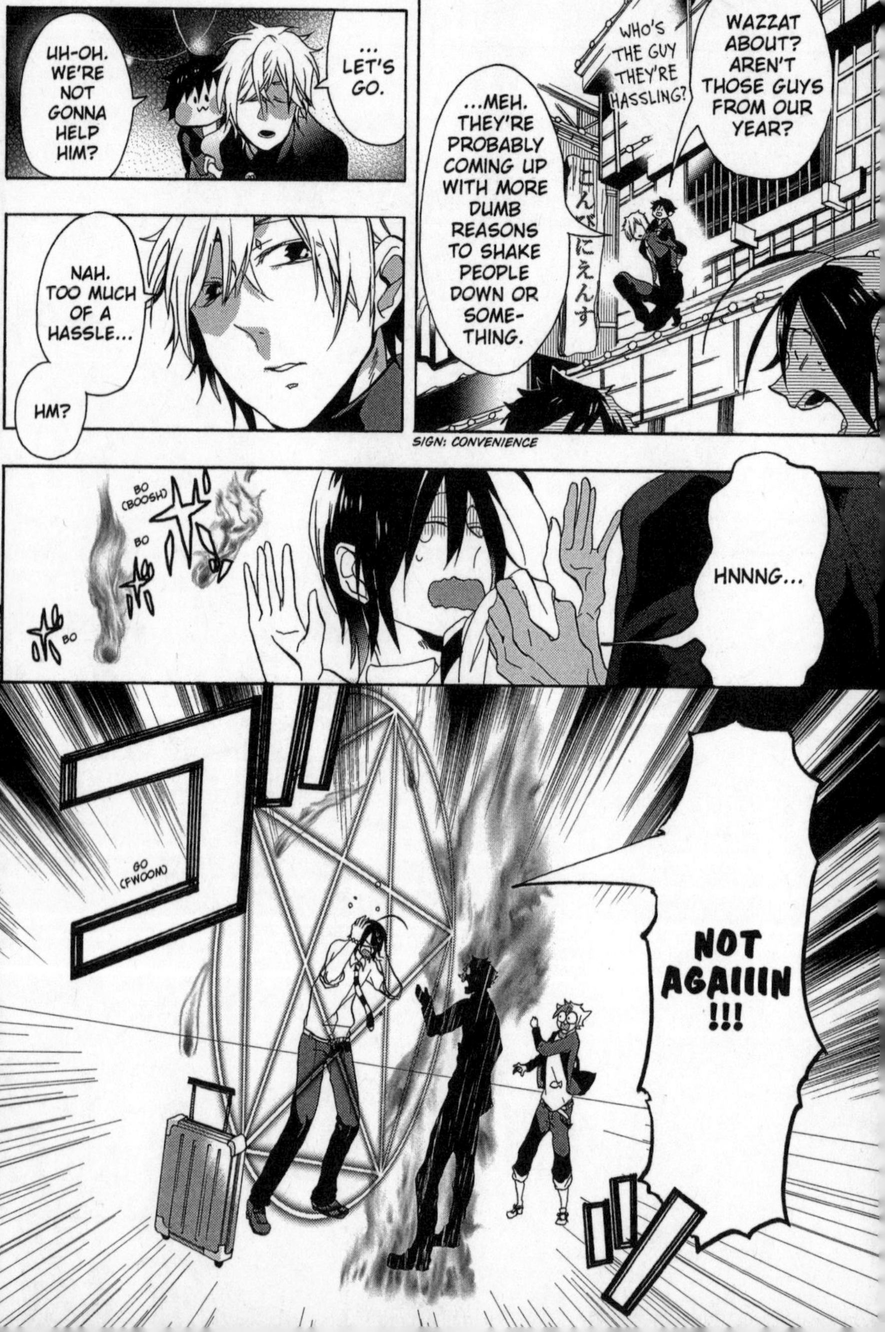
WAZZAT ABOUT? AREN'T THOSE GUYS FROM OUR YEAR?
WHO'S THE GUY THEY'RE HASSLING?
...MEH. THEY'RE PROBABLY COMING UP WITH MORE DUMB REASONS TO SHAKE PEOPLE DOWN OR SOME-THING.
にえんす
... LET'S GO.
UH-OH. WE'RE NOT GONNA HELP HIM?
NAH. TOO MUCH OF A HASSLE...
HM?
SIGN: CONVENIENCE
HNNNG...
BO (BOOSH)
BO
BO
NOT AGAIIIN!!!
GO (FWOOM)

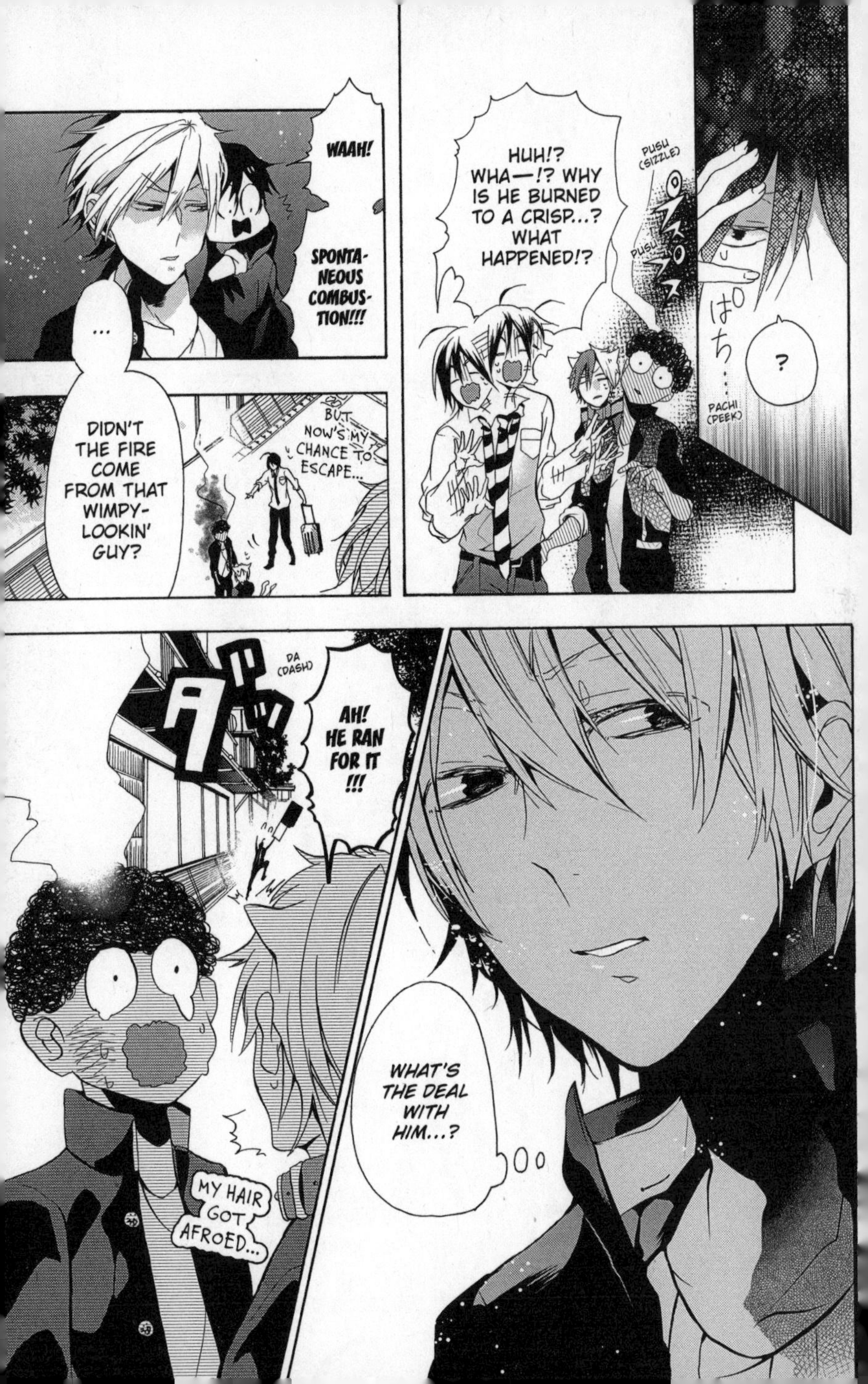
PUSU (SIZZLE)
PUSU
ぱち
PACHI (PEEK)
?
HUH!? WHA—!? WHY IS HE BURNED TO A CRISP...? WHAT HAPPENED!?
WAAH!
SPONTANEOUS COMBUSTION!!!
...
DIDN'T THE FIRE COME FROM THAT WIMPY-LOOKIN' GUY?
BUT NOW'S MY CHANCE TO ESCAPE...
WHAT'S THE DEAL WITH HIM...?
DA (DASH)
AH! HE RAN FOR IT!!!
MY HAIR GOT AFROED...

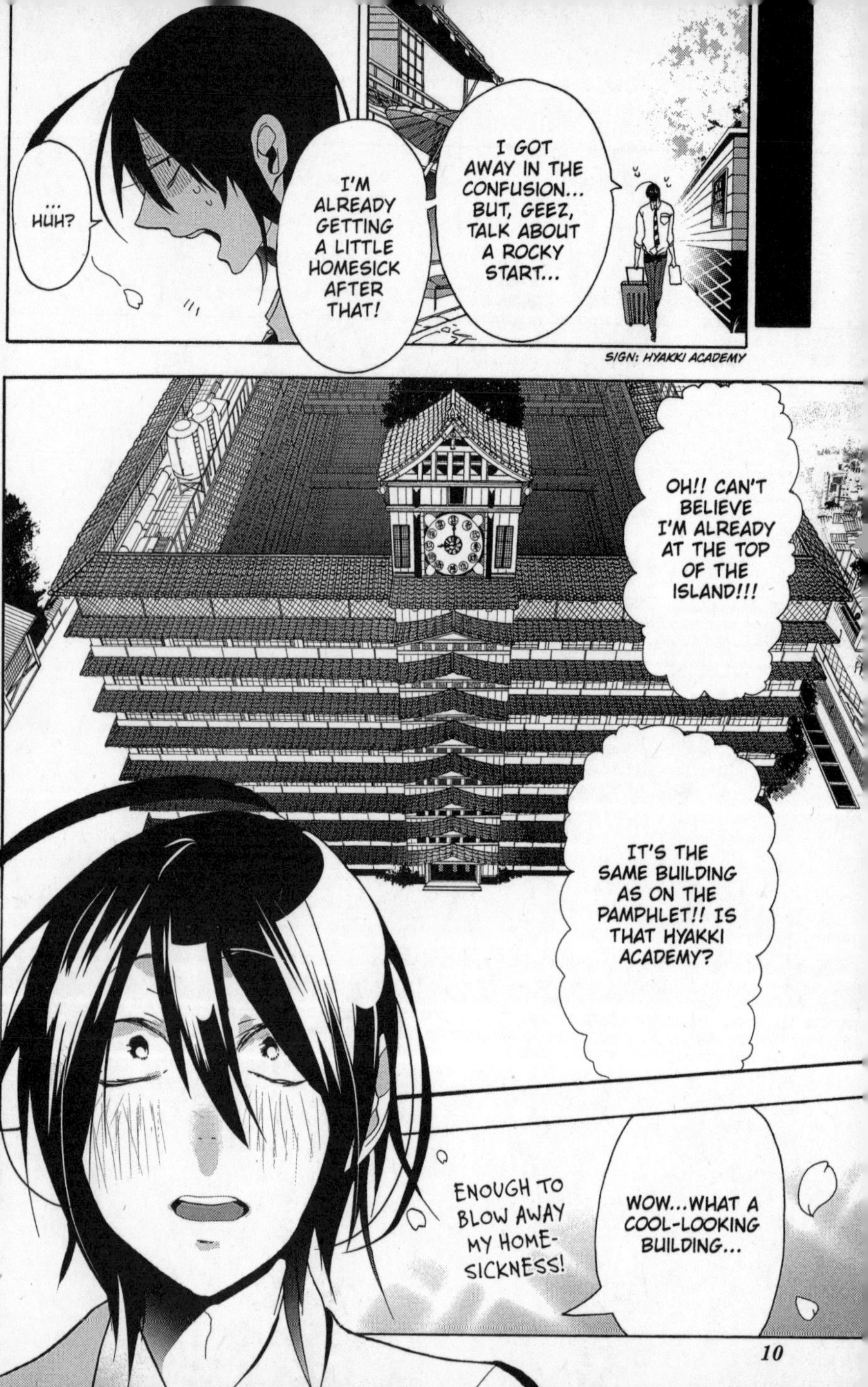
I GOT AWAY IN THE CONFUSION... BUT, GEEZ, TALK ABOUT A ROCKY START...
I'M ALREADY GETTING A LITTLE HOMESICK AFTER THAT!
...HUH?
SIGN: HYAKKI ACADEMY
OH!! CAN'T BELIEVE I'M ALREADY AT THE TOP OF THE ISLAND!!!
IT'S THE SAME BUILDING AS ON THE PAMPHLET!! IS THAT HYAKKI ACADEMY?
WOW...WHAT A COOL-LOOKING BUILDING...
ENOUGH TO BLOW AWAY MY HOME-SICKNESS!

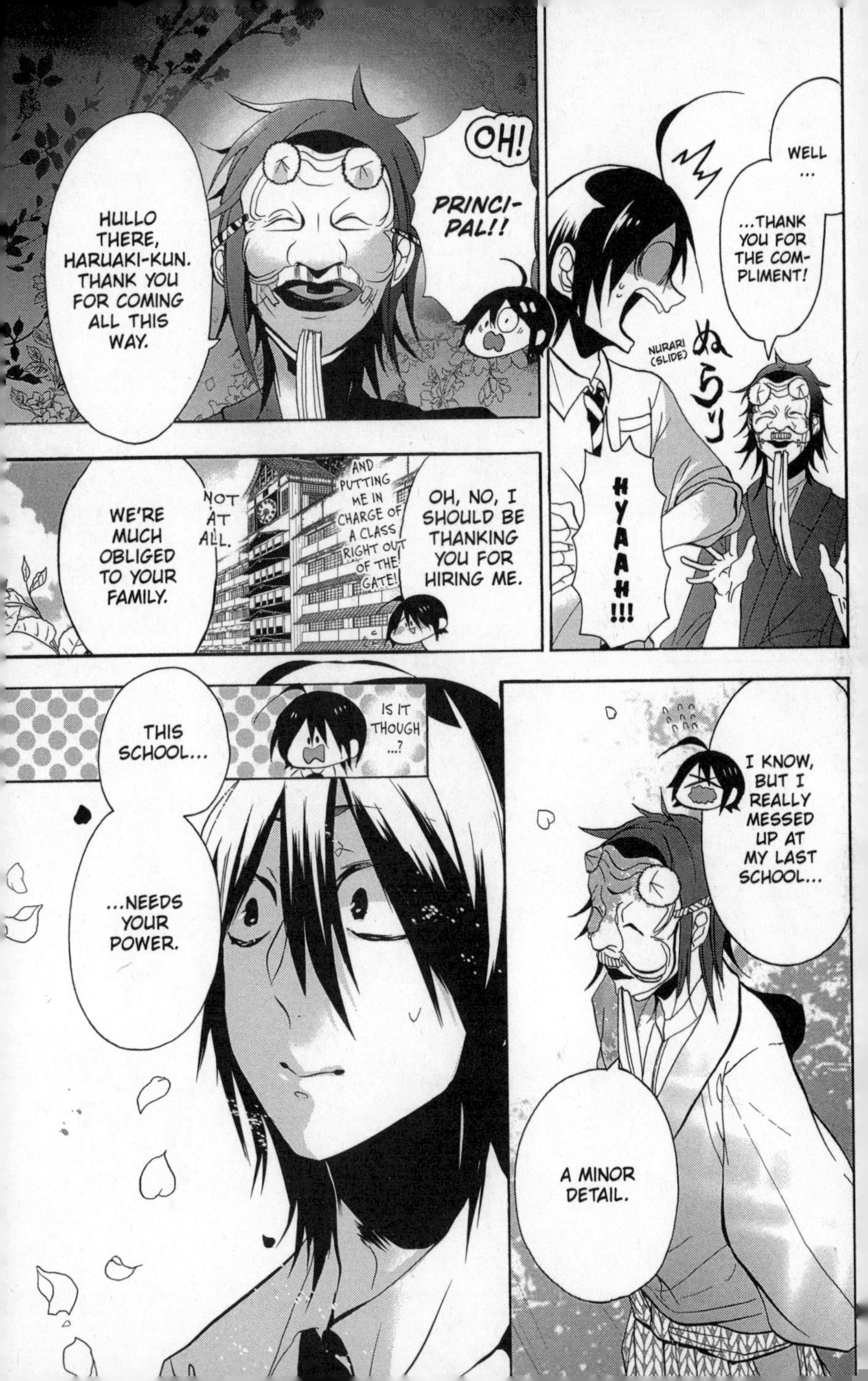
WELL ...
...THANK YOU FOR THE COMPLIMENT!
NURARI (SLIDE)
ぬらり
HYAAH!!!
OH!
PRINCIPAL!!
HULLO THERE, HARUAKI-KUN. THANK YOU FOR COMING ALL THIS WAY.
OH, NO, I SHOULD BE THANKING YOU FOR HIRING ME.
AND PUTTING ME IN CHARGE OF A CLASS RIGHT OUT OF THE GATE!
NOT AT ALL.
WE'RE MUCH OBLIGED TO YOUR FAMILY.
I KNOW, BUT I REALLY MESSED UP AT MY LAST SCHOOL...
A MINOR DETAIL.
THIS SCHOOL...
IS IT THOUGH ...?
...NEEDS YOUR POWER.

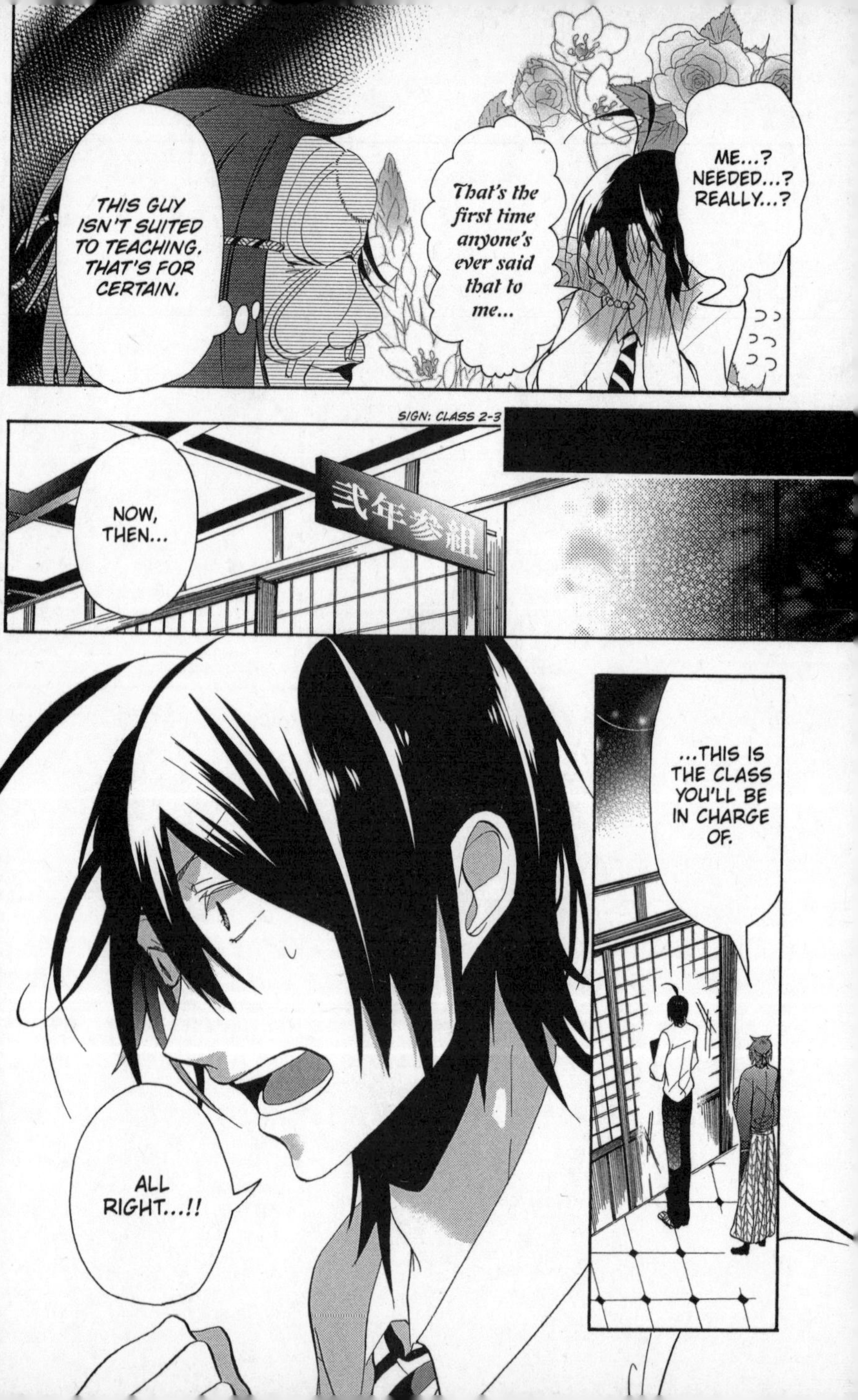
ME...? NEEDED...? REALLY...?
That's the first time anyone's ever said that to me...
THIS GUY ISN'T SUITED TO TEACHING. THAT'S FOR CERTAIN.
SIGN: CLASS 2-3
弐年参組
NOW, THEN...
...THIS IS THE CLASS YOU'LL BE IN CHARGE OF.
ALL RIGHT...!!

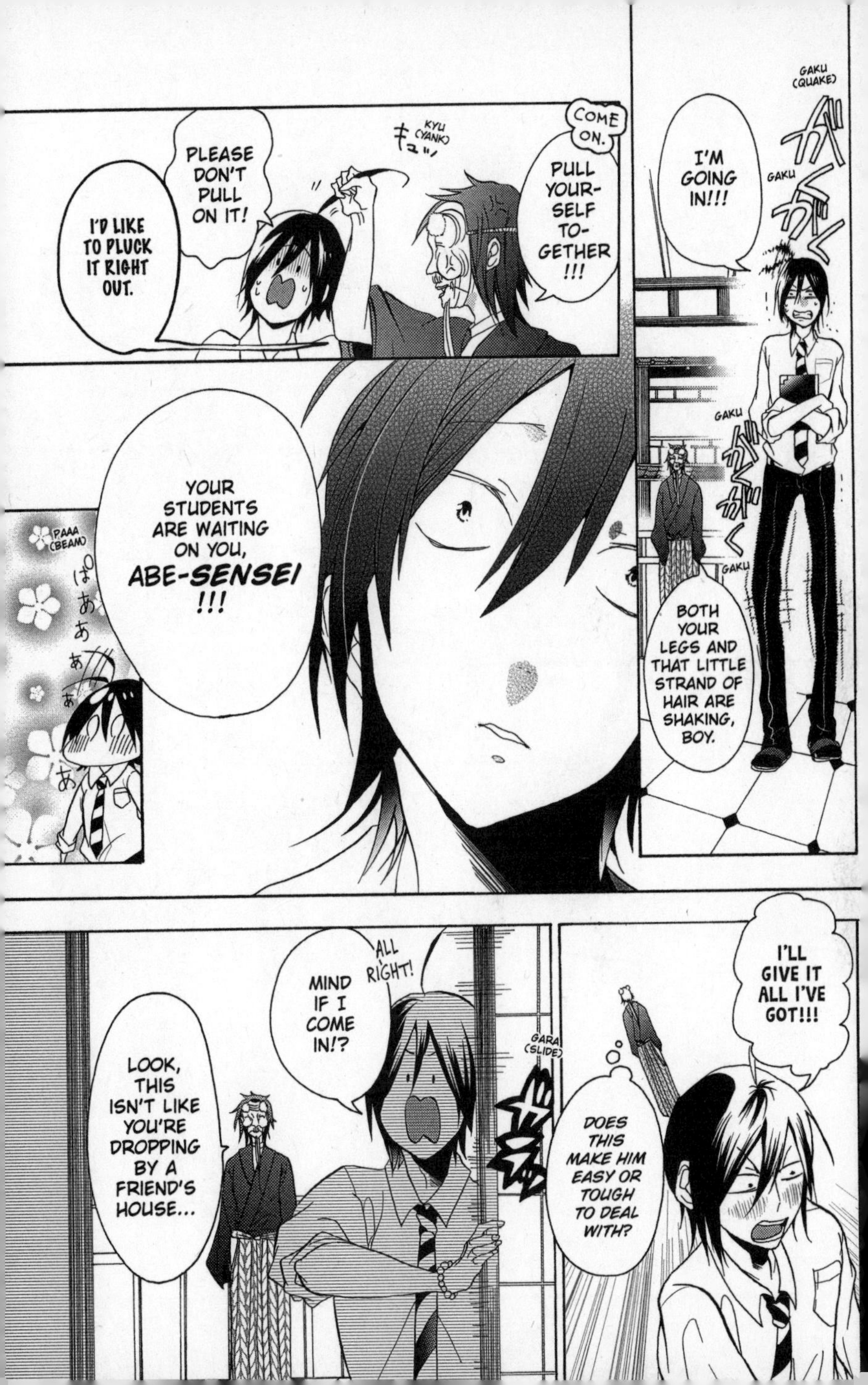
GAKU (QUAKE)
I'M GOING IN!!!
GAKU
GAKU
GAKU
BOTH YOUR LEGS AND THAT LITTLE STRAND OF HAIR ARE SHAKING, BOY.
COME ON.
PULL YOURSELF TOGETHER!!!
KYU (YANK)
PLEASE DON'T PULL ON IT!
I'D LIKE TO PLUCK IT RIGHT OUT.
YOUR STUDENTS ARE WAITING ON YOU, ABE-SENSEI!!!
PAAA (BEAM)
I'LL GIVE IT ALL I'VE GOT!!!
DOES THIS MAKE HIM EASY OR TOUGH TO DEAL WITH?
GARA (SLIDE)
ALL RIGHT!
MIND IF I COME IN!?
LOOK, THIS ISN'T LIKE YOU'RE DROPPING BY A FRIEND'S HOUSE...

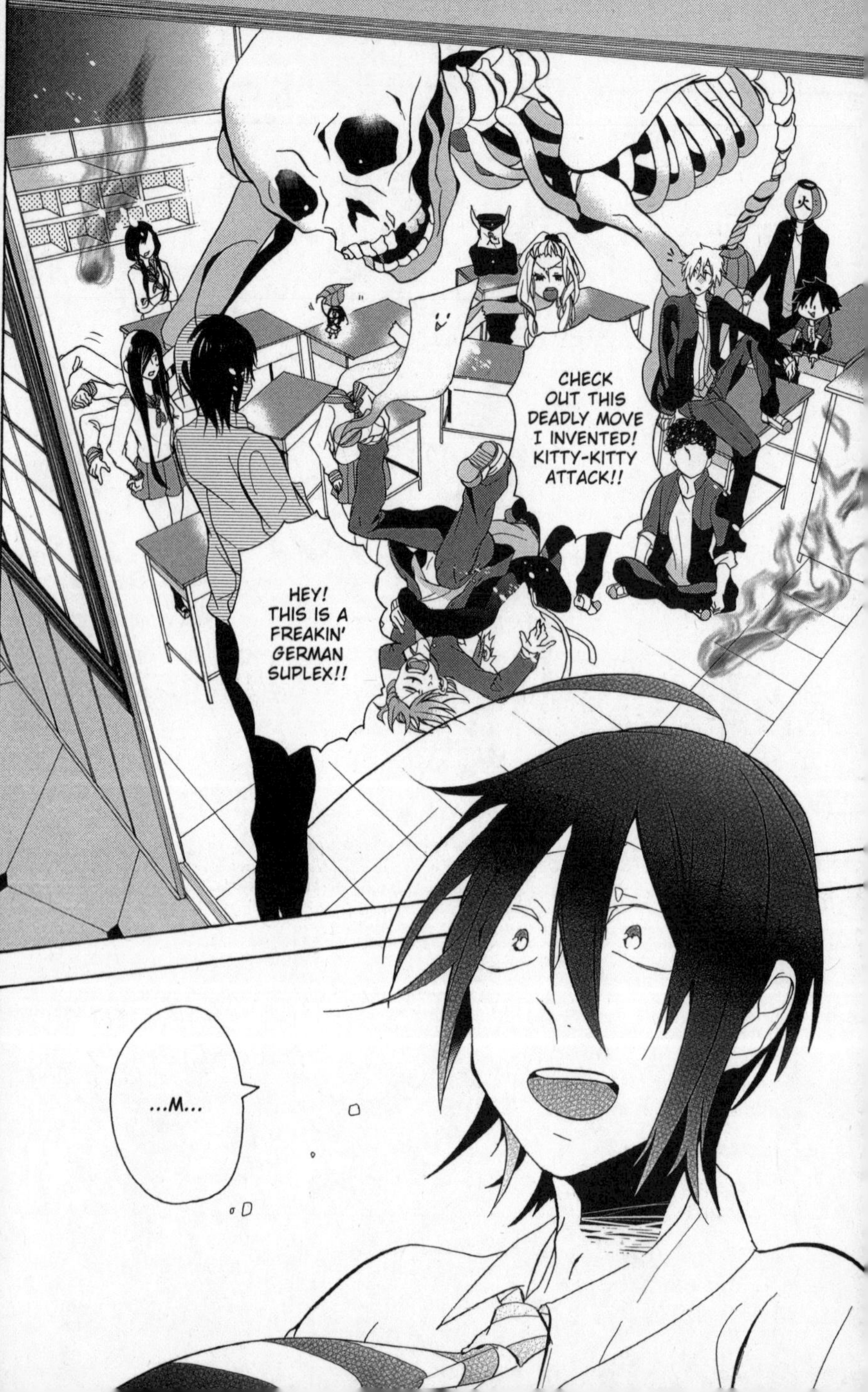
CHECK OUT THIS DEADLY MOVE I INVENTED! KITTY-KITTY ATTACK!!
HEY! THIS IS A FREAKIN' GERMAN SUPLEX!!
...M...

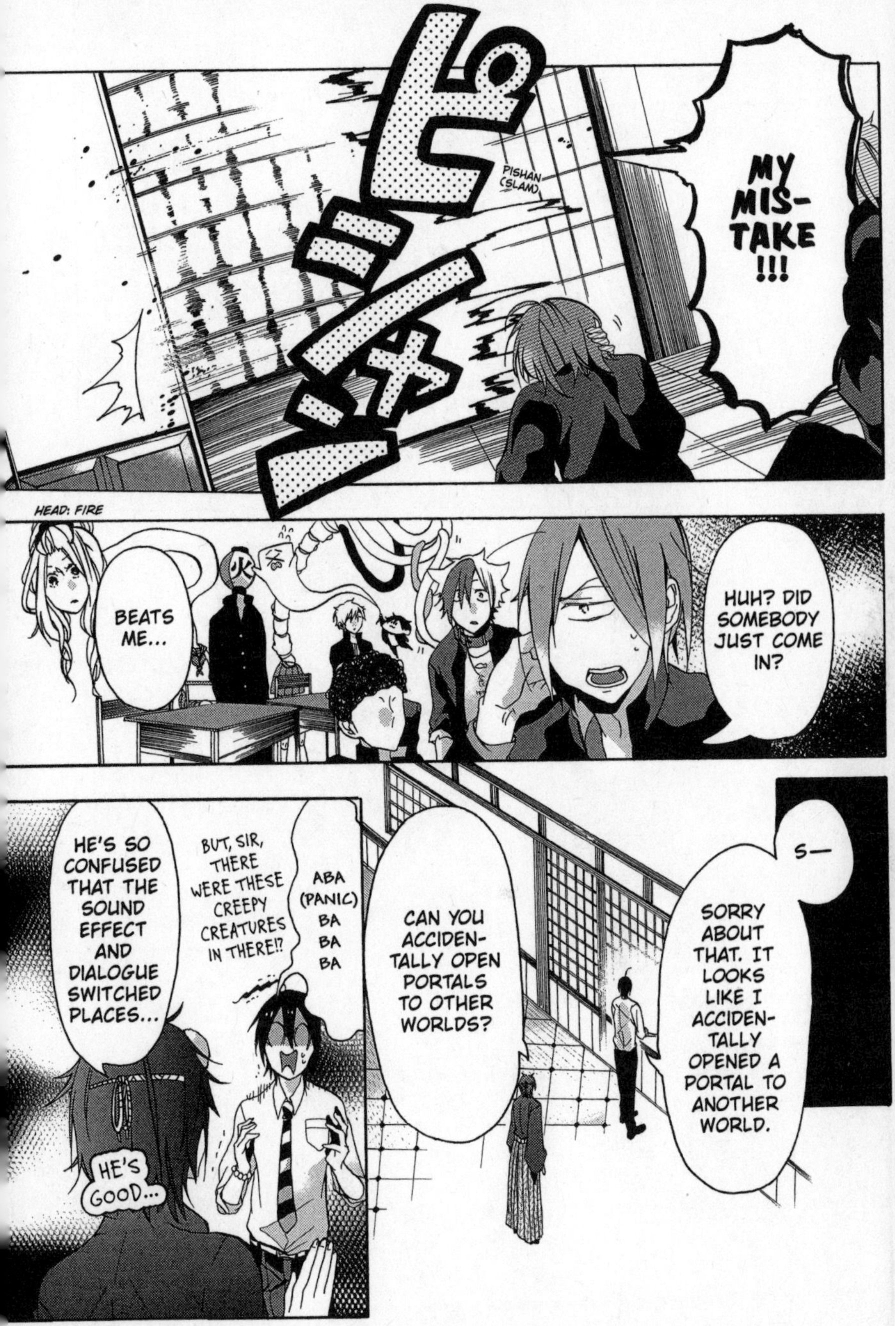
MY MIS-TAKE!!!
PISHAN (SLAM)
HEAD: FIRE
HUH? DID SOMEBODY JUST COME IN?
BEATS ME...
S—
SORRY ABOUT THAT. IT LOOKS LIKE I ACCIDEN-TALLY OPENED A PORTAL TO ANOTHER WORLD.
CAN YOU ACCIDEN-TALLY OPEN PORTALS TO OTHER WORLDS?
ABA (PANIC) BA BA BA
BUT, SIR, THERE WERE THESE CREEPY CREATURES IN THERE!?
HE'S SO CONFUSED THAT THE SOUND EFFECT AND DIALOGUE SWITCHED PLACES...
HE'S GOOD...

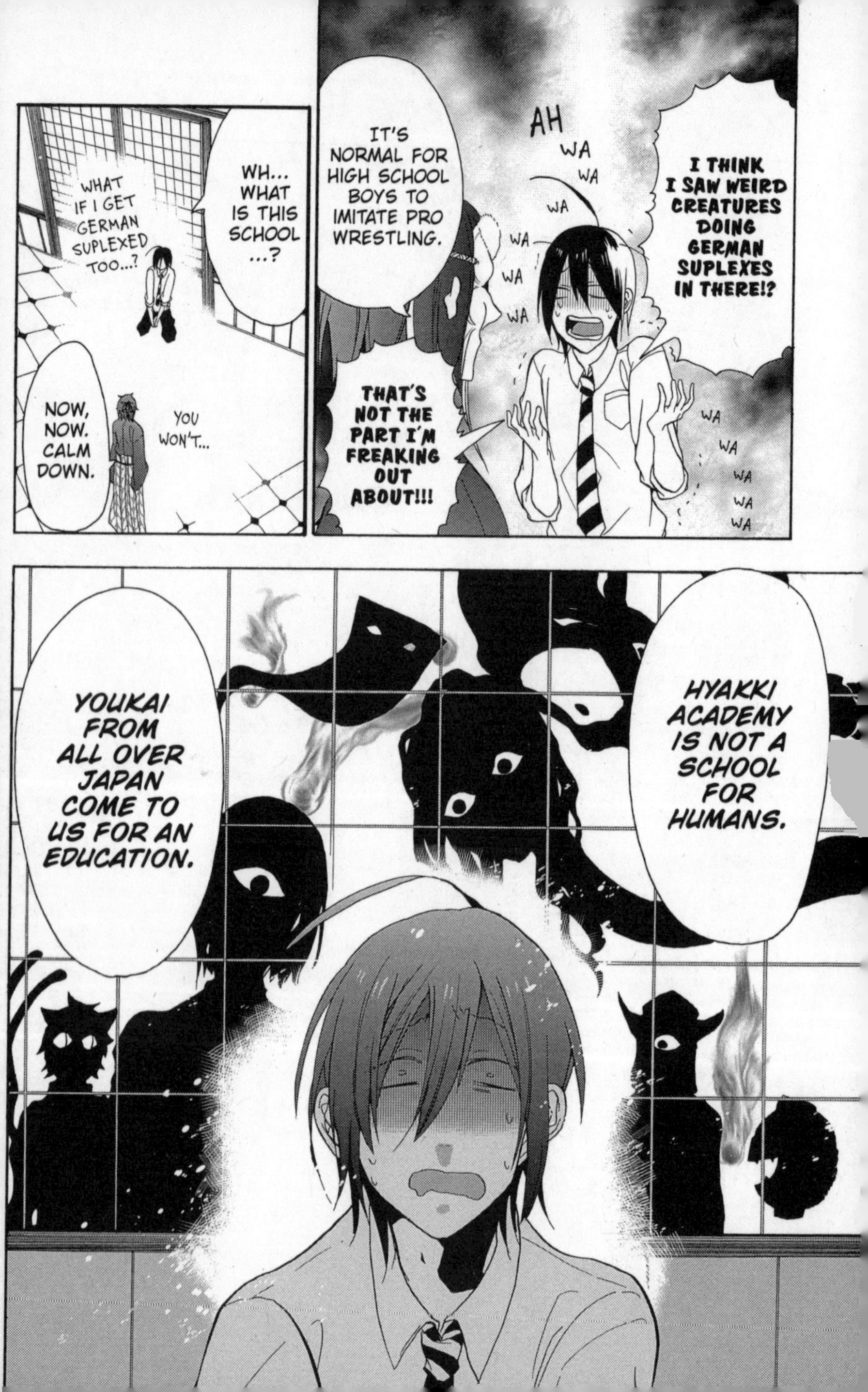
I THINK I SAW WEIRD CREATURES DOING GERMAN SUPLEXES IN THERE!?
AH WA WA WA WA WA WA
IT'S NORMAL FOR HIGH SCHOOL BOYS TO IMITATE PRO WRESTLING.
THAT'S NOT THE PART I'M FREAKING OUT ABOUT!!!
WA WA WA WA WA
WH... WHAT IS THIS SCHOOL ...?
WHAT IF I GET GERMAN SUPLEXED TOO...?
YOU WON'T...
NOW, NOW. CALM DOWN.
HYAKKI ACADEMY IS NOT A SCHOOL FOR HUMANS.
YOUKAI FROM ALL OVER JAPAN COME TO US FOR AN EDUCATION.

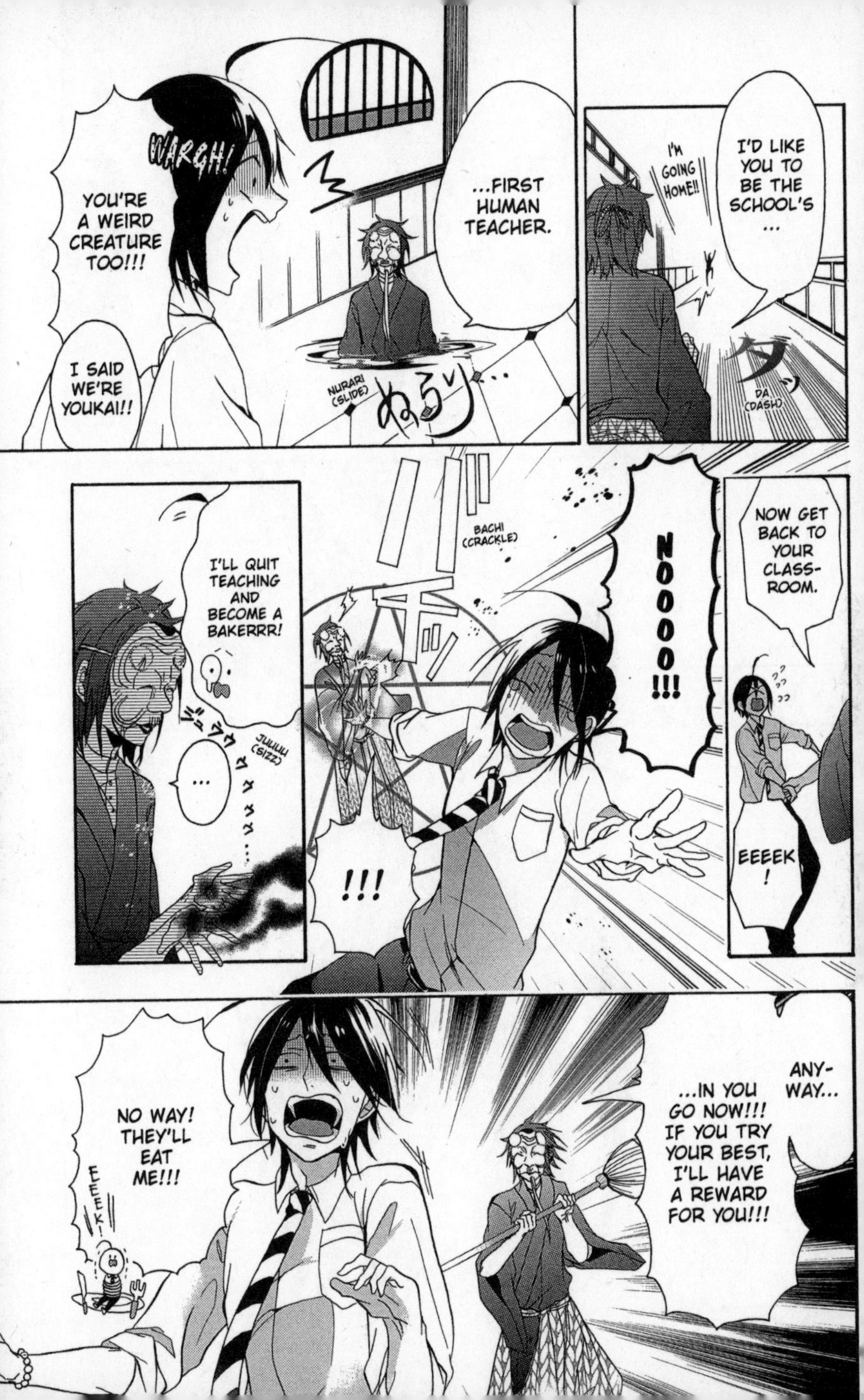

I'D LIKE YOU TO BE THE SCHOOL'S ...
I'M GOING HOME!!
DA (DASH)
...FIRST HUMAN TEACHER.
NURARI (SLIDE)
ぬらり
WARGH!
YOU'RE A WEIRD CREATURE TOO!!!
I SAID WE'RE YOUKAI!!
NOW GET BACK TO YOUR CLASS-ROOM.
EEEEK!
NOOOOO!!!
BACHI (CRACKLE)
!!!
I'LL QUIT TEACHING AND BECOME A BAKERRR!
JUUUU (SIZZ)
...
ANY-WAY...
...IN YOU GO NOW!!! IF YOU TRY YOUR BEST, I'LL HAVE A REWARD FOR YOU!!!
NO WAY! THEY'LL EAT ME!!!
EEEEK!

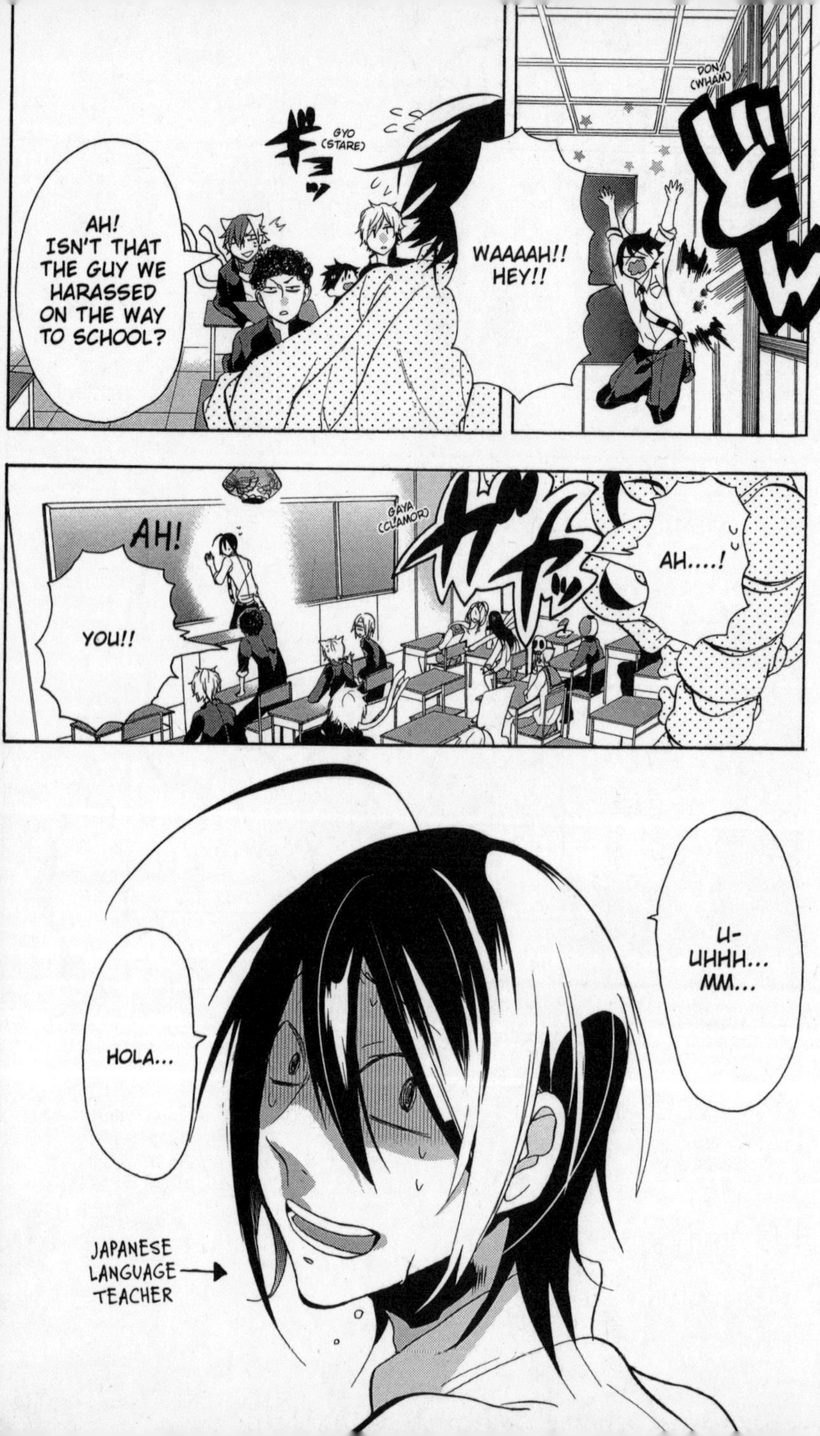
DON (WHAM)
WAAAAH!! HEY!!
GYO (STARE)
AH! ISN'T THAT THE GUY WE HARASSED ON THE WAY TO SCHOOL?
AH....!
GAYA (CLAMOR)
AH!
YOU!!
U-UHHH... MM...
HOLA...
JAPANESE LANGUAGE TEACHER

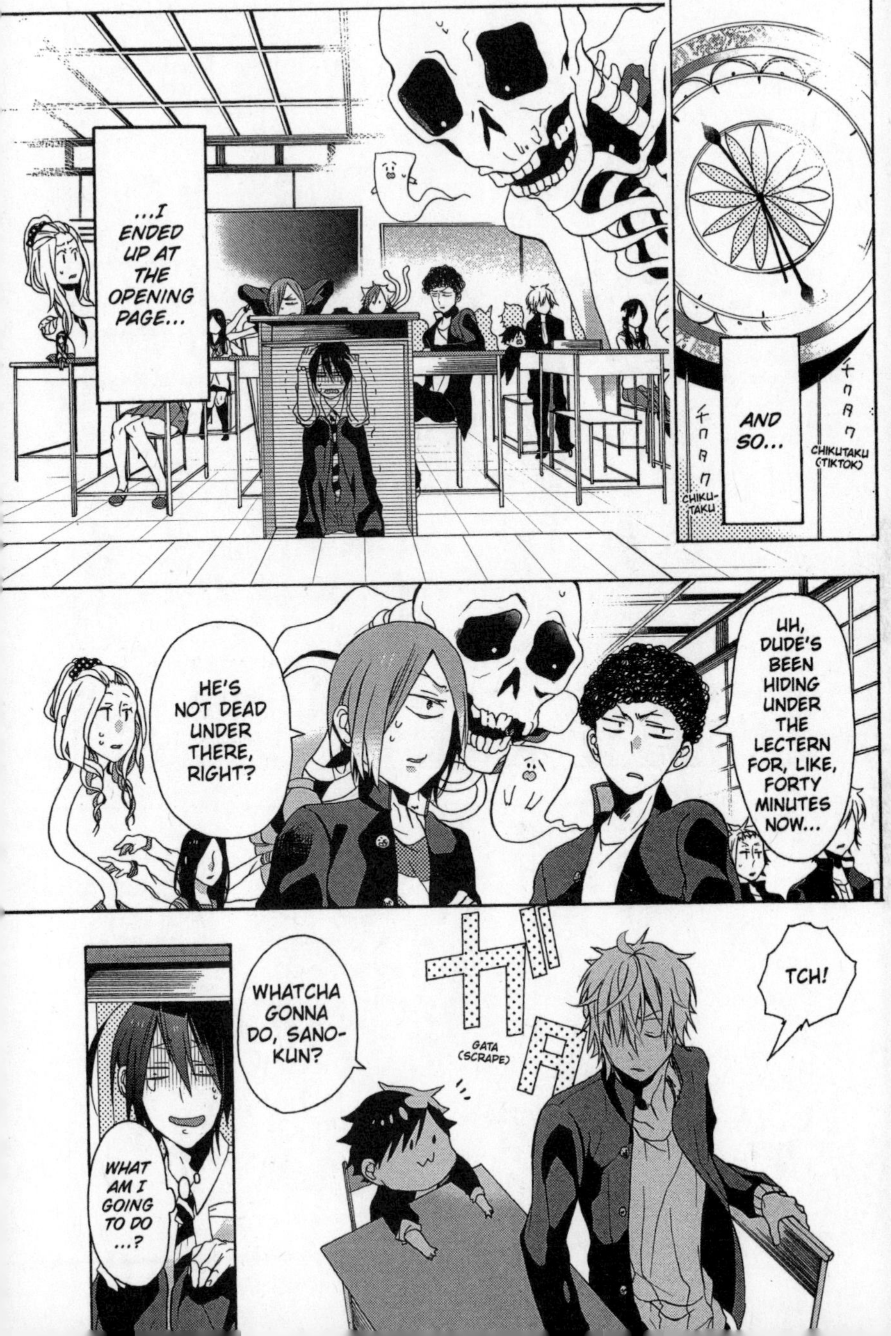
チクタク
CHIKUTAKU (TIKTOK)
AND SO...
チクタク
CHIKU-TAKU
...I ENDED UP AT THE OPENING PAGE...
UH, DUDE'S BEEN HIDING UNDER THE LECTERN FOR, LIKE, FORTY MINUTES NOW...
HE'S NOT DEAD UNDER THERE, RIGHT?
TCH!
ガタ
GATA (SCRAPE)
WHATCHA GONNA DO, SANO-KUN?
WHAT AM I GOING TO DO ...?

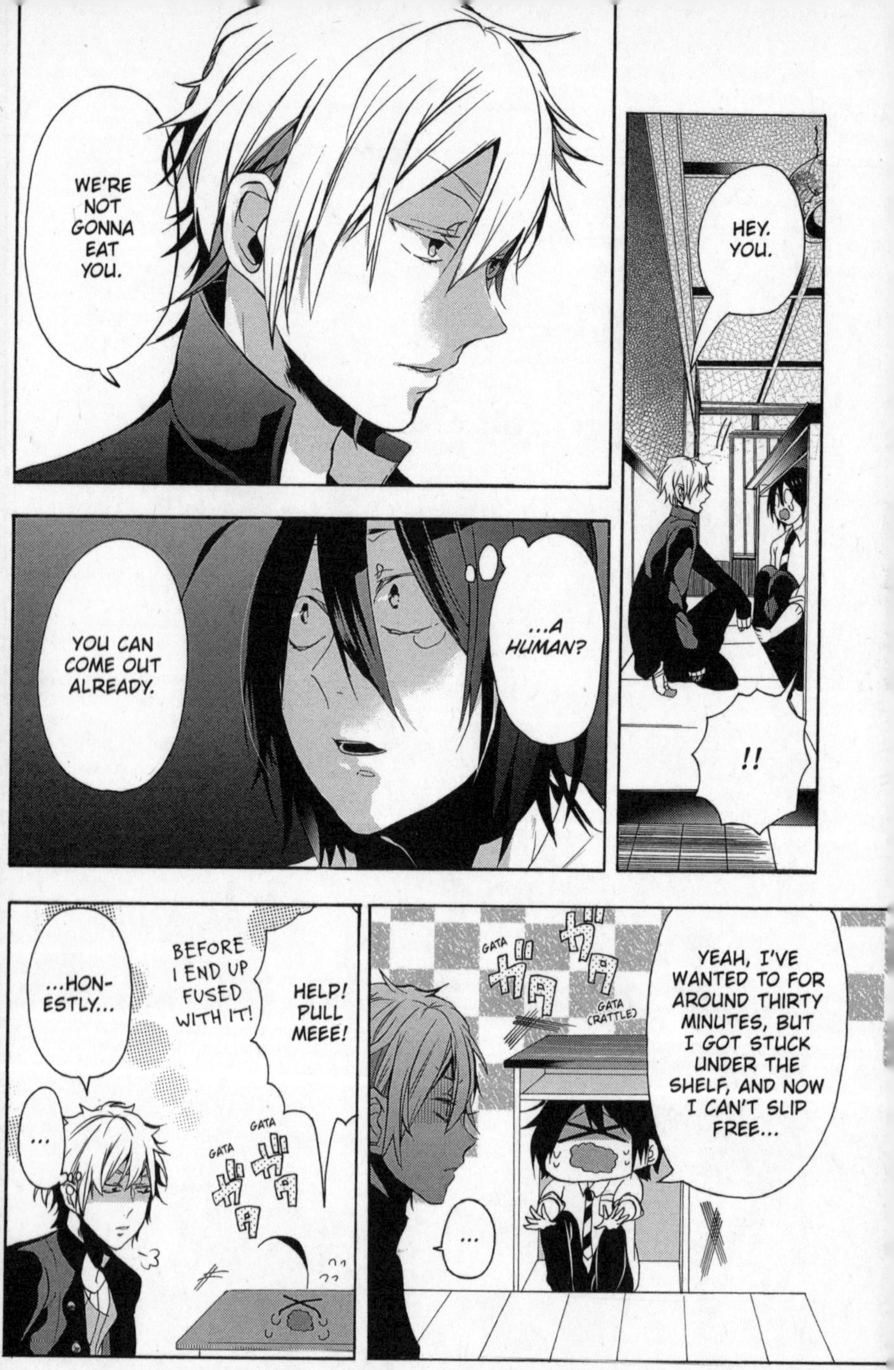
HEY. YOU.
!!
WE'RE NOT GONNA EAT YOU.
...A HUMAN?
YOU CAN COME OUT ALREADY.
GATA
GATA (RATTLE)
YEAH, I'VE WANTED TO FOR AROUND THIRTY MINUTES, BUT I GOT STUCK UNDER THE SHELF, AND NOW I CAN'T SLIP FREE...
...
HELP! PULL MEEE!
BEFORE I END UP FUSED WITH IT!
...HON-ESTLY...
...
GATA
GATA

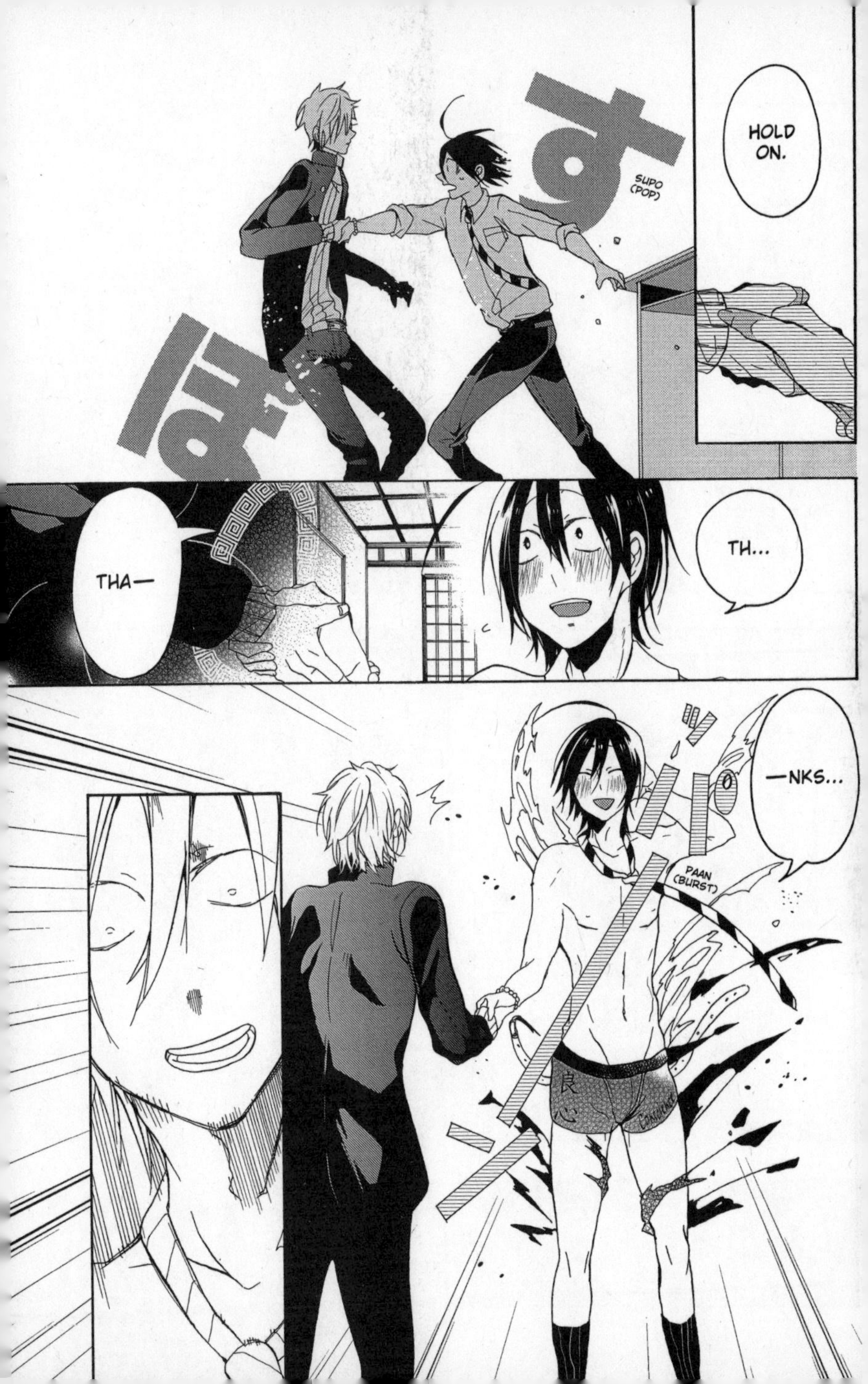
HOLD ON.
SUPO (POP)
TH...
THA—
—NKS...
PAAN (BURST)

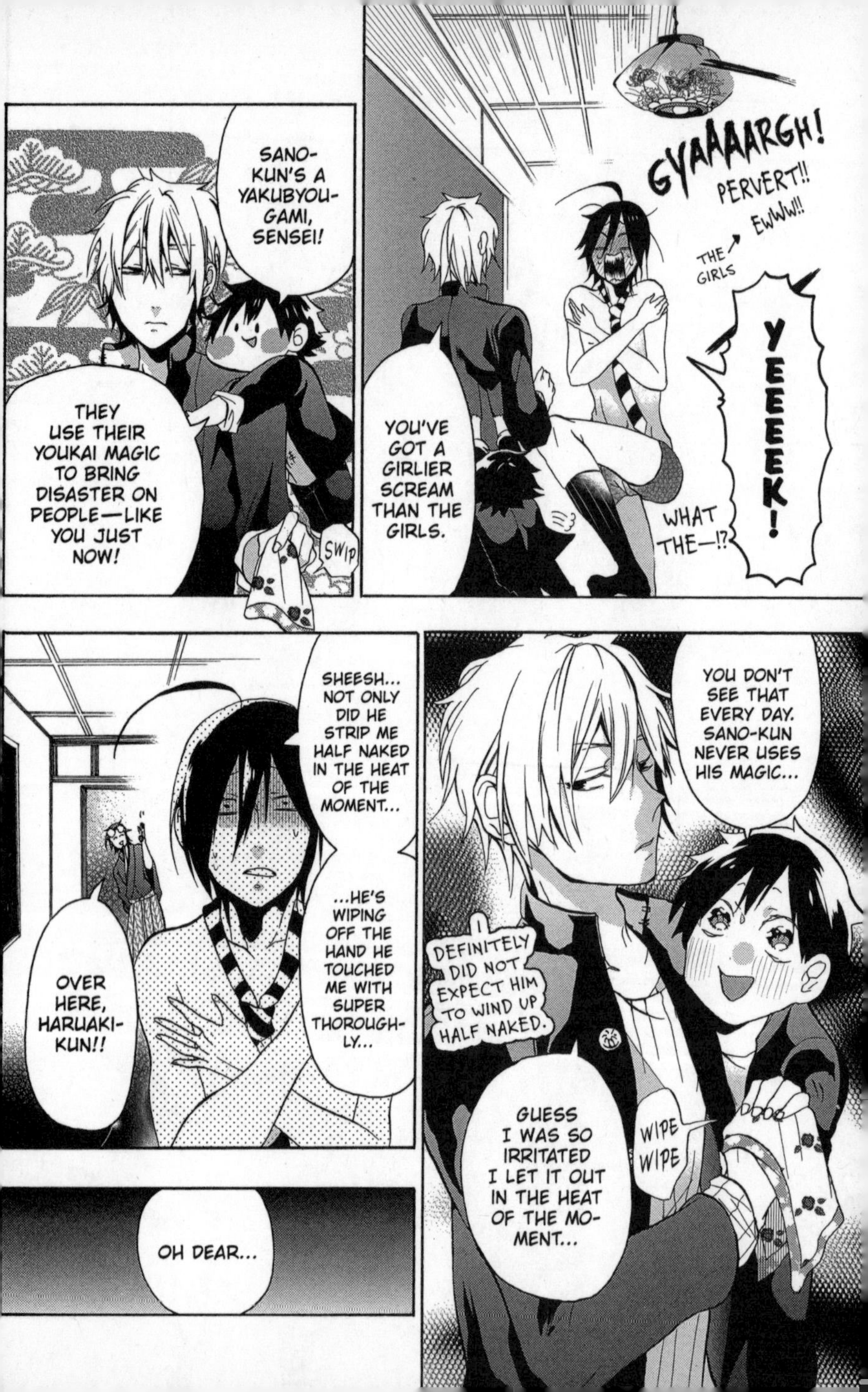
GYAAAARGH!
PERVERT!!
EWWW!!
THE GIRLS
YEEEEK!
WHAT THE—!?
YOU'VE GOT A GIRLIER SCREAM THAN THE GIRLS.
SANO-KUN'S A YAKUBYOU-GAMI, SENSEI!
SWIP
THEY USE THEIR YOUKAI MAGIC TO BRING DISASTER ON PEOPLE—LIKE YOU JUST NOW!
YOU DON'T SEE THAT EVERY DAY. SANO-KUN NEVER USES HIS MAGIC...
I DEFINITELY DID NOT EXPECT HIM TO WIND UP HALF NAKED.
WIPE WIPE
GUESS I WAS SO IRRITATED I LET IT OUT IN THE HEAT OF THE MO-MENT...
SHEESH... NOT ONLY DID HE STRIP ME HALF NAKED IN THE HEAT OF THE MOMENT...
...HE'S WIPING OFF THE HAND HE TOUCHED ME WITH SUPER THOROUGH-LY...
OVER HERE, HARUAKI-KUN!!
OH DEAR...

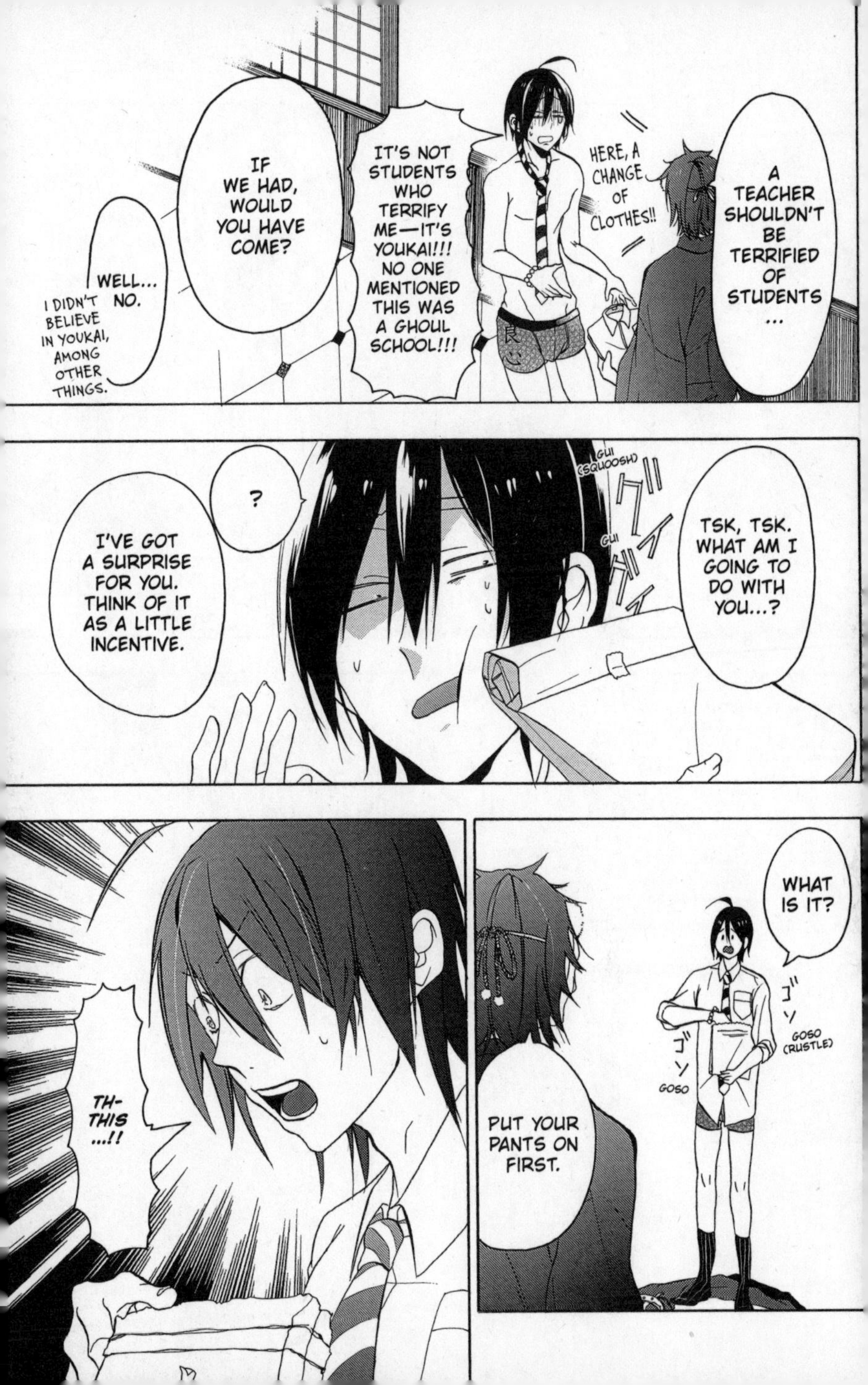
A TEACHER SHOULDN'T BE TERRIFIED OF STUDENTS...
HERE, A CHANGE OF CLOTHES!!
IT'S NOT STUDENTS WHO TERRIFY ME—IT'S YOUKAI!!! NO ONE MENTIONED THIS WAS A GHOUL SCHOOL!!!
IF WE HAD, WOULD YOU HAVE COME?
WELL... NO.
I DIDN'T BELIEVE IN YOUKAI, AMONG OTHER THINGS.
TSK, TSK. WHAT AM I GOING TO DO WITH YOU...?
グイ
GUI (SQUOOSH)
グイ
GUI
?
I'VE GOT A SURPRISE FOR YOU. THINK OF IT AS A LITTLE INCENTIVE.
WHAT IS IT?
ゴソ
GOSO (RUSTLE)
ゴソ
GOSO
PUT YOUR PANTS ON FIRST.
TH-THIS...!!

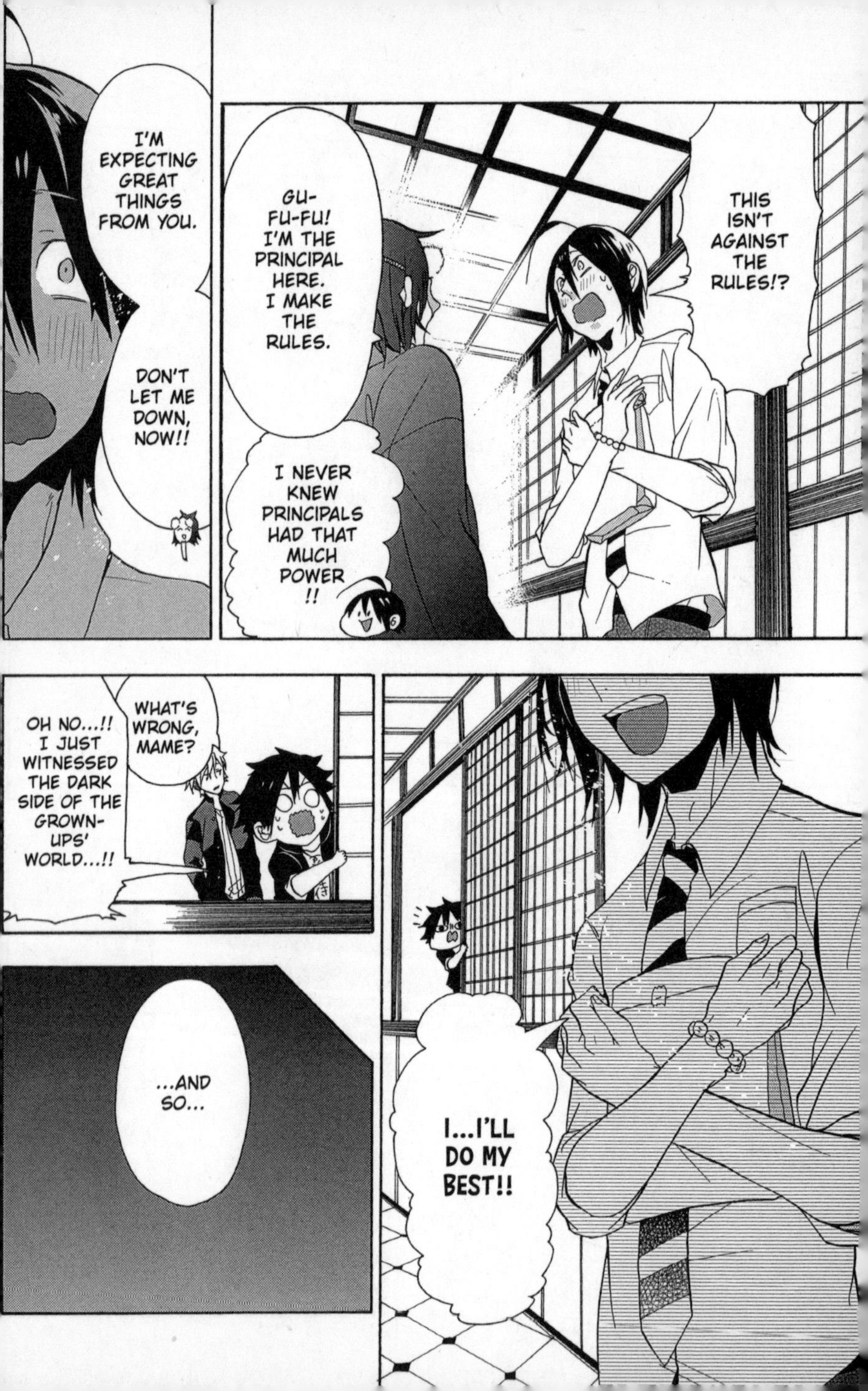
THIS ISN'T AGAINST THE RULES!?
GU-FU-FU! I'M THE PRINCIPAL HERE. I MAKE THE RULES.
I NEVER KNEW PRINCIPALS HAD THAT MUCH POWER!!
I'M EXPECTING GREAT THINGS FROM YOU.
DON'T LET ME DOWN, NOW!!
I...I'LL DO MY BEST!!
WHAT'S WRONG, MAME?
OH NO...!! I JUST WITNESSED THE DARK SIDE OF THE GROWN-UPS' WORLD...!!
...AND SO...

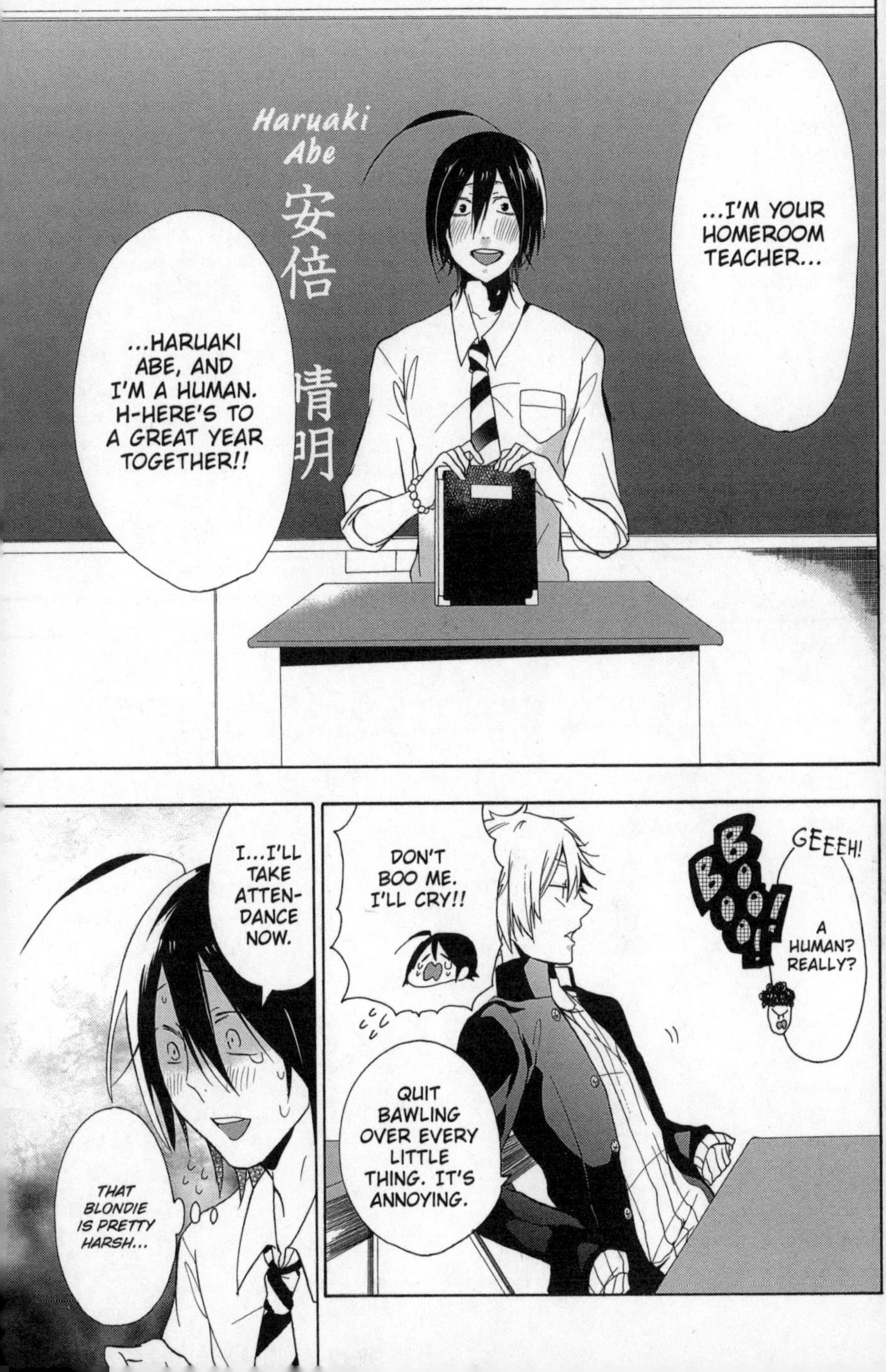

...I'M YOUR HOMEROOM TEACHER...
Haruaki Abe
安倍 晴明
...HARUAKI ABE, AND I'M A HUMAN. H-HERE'S TO A GREAT YEAR TOGETHER!!
GEEEH!
A HUMAN? REALLY?
DON'T BOO ME. I'LL CRY!!
QUIT BAWLING OVER EVERY LITTLE THING. IT'S ANNOYING.
I...I'LL TAKE ATTENDANCE NOW.
THAT BLONDIE IS PRETTY HARSH...

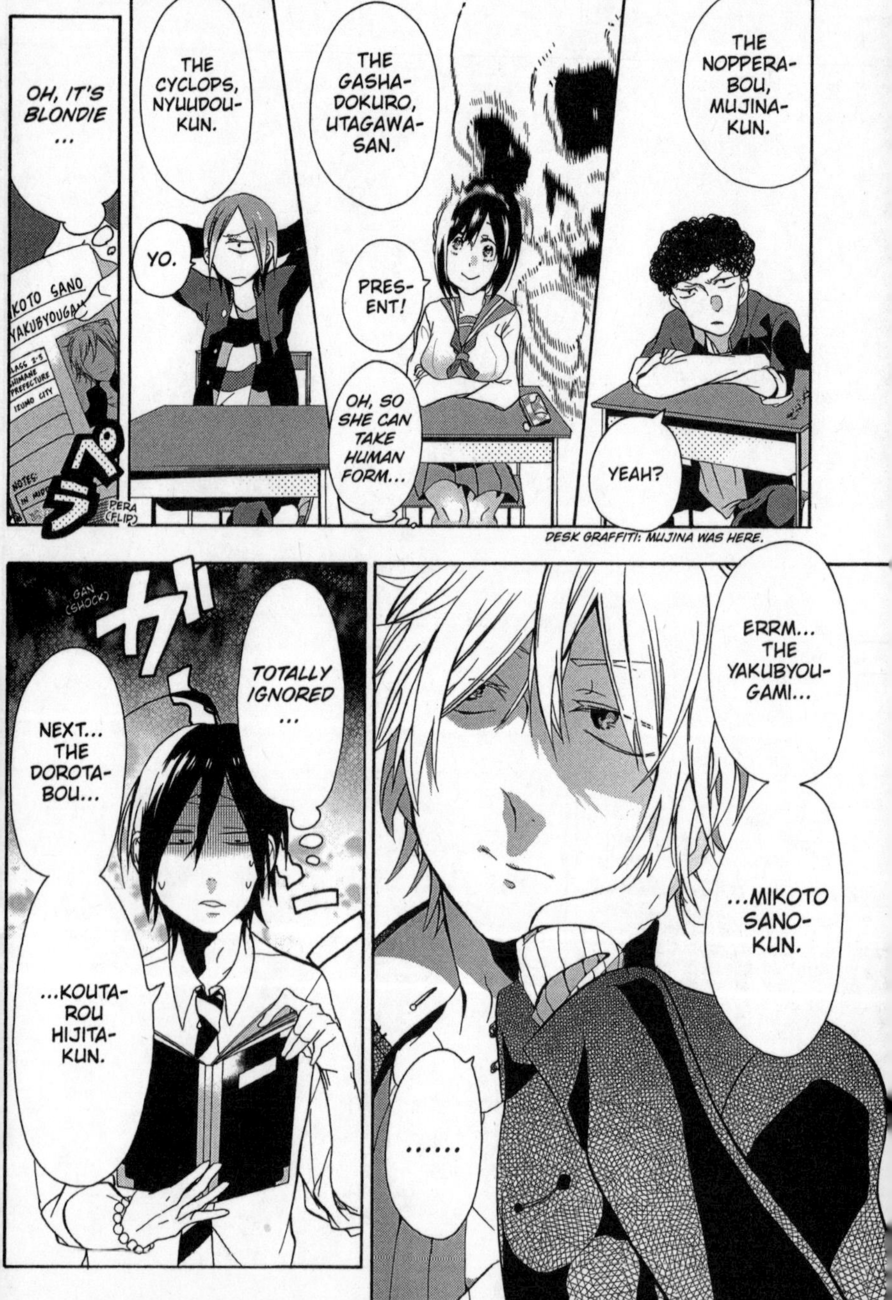
THE NOPPERA-BOU, MUJINA-KUN.
YEAH?
THE GASHA-DOKURO, UTAGAWA-SAN.
PRESENT!
OH, SO SHE CAN TAKE HUMAN FORM...
THE CYCLOPS, NYUUDOU-KUN.
YO.
OH, IT'S BLONDIE ...
KOTO SANO
YAKUBYOUGA
CLASS 2-3
SHIMANE PREFECTURE
IZUMO CITY
NOTES:
PERA (FLIP)
ERRM... THE YAKUBYOU-GAMI...
...MIKOTO SANO-KUN.
......
GAN (SHOCK)
TOTALLY IGNORED ...
NEXT... THE DOROTA-BOU...
...KOUTA-ROU HIJITA-KUN.
DESK GRAFFITI: MUJINA WAS HERE.

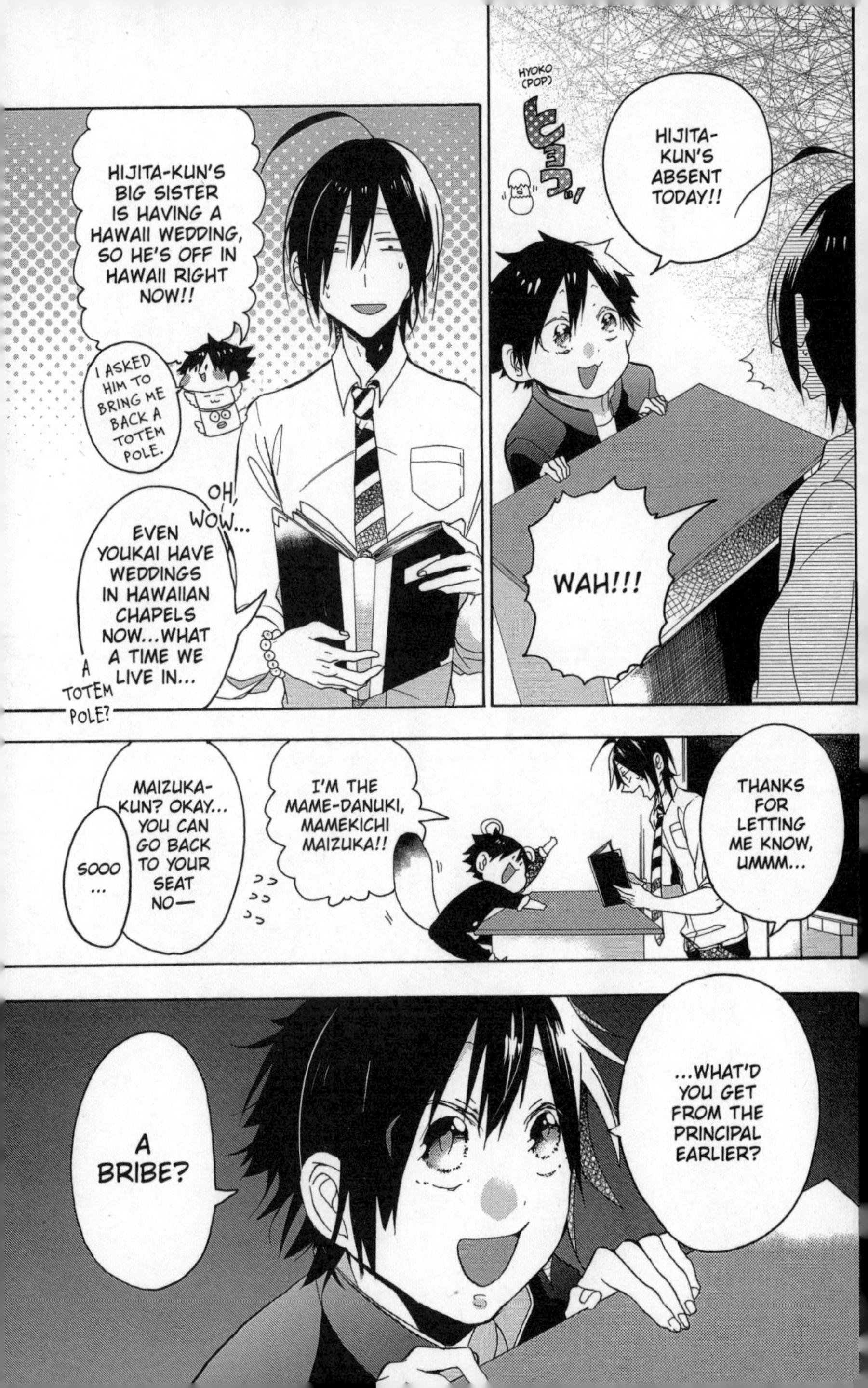
HIJITA-KUN'S ABSENT TODAY!!
HYOKO (POP)
WAH!!!
HIJITA-KUN'S BIG SISTER IS HAVING A HAWAII WEDDING, SO HE'S OFF IN HAWAII RIGHT NOW!!
I ASKED HIM TO BRING ME BACK A TOTEM POLE.
OH, WOW...
EVEN YOUKAI HAVE WEDDINGS IN HAWAIIAN CHAPELS NOW...WHAT A TIME WE LIVE IN...
A TOTEM POLE?
THANKS FOR LETTING ME KNOW, UMMM...
I'M THE MAME-DANUKI, MAMEKICHI MAIZUKA!!
MAIZUKA-KUN? OKAY... YOU CAN GO BACK TO YOUR SEAT NO—
SOOO ...
...WHAT'D YOU GET FROM THE PRINCIPAL EARLIER?
A BRIBE?

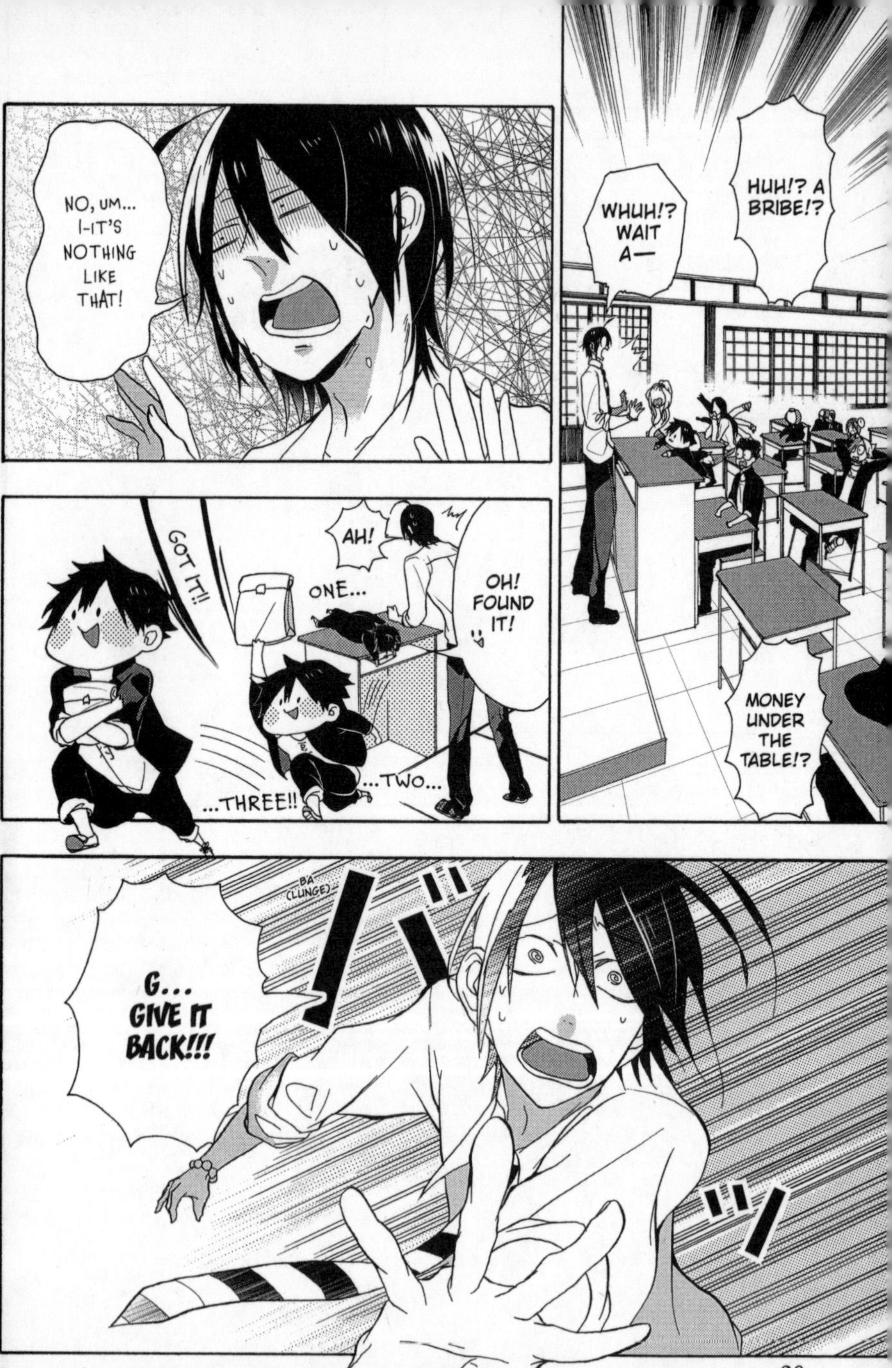
HUH!? A BRIBE!?
WHUH!? WAIT A—
MONEY UNDER THE TABLE!?
NO, UM... I-IT'S NOTHING LIKE THAT!
OH! FOUND IT!
AH!
ONE...
...TWO...
GOT IT!!
...THREE!!
BA (LUNGE)
G... GIVE IT BACK!!!

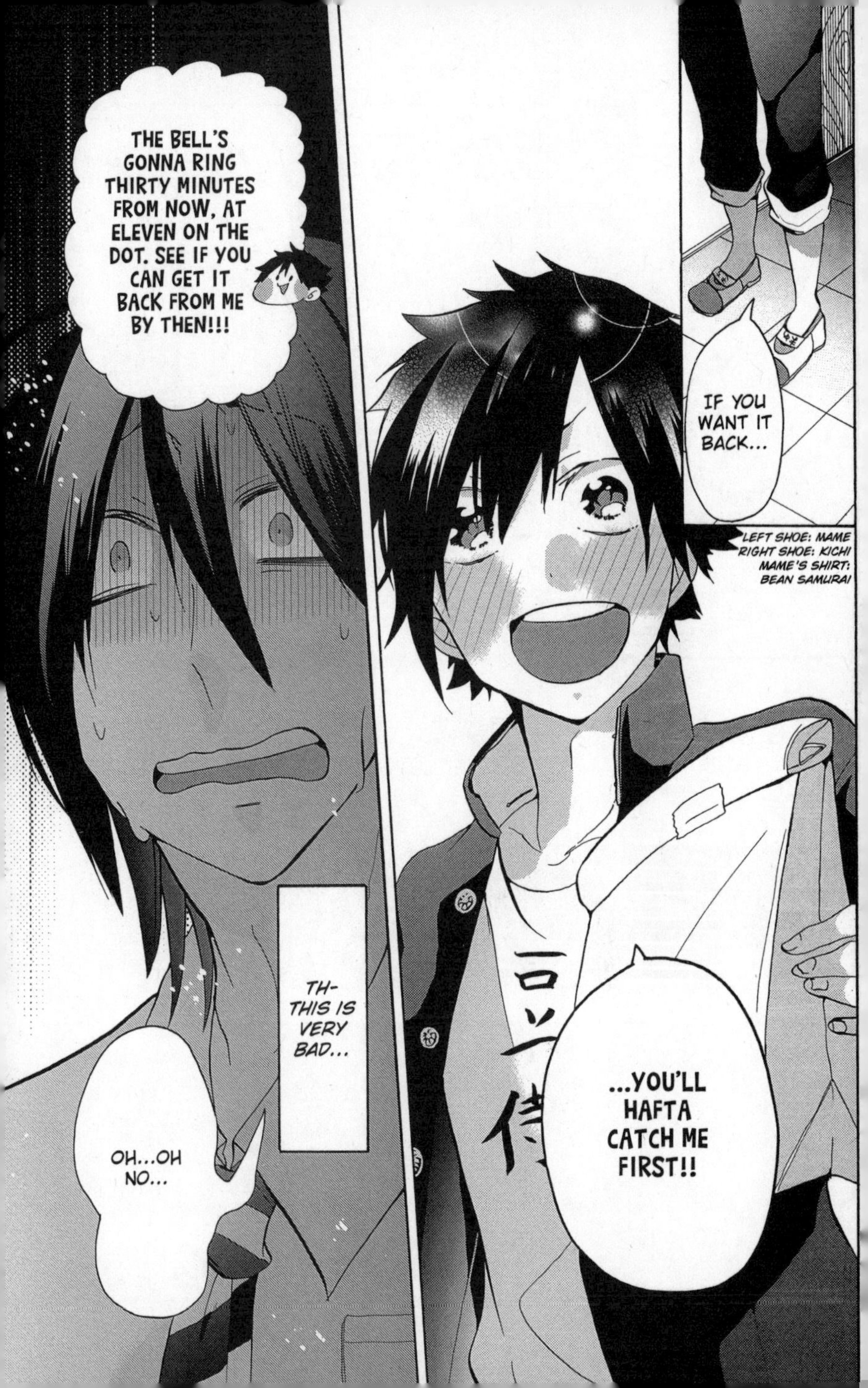
IF YOU WANT IT BACK...
LEFT SHOE: MAME
RIGHT SHOE: KICHI
MAME'S SHIRT: BEAN SAMURAI
...YOU'LL HAFTA CATCH ME FIRST!!
THE BELL'S GONNA RING THIRTY MINUTES FROM NOW, AT ELEVEN ON THE DOT. SEE IF YOU CAN GET IT BACK FROM ME BY THEN!!!
TH- THIS IS VERY BAD...
OH...OH NO...

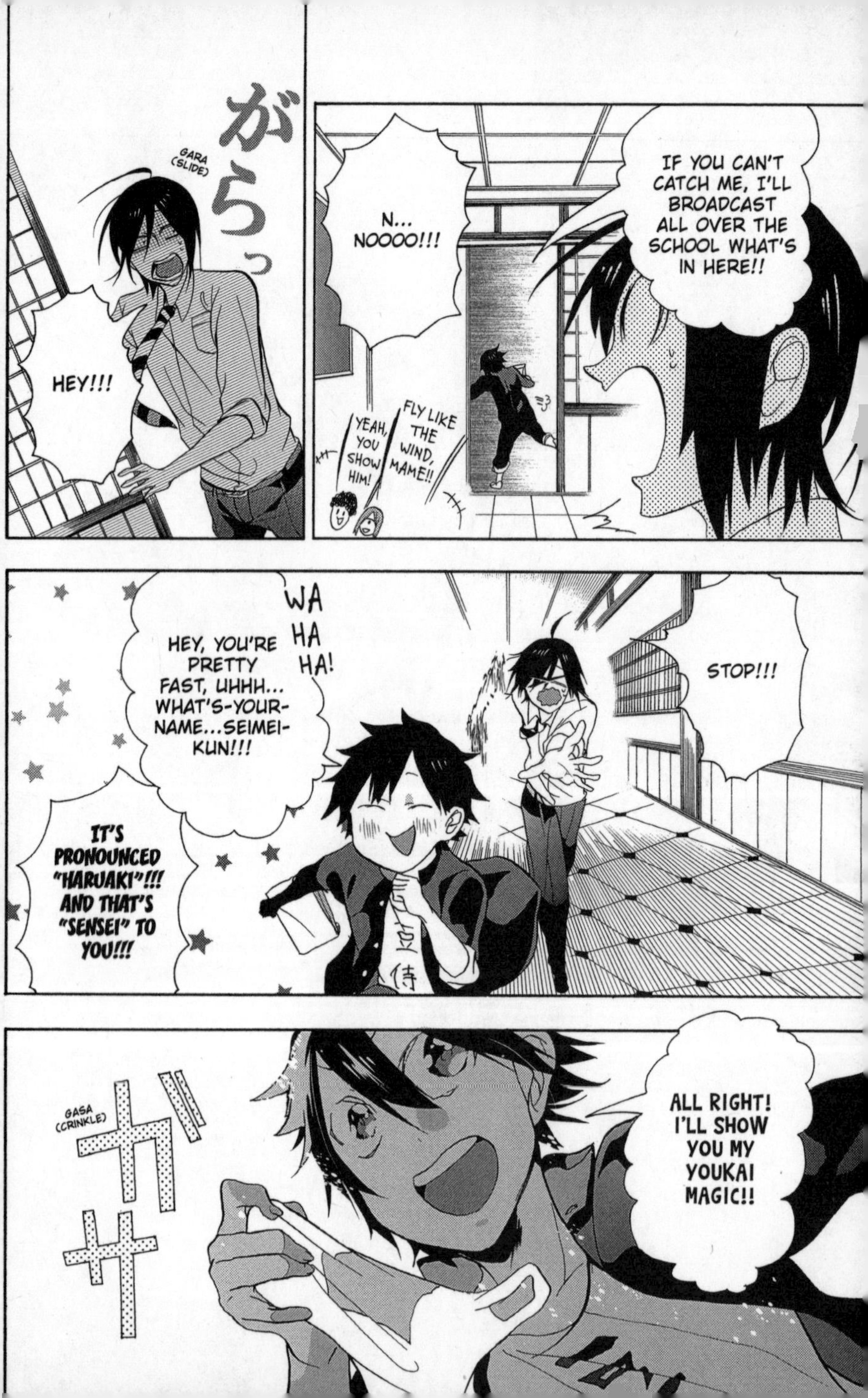
IF YOU CAN'T CATCH ME, I'LL BROADCAST ALL OVER THE SCHOOL WHAT'S IN HERE!!
N... NOOOO!!!
FLY LIKE THE WIND, MAME!!
YEAH, YOU SHOW HIM!
がらっ
GARA (SLIDE)
HEY!!!
STOP!!!
WA HA HA!
HEY, YOU'RE PRETTY FAST, UHHH... WHAT'S-YOUR-NAME...SEIMEI-KUN!!!
IT'S PRONOUNCED "HARUAKI"!!! AND THAT'S "SENSEI" TO YOU!!!
ALL RIGHT! I'LL SHOW YOU MY YOUKAI MAGIC!!
ガサッ
GASA (CRINKLE)

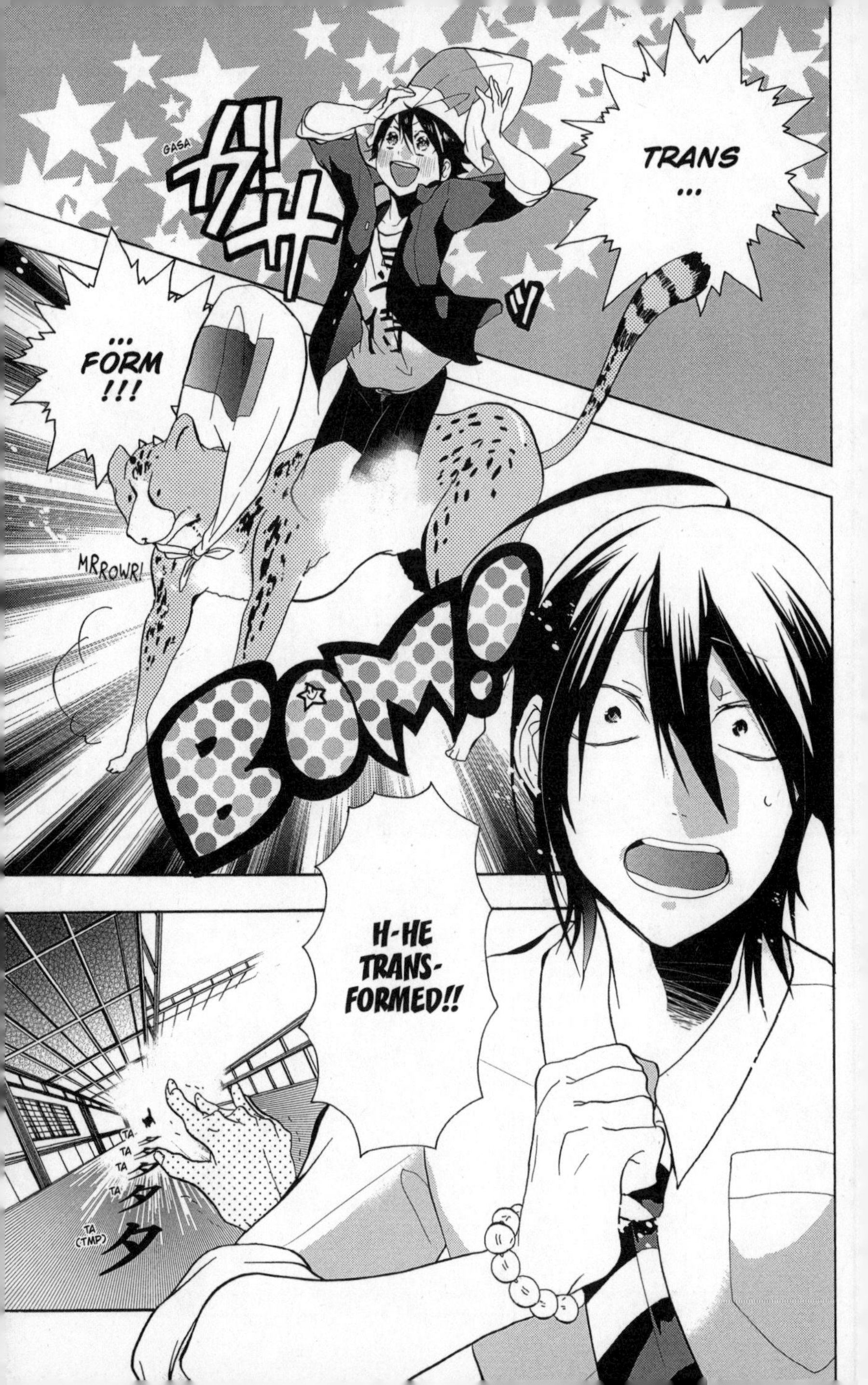
TRANS ...
GASA
... FÖRM !!!
MRROWR!
BOOM!
H-HE TRANS-FORMED!!
TA TA TA TA TA (TMP)

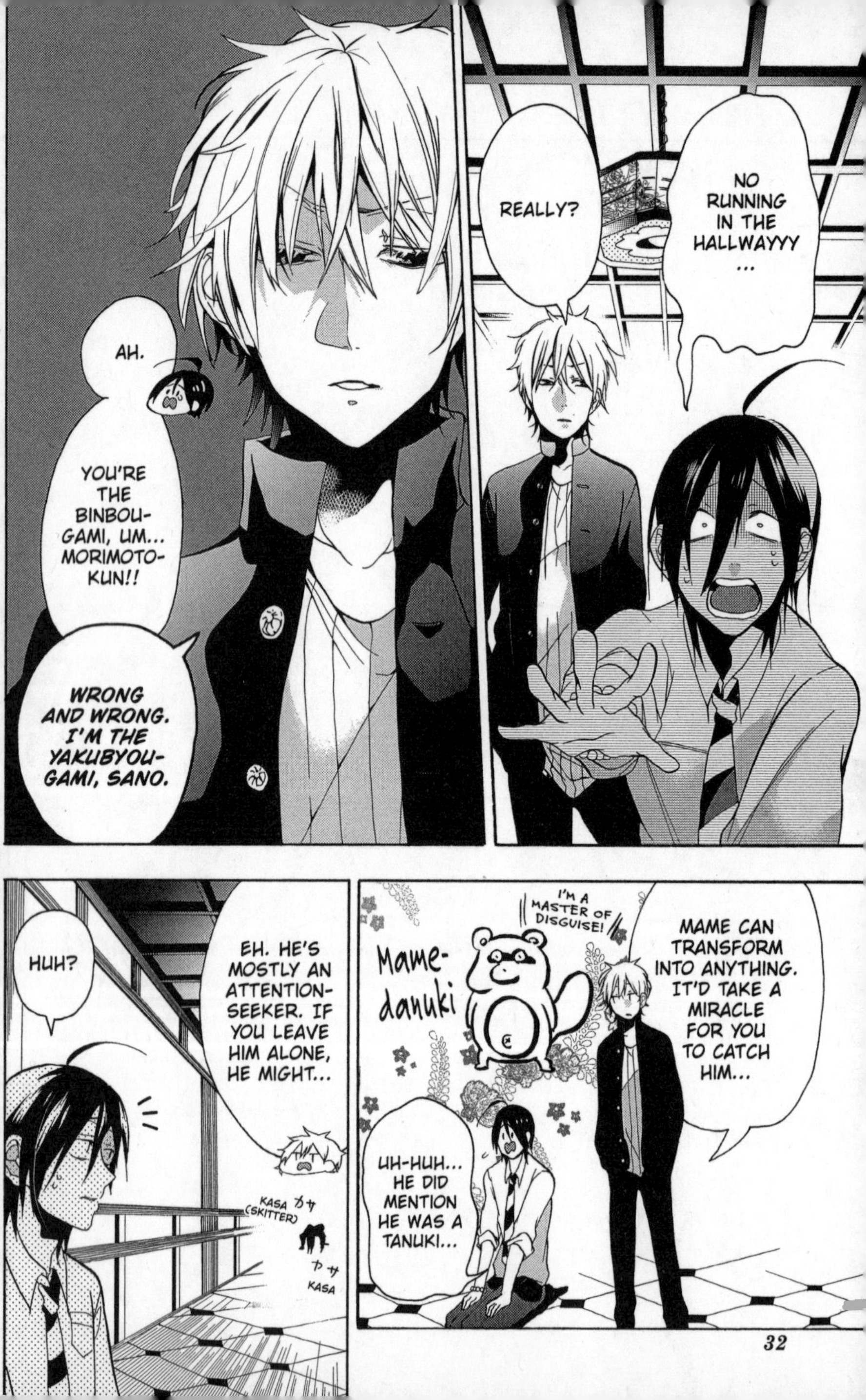
NO RUNNING IN THE HALLWAYYY ...
REALLY?
AH.
YOU'RE THE BINBOU-GAMI, UM... MORIMOTO-KUN!!
WRONG AND WRONG. I'M THE YAKUBYOU-GAMI, SANO.
MAME CAN TRANSFORM INTO ANYTHING. IT'D TAKE A MIRACLE FOR YOU TO CATCH HIM...
I'M A MASTER OF DISGUISE!
Mame-danuki
UH-HUH... HE DID MENTION HE WAS A TANUKI...
EH. HE'S MOSTLY AN ATTENTION-SEEKER. IF YOU LEAVE HIM ALONE, HE MIGHT...
HUH?
KASA カサ (SKITTER)
カサ KASA

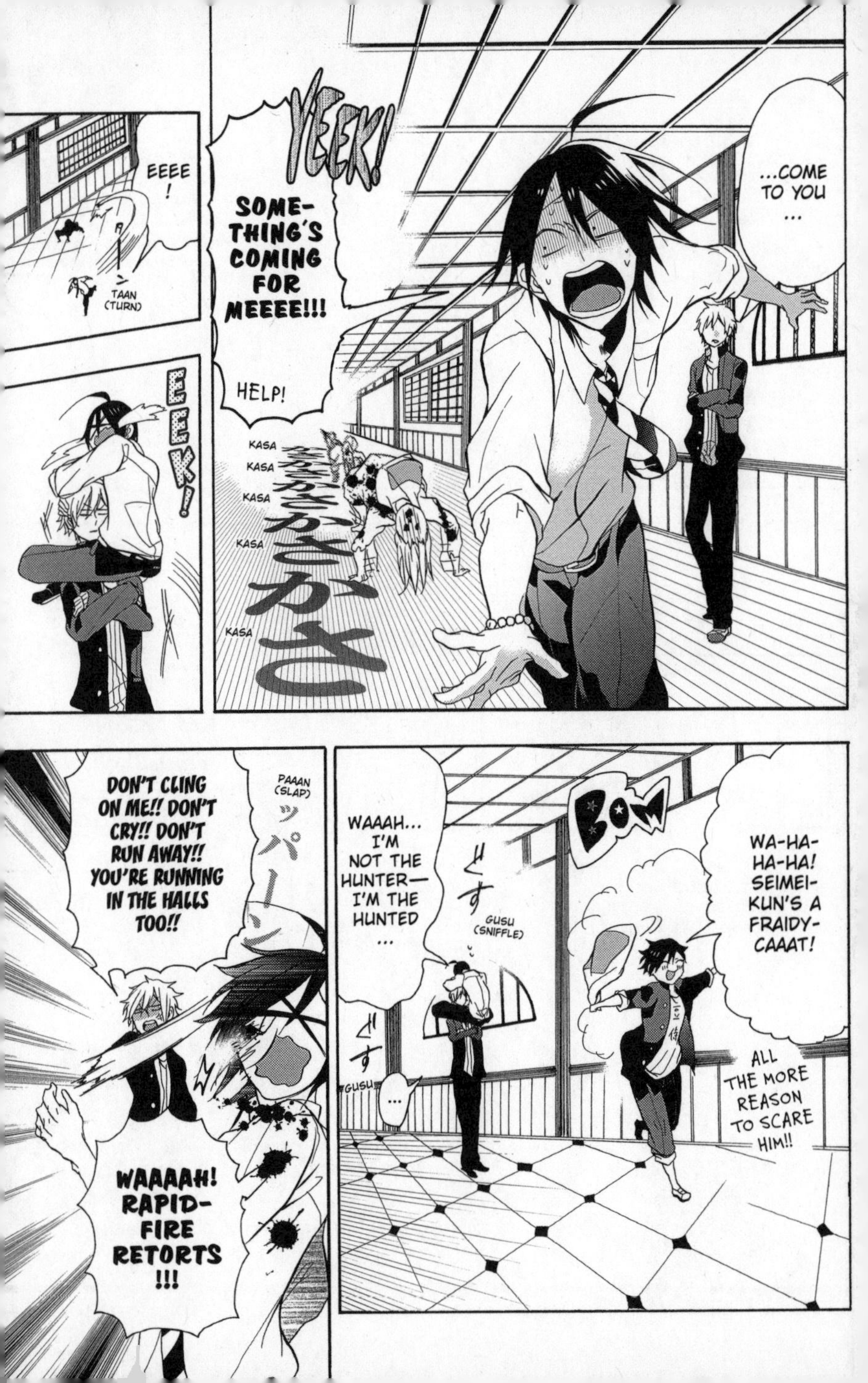
...COME TO YOU ...
YEEK!
SOMETHING'S COMING FOR MEEEE!!!
HELP!
KASA KASA KASA KASA KASA
EEEE !
TAAN (TURN)
EEEK!
WA-HA-HA-HA! SEIMEI-KUN'S A FRAIDY-CAAAT!
BOW
ALL THE MORE REASON TO SCARE HIM!!
GUSU (SNIFFLE)
WAAAH... I'M NOT THE HUNTER— I'M THE HUNTED ...
GUSU
...
DON'T CLING ON ME!! DON'T CRY!! DON'T RUN AWAY!! YOU'RE RUNNING IN THE HALLS TOO!!
PAAAN (SLAP)
WAAAAH! RAPID-FIRE RETORTS !!!

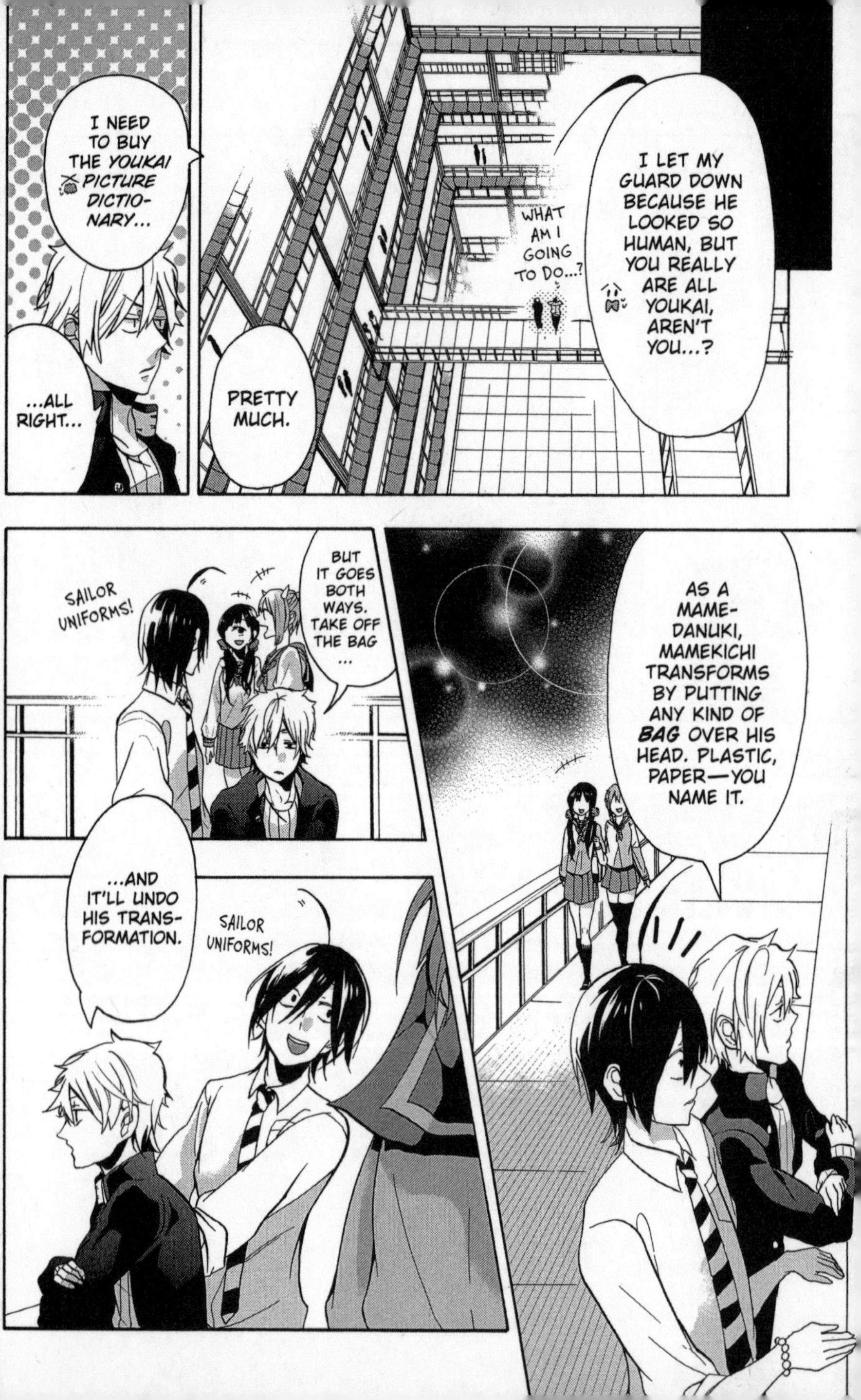
I LET MY GUARD DOWN BECAUSE HE LOOKED SO HUMAN, BUT YOU REALLY ARE ALL YOUKAI, AREN'T YOU...?
WHAT AM I GOING TO DO...?
PRETTY MUCH.
I NEED TO BUY THE *YOUKAI PICTURE DICTIONARY*...
...ALL RIGHT...
AS A MAME-DANUKI, MAMEKICHI TRANSFORMS BY PUTTING ANY KIND OF **BAG** OVER HIS HEAD. PLASTIC, PAPER—YOU NAME IT.
BUT IT GOES BOTH WAYS. TAKE OFF THE BAG...
SAILOR UNIFORMS!
...AND IT'LL UNDO HIS TRANSFORMATION.
SAILOR UNIFORMS!

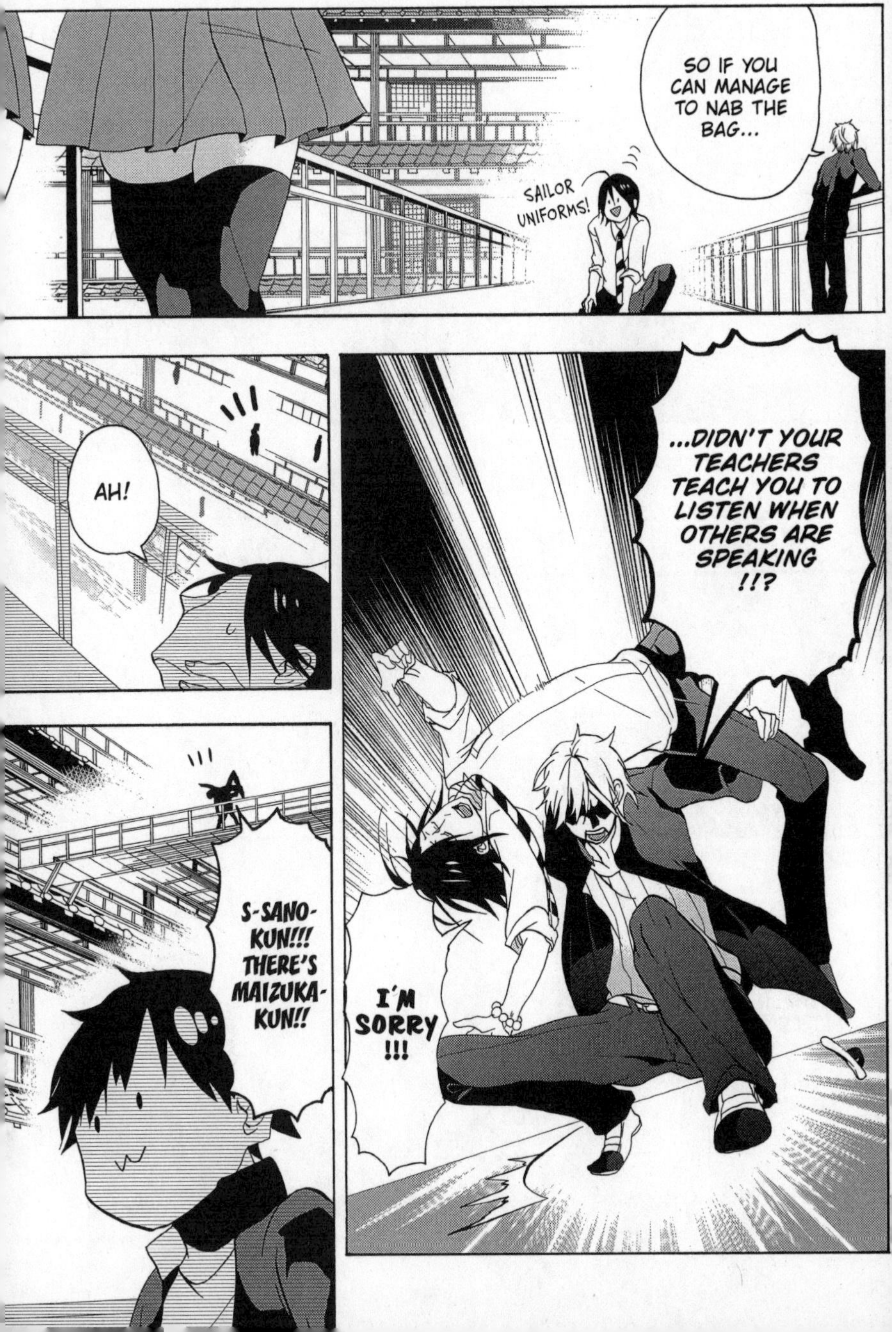
SO IF YOU CAN MANAGE TO NAB THE BAG...
SAILOR UNIFORMS!
...DIDN'T YOUR TEACHERS TEACH YOU TO LISTEN WHEN OTHERS ARE SPEAKING !!?
I'M SORRY !!!
AH!
S-SANO-KUN!!! THERE'S MAIZUKA-KUN!!

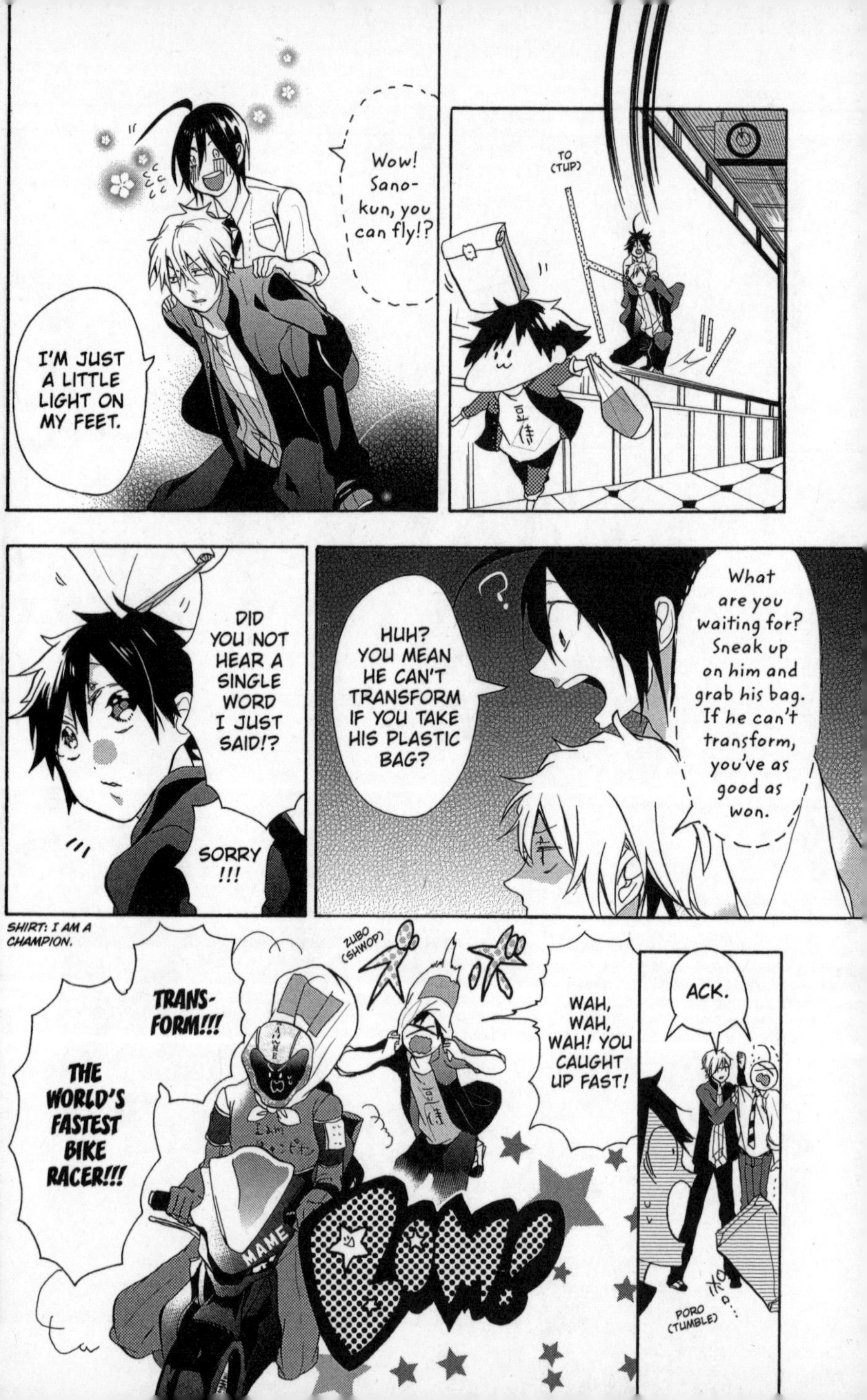
TO (TUP)
Wow! Sano-kun, you can fly!?
I'M JUST A LITTLE LIGHT ON MY FEET.
What are you waiting for? Sneak up on him and grab his bag. If he can't transform, you've as good as won.
HUH? YOU MEAN HE CAN'T TRANSFORM IF YOU TAKE HIS PLASTIC BAG?
DID YOU NOT HEAR A SINGLE WORD I JUST SAID!?
SORRY!!!
ACK.
PORO (TUMBLE)
WAH, WAH, WAH! YOU CAUGHT UP FAST!
ZUBO (SHWOP)
TRANS-FORM!!!
THE WORLD'S FASTEST BIKE RACER!!!
MAME
SHIRT: I AM A CHAMPION.

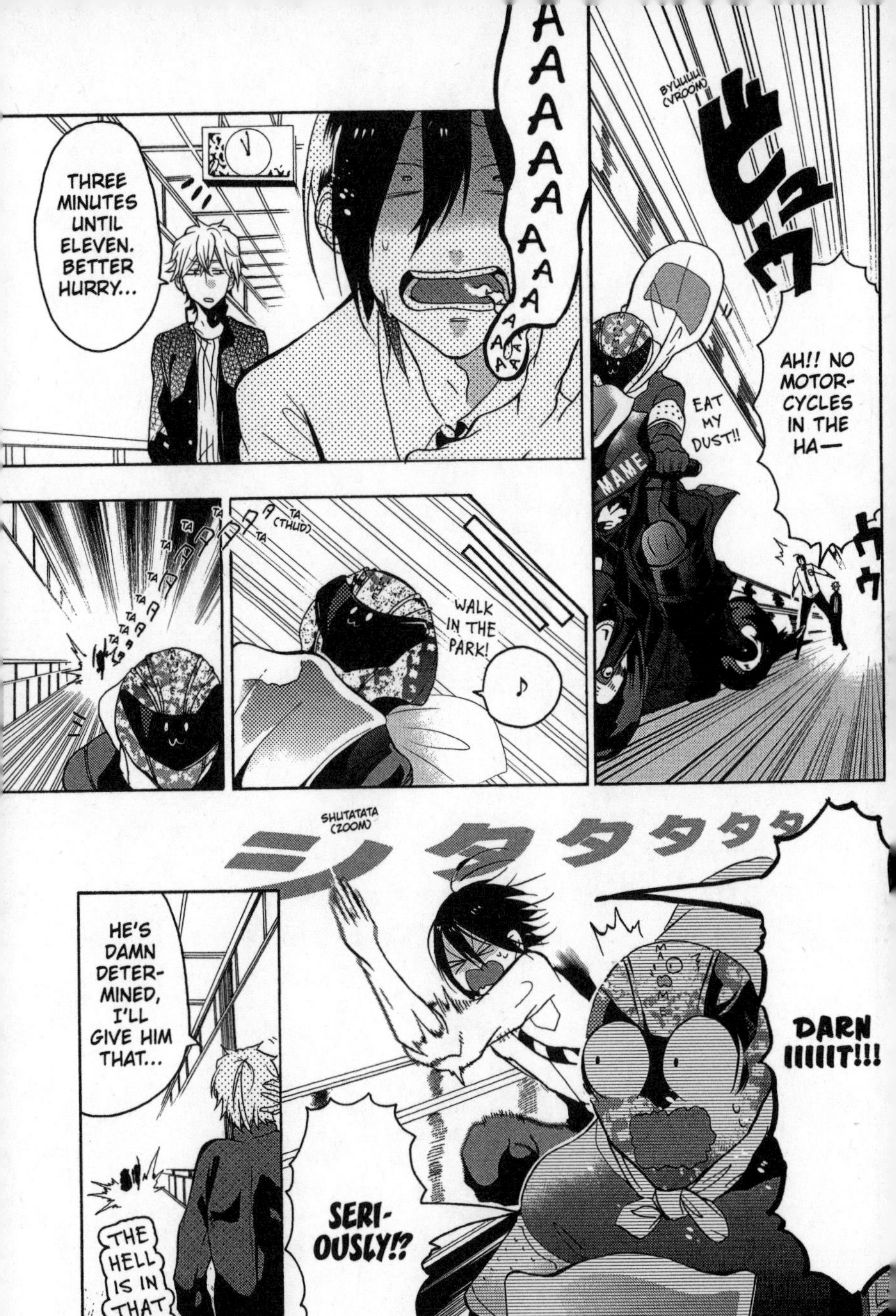
BYUUUU (VROOM)
EAT MY DUST!!
AH!! NO MOTOR-CYCLES IN THE HA—
THREE MINUTES UNTIL ELEVEN. BETTER HURRY...
AAAAAAAAAAAAAA
TA (THUD) TA
WALK IN THE PARK!
♪
TA TA TA TA TA TA TA TA
SHUTATATA (ZOOM)
DARN IIIIIT!!!
SERI-OUSLY!?
HE'S DAMN DETER-MINED, I'LL GIVE HIM THAT...
THE HELL IS IN THAT PAPER BAG?

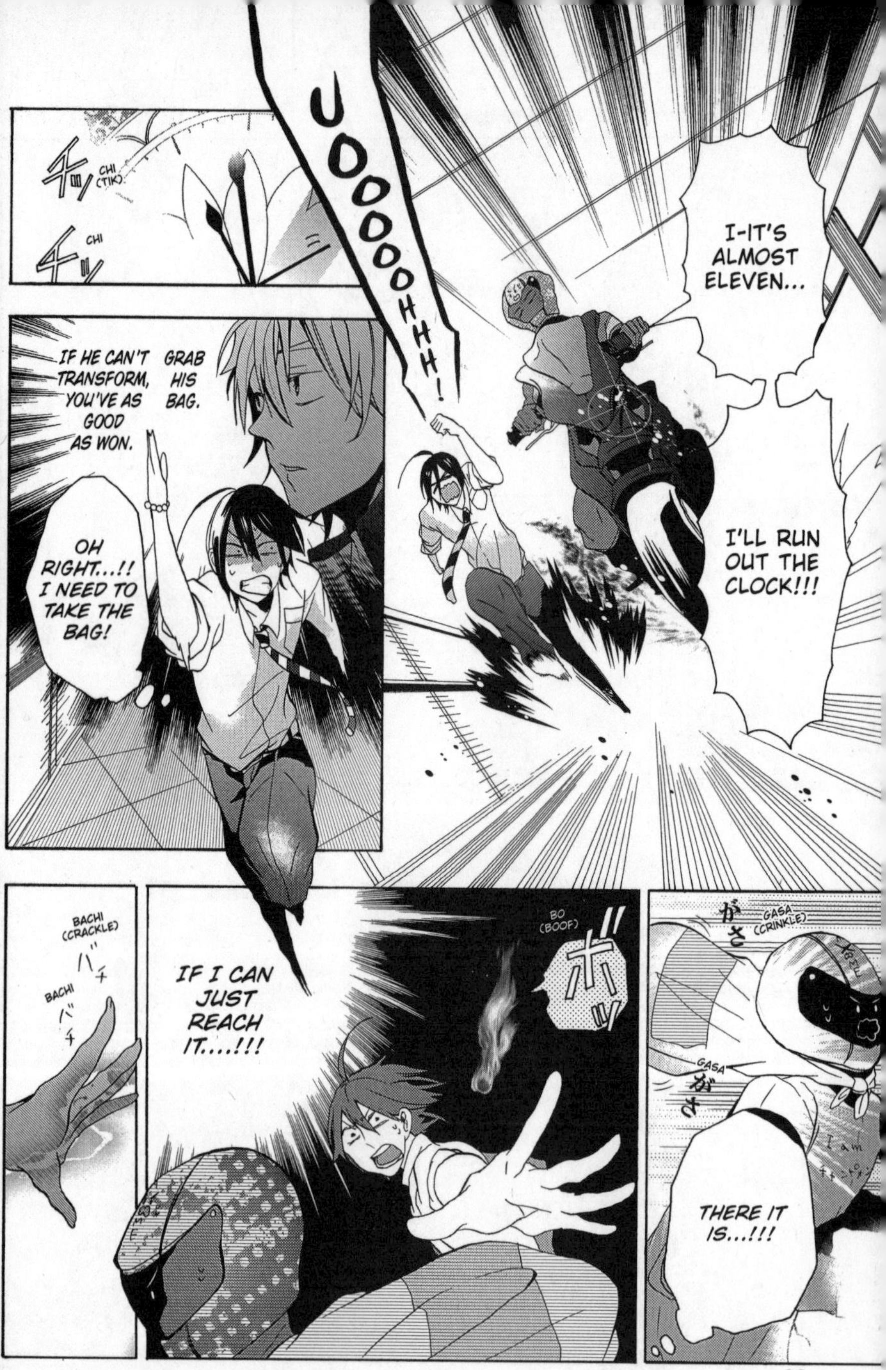
UOOOOOOHHH!
I-IT'S ALMOST ELEVEN...
I'LL RUN OUT THE CLOCK!!!
チッ
CHI (TIK)
チッ
CHI
GRAB HIS BAG.
IF HE CAN'T TRANSFORM, YOU'VE AS GOOD AS WON.
OH RIGHT...!! I NEED TO TAKE THE BAG!
がさ
GASA (CRINKLE)
がさ
GASA
THERE IT IS...!!!
ボッ
BO (BOOF)
IF I CAN JUST REACH IT....!!!
バチ
BACHI (CRACKLE)
バチ
BACHI

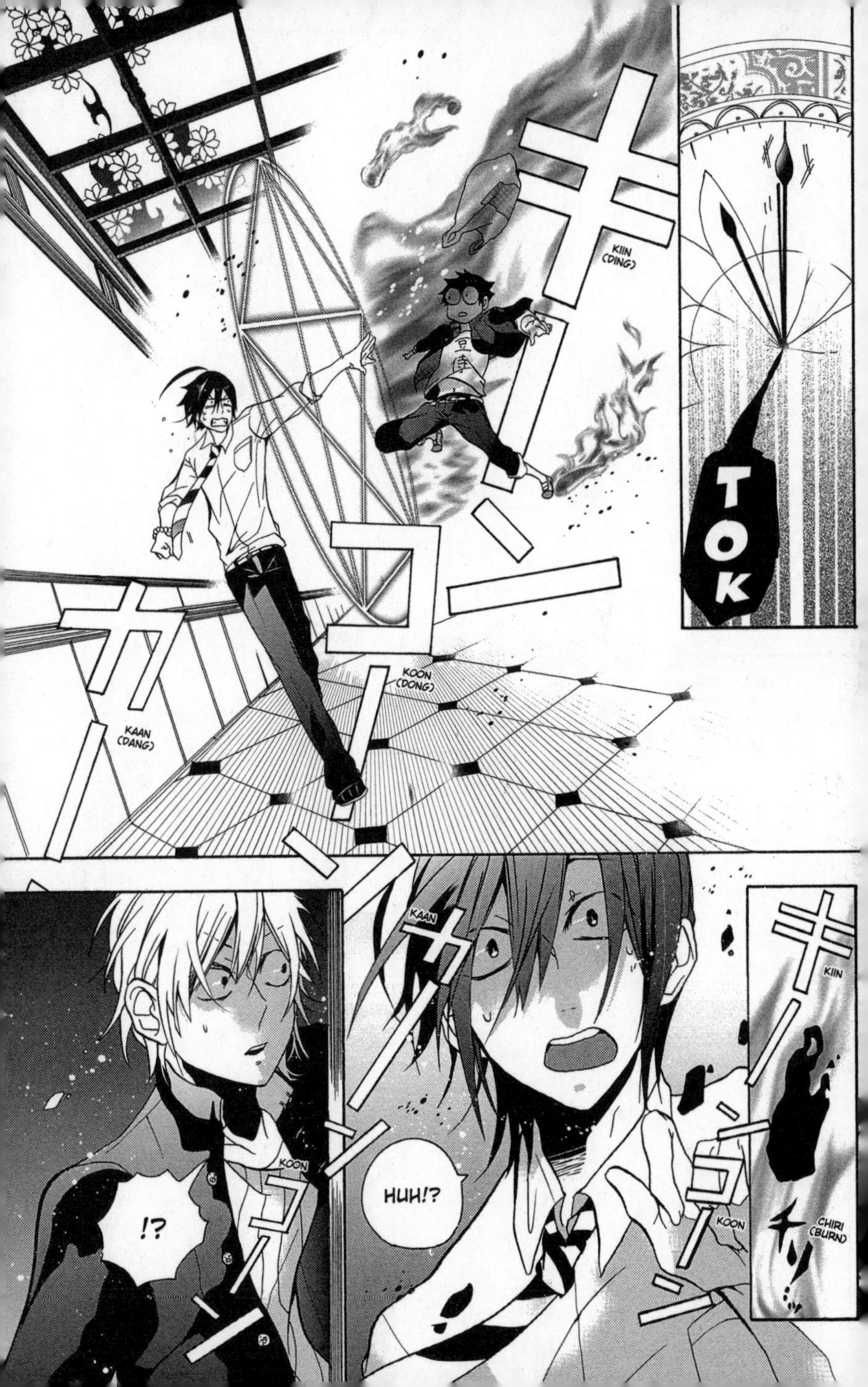
TOK
KIIN (DING)
KOON (DONG)
KAAN (DANG)
KIIN
CHIRI (BURN)
KAAN
HUH!?
KOON
!?
KOON

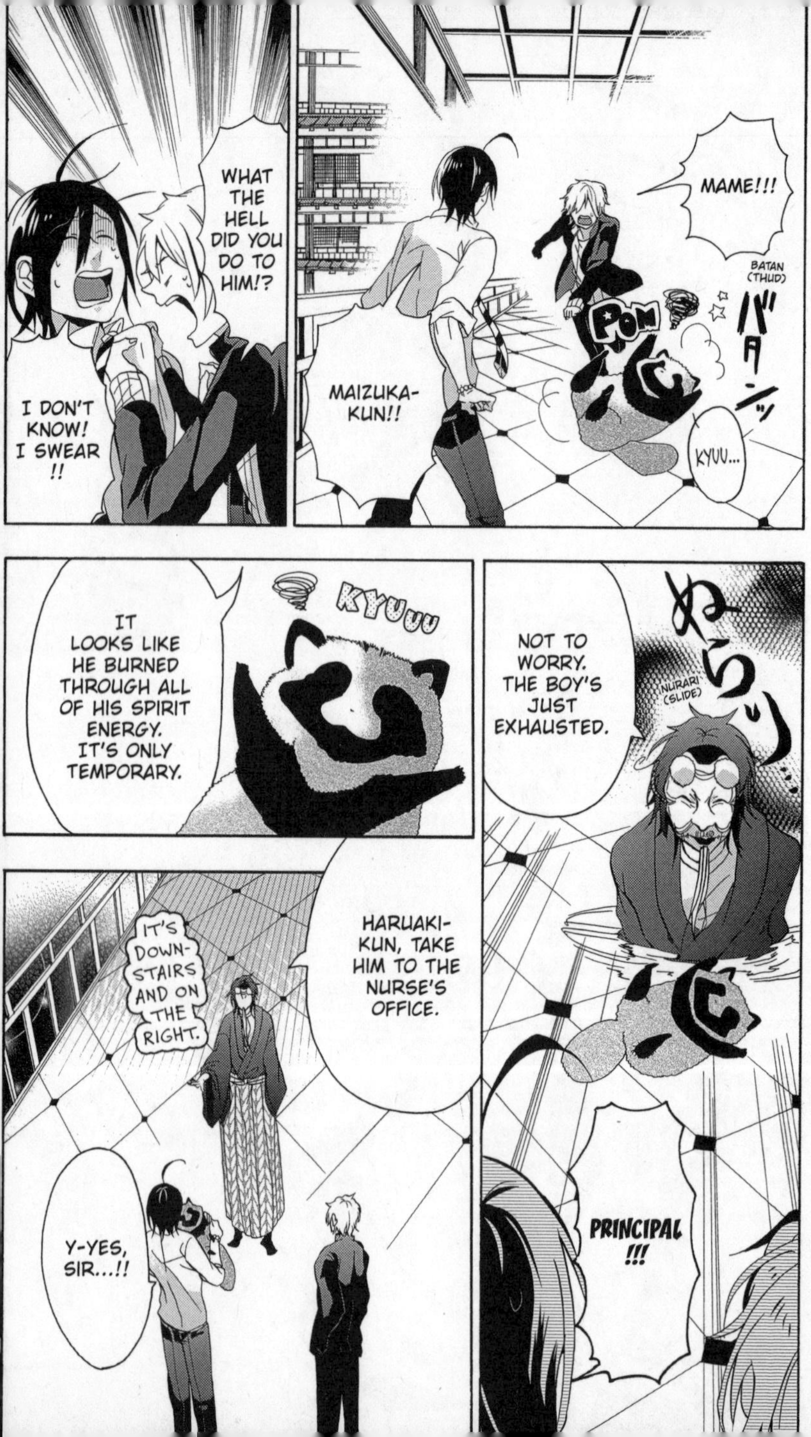
MAME!!!
BATAN (THUD)
バターッ
POM
KYUU...
MAIZUKA-KUN!!
WHAT THE HELL DID YOU DO TO HIM!?
I DON'T KNOW! I SWEAR!!
NURARI (SLIDE)
ぬらり
NOT TO WORRY. THE BOY'S JUST EXHAUSTED.
PRINCIPAL!!!
KYUUU
IT LOOKS LIKE HE BURNED THROUGH ALL OF HIS SPIRIT ENERGY. IT'S ONLY TEMPORARY.
HARUAKI-KUN, TAKE HIM TO THE NURSE'S OFFICE.
IT'S DOWNSTAIRS AND ON THE RIGHT.
Y-YES, SIR...!!

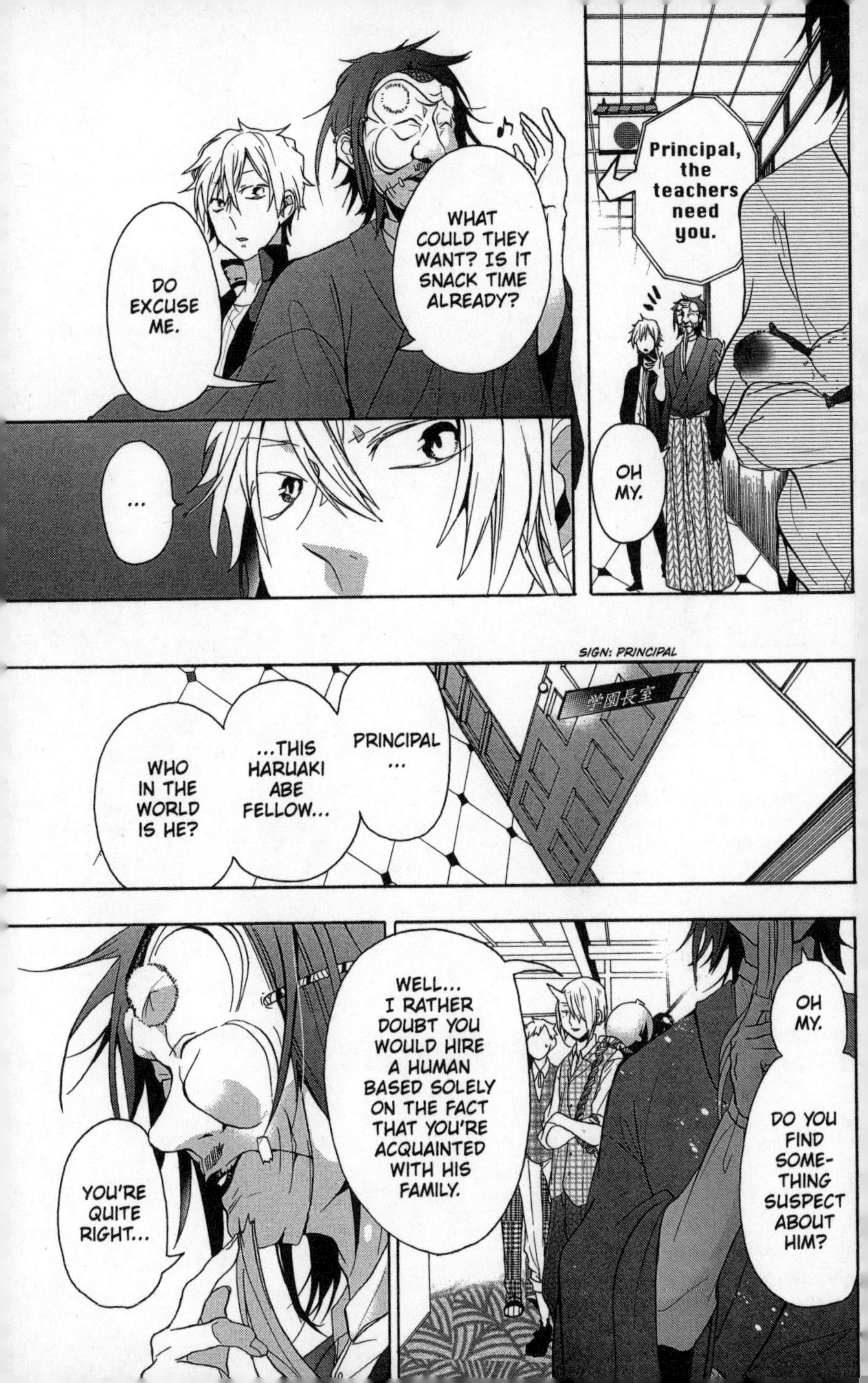
Principal, the teachers need you.
OH MY.
WHAT COULD THEY WANT? IS IT SNACK TIME ALREADY?
DO EXCUSE ME.
...
SIGN: PRINCIPAL
学園長室
PRINCIPAL...
...THIS HARUAKI ABE FELLOW...
WHO IN THE WORLD IS HE?
OH MY.
DO YOU FIND SOMETHING SUSPECT ABOUT HIM?
WELL... I RATHER DOUBT YOU WOULD HIRE A HUMAN BASED SOLELY ON THE FACT THAT YOU'RE ACQUAINTED WITH HIS FAMILY.
YOU'RE QUITE RIGHT...

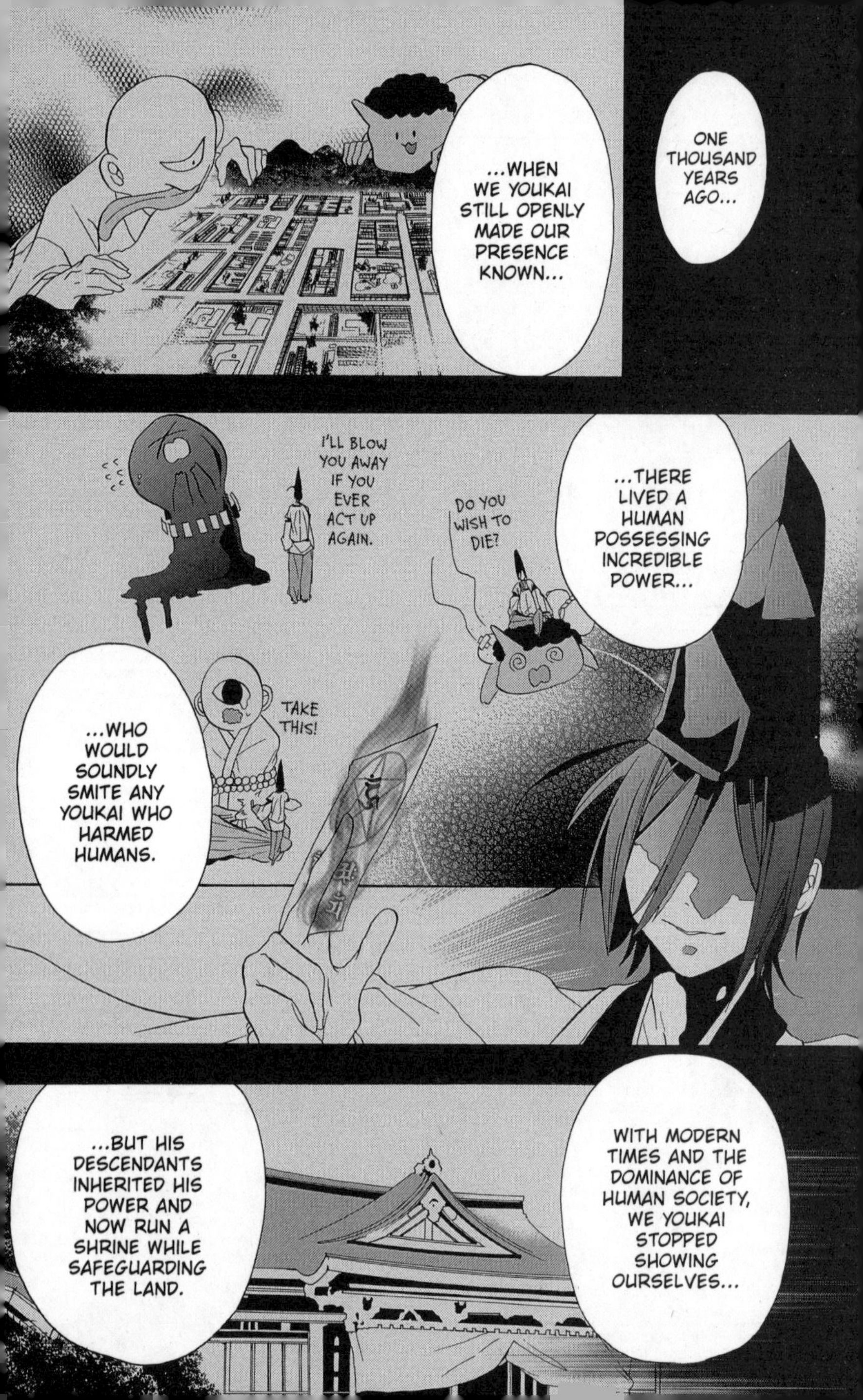
ONE THOUSAND YEARS AGO...
...WHEN WE YOUKAI STILL OPENLY MADE OUR PRESENCE KNOWN...
...THERE LIVED A HUMAN POSSESSING INCREDIBLE POWER...
DO YOU WISH TO DIE?
I'LL BLOW YOU AWAY IF YOU EVER ACT UP AGAIN.
TAKE THIS!
...WHO WOULD SOUNDLY SMITE ANY YOUKAI WHO HARMED HUMANS.
WITH MODERN TIMES AND THE DOMINANCE OF HUMAN SOCIETY, WE YOUKAI STOPPED SHOWING OURSELVES...
...BUT HIS DESCENDANTS INHERITED HIS POWER AND NOW RUN A SHRINE WHILE SAFEGUARDING THE LAND.

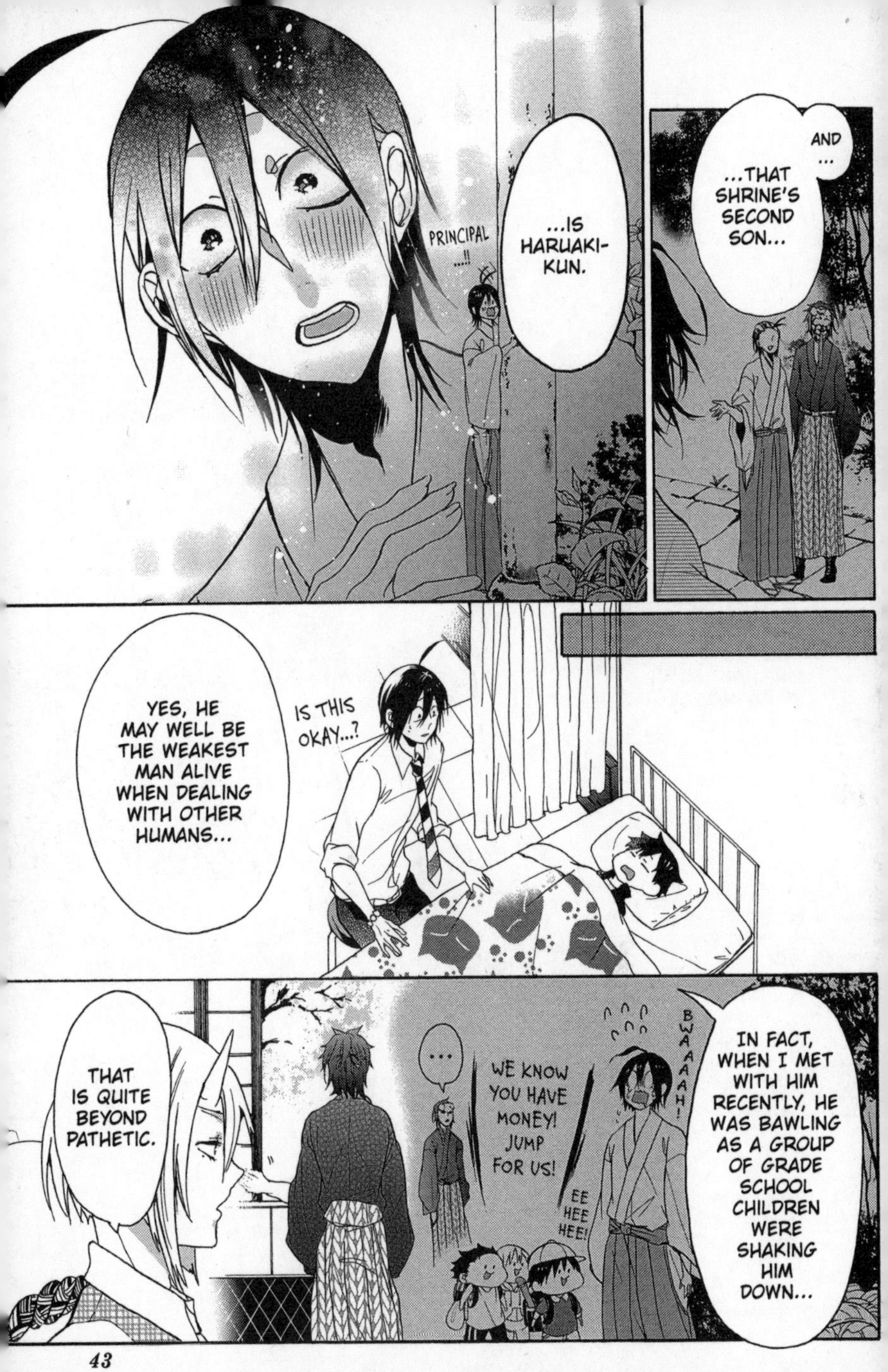
AND...
...THAT SHRINE'S SECOND SON...
...IS HARUAKI-KUN.
PRINCIPAL ...!!
YES, HE MAY WELL BE THE WEAKEST MAN ALIVE WHEN DEALING WITH OTHER HUMANS...
IS THIS OKAY...?
IN FACT, WHEN I MET WITH HIM RECENTLY, HE WAS BAWLING AS A GROUP OF GRADE SCHOOL CHILDREN WERE SHAKING HIM DOWN...
BWAAAAH!
WE KNOW YOU HAVE MONEY! JUMP FOR US!
EE HEE HEE!
...
THAT IS QUITE BEYOND PATHETIC.

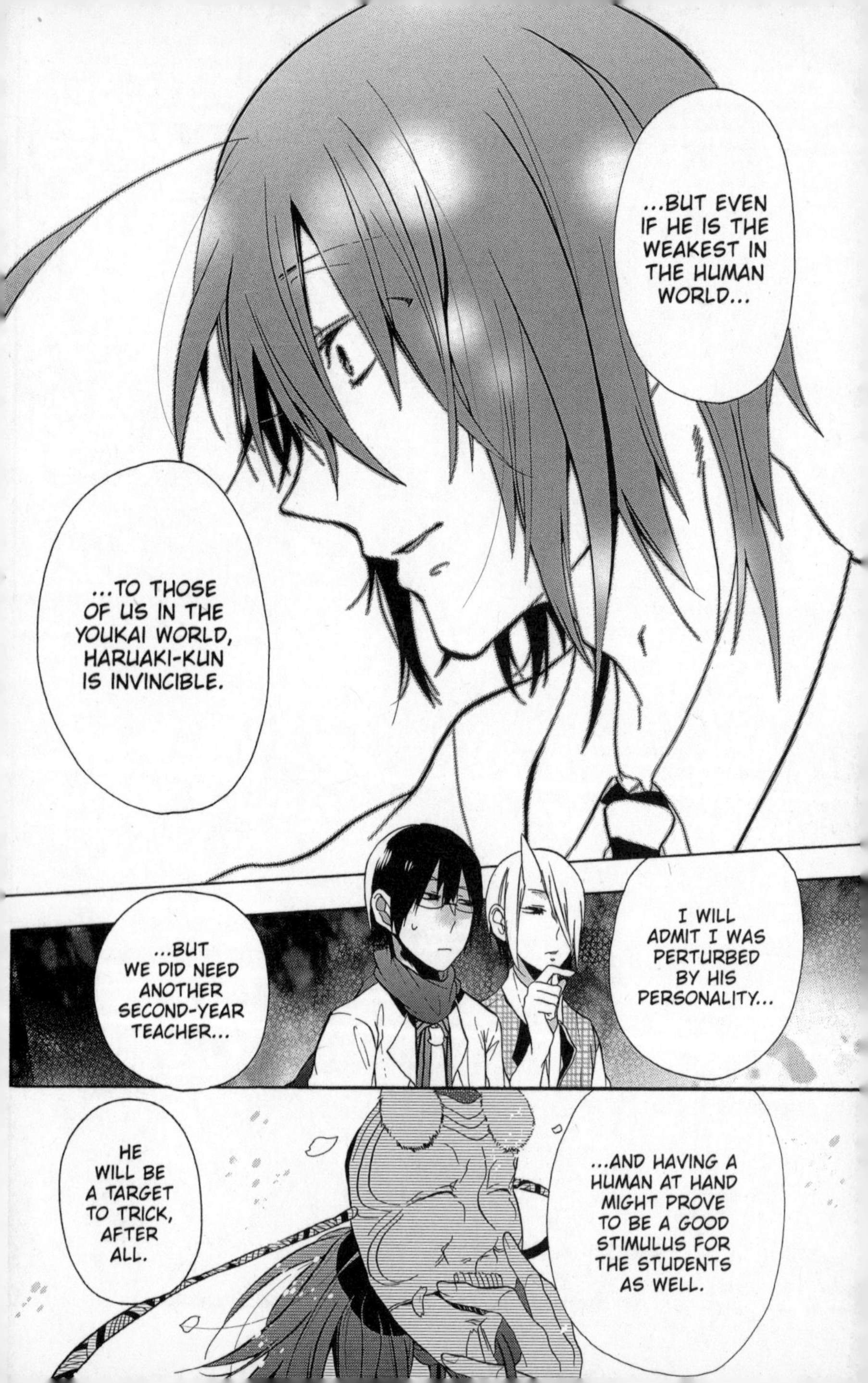
...BUT EVEN IF HE IS THE WEAKEST IN THE HUMAN WORLD...
...TO THOSE OF US IN THE YOUKAI WORLD, HARUAKI-KUN IS INVINCIBLE.
I WILL ADMIT I WAS PERTURBED BY HIS PERSONALITY...
...BUT WE DID NEED ANOTHER SECOND-YEAR TEACHER...
...AND HAVING A HUMAN AT HAND MIGHT PROVE TO BE A GOOD STIMULUS FOR THE STUDENTS AS WELL.
HE WILL BE A TARGET TO TRICK, AFTER ALL.

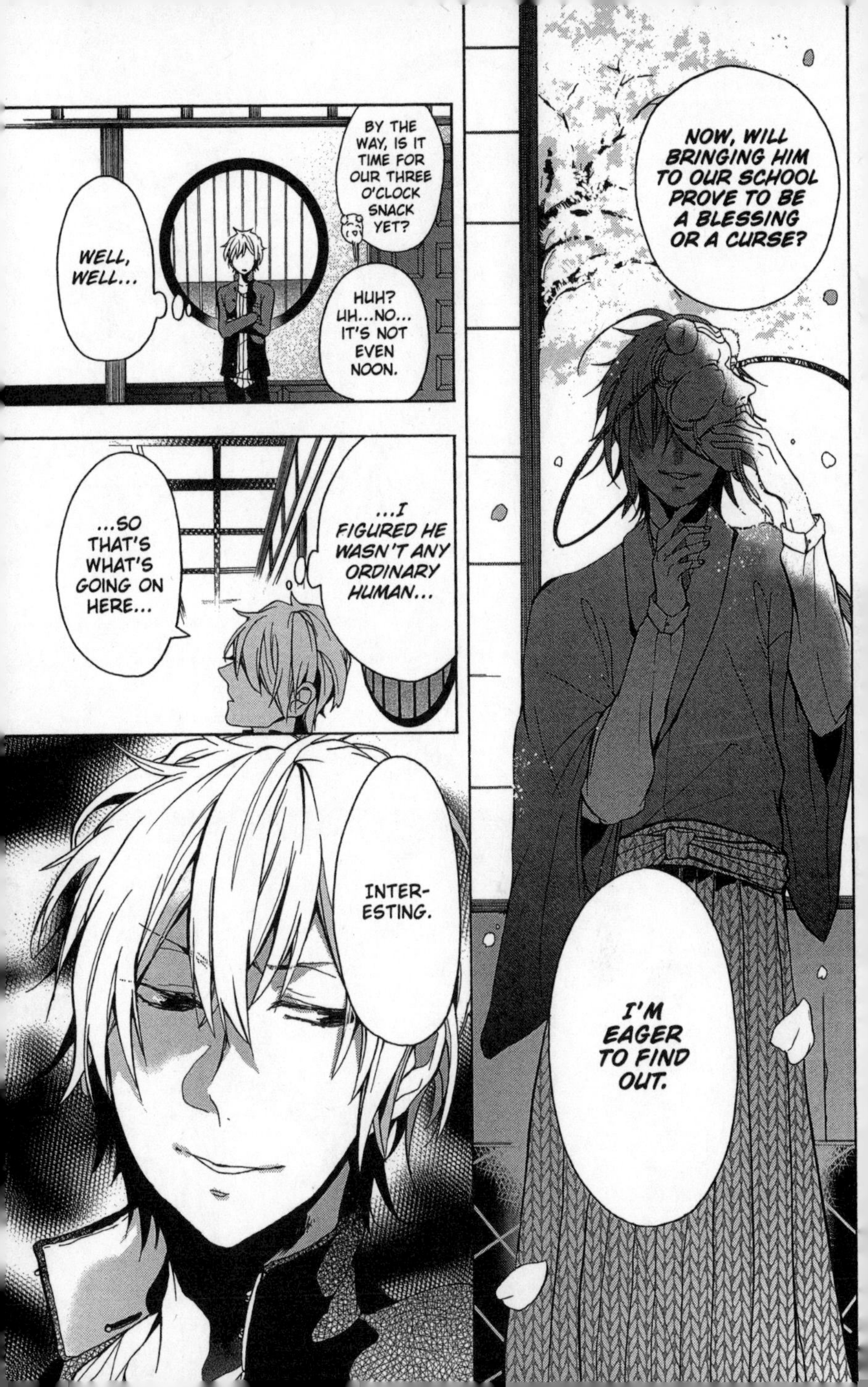
NOW, WILL BRINGING HIM TO OUR SCHOOL PROVE TO BE A BLESSING OR A CURSE?
I'M EAGER TO FIND OUT.
BY THE WAY, IS IT TIME FOR OUR THREE O'CLOCK SNACK YET?
HUH? UH...NO... IT'S NOT EVEN NOON.
WELL, WELL...
...I FIGURED HE WASN'T ANY ORDINARY HUMAN...
...SO THAT'S WHAT'S GOING ON HERE...
INTER-ESTING.

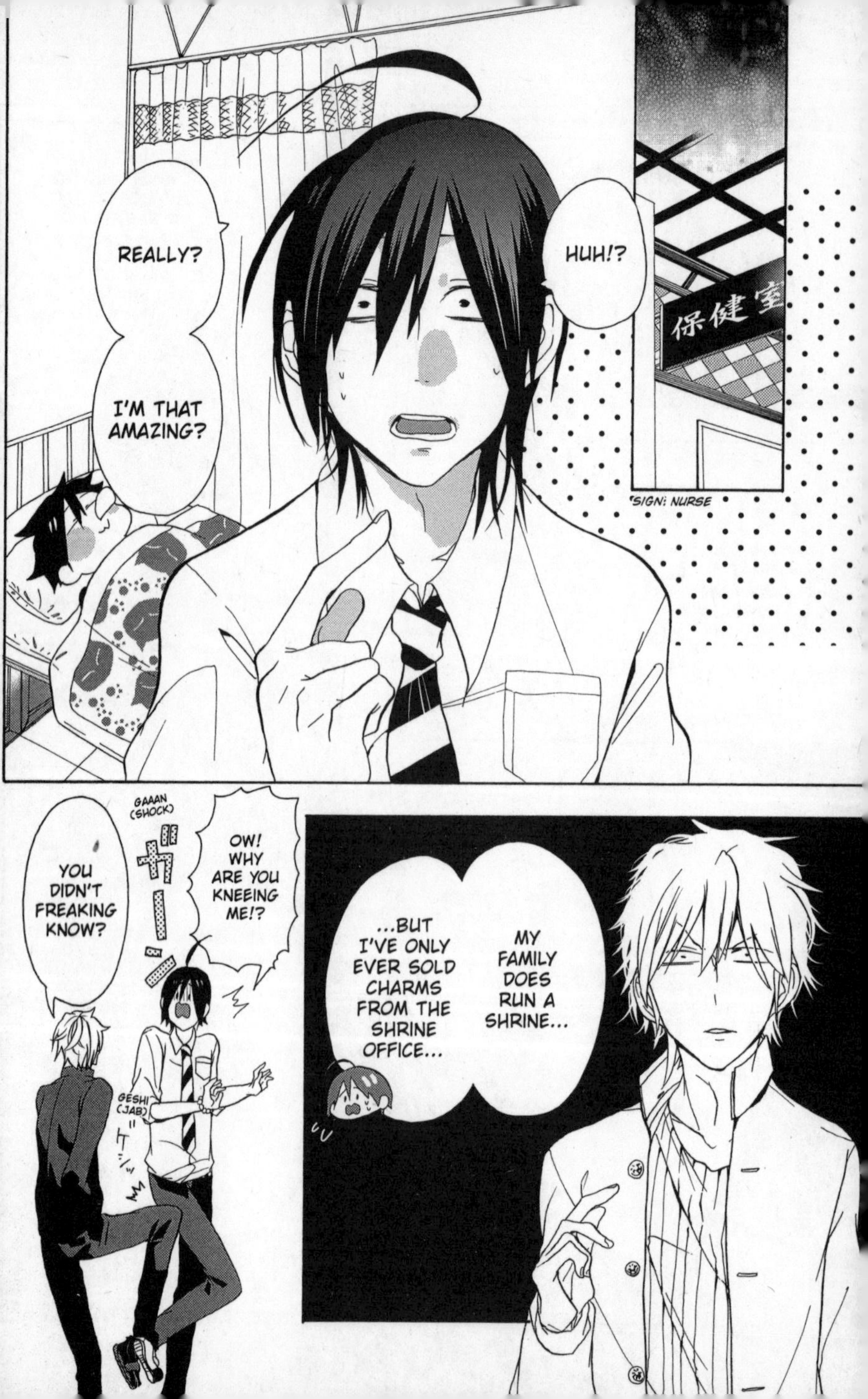
保健室
*SIGN: NURSE
HUH!?
REALLY?
I'M THAT AMAZING?
MY FAMILY DOES RUN A SHRINE...
...BUT I'VE ONLY EVER SOLD CHARMS FROM THE SHRINE OFFICE...
OW! WHY ARE YOU KNEEING ME!?
GAAAN (SHOCK)
YOU DIDN'T FREAKING KNOW?
GESHI (JAB)

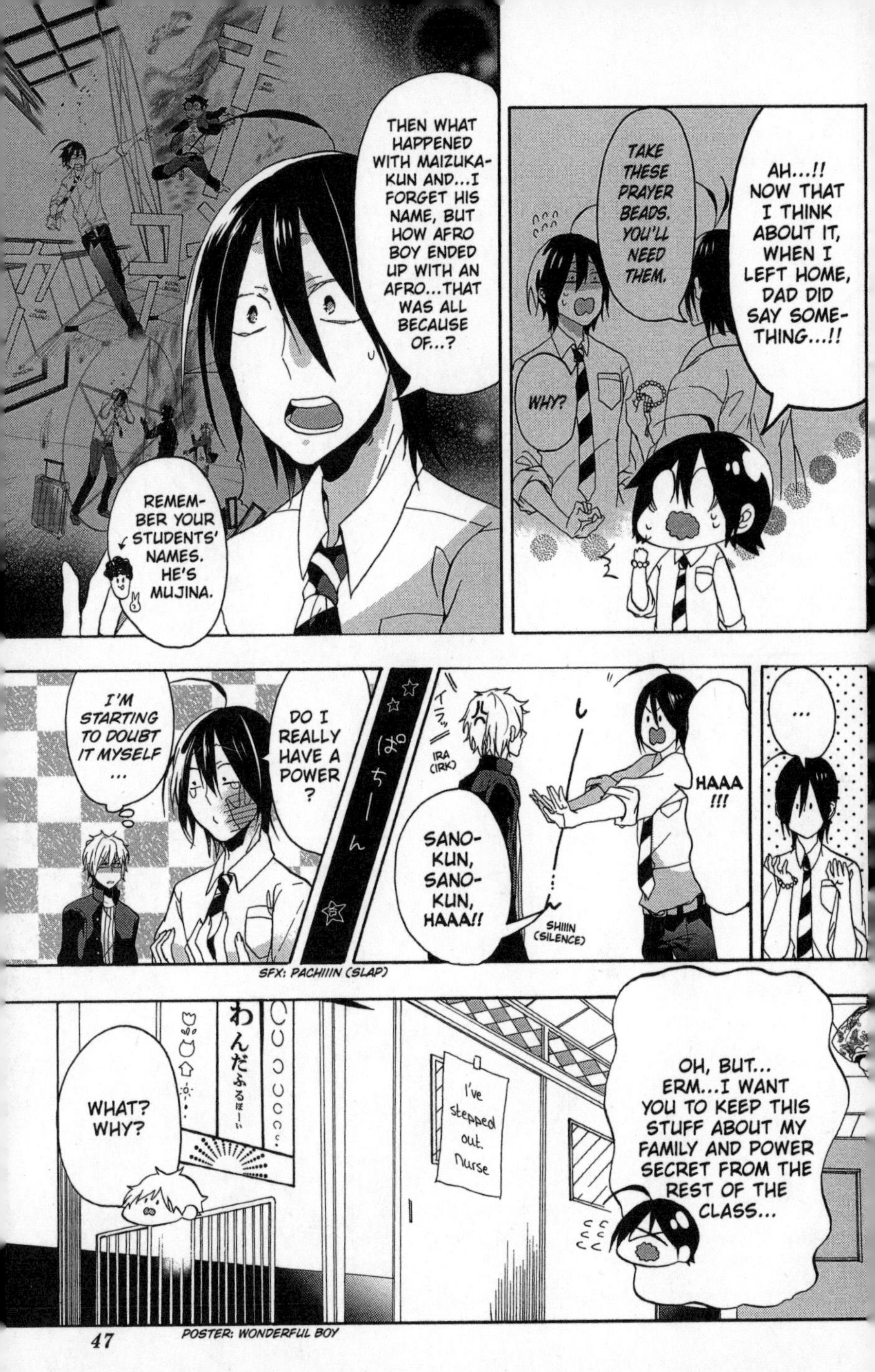
AH...!! NOW THAT I THINK ABOUT IT, WHEN I LEFT HOME, DAD DID SAY SOMETHING...!!
TAKE THESE PRAYER BEADS. YOU'LL NEED THEM.
WHY?
THEN WHAT HAPPENED WITH MAIZUKA-KUN AND...I FORGET HIS NAME, BUT HOW AFRO BOY ENDED UP WITH AN AFRO...THAT WAS ALL BECAUSE OF...?
REMEMBER YOUR STUDENTS' NAMES. HE'S MUJINA.
...
HAAA!!!
し...ん
イラッ
IRA (IRK)
SANO-KUN, SANO-KUN, HAAA!!
SHIIIN (SILENCE)
ぱちーん
DO I REALLY HAVE A POWER?
I'M STARTING TO DOUBT IT MYSELF...
OH, BUT...ERM...I WANT YOU TO KEEP THIS STUFF ABOUT MY FAMILY AND POWER SECRET FROM THE REST OF THE CLASS...
I've stepped out. Nurse
わんだふるぼーい
WHAT? WHY?
SFX: PACHIIIN (SLAP)

POSTER: WONDERFUL BOY

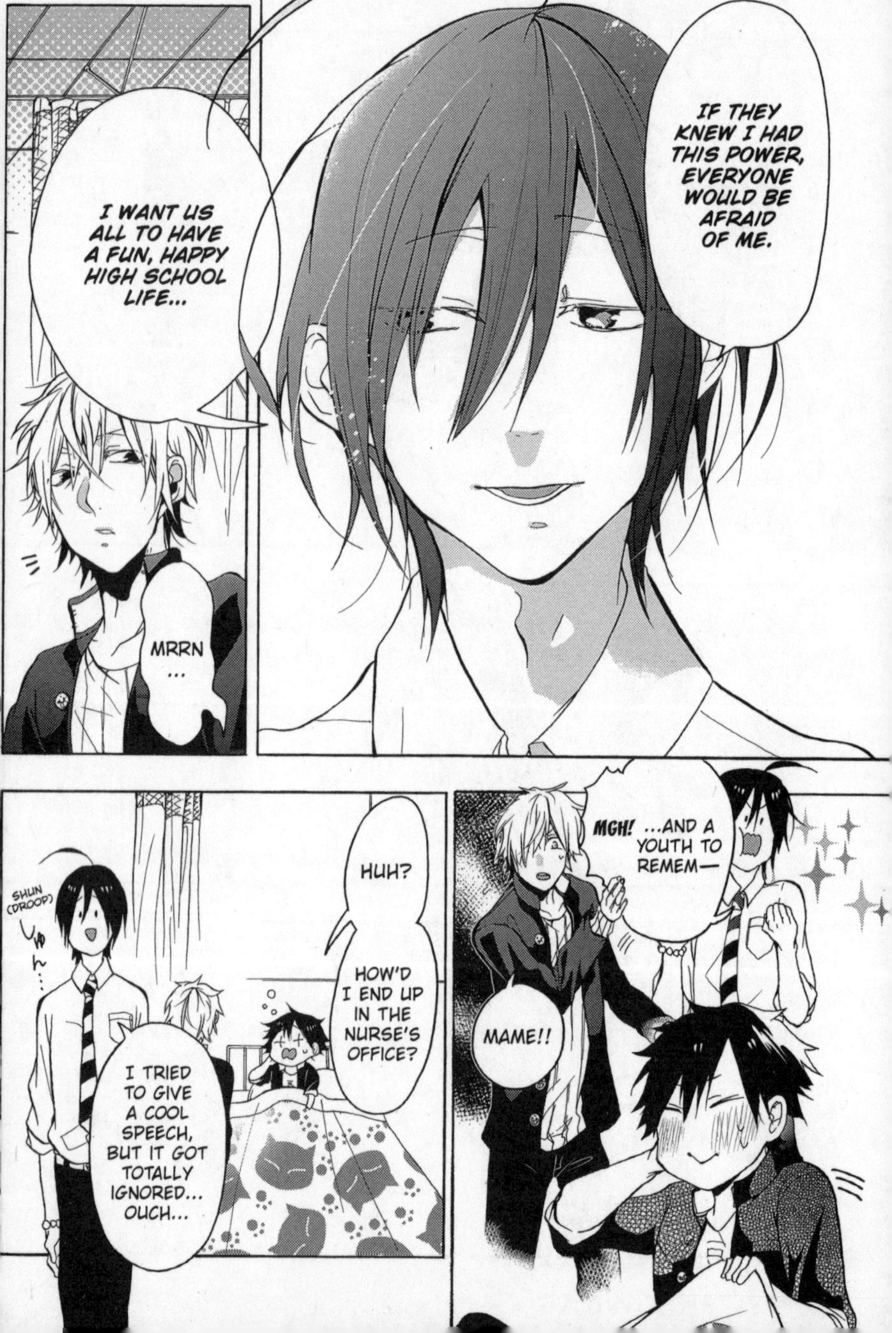
IF THEY KNEW I HAD THIS POWER, EVERYONE WOULD BE AFRAID OF ME.
I WANT US ALL TO HAVE A FUN, HAPPY HIGH SCHOOL LIFE...
MRRN ...
MGH! ...AND A YOUTH TO REMEM—
MAME!!
HUH?
HOW'D I END UP IN THE NURSE'S OFFICE?
SHUN (DROOP)
しゅん…
I TRIED TO GIVE A COOL SPEECH, BUT IT GOT TOTALLY IGNORED... OUCH...

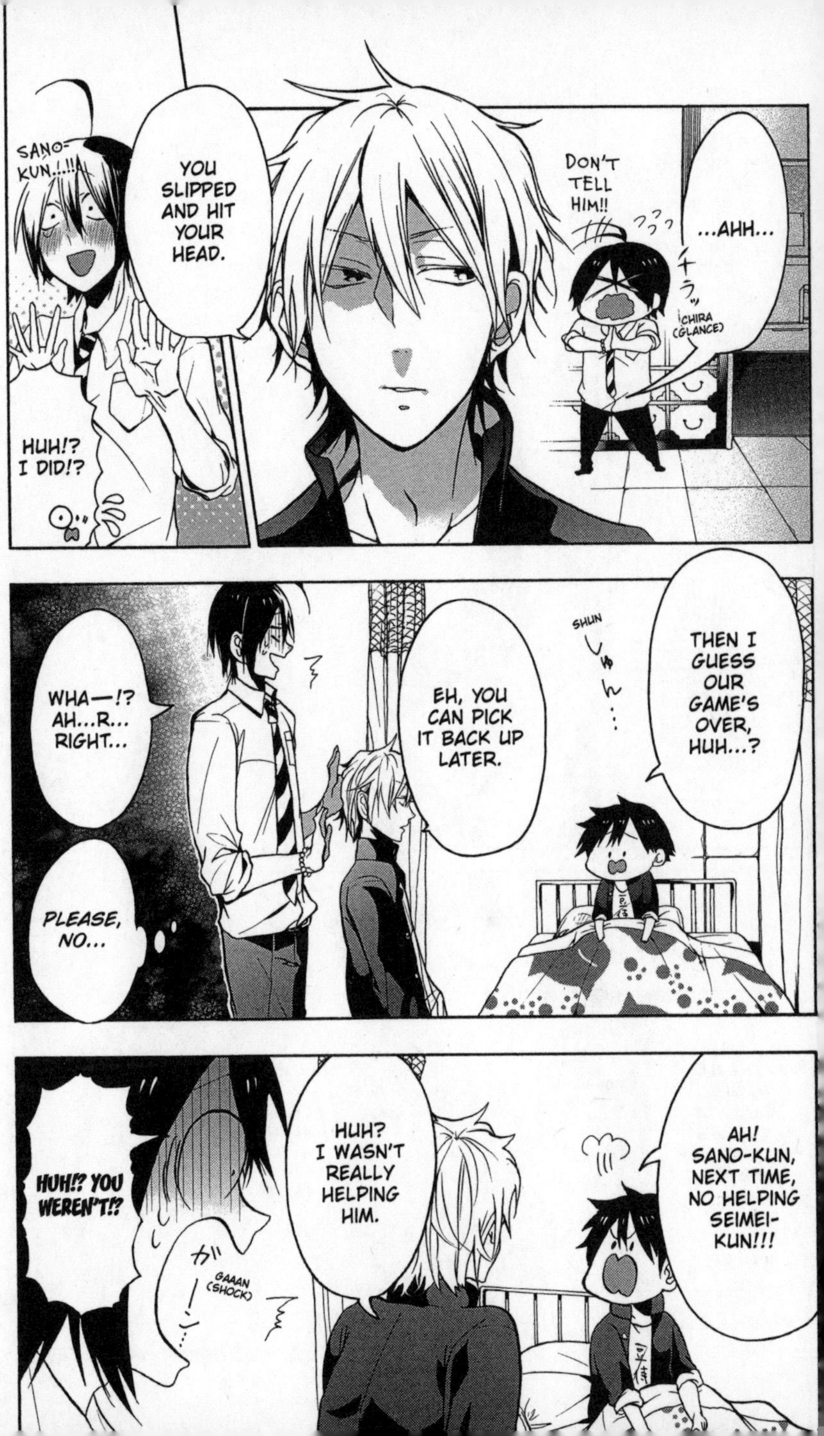
...AHH...
DON'T TELL HIM!!
CHIRA (GLANCE)
YOU SLIPPED AND HIT YOUR HEAD.
SANO-KUN...!!
HUH!? I DID!?
THEN I GUESS OUR GAME'S OVER, HUH...?
SHUN
EH, YOU CAN PICK IT BACK UP LATER.
WHA—!? AH...R... RIGHT...
PLEASE, NO...
AH! SANO-KUN, NEXT TIME, NO HELPING SEIMEI-KUN!!!
HUH? I WASN'T REALLY HELPING HIM.
HUH!? YOU WEREN'T!?
GAAAN (SHOCK)

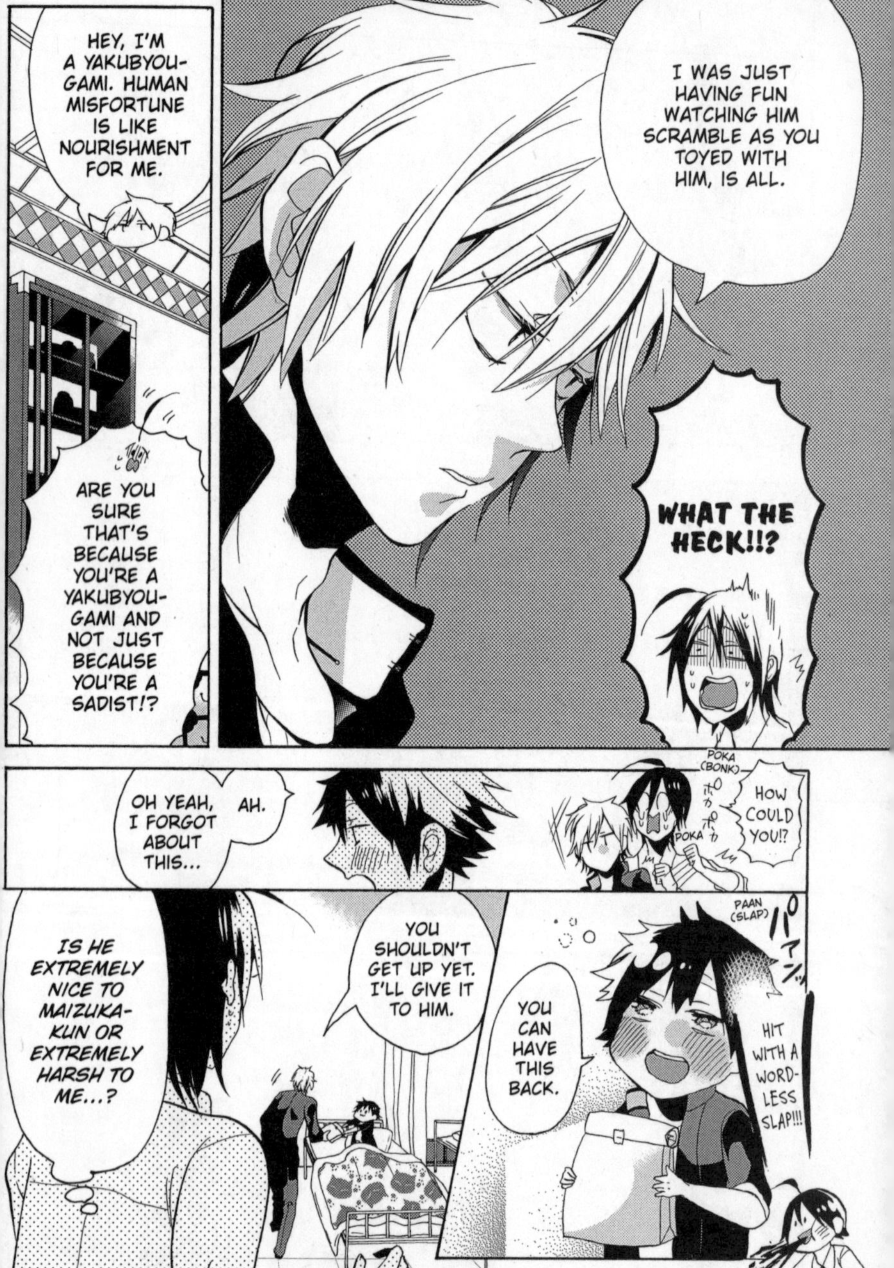
I WAS JUST HAVING FUN WATCHING HIM SCRAMBLE AS YOU TOYED WITH HIM, IS ALL.
WHAT THE HECK!!?
HEY, I'M A YAKUBYOU-GAMI. HUMAN MISFORTUNE IS LIKE NOURISHMENT FOR ME.
ARE YOU SURE THAT'S BECAUSE YOU'RE A YAKUBYOU-GAMI AND NOT JUST BECAUSE YOU'RE A SADIST!?
POKA (BONK)
POKA
HOW COULD YOU!?
AH.
OH YEAH, I FORGOT ABOUT THIS...
PAAN (SLAP)
YOU CAN HAVE THIS BACK.
HIT WITH A WORD-LESS SLAP!!!
YOU SHOULDN'T GET UP YET. I'LL GIVE IT TO HIM.
IS HE EXTREMELY NICE TO MAIZUKA-KUN OR EXTREMELY HARSH TO ME...?

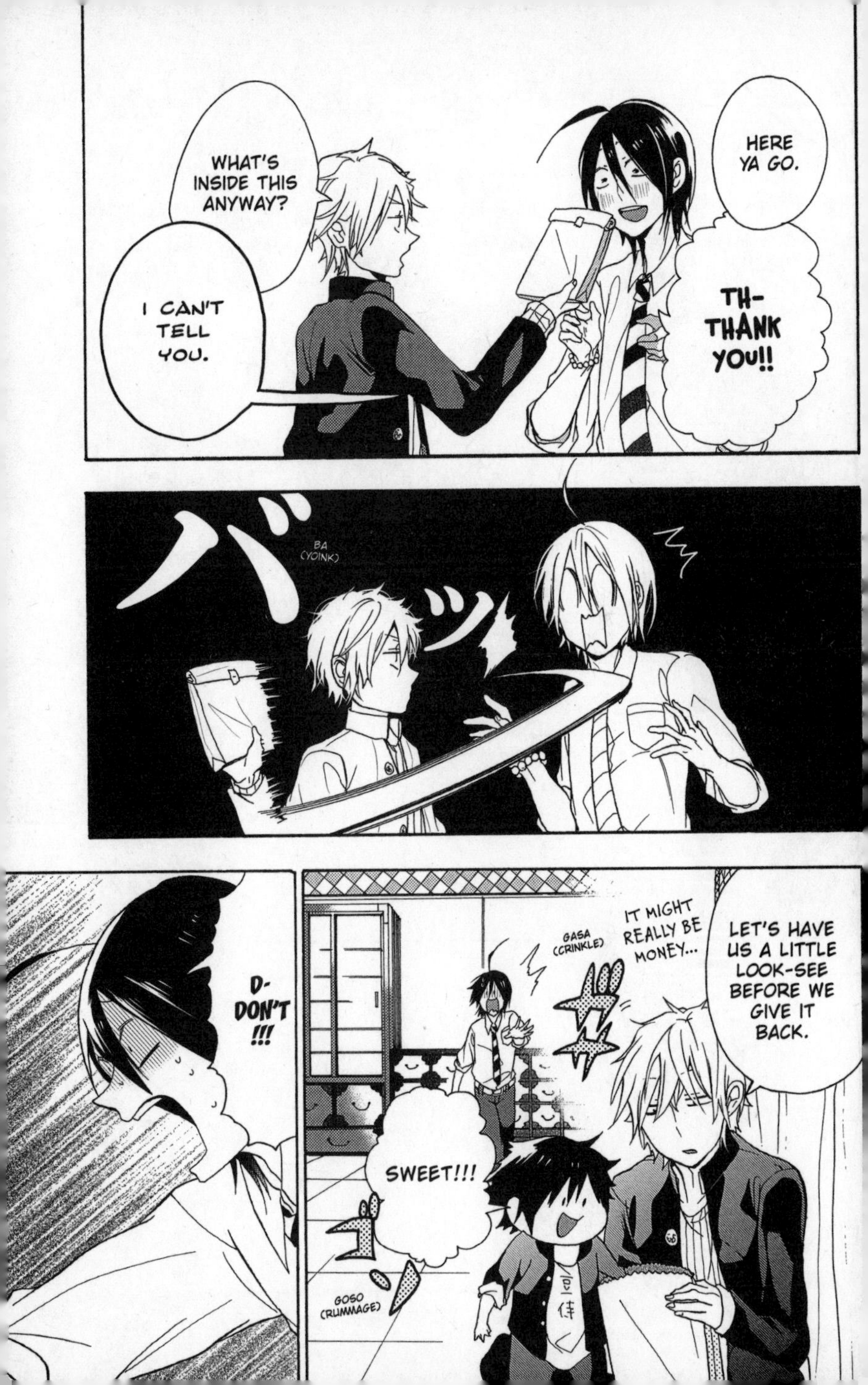
HERE YA GO.
TH- THANK YOU!!
WHAT'S INSIDE THIS ANYWAY?
I CAN'T TELL YOU.
BA (YOINK)
LET'S HAVE US A LITTLE LOOK-SEE BEFORE WE GIVE IT BACK.
IT MIGHT REALLY BE MONEY...
GASA (CRINKLE)
SWEET!!!
GOSO (RUMMAGE)
D- DON'T !!!

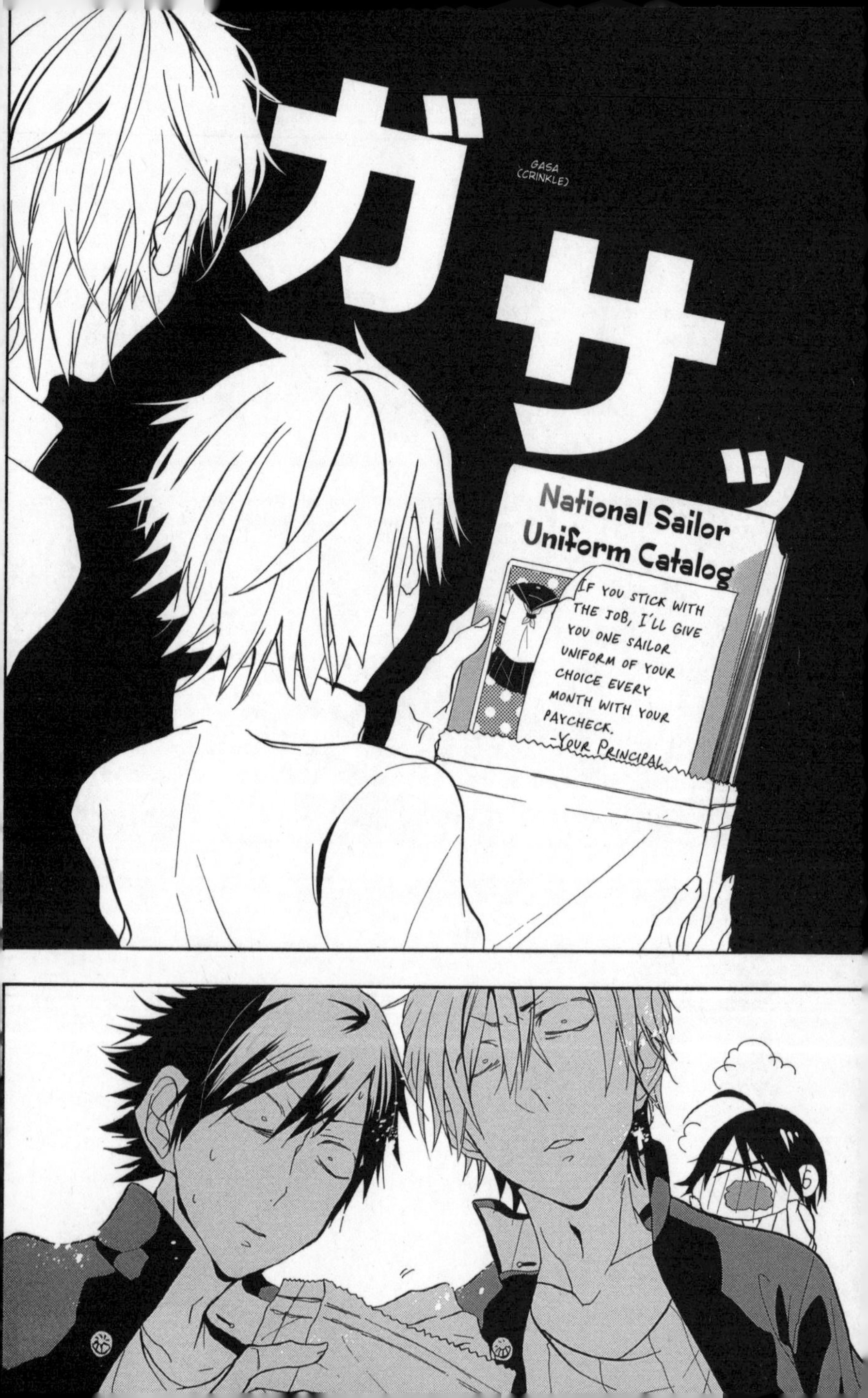
ガサッ
GASA (CRINKLE)
National Sailor Uniform Catalog
IF YOU STICK WITH THE JOB, I'LL GIVE YOU ONE SAILOR UNIFORM OF YOUR CHOICE EVERY MONTH WITH YOUR PAYCHECK.
-YOUR PRINCIPAL

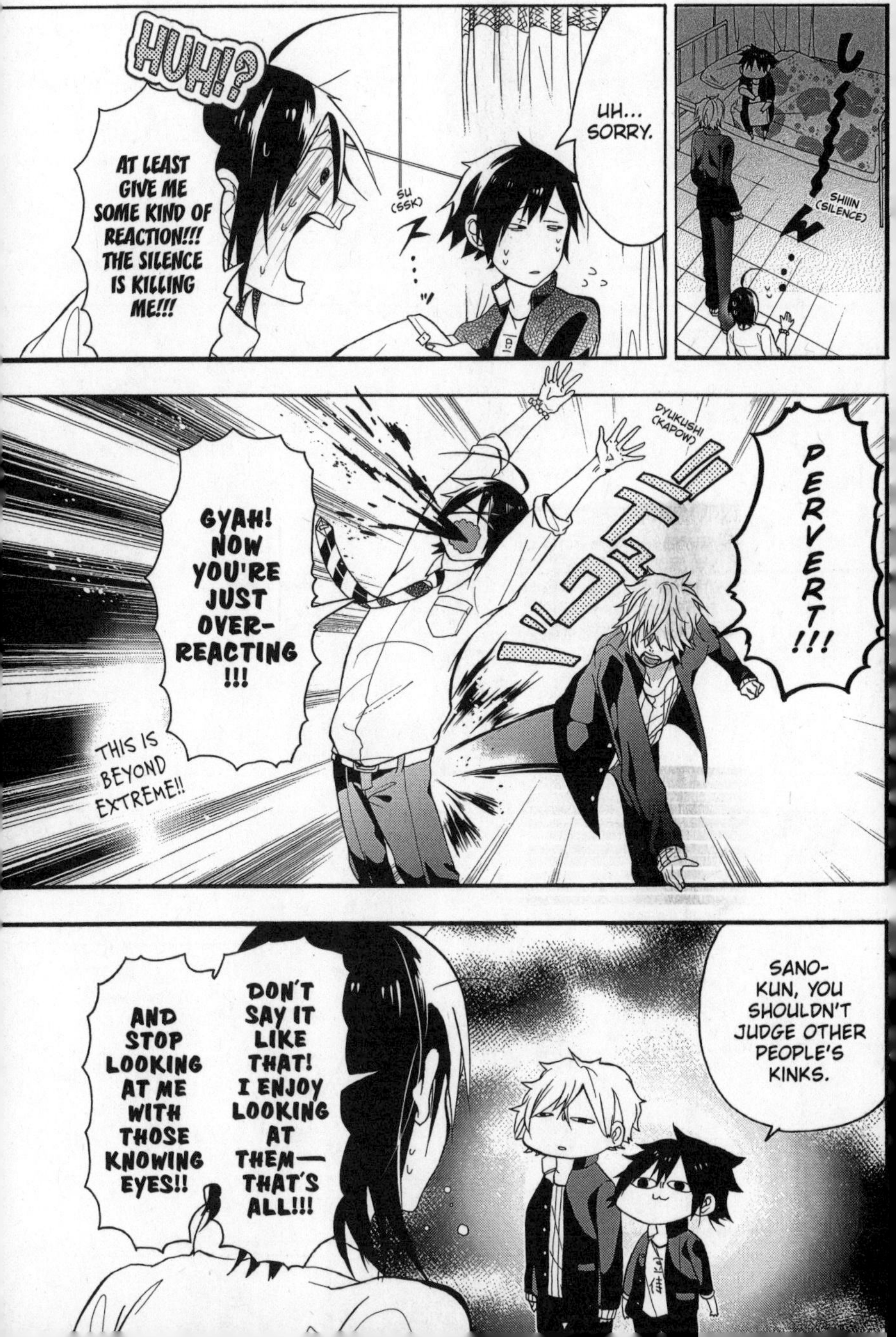
SHIIIN (SILENCE)
UH... SORRY.
SU (SSK)
HUH!?
AT LEAST GIVE ME SOME KIND OF REACTION!!! THE SILENCE IS KILLING ME!!!
PERVERT!!!
DYUKUSHI (KAPOW)
GYAH! NOW YOU'RE JUST OVER-REACTING!!!
THIS IS BEYOND EXTREME!!
SANO-KUN, YOU SHOULDN'T JUDGE OTHER PEOPLE'S KINKS.
DON'T SAY IT LIKE THAT! I ENJOY LOOKING AT THEM—THAT'S ALL!!!
AND STOP LOOKING AT ME WITH THOSE KNOWING EYES!!

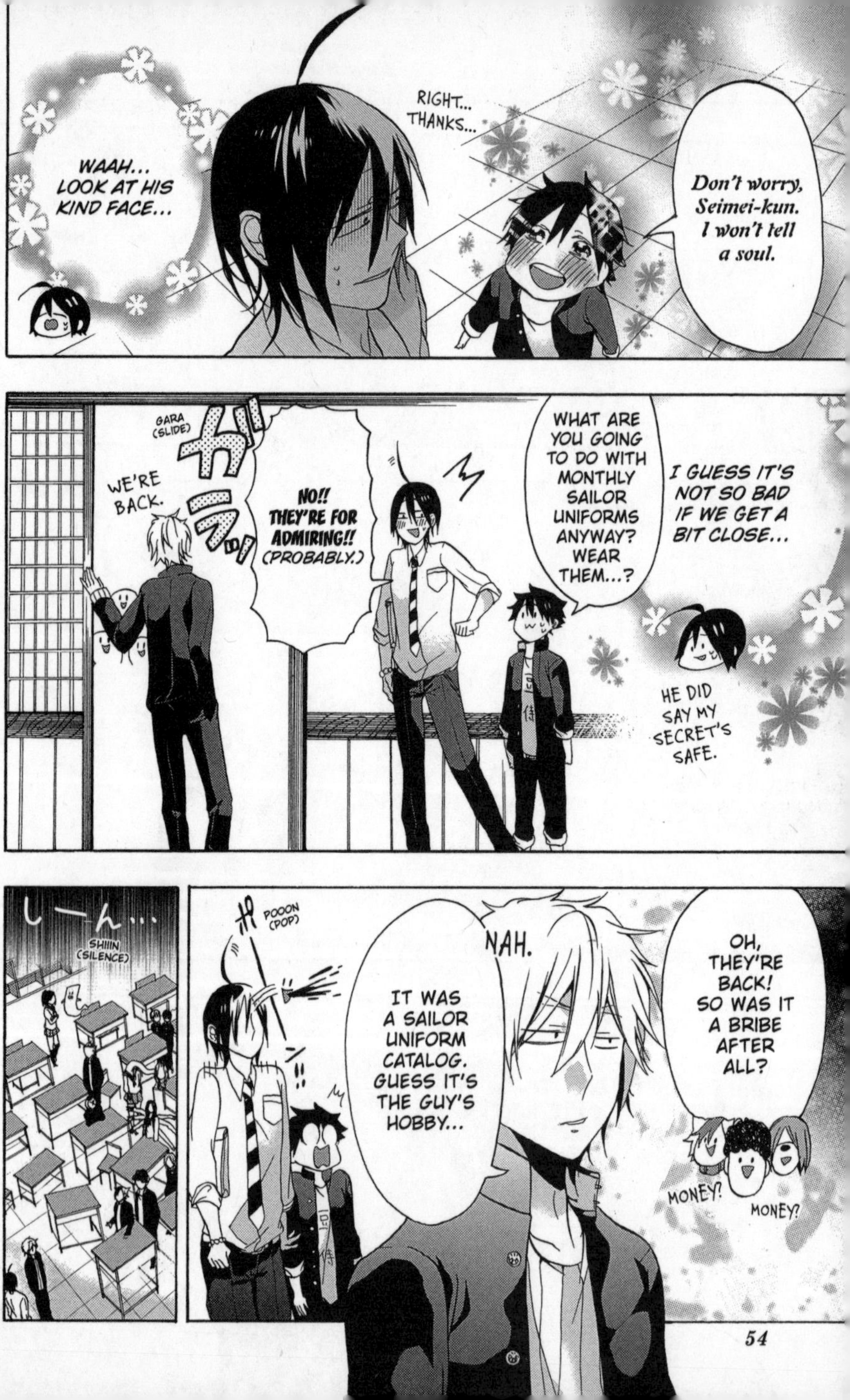
Don't worry, Seimei-kun. I won't tell a soul.
RIGHT... THANKS...
WAAH... LOOK AT HIS KIND FACE...
I GUESS IT'S NOT SO BAD IF WE GET A BIT CLOSE...
HE DID SAY MY SECRET'S SAFE.
WHAT ARE YOU GOING TO DO WITH MONTHLY SAILOR UNIFORMS ANYWAY? WEAR THEM...?
NO!! THEY'RE FOR ADMIRING!! (PROBABLY.)
ガラッ
GARA (SLIDE)
WE'RE BACK.
OH, THEY'RE BACK! SO WAS IT A BRIBE AFTER ALL?
MONEY?
MONEY?
NAH.
IT WAS A SAILOR UNIFORM CATALOG. GUESS IT'S THE GUY'S HOBBY...
POOON (POP)
しーん…
SHIIIN (SILENCE)

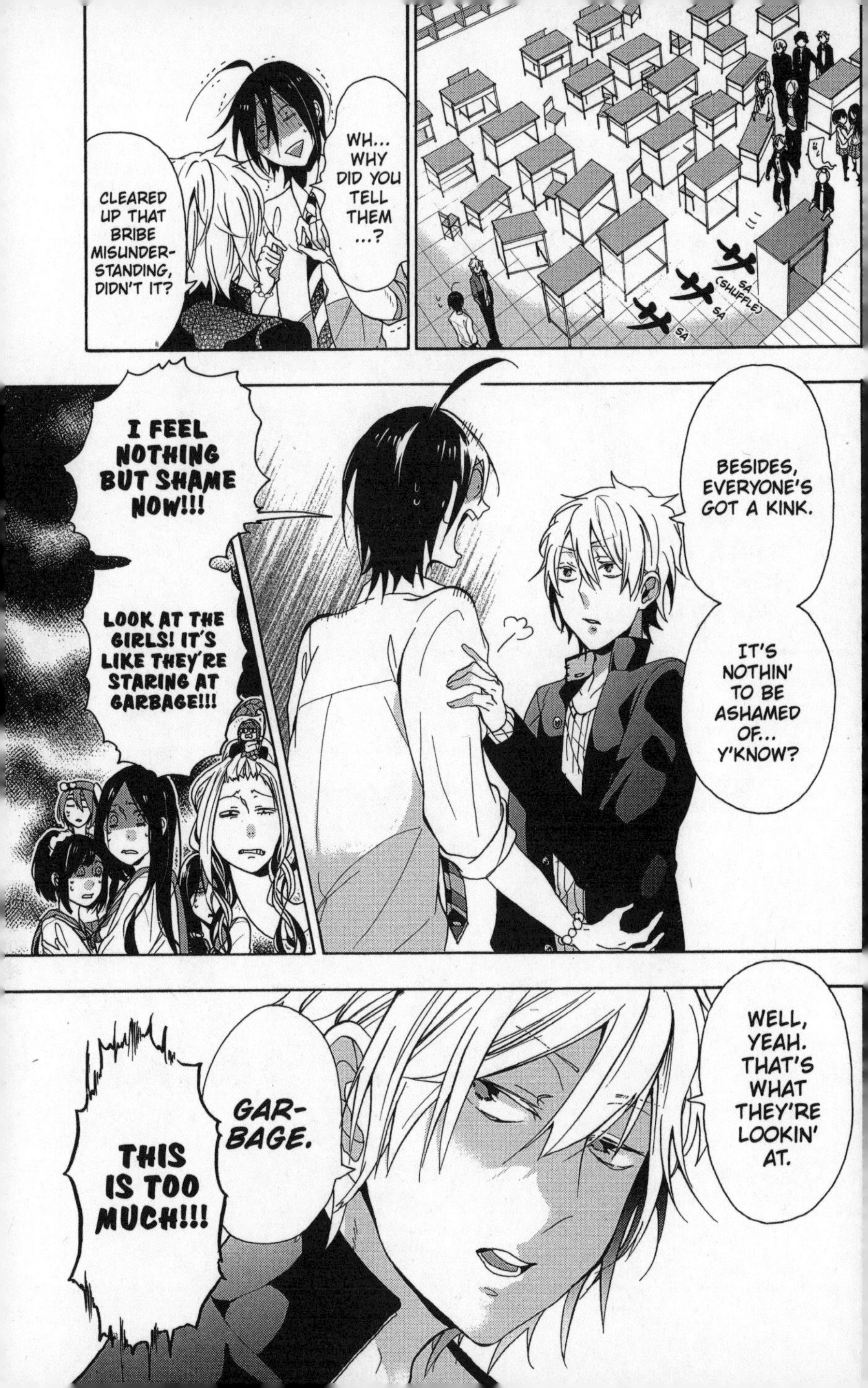
SA SA SA
(SHUFFLE)
WH... WHY DID YOU TELL THEM ...?
CLEARED UP THAT BRIBE MISUNDER-STANDING, DIDN'T IT?
BESIDES, EVERYONE'S GOT A KINK.
IT'S NOTHIN' TO BE ASHAMED OF... Y'KNOW?
I FEEL NOTHING BUT SHAME NOW!!!
LOOK AT THE GIRLS! IT'S LIKE THEY'RE STARING AT GARBAGE!!!
WELL, YEAH. THAT'S WHAT THEY'RE LOOKIN' AT.
GAR-BAGE.
THIS IS TOO MUCH!!!

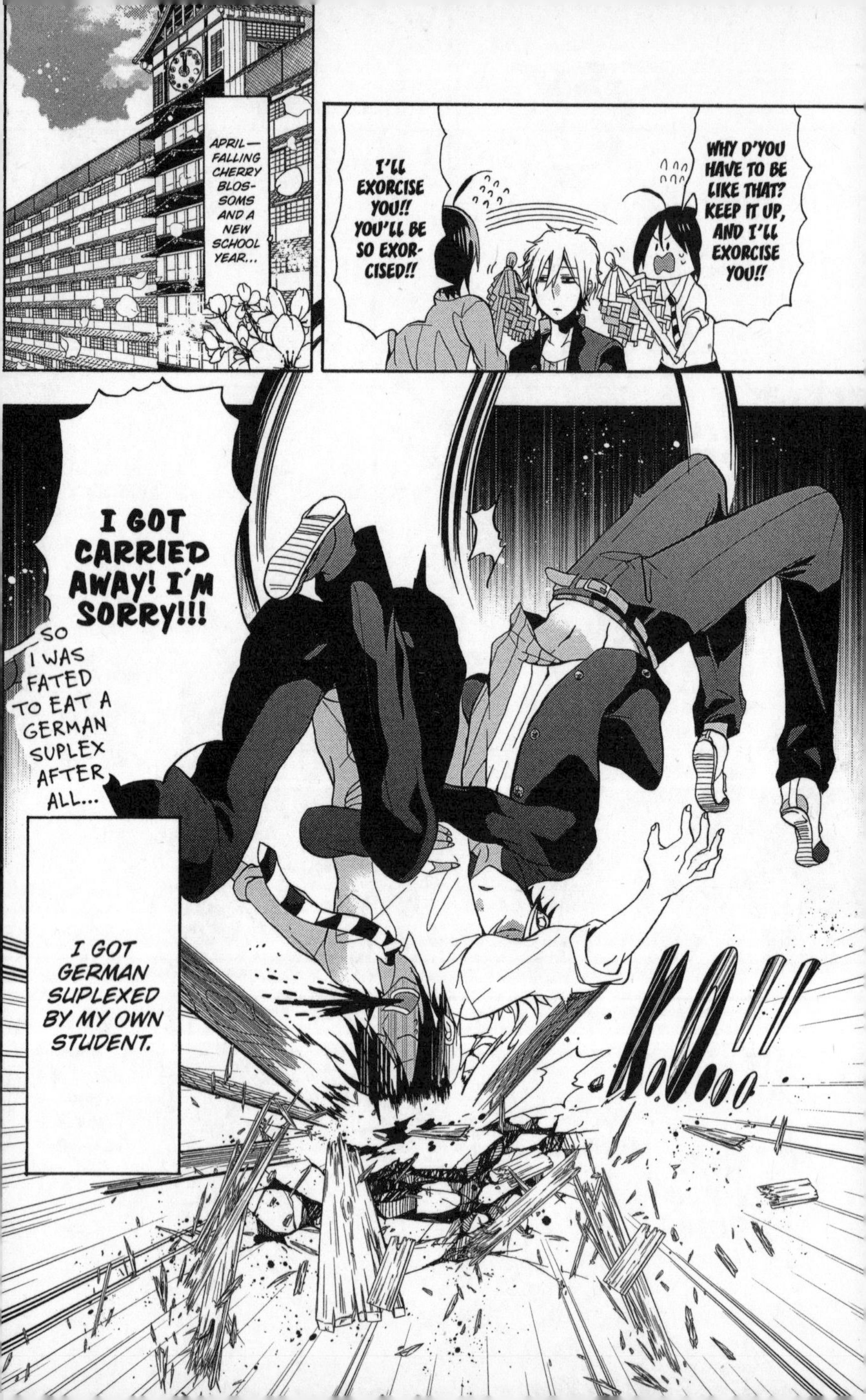
WHY D'YOU HAVE TO BE LIKE THAT? KEEP IT UP, AND I'LL EXORCISE YOU!!
I'LL EXORCISE YOU!! YOU'LL BE SO EXORCISED!!
APRIL—FALLING CHERRY BLOSSOMS AND A NEW SCHOOL YEAR...
I GOT CARRIED AWAY! I'M SORRY!!!
SO I WAS FATED TO EAT A GERMAN SUPLEX AFTER ALL...
I GOT GERMAN SUPLEXED BY MY OWN STUDENT.
K.O...!!

Second Period

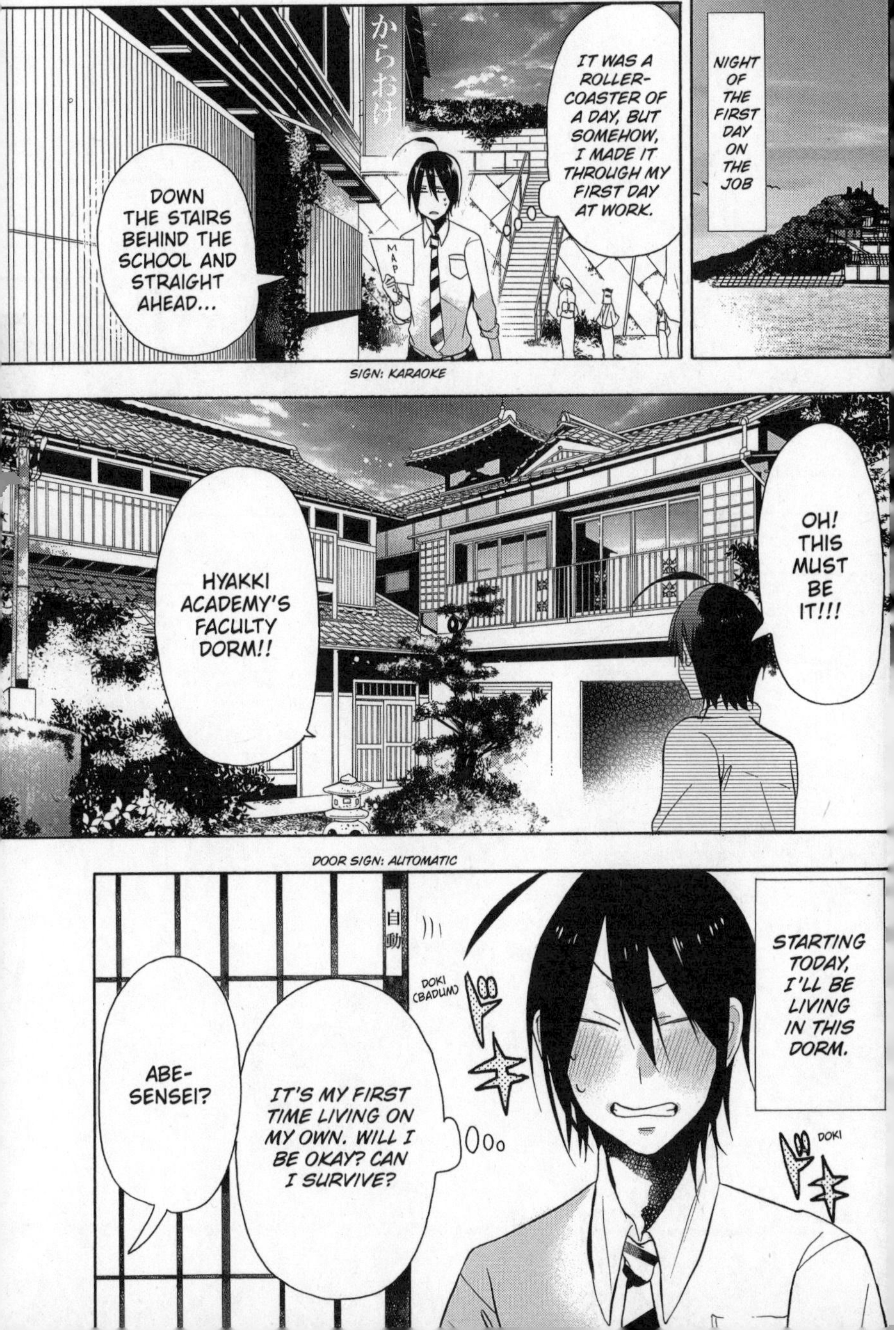
NIGHT OF THE FIRST DAY ON THE JOB
IT WAS A ROLLER-COASTER OF A DAY, BUT SOMEHOW, I MADE IT THROUGH MY FIRST DAY AT WORK.
からおけ
MAP
DOWN THE STAIRS BEHIND THE SCHOOL AND STRAIGHT AHEAD...
SIGN: KARAOKE
OH! THIS MUST BE IT!!!
HYAKKI ACADEMY'S FACULTY DORM!!
DOOR SIGN: AUTOMATIC
STARTING TODAY, I'LL BE LIVING IN THIS DORM.
DOKI
IT'S MY FIRST TIME LIVING ON MY OWN. WILL I BE OKAY? CAN I SURVIVE?
DOKI (BADUM)
自動
ABE-SENSEI?

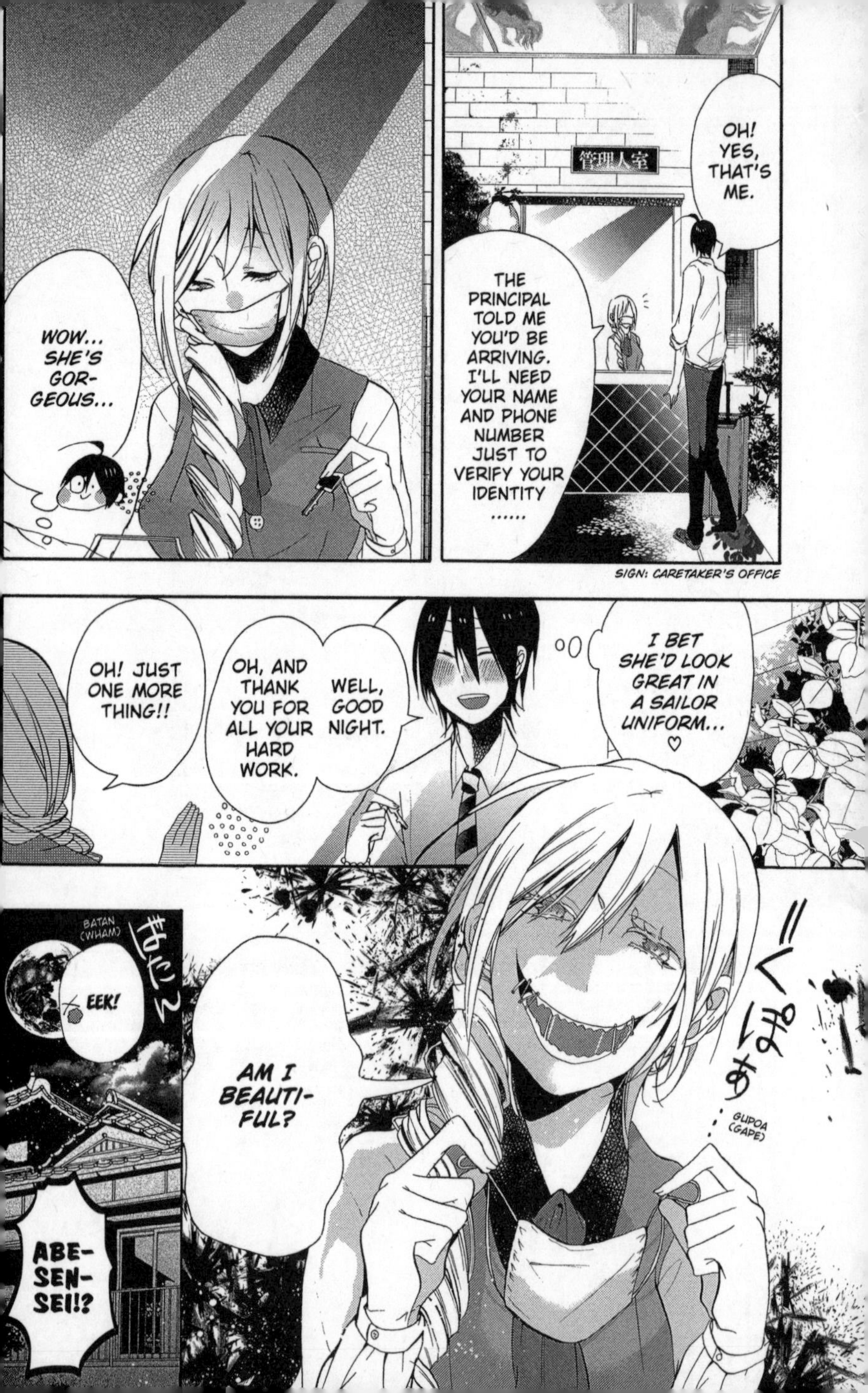
OH! YES, THAT'S ME.
管理人室
THE PRINCIPAL TOLD ME YOU'D BE ARRIVING. I'LL NEED YOUR NAME AND PHONE NUMBER JUST TO VERIFY YOUR IDENTITY ......
WOW... SHE'S GOR-GEOUS...
SIGN: CARETAKER'S OFFICE
I BET SHE'D LOOK GREAT IN A SAILOR UNIFORM... ♡
WELL, GOOD NIGHT.
OH, AND THANK YOU FOR ALL YOUR HARD WORK.
OH! JUST ONE MORE THING!!
ぐぽぁ
GUPOA (GAPE)
AM I BEAUTI-FUL?
ばたん
BATAN (WHAM)
EEK!
ABE-SEN-SEI!?

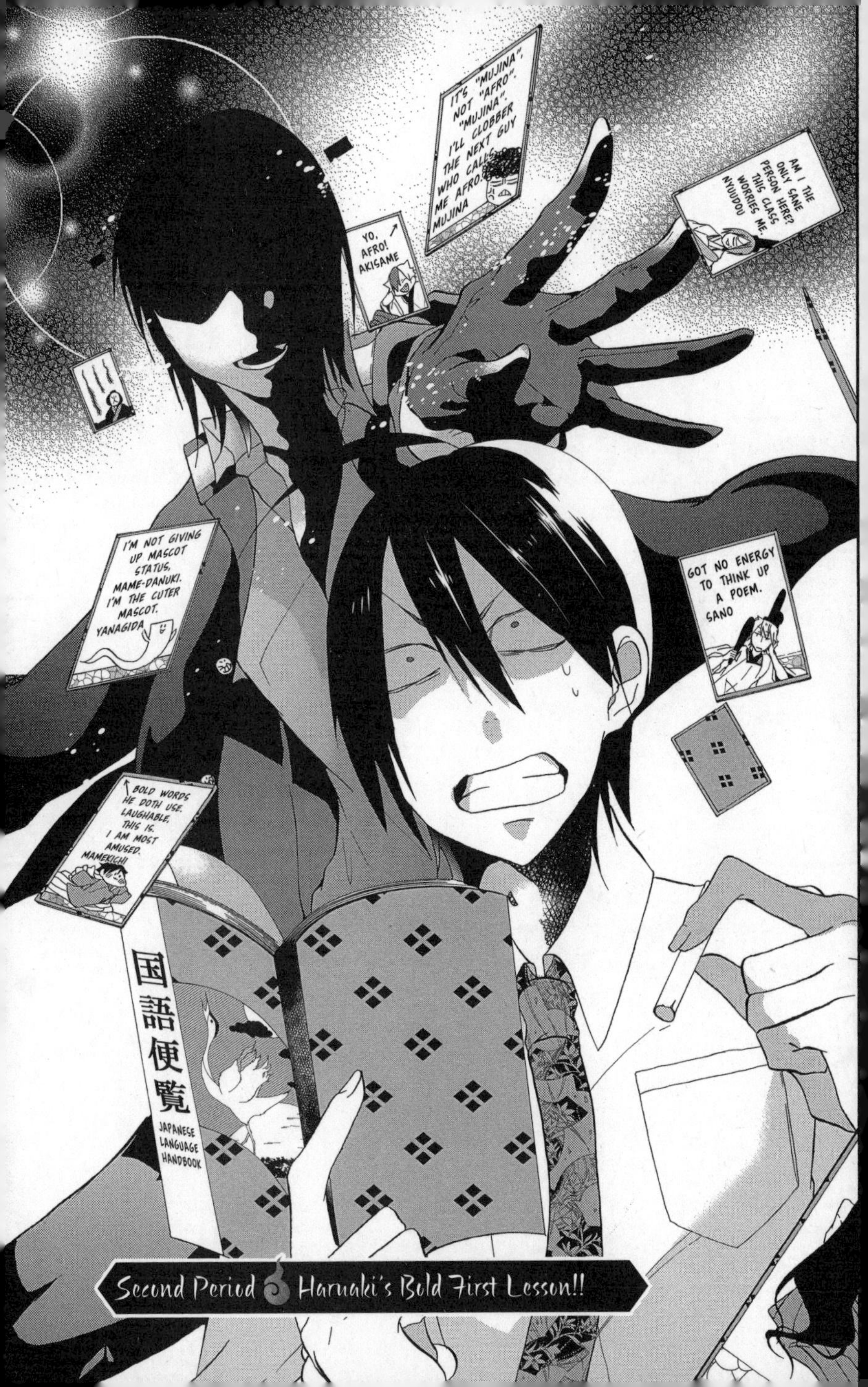
AM I THE ONLY SANE PERSON HERE? THIS CLASS WORRIES ME. NYUUDOU
IT'S "MUJINA", NOT "AFRO". "MUJINA" I'LL CLOBBER THE NEXT GUY WHO CALLS ME AFRO. MUJINA
YO, AFRO! AKISAME
GOT NO ENERGY TO THINK UP A POEM. SANO
I'M NOT GIVING UP MASCOT STATUS, MAME-DANUKI. I'M THE CUTER MASCOT. YANAGIDA
BOLD WORDS HE DOTH USE. LAUGHABLE, THIS IS. I AM MOST AMUSED. MAMEKICHI
国語便覧
JAPANESE LANGUAGE HANDBOOK
Second Period 3 Haruaki's Bold First Lesson!!

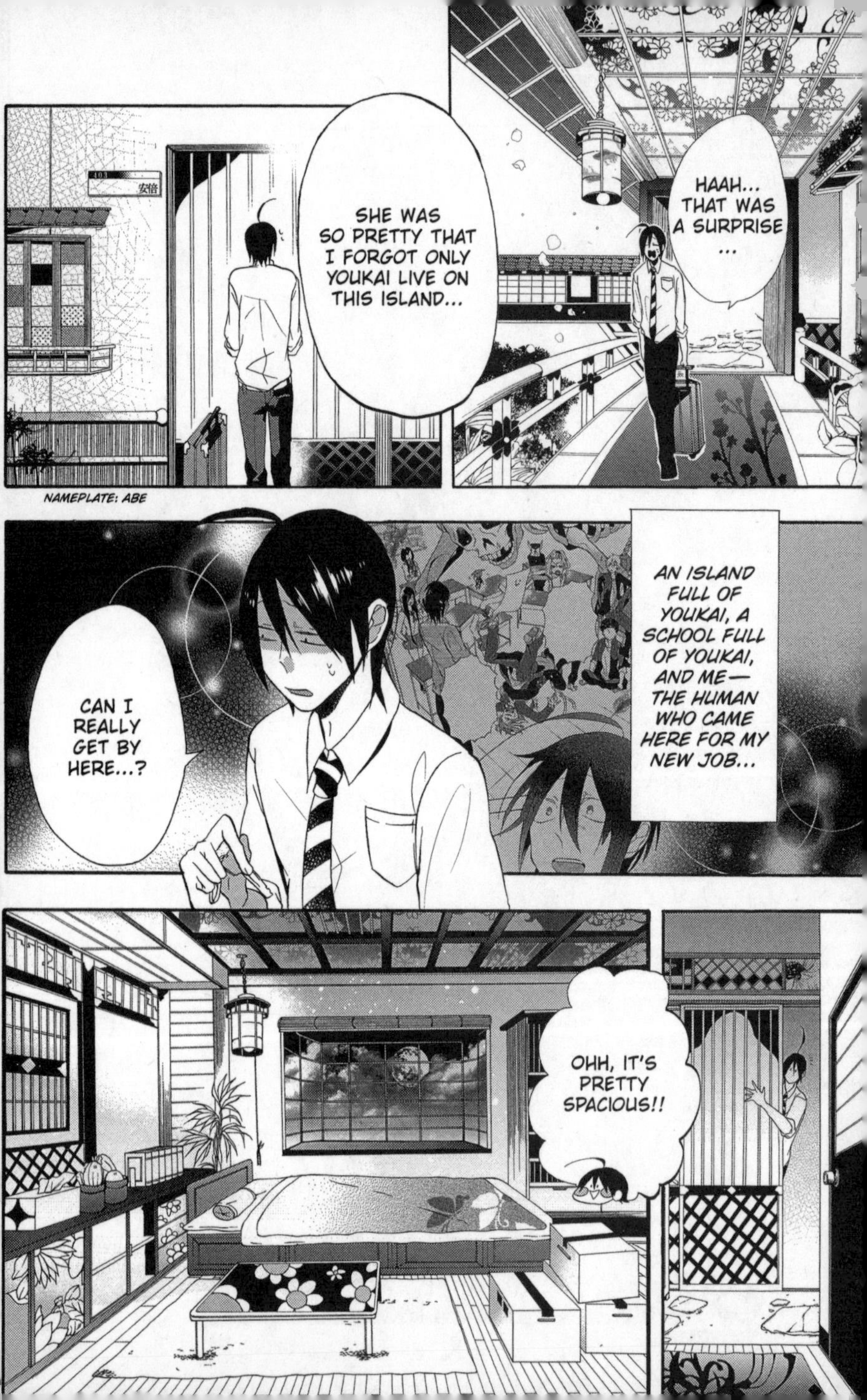
HAAH... THAT WAS A SURPRISE ...
SHE WAS SO PRETTY THAT I FORGOT ONLY YOUKAI LIVE ON THIS ISLAND...
安倍
NAMEPLATE: ABE
AN ISLAND FULL OF YOUKAI, A SCHOOL FULL OF YOUKAI, AND ME—THE HUMAN WHO CAME HERE FOR MY NEW JOB...
CAN I REALLY GET BY HERE...?
OHH, IT'S PRETTY SPACIOUS!!

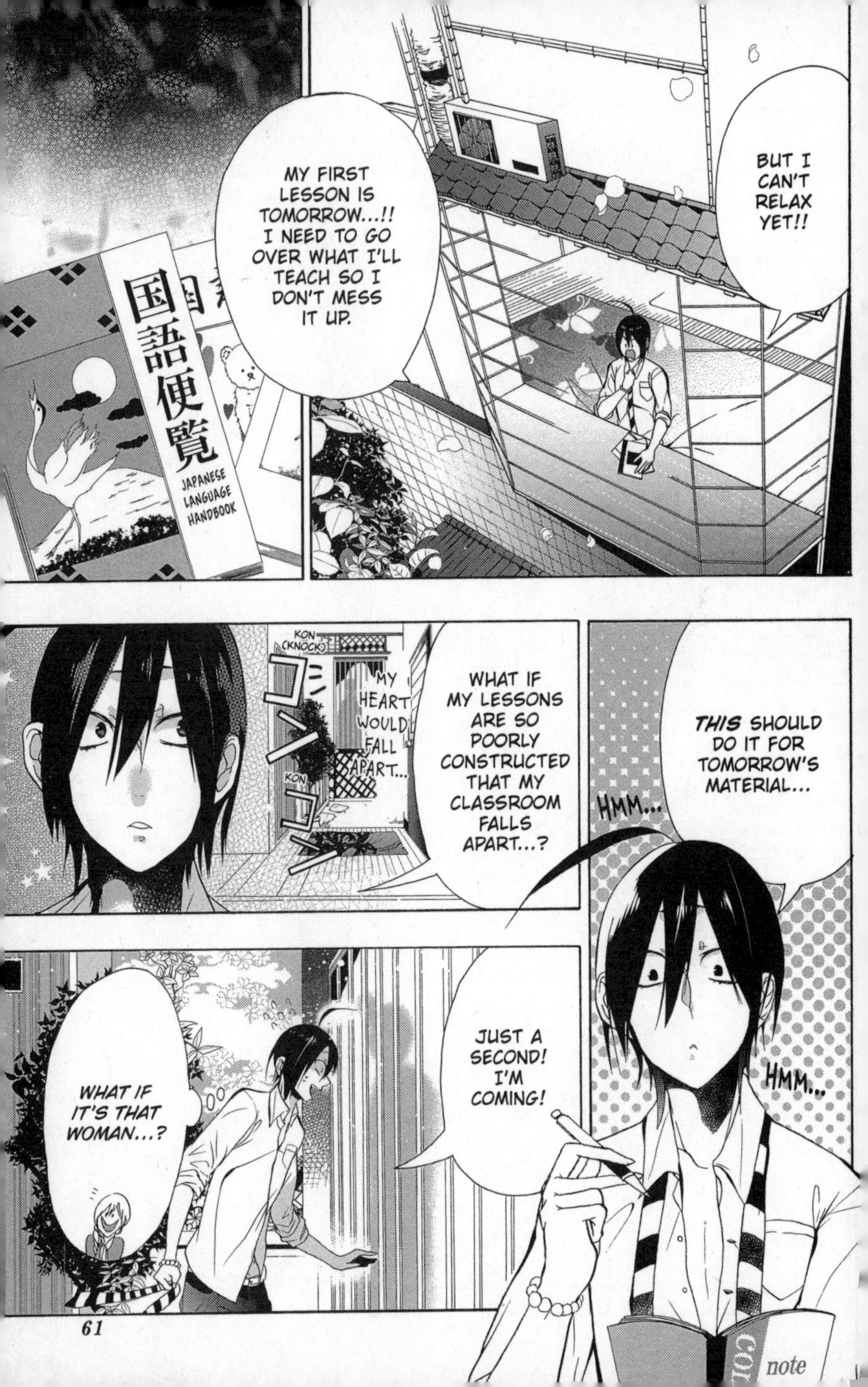
BUT I CAN'T RELAX YET!!
MY FIRST LESSON IS TOMORROW...!! I NEED TO GO OVER WHAT I'LL TEACH SO I DON'T MESS IT UP.
国語便覧
JAPANESE LANGUAGE HANDBOOK
HMM...
THIS SHOULD DO IT FOR TOMORROW'S MATERIAL...
HMM...
note
KON (KNOCK)
KON
WHAT IF MY LESSONS ARE SO POORLY CONSTRUCTED THAT MY CLASSROOM FALLS APART...?
MY HEART WOULD FALL APART...
JUST A SECOND! I'M COMING!
WHAT IF IT'S THAT WOMAN...?

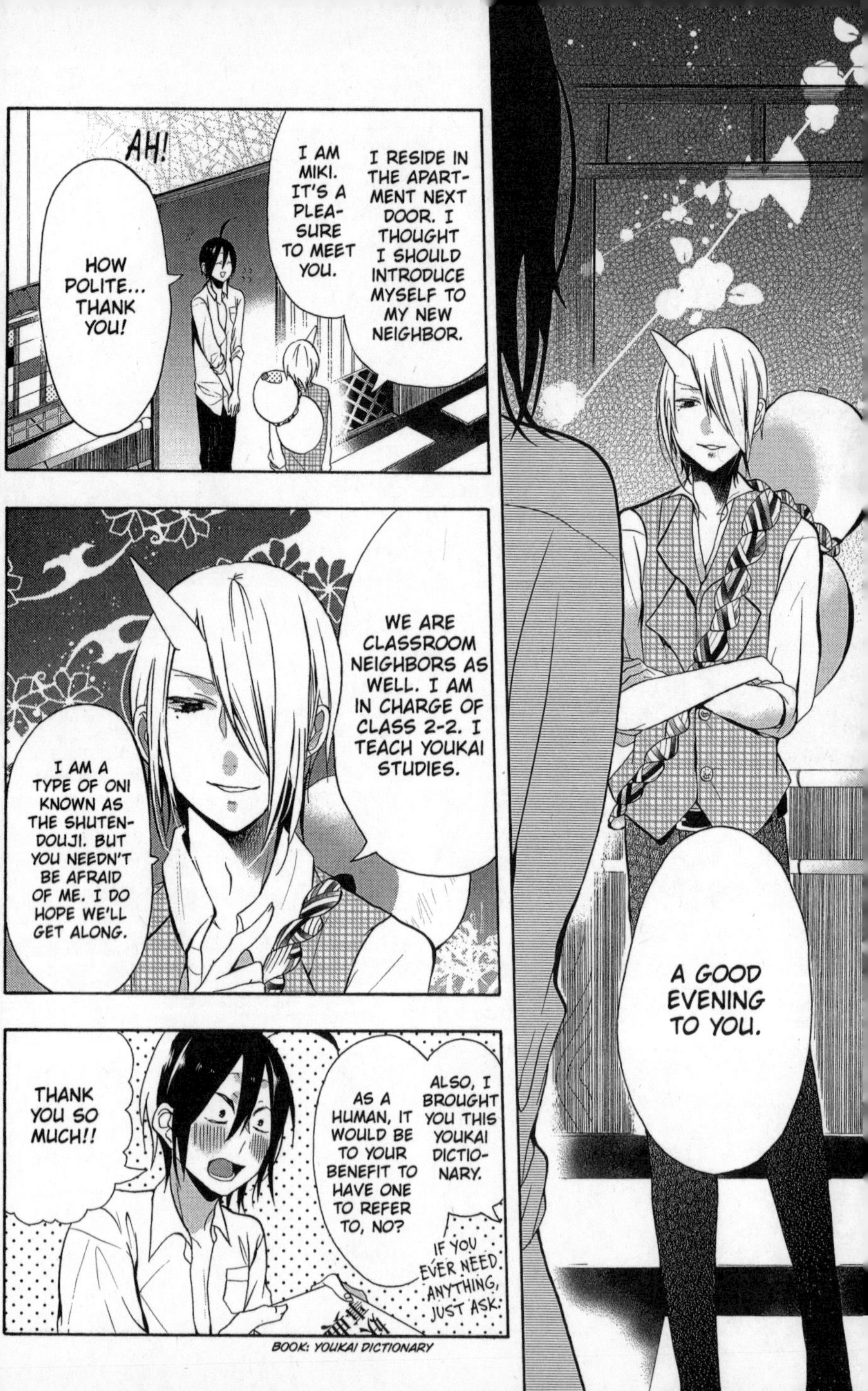
A GOOD EVENING TO YOU.
I RESIDE IN THE APARTMENT NEXT DOOR. I THOUGHT I SHOULD INTRODUCE MYSELF TO MY NEW NEIGHBOR.
I AM MIKI. IT'S A PLEASURE TO MEET YOU.
AH!
HOW POLITE... THANK YOU!
WE ARE CLASSROOM NEIGHBORS AS WELL. I AM IN CHARGE OF CLASS 2-2. I TEACH YOUKAI STUDIES.
I AM A TYPE OF ONI KNOWN AS THE SHUTEN-DOUJI. BUT YOU NEEDN'T BE AFRAID OF ME. I DO HOPE WE'LL GET ALONG.
ALSO, I BROUGHT YOU THIS YOUKAI DICTIONARY.
AS A HUMAN, IT WOULD BE TO YOUR BENEFIT TO HAVE ONE TO REFER TO, NO?
IF YOU EVER NEED ANYTHING, JUST ASK.
THANK YOU SO MUCH!!
BOOK: YOUKAI DICTIONARY

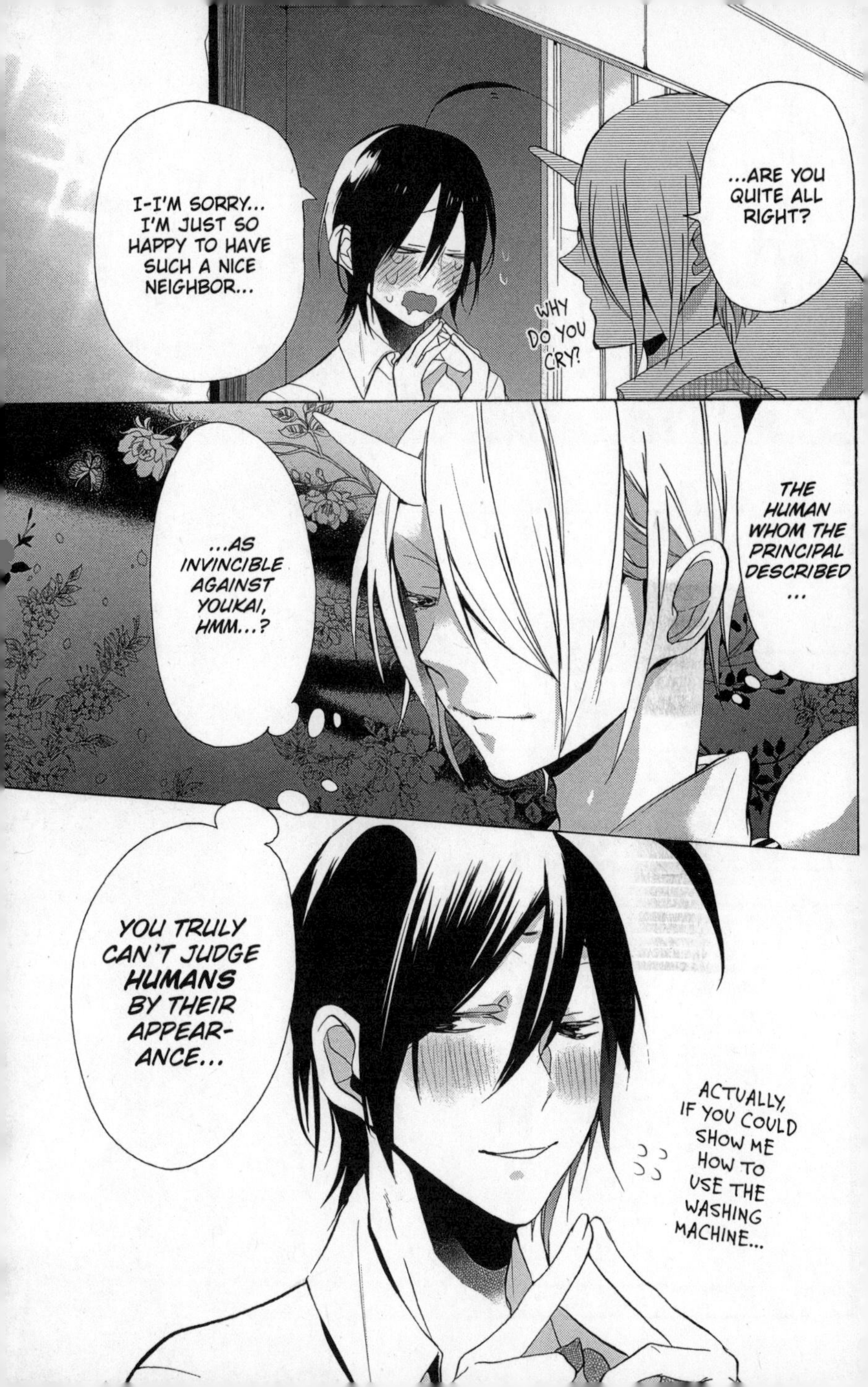
...ARE YOU QUITE ALL RIGHT?
WHY DO YOU CRY?
I-I'M SORRY... I'M JUST SO HAPPY TO HAVE SUCH A NICE NEIGHBOR...
THE HUMAN WHOM THE PRINCIPAL DESCRIBED...
...AS INVINCIBLE AGAINST YOUKAI, HMM...?
YOU TRULY CAN'T JUDGE HUMANS BY THEIR APPEARANCE...
ACTUALLY, IF YOU COULD SHOW ME HOW TO USE THE WASHING MACHINE...

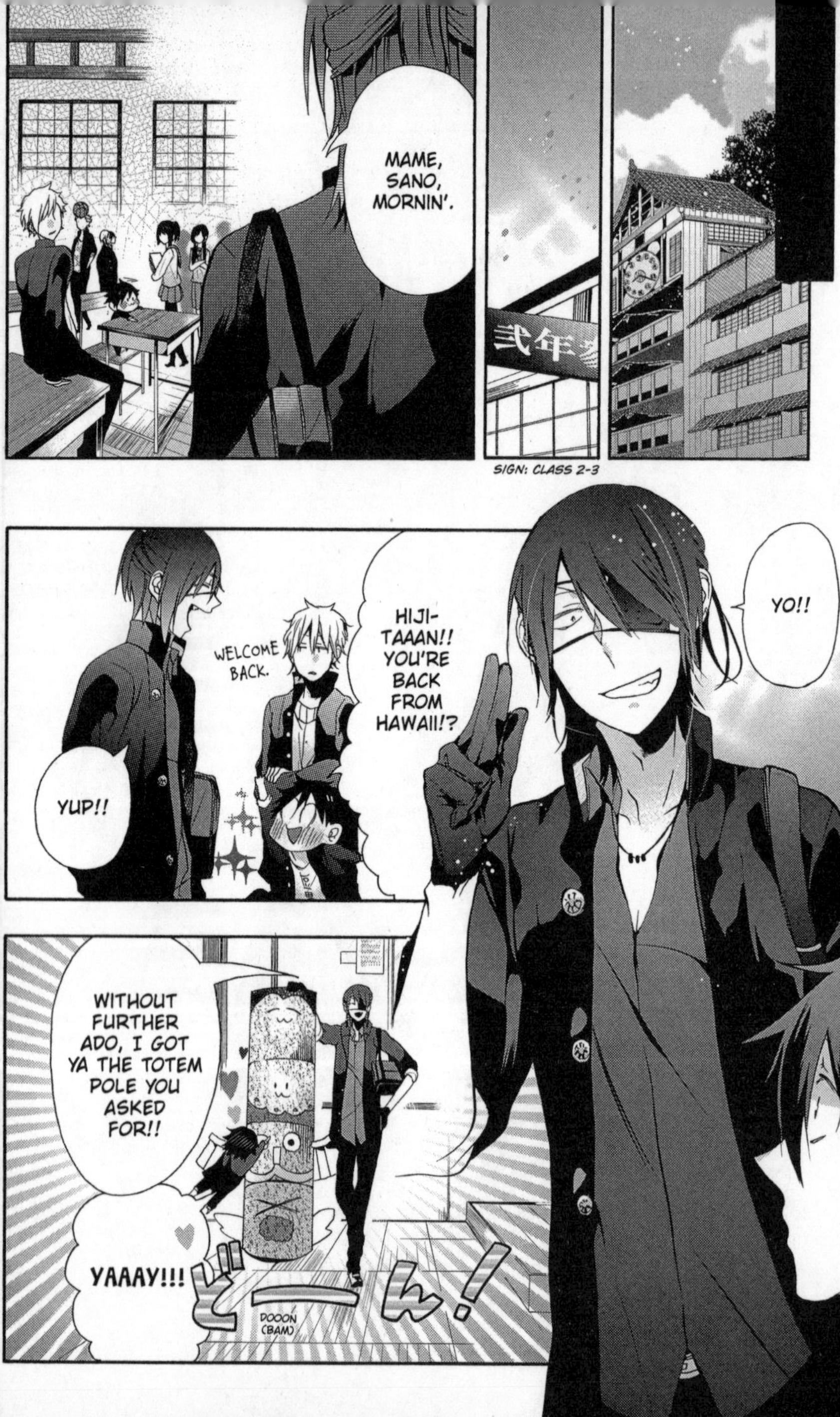
SIGN: CLASS 2-3
MAME, SANO, MORNIN'.
YO!!
HIJI-TAAAN!! YOU'RE BACK FROM HAWAII!?
WELCOME BACK.
YUP!!
WITHOUT FURTHER ADO, I GOT YA THE TOTEM POLE YOU ASKED FOR!!
YAAAY!!!
DOOON (BAM)

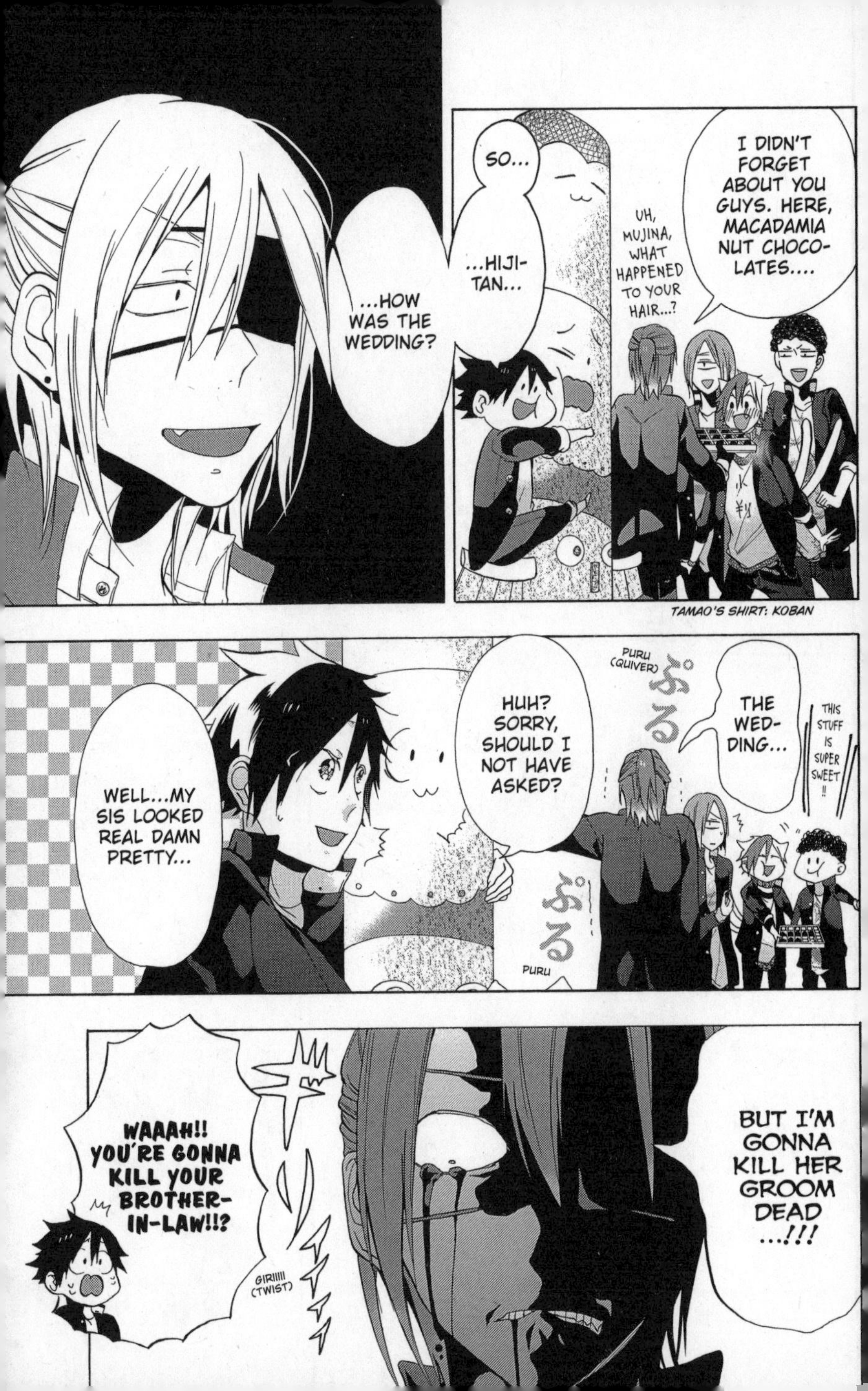
I DIDN'T FORGET ABOUT YOU GUYS. HERE, MACADAMIA NUT CHOCO-LATES....
UH, MUJINA, WHAT HAPPENED TO YOUR HAIR...?
SO...
...HIJI-TAN...
...HOW WAS THE WEDDING?
TAMAO'S SHIRT: KOBAN
THIS STUFF IS SUPER SWEET!!
ぷる
PURU (QUIVER)
THE WED-DING...
HUH? SORRY, SHOULD I NOT HAVE ASKED?
ぷる
PURU
WELL...MY SIS LOOKED REAL DAMN PRETTY...
BUT I'M GONNA KILL HER GROOM DEAD ...!!!
GIRIIIII (TWIST)
WAAAH!! YOU'RE GONNA KILL YOUR BROTHER-IN-LAW!!?

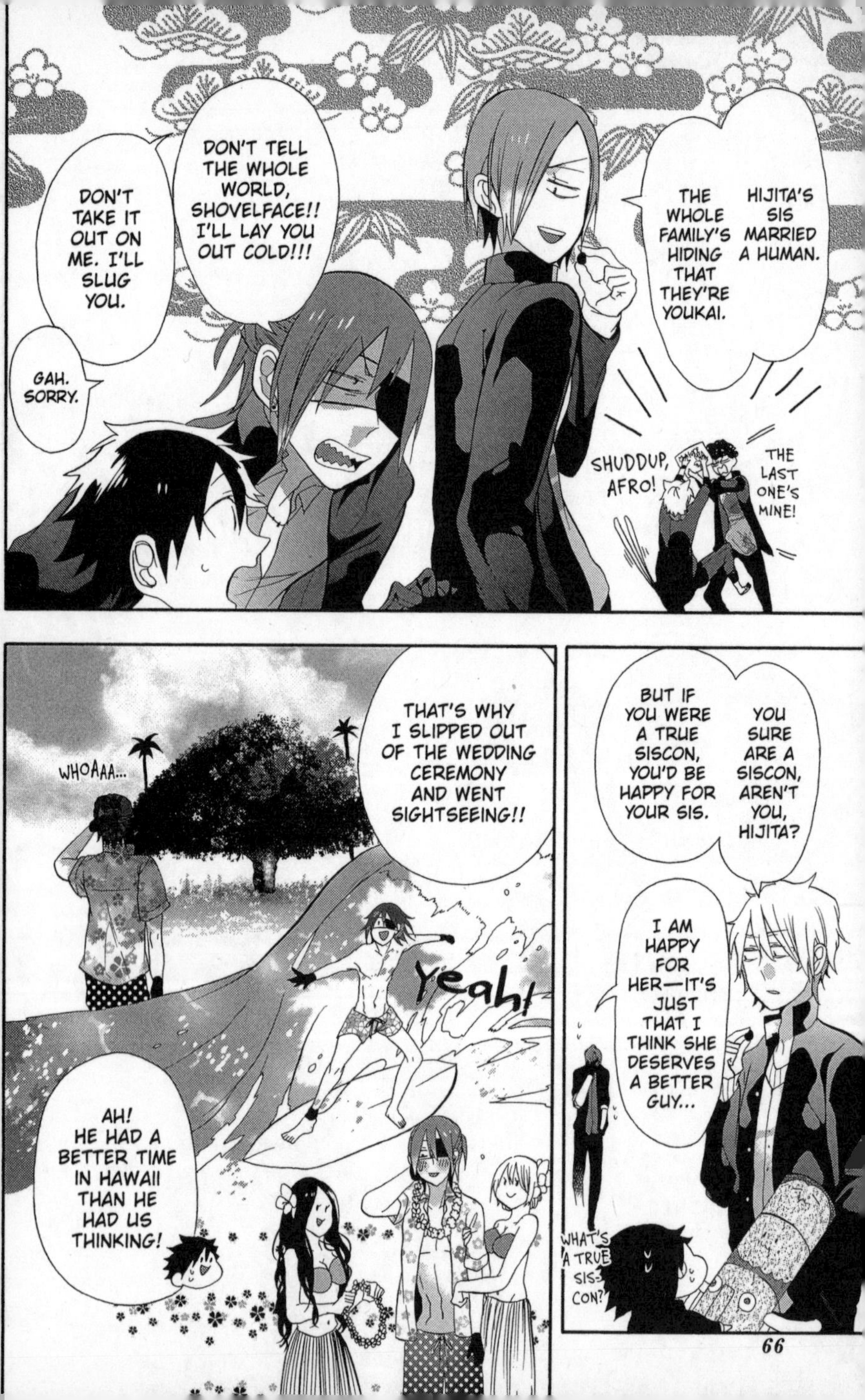
HIJITA'S SIS MARRIED A HUMAN.
THE WHOLE FAMILY'S HIDING THAT THEY'RE YOUKAI.
DON'T TELL THE WHOLE WORLD, SHOVELFACE!! I'LL LAY YOU OUT COLD!!!
DON'T TAKE IT OUT ON ME. I'LL SLUG YOU.
GAH. SORRY.
THE LAST ONE'S MINE!
SHUDDUP, AFRO!
YOU SURE ARE A SISCON, AREN'T YOU, HIJITA?
BUT IF YOU WERE A TRUE SISCON, YOU'D BE HAPPY FOR YOUR SIS.
I AM HAPPY FOR HER—IT'S JUST THAT I THINK SHE DESERVES A BETTER GUY...
WHAT'S A TRUE SIS-CON?
THAT'S WHY I SLIPPED OUT OF THE WEDDING CEREMONY AND WENT SIGHTSEEING!!
WHOAAA...
Yeah!
AH! HE HAD A BETTER TIME IN HAWAII THAN HE HAD US THINKING!

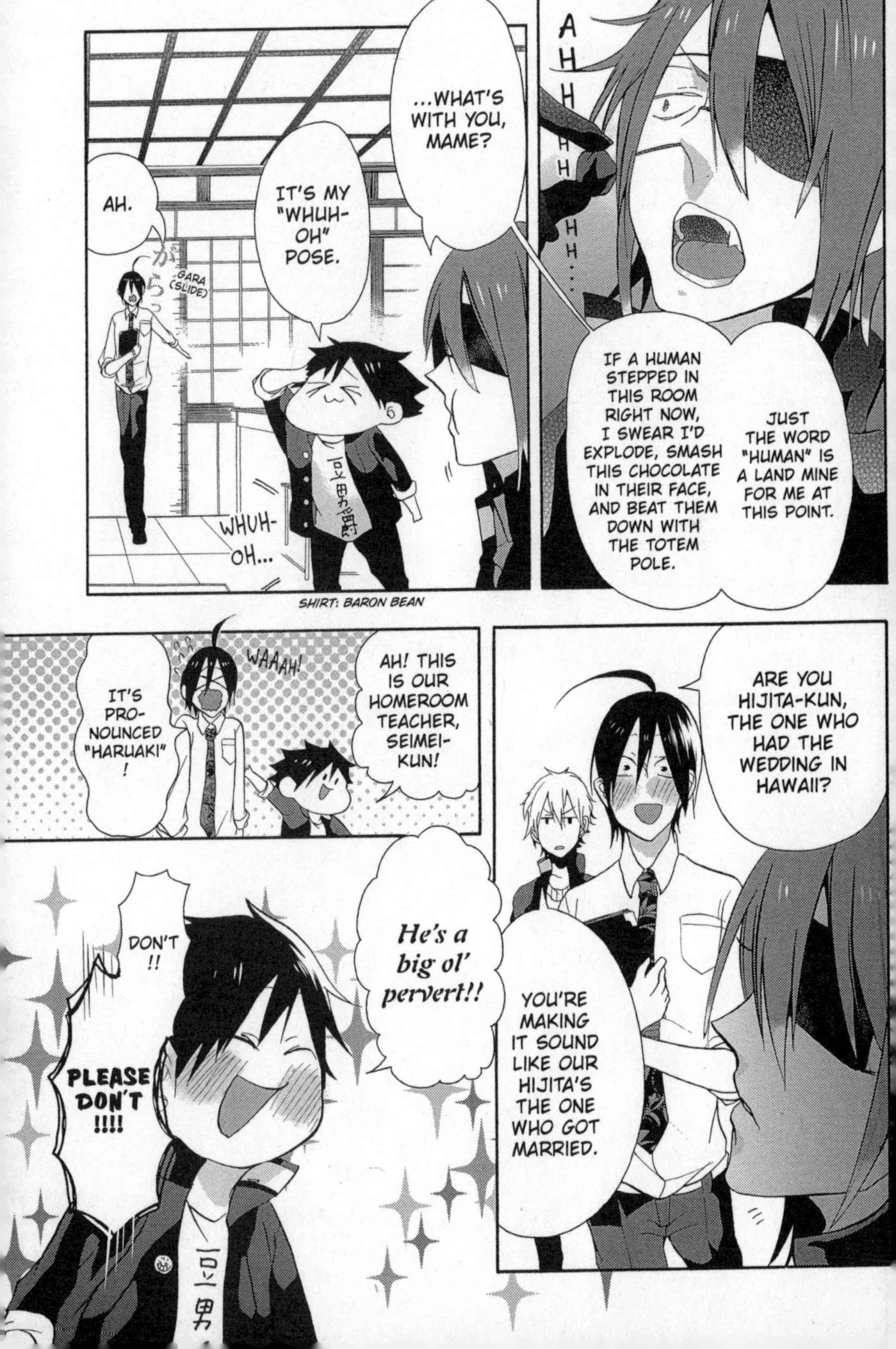
AHHHHHH...
JUST THE WORD "HUMAN" IS A LAND MINE FOR ME AT THIS POINT.
IF A HUMAN STEPPED IN THIS ROOM RIGHT NOW, I SWEAR I'D EXPLODE, SMASH THIS CHOCOLATE IN THEIR FACE, AND BEAT THEM DOWN WITH THE TOTEM POLE.
...WHAT'S WITH YOU, MAME?
IT'S MY "WHUH-OH" POSE.
WHUH-OH...
AH.
GARA (SLIDE)
SHIRT: BARON BEAN
ARE YOU HIJITA-KUN, THE ONE WHO HAD THE WEDDING IN HAWAII?
AH! THIS IS OUR HOMEROOM TEACHER, SEIMEI-KUN!
WAAAH!
IT'S PRO-NOUNCED "HARUAKI"!
YOU'RE MAKING IT SOUND LIKE OUR HIJITA'S THE ONE WHO GOT MARRIED.
He's a big ol' pervert!!
DON'T!!
PLEASE DON'T!!!!

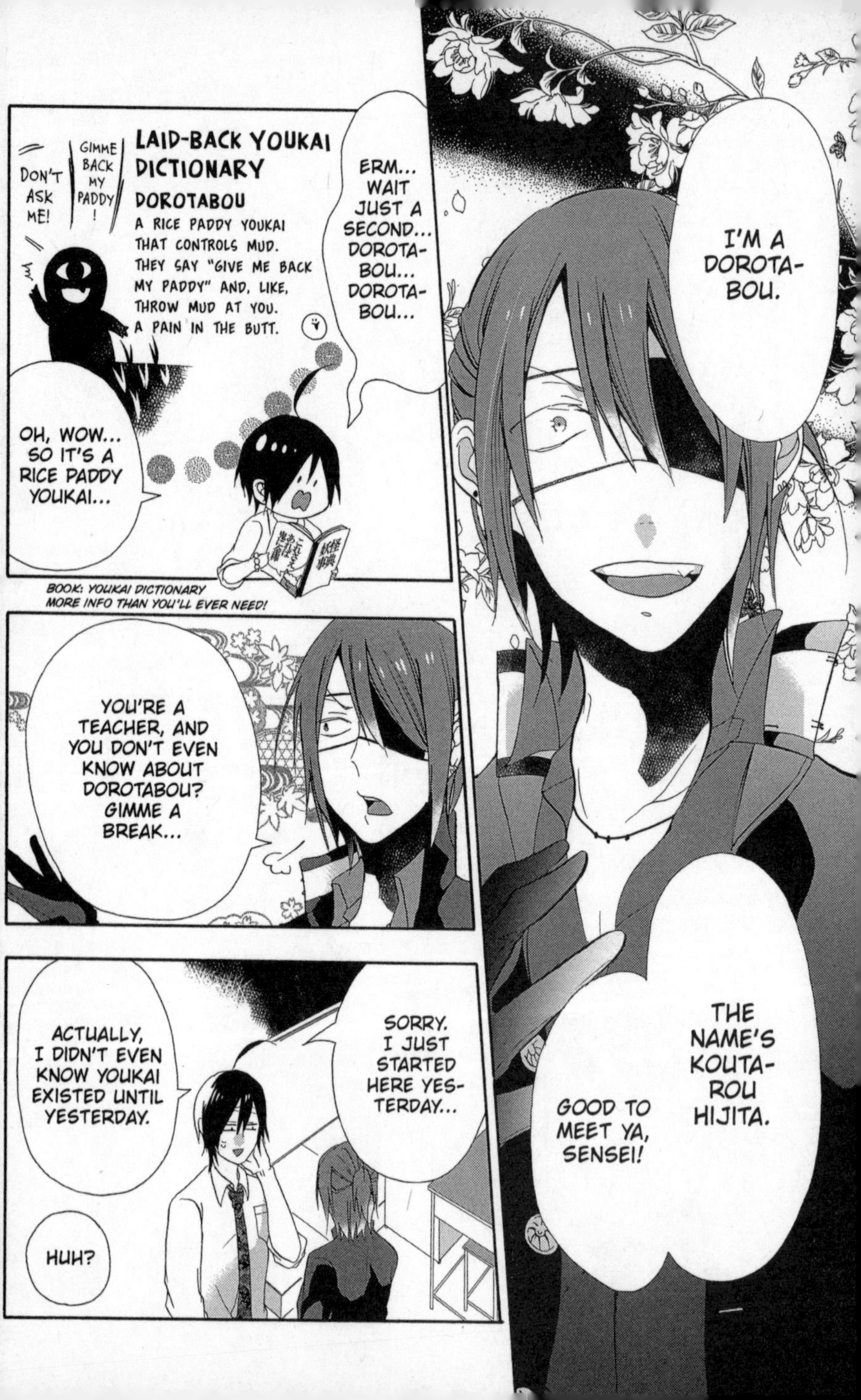
I'M A DOROTA-BOU.
THE NAME'S KOUTA-ROU HIJITA.
GOOD TO MEET YA, SENSEI!
ERM... WAIT JUST A SECOND... DOROTA-BOU... DOROTA-BOU...
LAID-BACK YOUKAI DICTIONARY
DOROTABOU
A RICE PADDY YOUKAI THAT CONTROLS MUD. THEY SAY "GIVE ME BACK MY PADDY" AND, LIKE, THROW MUD AT YOU. A PAIN IN THE BUTT.
GIMME BACK MY PADDY!
DON'T ASK ME!
OH, WOW... SO IT'S A RICE PADDY YOUKAI...
BOOK: YOUKAI DICTIONARY
MORE INFO THAN YOU'LL EVER NEED!
YOU'RE A TEACHER, AND YOU DON'T EVEN KNOW ABOUT DOROTABOU? GIMME A BREAK...
SORRY. I JUST STARTED HERE YES-TERDAY...
ACTUALLY, I DIDN'T EVEN KNOW YOUKAI EXISTED UNTIL YESTERDAY.
HUH?

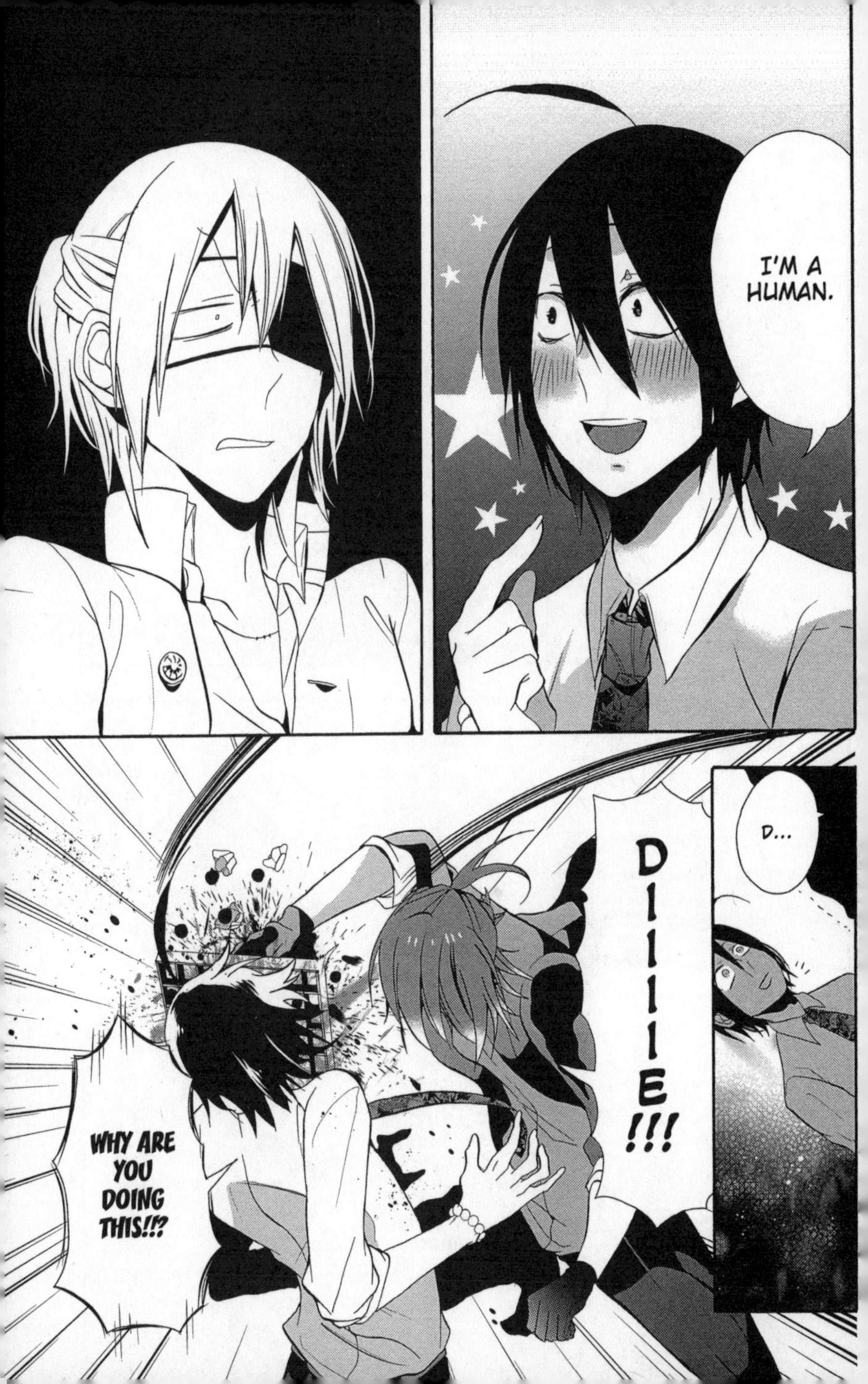
I'M A HUMAN.
D...
DIIIIE!!!
WHY ARE YOU DOING THIS!!?

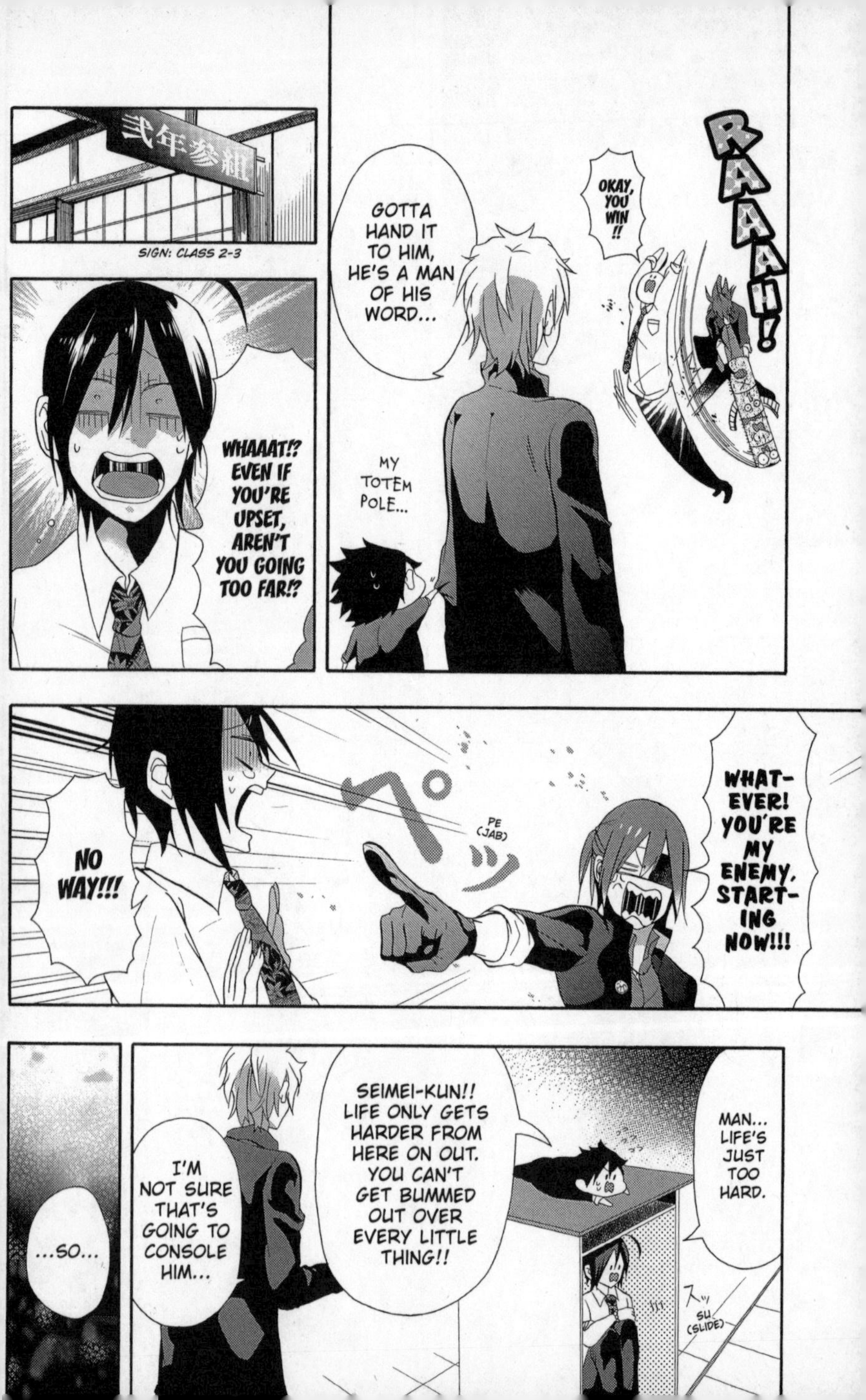
RAAAAH!
OKAY, YOU WIN!!
GOTTA HAND IT TO HIM, HE'S A MAN OF HIS WORD...
MY TOTEM POLE...
弐年参組
SIGN: CLASS 2-3
WHAAAT!? EVEN IF YOU'RE UPSET, AREN'T YOU GOING TOO FAR!?
WHAT-EVER! YOU'RE MY ENEMY, START-ING NOW!!!
ペッ
PE (JAB)
NO WAY!!!
MAN... LIFE'S JUST TOO HARD.
スッ
SU (SLIDE)
SEIMEI-KUN!! LIFE ONLY GETS HARDER FROM HERE ON OUT. YOU CAN'T GET BUMMED OUT OVER EVERY LITTLE THING!!
I'M NOT SURE THAT'S GOING TO CONSOLE HIM...
...SO...

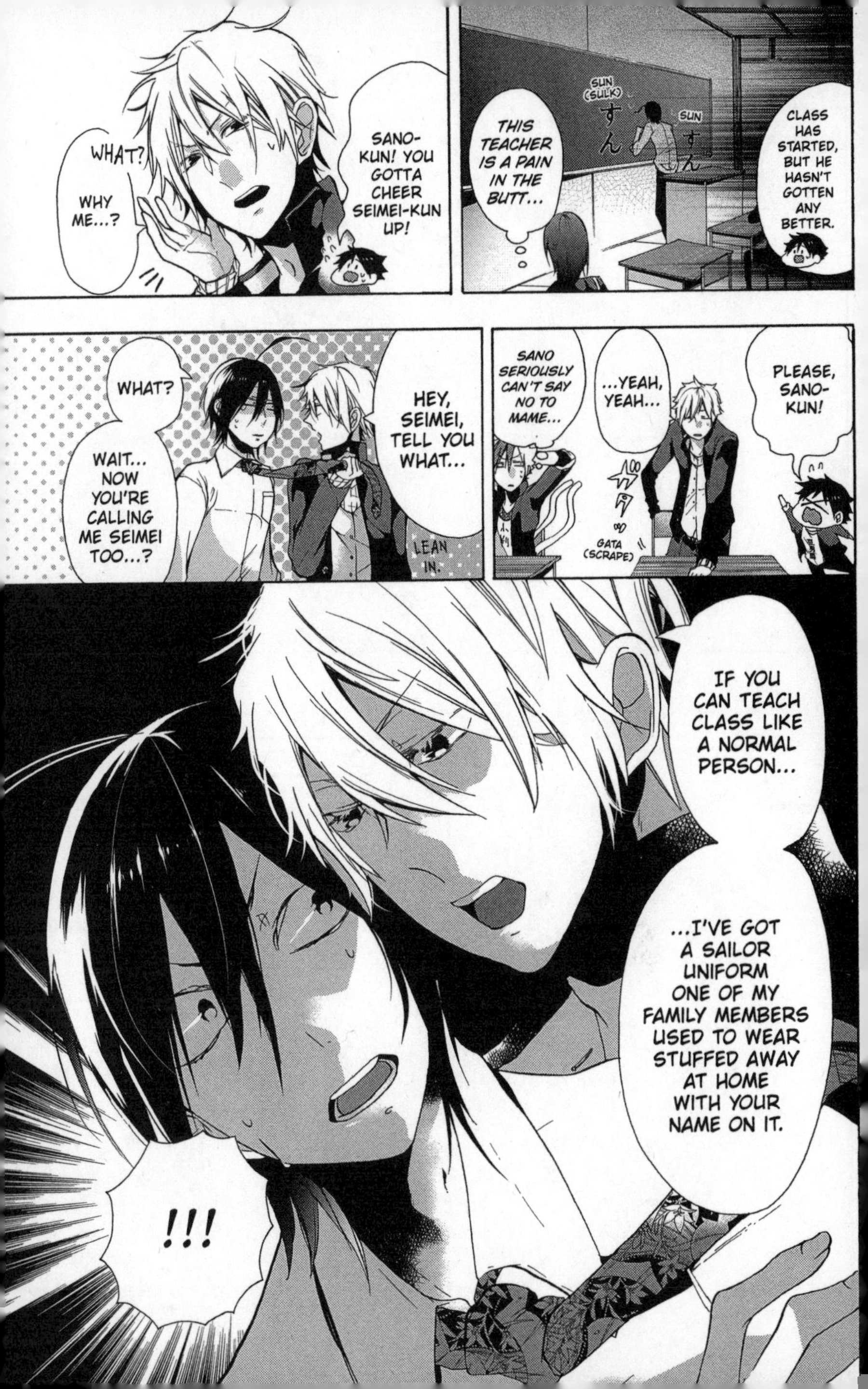
CLASS HAS STARTED, BUT HE HASN'T GOTTEN ANY BETTER.
SUN
すん
SUN (SULK)
すん
THIS TEACHER IS A PAIN IN THE BUTT…
SANO-KUN! YOU GOTTA CHEER SEIMEI-KUN UP!
WHAT?
WHY ME…?
PLEASE, SANO-KUN!
…YEAH, YEAH…
SANO SERIOUSLY CAN'T SAY NO TO MAME…
GATA (SCRAPE)
HEY, SEIMEI, TELL YOU WHAT…
LEAN IN.
WHAT?
WAIT… NOW YOU'RE CALLING ME SEIMEI TOO…?
IF YOU CAN TEACH CLASS LIKE A NORMAL PERSON…
…I'VE GOT A SAILOR UNIFORM ONE OF MY FAMILY MEMBERS USED TO WEAR STUFFED AWAY AT HOME WITH YOUR NAME ON IT.
!!!

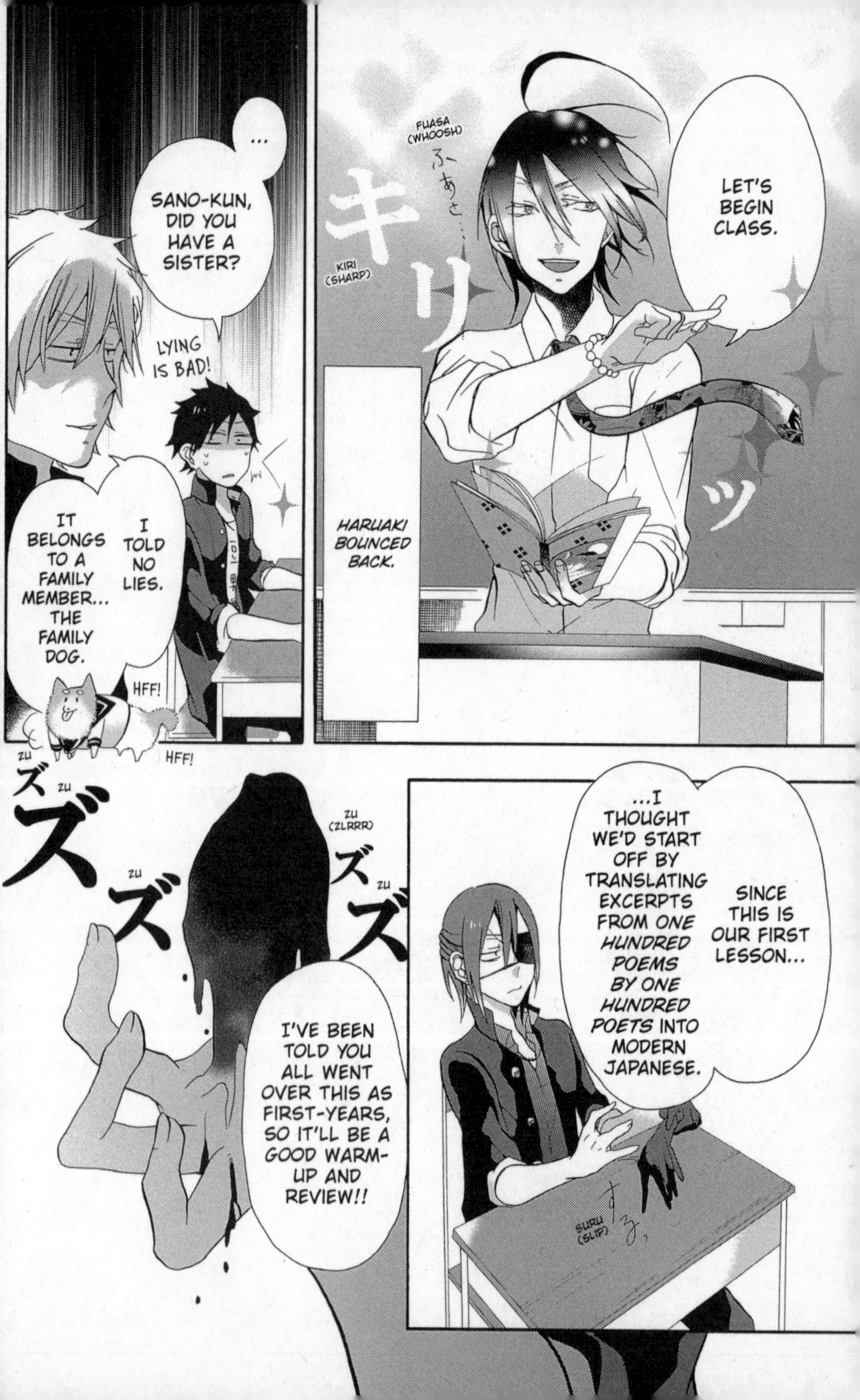
FUASA (WHOOSH)
ふあさ…
LET'S BEGIN CLASS.
KIRI (SHARP)
キリッ
HARUAKI BOUNCED BACK.
…
SANO-KUN, DID YOU HAVE A SISTER?
LYING IS BAD!
I TOLD NO LIES.
IT BELONGS TO A FAMILY MEMBER… THE FAMILY DOG.
HFF!
HFF!
SINCE THIS IS OUR FIRST LESSON…
…I THOUGHT WE'D START OFF BY TRANSLATING EXCERPTS FROM ONE *HUNDRED POEMS BY ONE HUNDRED POETS* INTO MODERN JAPANESE.
SURU (SLIP)
する
ZU (ZLRRR)
ズ ZU
ズ ZU
ズ ZU
ズ ZU
I'VE BEEN TOLD YOU ALL WENT OVER THIS AS FIRST-YEARS, SO IT'LL BE A GOOD WARM-UP AND REVIEW!!

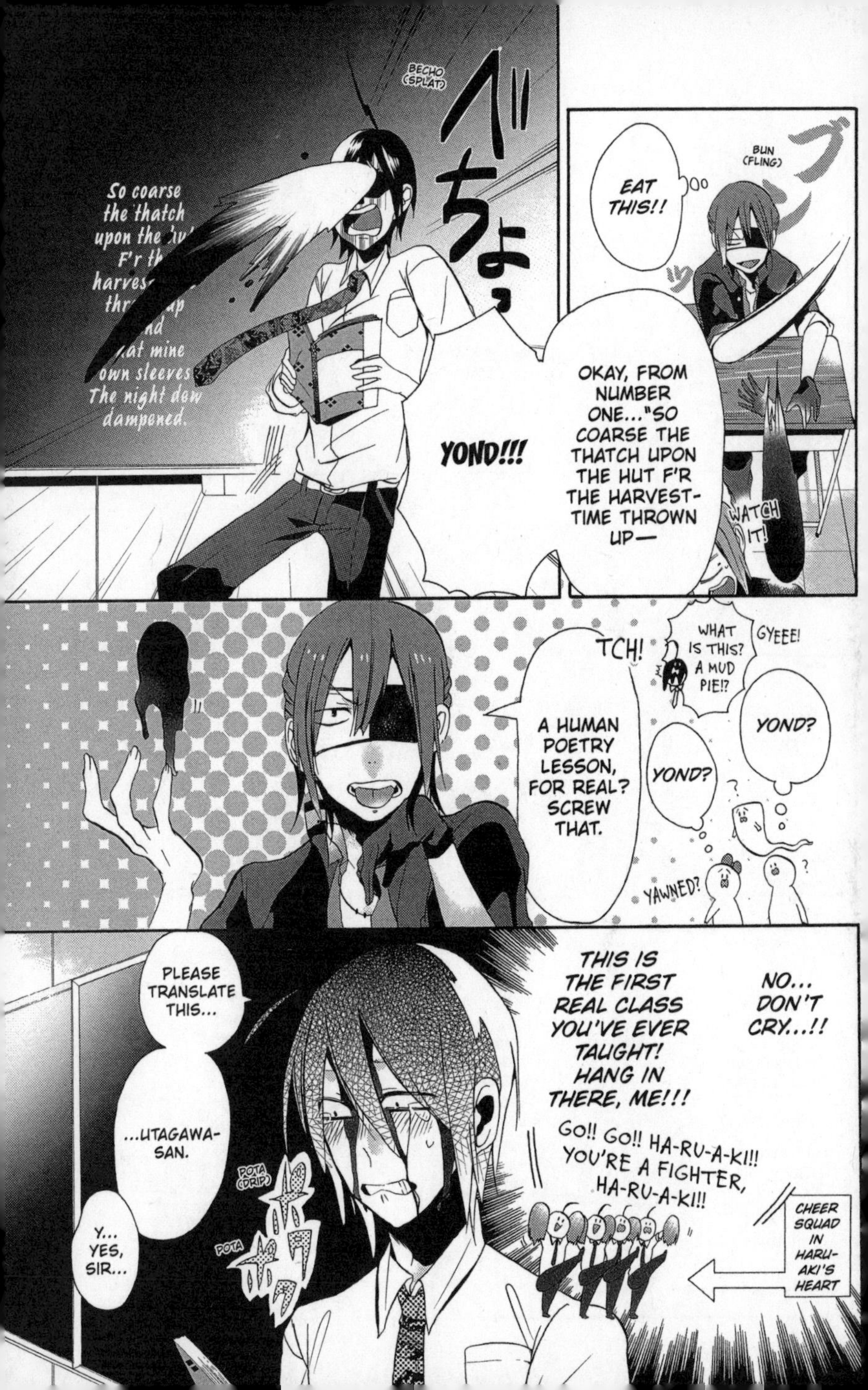
OKAY, FROM NUMBER ONE..."SO COARSE THE THATCH UPON THE HUT F'R THE HARVEST-TIME THROWN UP—
BUN (FLING)
EAT THIS!!
WATCH IT!
BECHO (SPLAT)
YOND!!!
So coarse the thatch upon the
harves
own sleeves The night dew dampened.
GYEEE!
WHAT IS THIS? A MUD PIE!?
YOND?
YOND?
YAWNED?
TCH!
A HUMAN POETRY LESSON, FOR REAL? SCREW THAT.
NO... DON'T CRY...!!
THIS IS THE FIRST REAL CLASS YOU'VE EVER TAUGHT! HANG IN THERE, ME!!!
GO!! GO!! HA-RU-A-KI!! YOU'RE A FIGHTER, HA-RU-A-KI!!
CHEER SQUAD IN HARU-AKI'S HEART
PLEASE TRANSLATE THIS...
...UTAGAWA-SAN.
POTA (DRIP)
POTA
Y... YES, SIR...

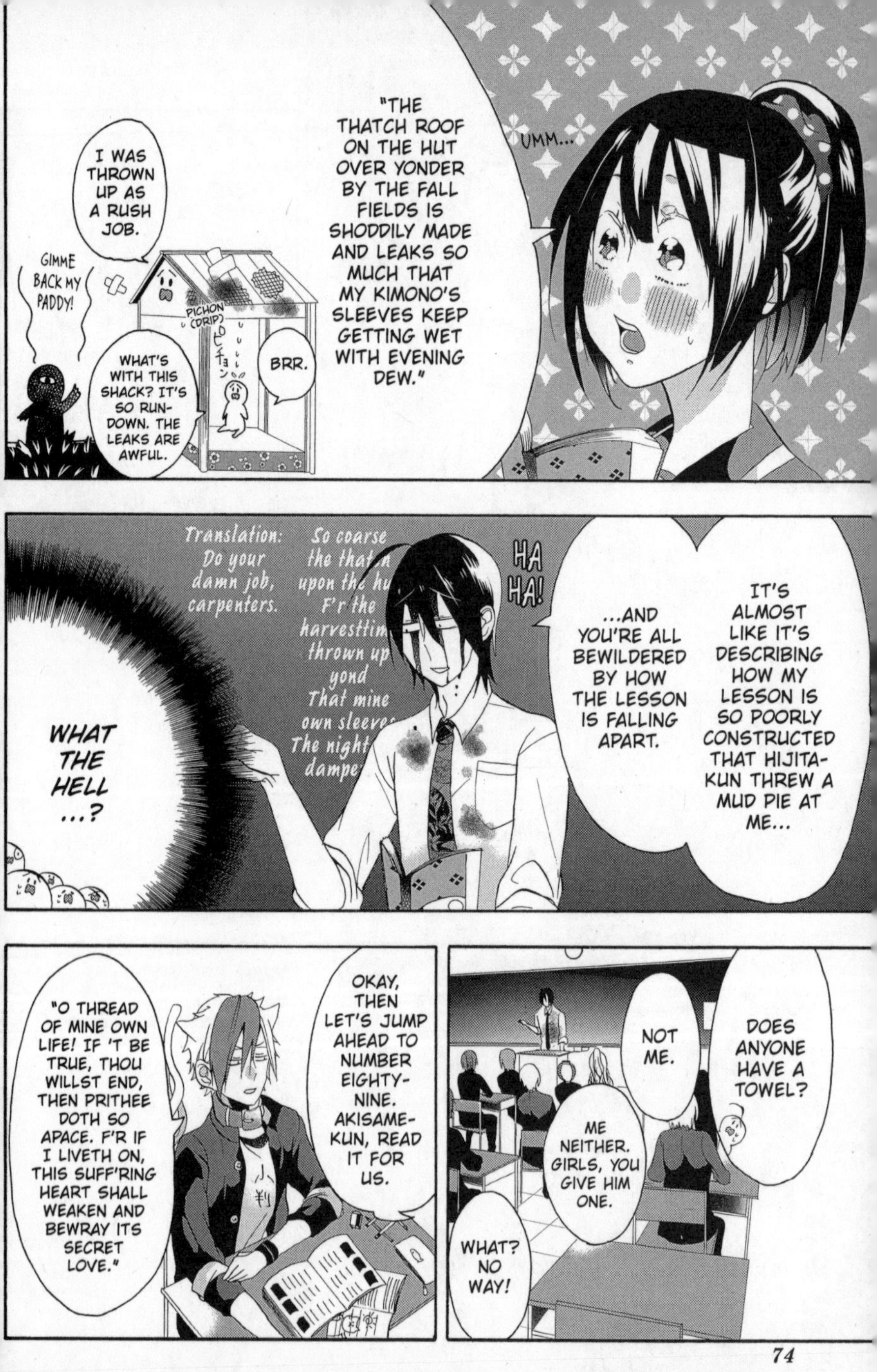
UMM...
"THE THATCH ROOF ON THE HUT OVER YONDER BY THE FALL FIELDS IS SHODDILY MADE AND LEAKS SO MUCH THAT MY KIMONO'S SLEEVES KEEP GETTING WET WITH EVENING DEW."
I WAS THROWN UP AS A RUSH JOB.
BRR.
PICHON (DRIP)
WHAT'S WITH THIS SHACK? IT'S SO RUN-DOWN. THE LEAKS ARE AWFUL.
GIMME BACK MY PADDY!
IT'S ALMOST LIKE IT'S DESCRIBING HOW MY LESSON IS SO POORLY CONSTRUCTED THAT HIJITA-KUN THREW A MUD PIE AT ME...
...AND YOU'RE ALL BEWILDERED BY HOW THE LESSON IS FALLING APART.
HA HA!
Translation: Do your damn job, carpenters.
WHAT THE HELL ...?
DOES ANYONE HAVE A TOWEL?
NOT ME.
ME NEITHER. GIRLS, YOU GIVE HIM ONE.
WHAT? NO WAY!
OKAY, THEN LET'S JUMP AHEAD TO NUMBER EIGHTY-NINE. AKISAME-KUN, READ IT FOR US.
"O THREAD OF MINE OWN LIFE! IF 'T BE TRUE, THOU WILLST END, THEN PRITHEE DOTH SO APACE. F'R IF I LIVETH ON, THIS SUFF'RING HEART SHALL WEAKEN AND BEWRAY ITS SECRET LOVE."

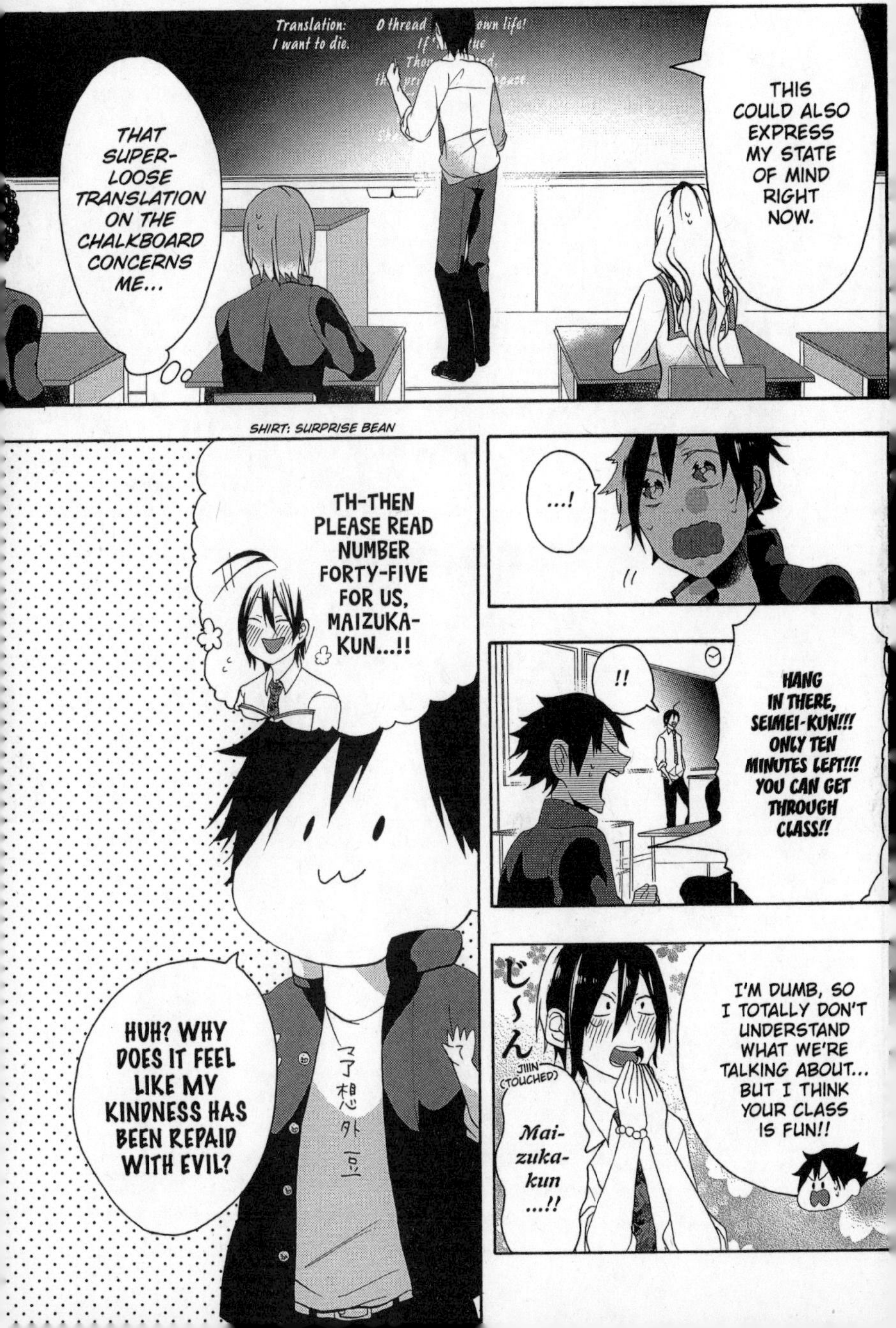
THIS COULD ALSO EXPRESS MY STATE OF MIND RIGHT NOW.
Translation:
I want to die.
THAT SUPER-LOOSE TRANSLATION ON THE CHALKBOARD CONCERNS ME...
...!
!!
HANG IN THERE, SEIMEI-KUN!!! ONLY TEN MINUTES LEFT!!! YOU CAN GET THROUGH CLASS!!
I'M DUMB, SO I TOTALLY DON'T UNDERSTAND WHAT WE'RE TALKING ABOUT... BUT I THINK YOUR CLASS IS FUN!!
じ〜ん
JIIIN (TOUCHED)
Mai-zuka-kun...!!
SHIRT: SURPRISE BEAN
TH-THEN PLEASE READ NUMBER FORTY-FIVE FOR US, MAIZUKA-KUN...!!
予想外豆
HUH? WHY DOES IT FEEL LIKE MY KINDNESS HAS BEEN REPAID WITH EVIL?

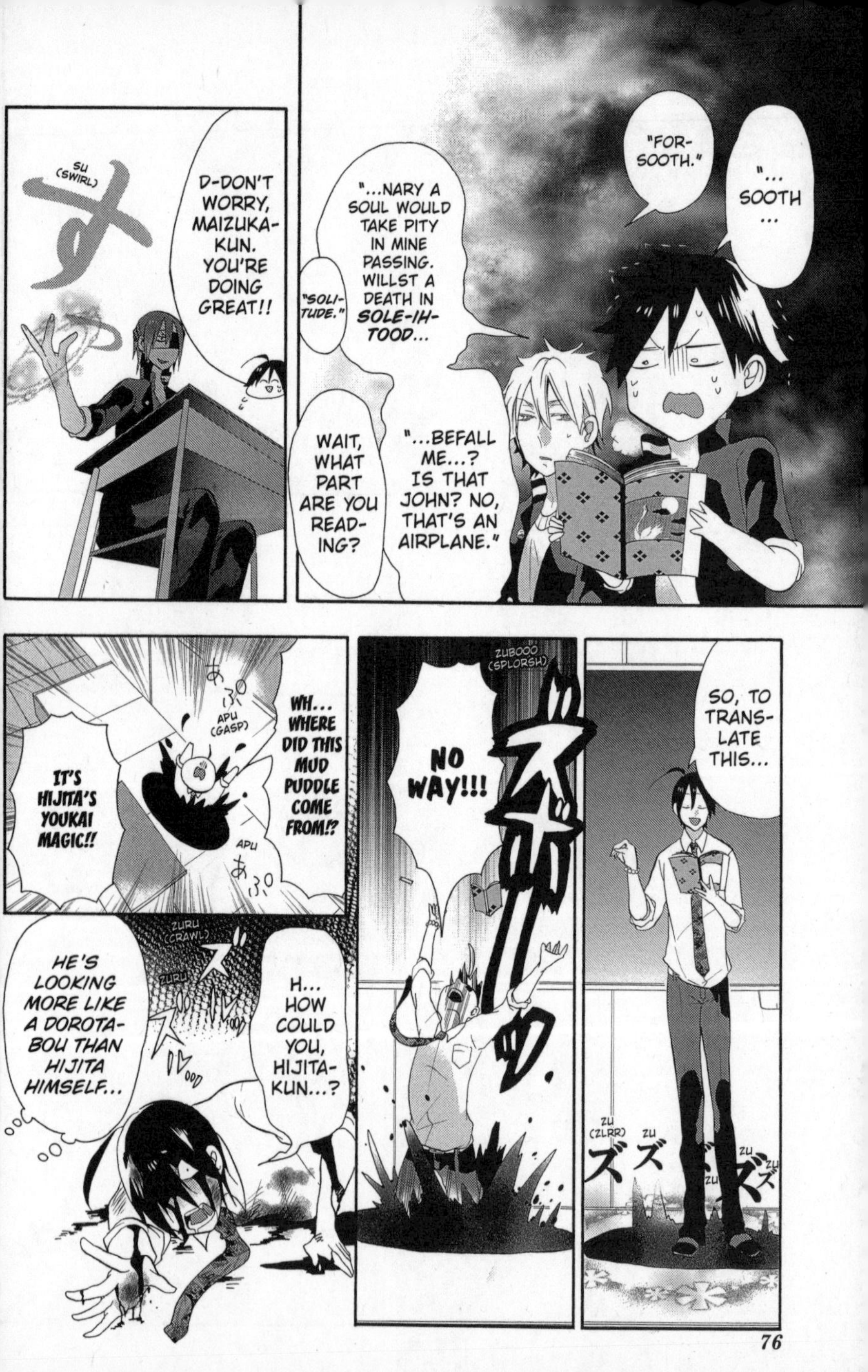
"...SOOTH..."
"FOR-SOOTH."
"...NARY A SOUL WOULD TAKE PITY IN MINE PASSING. WILLST A DEATH IN SOLE-IH-TOOD...
"SOLI-TUDE."
"...BEFALL ME...? IS THAT JOHN? NO, THAT'S AN AIRPLANE."
WAIT, WHAT PART ARE YOU READ-ING?
SU (SWIRL)
D-DON'T WORRY, MAIZUKA-KUN. YOU'RE DOING GREAT!!
SO, TO TRANS-LATE THIS...
ZU (ZLRR) ZU ZU ZU ZU
ZUBOOO (SPLORSH)
NO WAY!!!
WH... WHERE DID THIS MUD PUDDLE COME FROM!?
APU (GASP)
APU
IT'S HIJITA'S YOUKAI MAGIC!!
H... HOW COULD YOU, HIJITA-KUN...?
ZURU (CRAWL)
ZURU
HE'S LOOKING MORE LIKE A DOROTA-BOU THAN HIJITA HIMSELF...

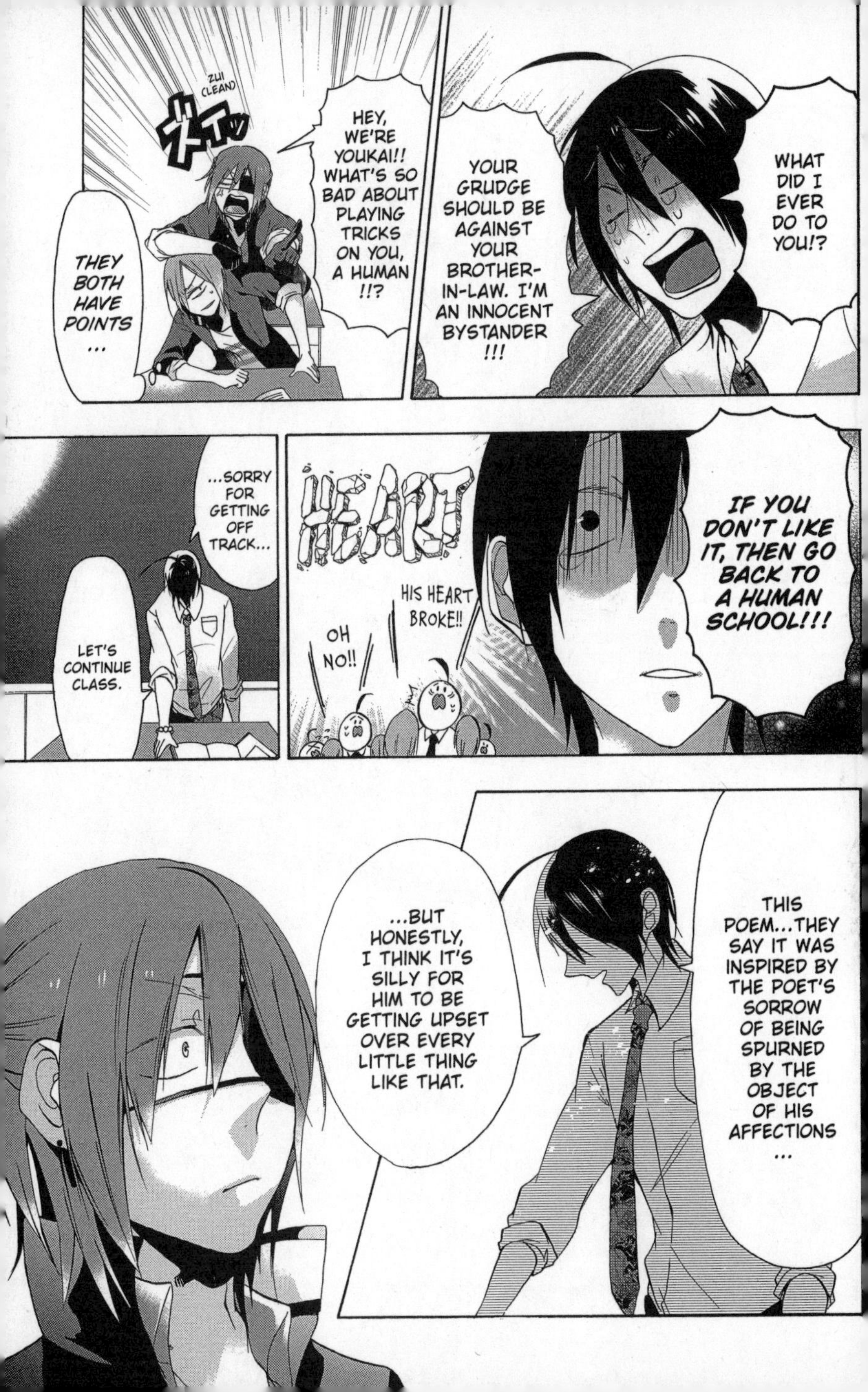
WHAT DID I EVER DO TO YOU!?
YOUR GRUDGE SHOULD BE AGAINST YOUR BROTHER-IN-LAW. I'M AN INNOCENT BYSTANDER!!!
HEY, WE'RE YOUKAI!! WHAT'S SO BAD ABOUT PLAYING TRICKS ON YOU, A HUMAN!!?
ZUI (CLEAN)
THEY BOTH HAVE POINTS...
IF YOU DON'T LIKE IT, THEN GO BACK TO A HUMAN SCHOOL!!!
HEART
HIS HEART BROKE!!
OH NO!!
...SORRY FOR GETTING OFF TRACK...
LET'S CONTINUE CLASS.
THIS POEM...THEY SAY IT WAS INSPIRED BY THE POET'S SORROW OF BEING SPURNED BY THE OBJECT OF HIS AFFECTIONS...
...BUT HONESTLY, I THINK IT'S SILLY FOR HIM TO BE GETTING UPSET OVER EVERY LITTLE THING LIKE THAT.

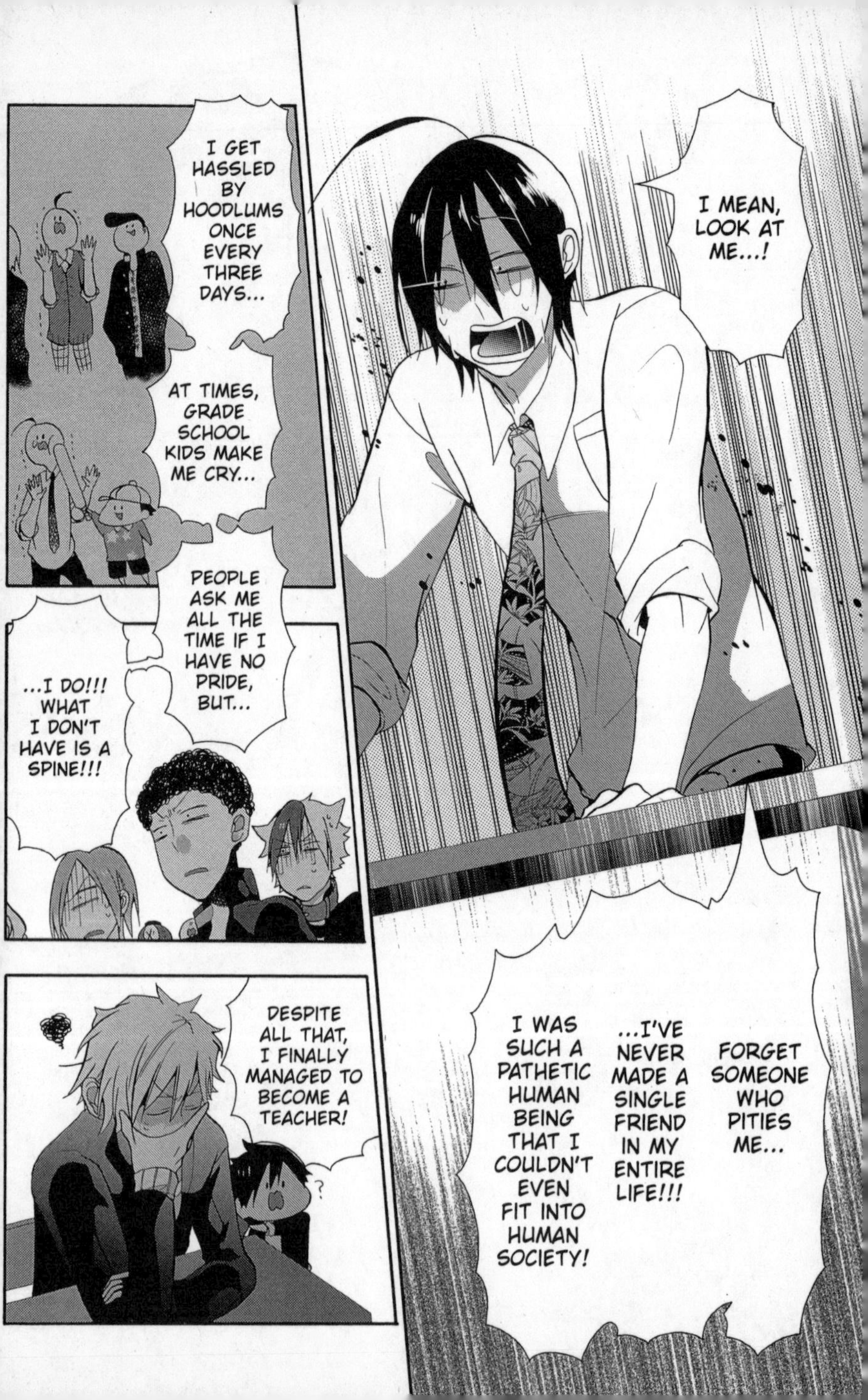
I MEAN, LOOK AT ME...!
I GET HASSLED BY HOODLUMS ONCE EVERY THREE DAYS...
AT TIMES, GRADE SCHOOL KIDS MAKE ME CRY...
PEOPLE ASK ME ALL THE TIME IF I HAVE NO PRIDE, BUT...
...I DO!!! WHAT I DON'T HAVE IS A SPINE!!!
DESPITE ALL THAT, I FINALLY MANAGED TO BECOME A TEACHER!
I WAS SUCH A PATHETIC HUMAN BEING THAT I COULDN'T EVEN FIT INTO HUMAN SOCIETY!
...I'VE NEVER MADE A SINGLE FRIEND IN MY ENTIRE LIFE!!!
FORGET SOMEONE WHO PITIES ME...

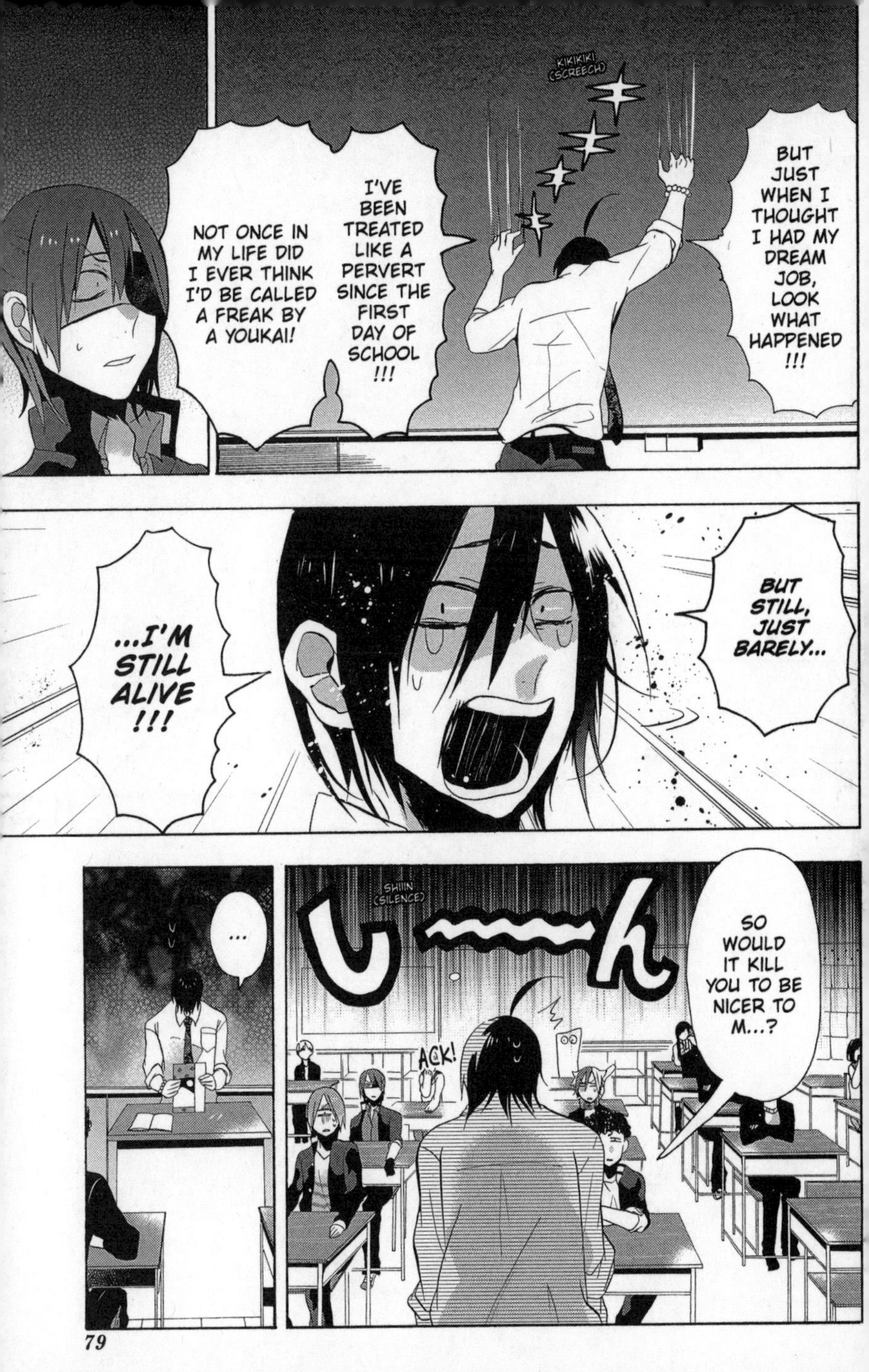
KIKIKIKI (SCREECH)
BUT JUST WHEN I THOUGHT I HAD MY DREAM JOB, LOOK WHAT HAPPENED!!!
I'VE BEEN TREATED LIKE A PERVERT SINCE THE FIRST DAY OF SCHOOL!!!
NOT ONCE IN MY LIFE DID I EVER THINK I'D BE CALLED A FREAK BY A YOUKAI!
BUT STILL, JUST BARELY...
...I'M STILL ALIVE!!!
SHIIN (SILENCE)
U—h
SO WOULD IT KILL YOU TO BE NICER TO M...?
ACK!
...

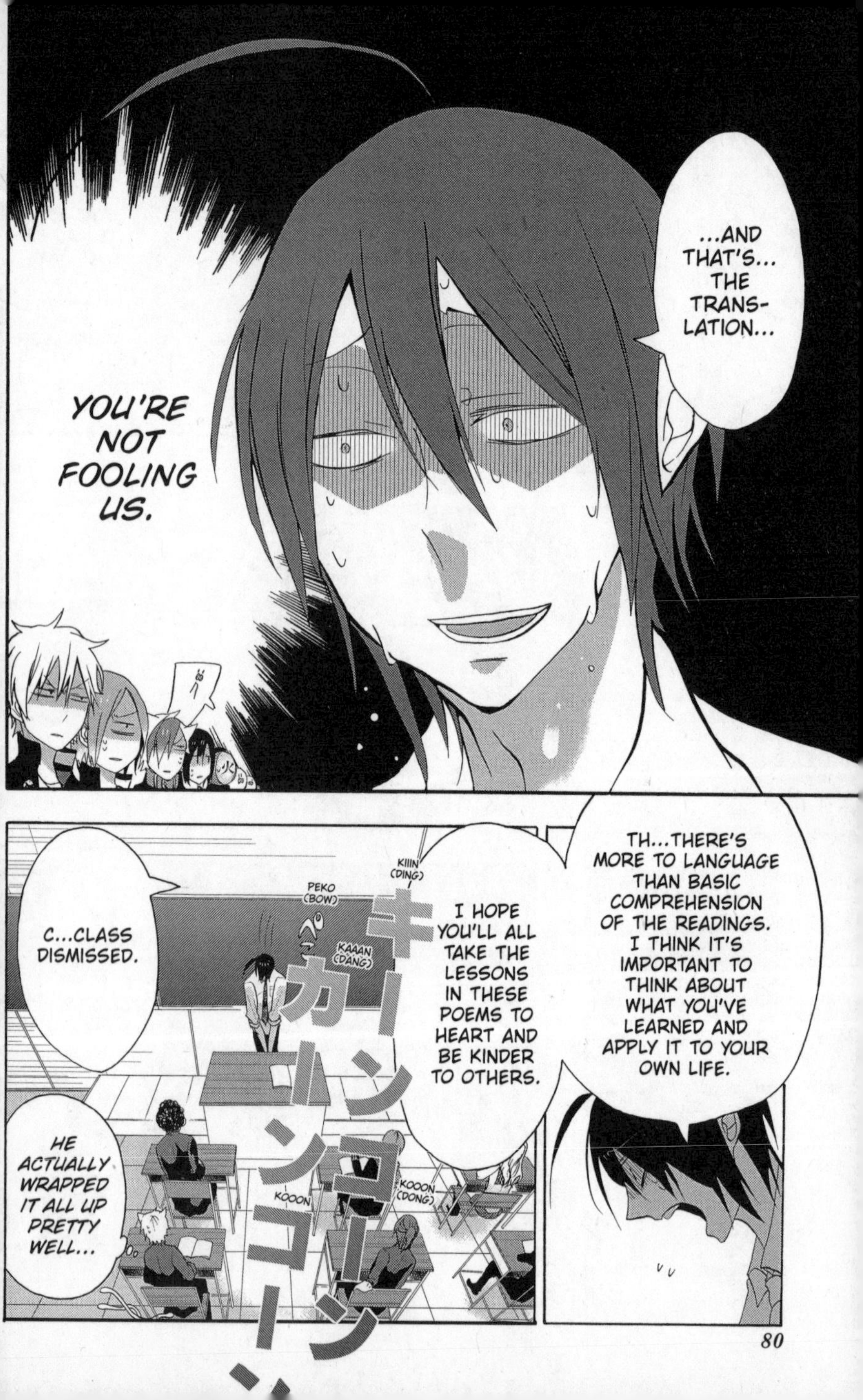
...AND THAT'S... THE TRANS-LATION...
YOU'RE NOT FOOLING US.
TH...THERE'S MORE TO LANGUAGE THAN BASIC COMPREHENSION OF THE READINGS. I THINK IT'S IMPORTANT TO THINK ABOUT WHAT YOU'VE LEARNED AND APPLY IT TO YOUR OWN LIFE.
I HOPE YOU'LL ALL TAKE THE LESSONS IN THESE POEMS TO HEART AND BE KINDER TO OTHERS.
KIIN (DING)
PEKO (BOW)
KAAAN (DANG)
C...CLASS DISMISSED.
KOOON (DONG)
KOOON
HE ACTUALLY WRAPPED IT ALL UP PRETTY WELL...

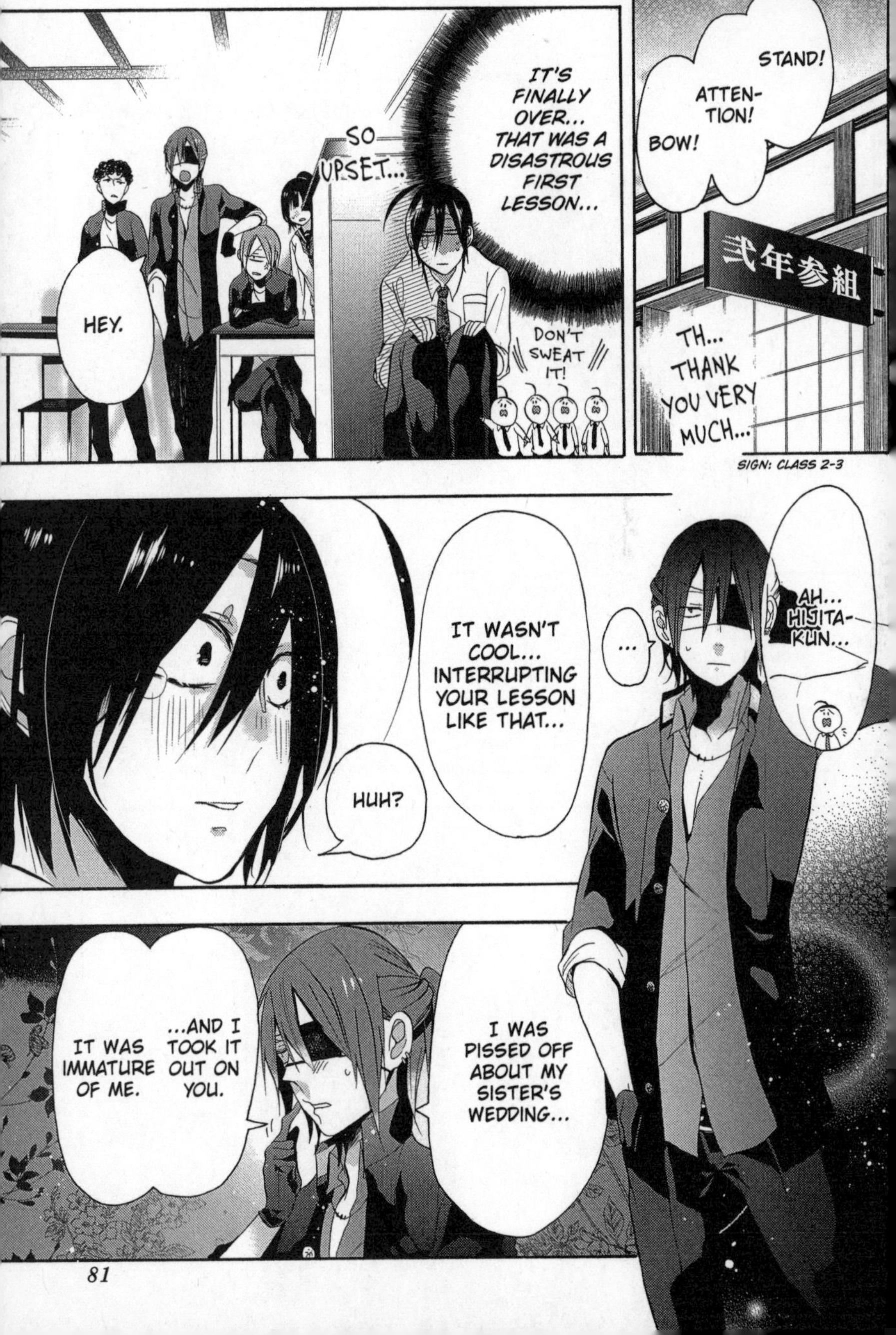
STAND!
ATTEN-TION!
BOW!
TH... THANK YOU VERY MUCH...
弐年参組
SIGN: CLASS 2-3
IT'S FINALLY OVER... THAT WAS A DISASTROUS FIRST LESSON...
SO UPSET...
DON'T SWEAT IT!
HEY.
AH... HIJITA-KUN...
...
IT WASN'T COOL... INTERRUPTING YOUR LESSON LIKE THAT...
HUH?
I WAS PISSED OFF ABOUT MY SISTER'S WEDDING...
...AND I TOOK IT OUT ON YOU.
IT WAS IMMATURE OF ME.

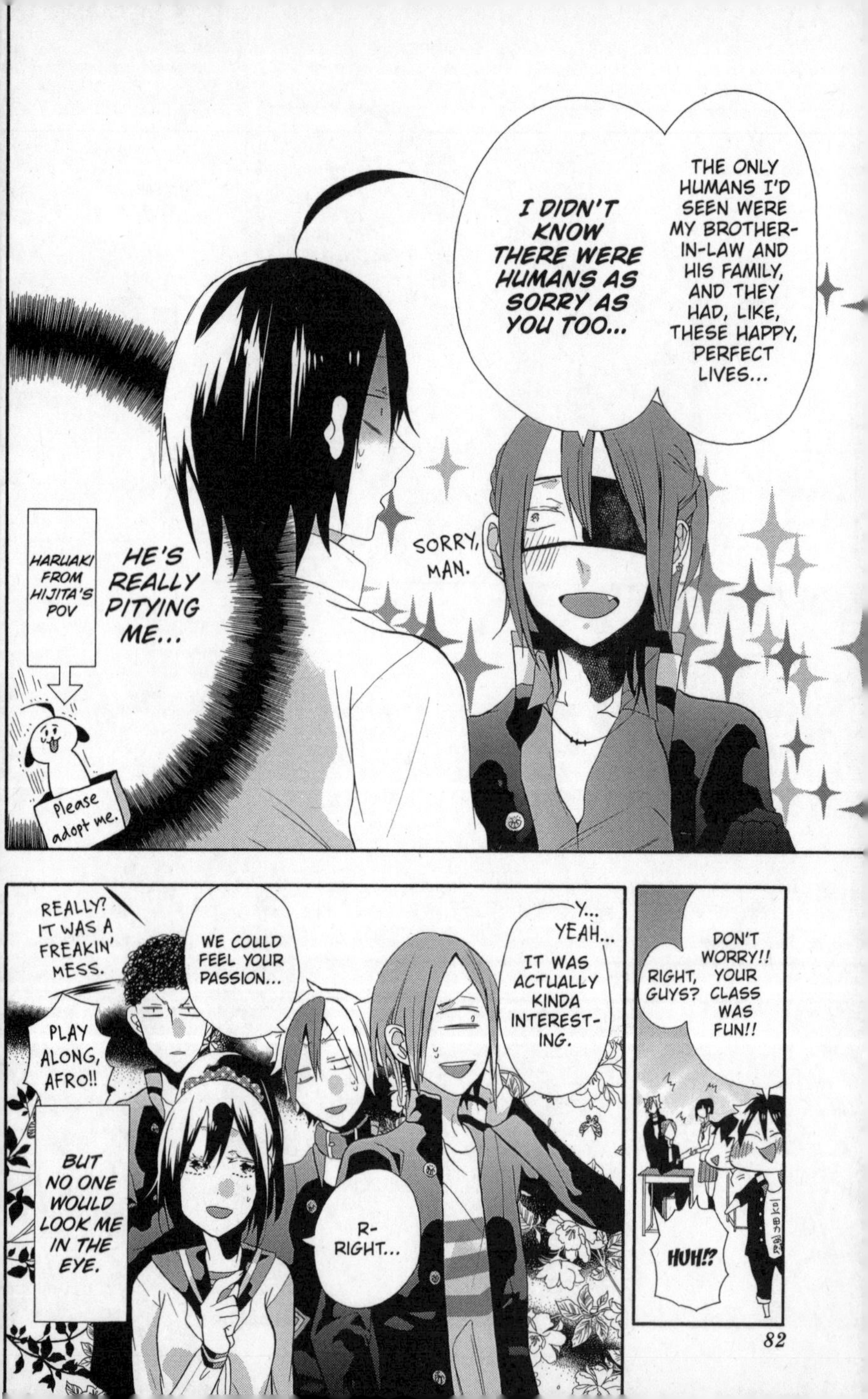
THE ONLY HUMANS I'D SEEN WERE MY BROTHER-IN-LAW AND HIS FAMILY, AND THEY HAD, LIKE, THESE HAPPY, PERFECT LIVES...
I DIDN'T KNOW THERE WERE HUMANS AS SORRY AS YOU TOO...
SORRY, MAN.
HE'S REALLY PITYING ME...
HARUAKI FROM HIJITA'S POV
Please adopt me.
DON'T WORRY!! YOUR CLASS WAS FUN!!
RIGHT, GUYS?
HUH!?
Y... YEAH... IT WAS ACTUALLY KINDA INTEREST-ING.
WE COULD FEEL YOUR PASSION...
REALLY? IT WAS A FREAKIN' MESS.
PLAY ALONG, AFRO!!
R-RIGHT...
BUT NO ONE WOULD LOOK ME IN THE EYE.

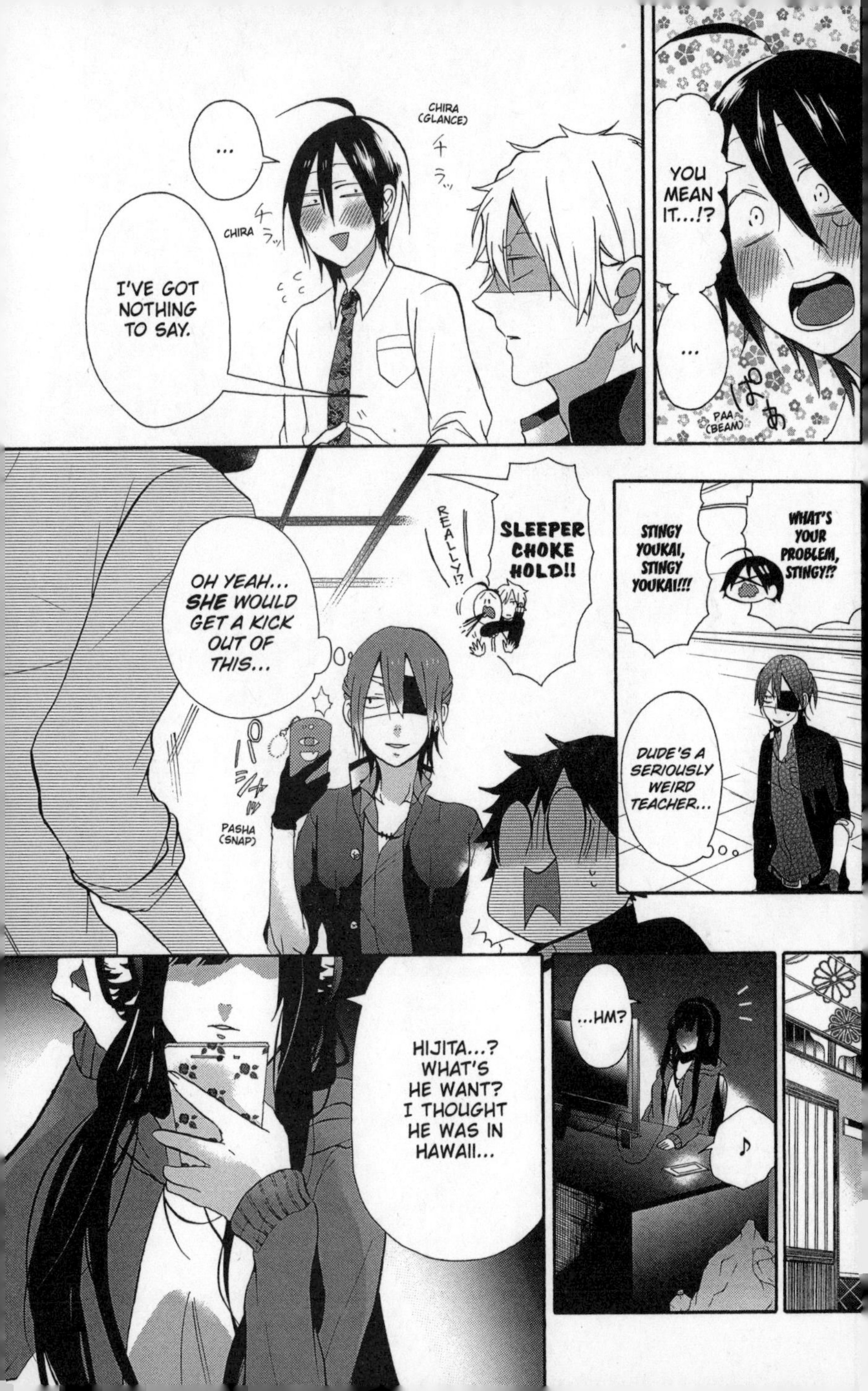

YOU MEAN IT...!?
...
ぱあ
PAA (BEAM)
CHIRA (GLANCE)
チラッ
...
チラッ
CHIRA
I'VE GOT NOTHING TO SAY.
WHAT'S YOUR PROBLEM, STINGY!?
STINGY YOUKAI, STINGY YOUKAI!!!
DUDE'S A SERIOUSLY WEIRD TEACHER...
SLEEPER CHOKE HOLD!!
REALLY!?
OH YEAH... SHE WOULD GET A KICK OUT OF THIS...
パシャ
PASHA (SNAP)
...HM?
♪
HIJITA...? WHAT'S HE WANT? I THOUGHT HE WAS IN HAWAII...

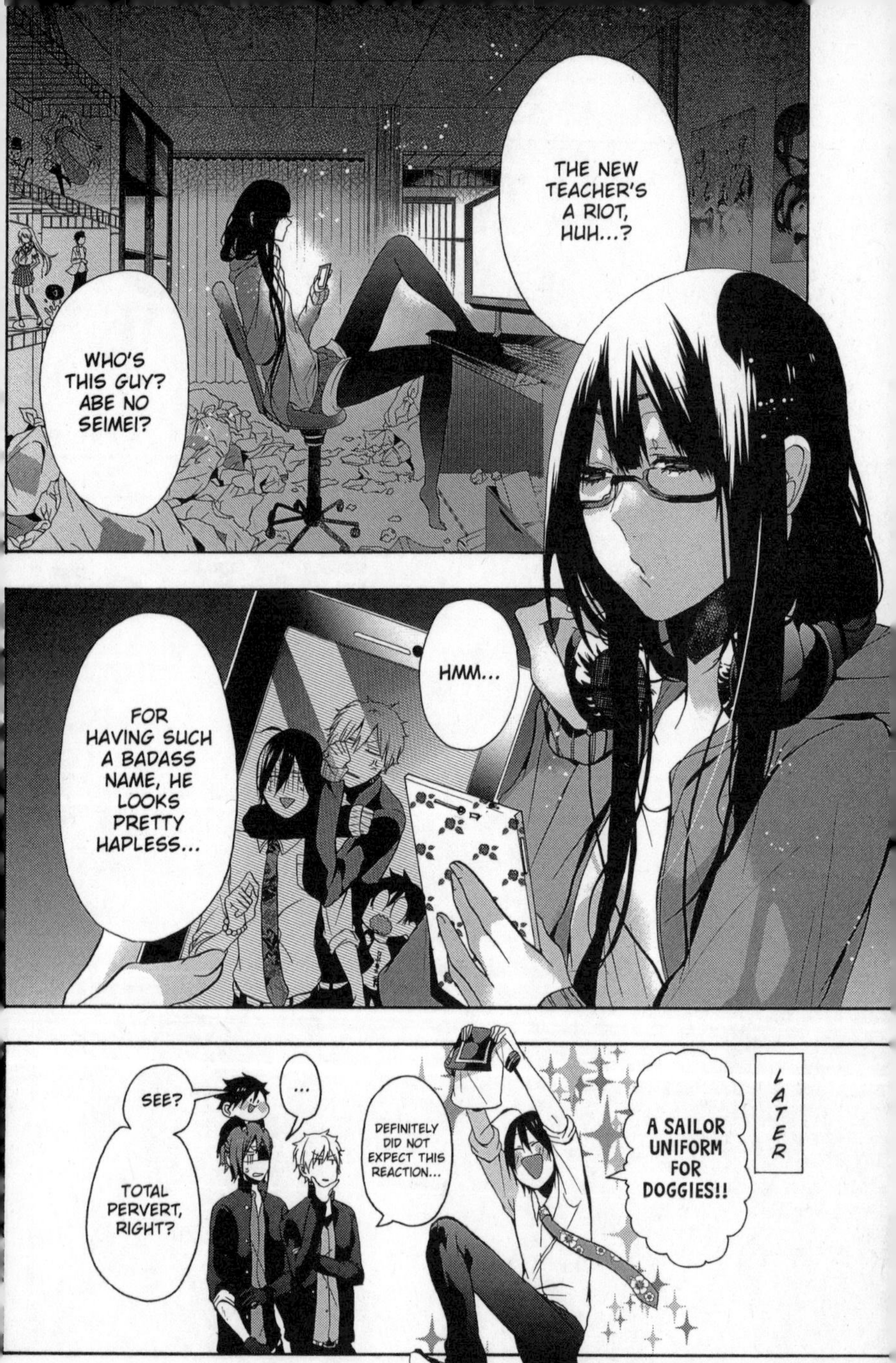
THE NEW TEACHER'S A RIOT, HUH...?
WHO'S THIS GUY? ABE NO SEIMEI?
HMM...
FOR HAVING SUCH A BADASS NAME, HE LOOKS PRETTY HAPLESS...
LATER
A SAILOR UNIFORM FOR DOGGIES!!
DEFINITELY DID NOT EXPECT THIS REACTION...
...
SEE?
TOTAL PERVERT, RIGHT?

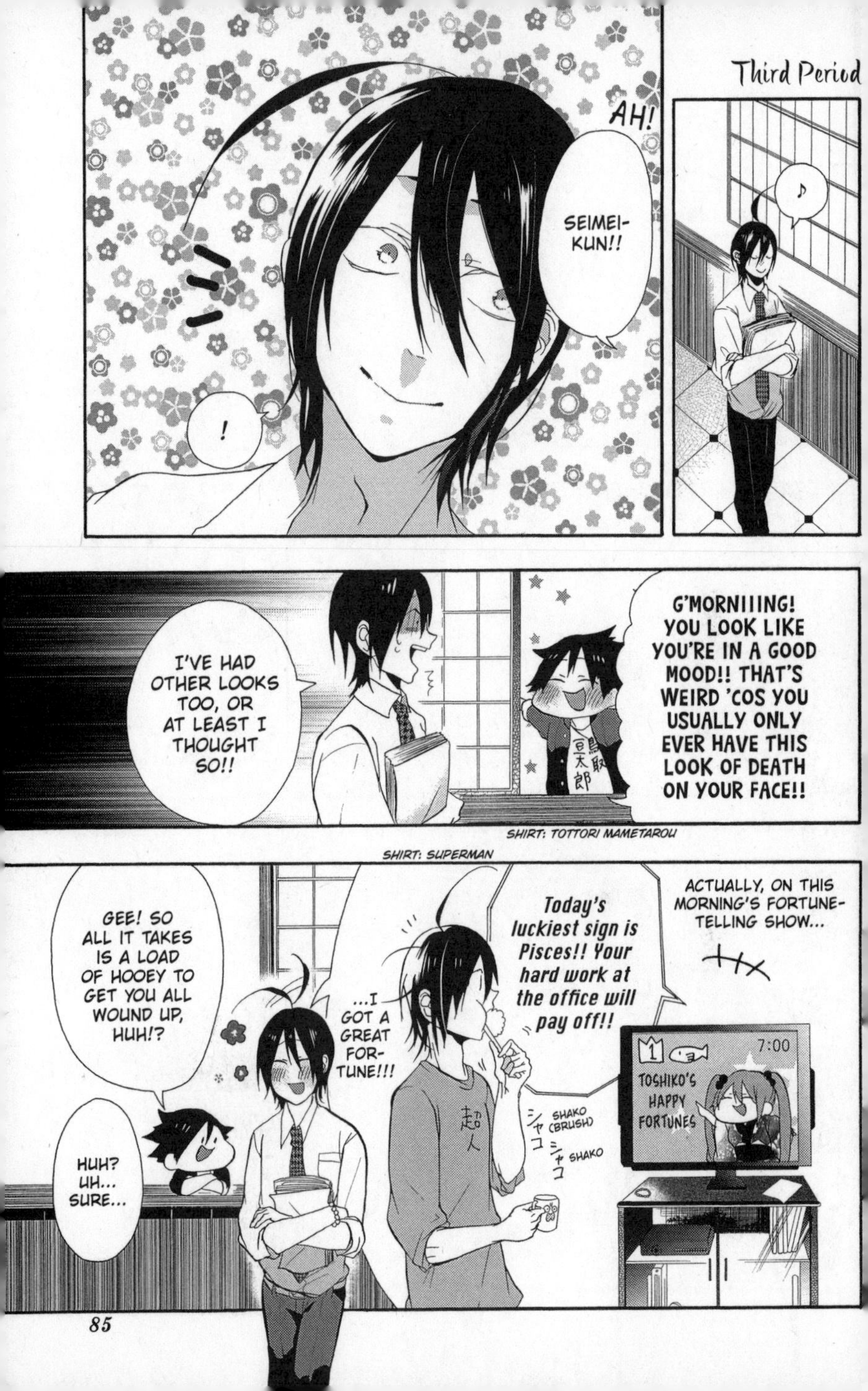
♪
AH!
SEIMEI-KUN!!
!
G'MORNIIIING! YOU LOOK LIKE YOU'RE IN A GOOD MOOD!! THAT'S WEIRD 'COS YOU USUALLY ONLY EVER HAVE THIS LOOK OF DEATH ON YOUR FACE!!
I'VE HAD OTHER LOOKS TOO, OR AT LEAST I THOUGHT SO!!
SHIRT: TOTTORI MAMETAROU
SHIRT: SUPERMAN
ACTUALLY, ON THIS MORNING'S FORTUNE-TELLING SHOW...
1
7:00
TOSHIKO'S HAPPY FORTUNES
Today's luckiest sign is Pisces!! Your hard work at the office will pay off!!
SHAKO (BRUSH)
SHAKO
...I GOT A GREAT FOR-TUNE!!!
GEE! SO ALL IT TAKES IS A LOAD OF HOOEY TO GET YOU ALL WOUND UP, HUH!?
HUH? UH... SURE...

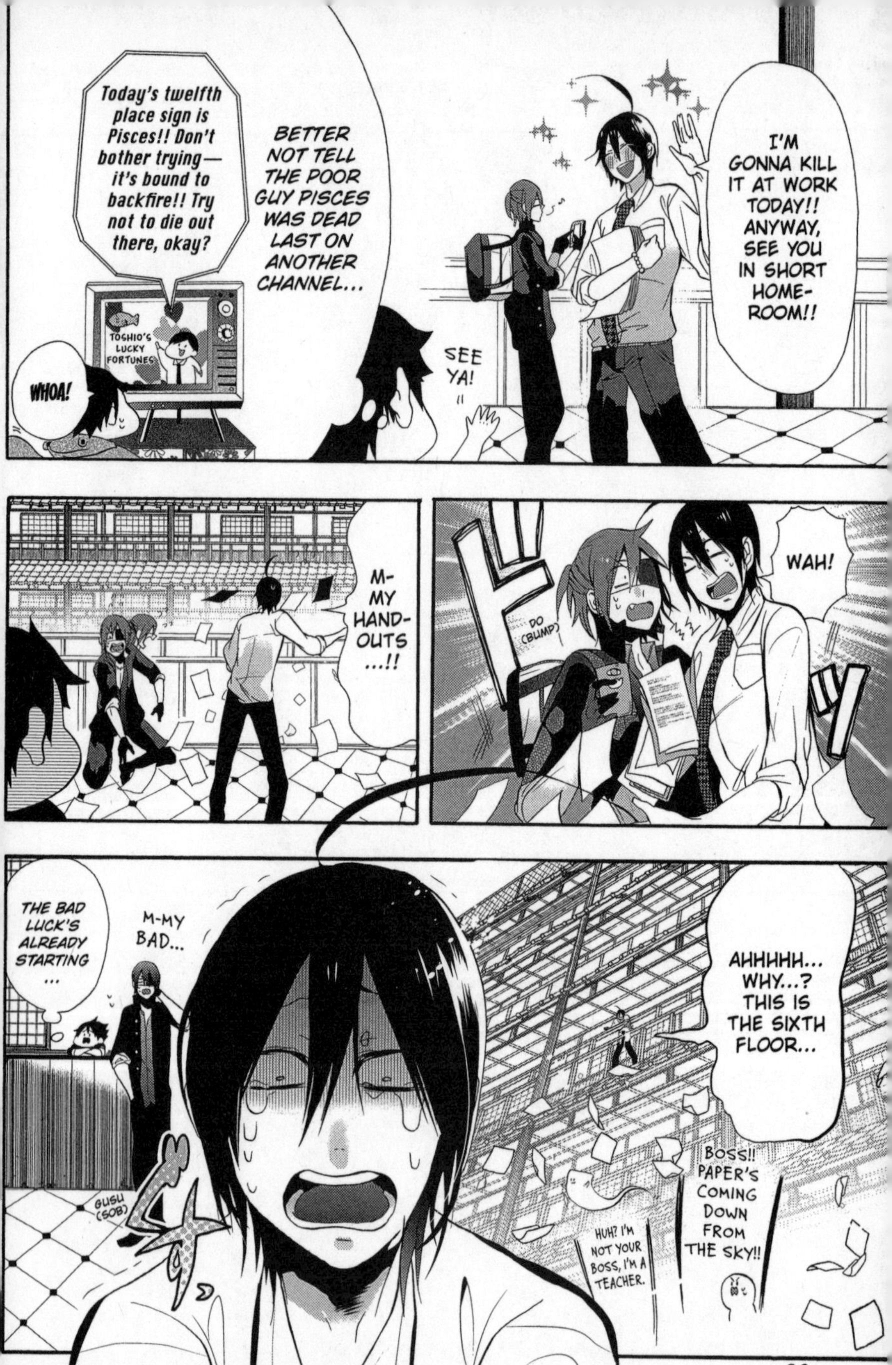
I'M GONNA KILL IT AT WORK TODAY!! ANYWAY, SEE YOU IN SHORT HOME-ROOM!!
SEE YA!
BETTER NOT TELL THE POOR GUY PISCES WAS DEAD LAST ON ANOTHER CHANNEL...
Today's twelfth place sign is Pisces!! Don't bother trying—it's bound to backfire!! Try not to die out there, okay?
TOSHIO'S LUCKY FORTUNES
WHOA!
WAH!
DO (BUMP)
M-MY HAND-OUTS...!!
AHHHHH... WHY...? THIS IS THE SIXTH FLOOR...
BOSS!! PAPER'S COMING DOWN FROM THE SKY!!
HUH? I'M NOT YOUR BOSS, I'M A TEACHER.
GUSU (SOB)
M-MY BAD...
THE BAD LUCK'S ALREADY STARTING...

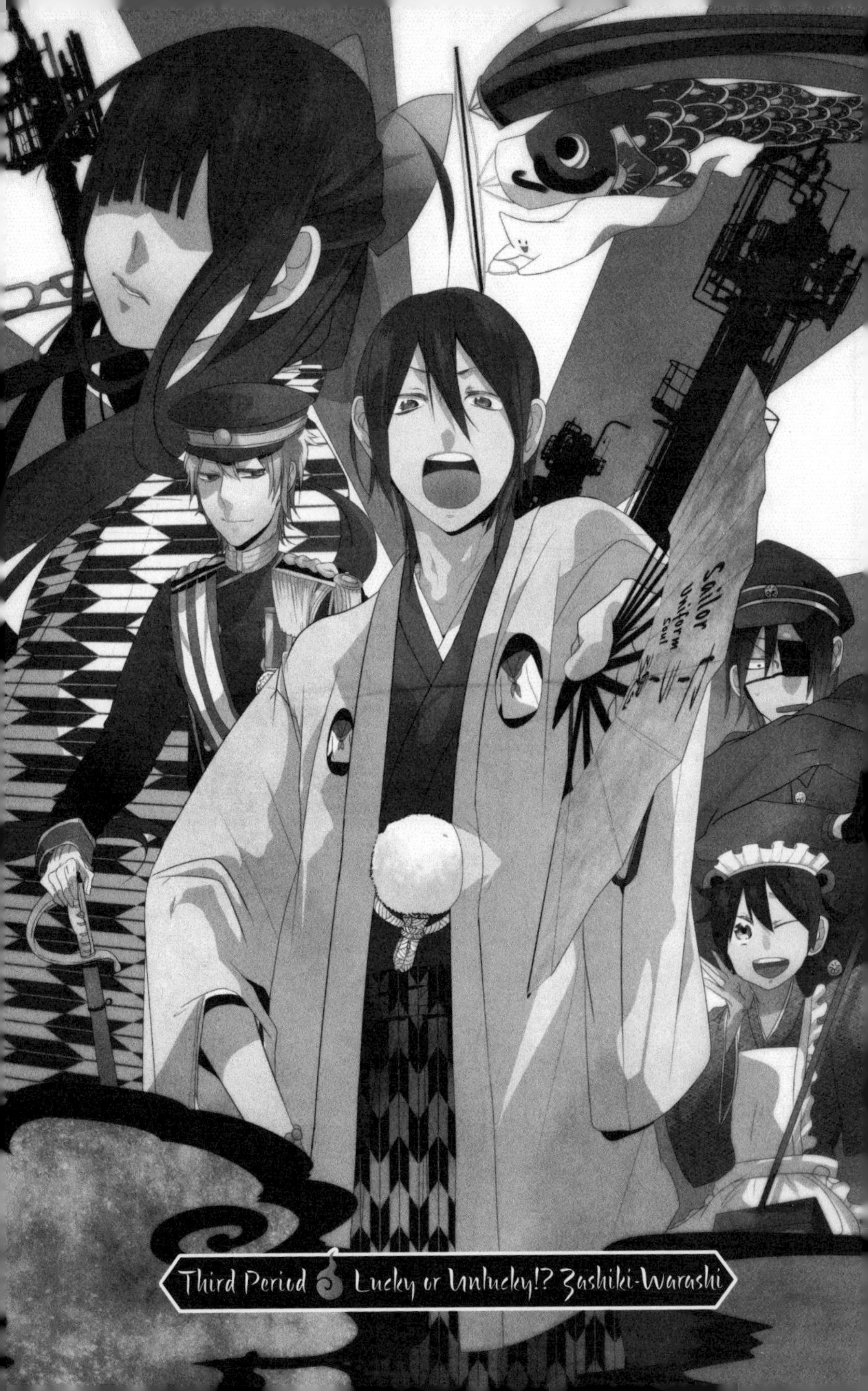
Sailor Uniform Soul
Third Period Lucky or Unlucky!? Zashiki-Warashi

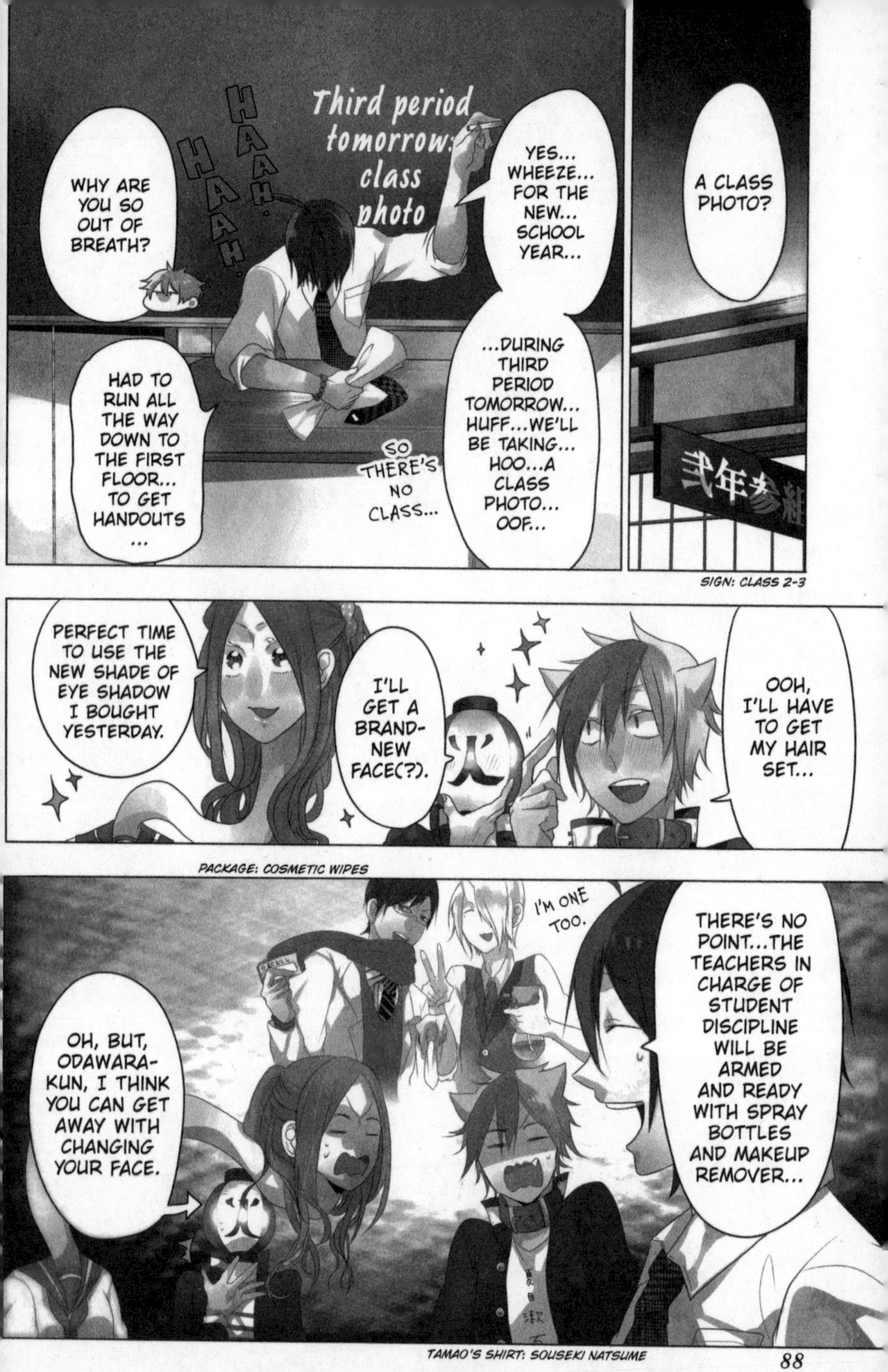
A CLASS PHOTO?
Third period tomorrow: class photo
YES... WHEEZE... FOR THE NEW... SCHOOL YEAR...
HAAAH HAAAH.
WHY ARE YOU SO OUT OF BREATH?
HAD TO RUN ALL THE WAY DOWN TO THE FIRST FLOOR... TO GET HANDOUTS...
...DURING THIRD PERIOD TOMORROW... HUFF...WE'LL BE TAKING... HOO...A CLASS PHOTO... OOF...
SO THERE'S NO CLASS...
弐年参組
OOH, I'LL HAVE TO GET MY HAIR SET...
I'LL GET A BRAND-NEW FACE(?).
PERFECT TIME TO USE THE NEW SHADE OF EYE SHADOW I BOUGHT YESTERDAY.
THERE'S NO POINT...THE TEACHERS IN CHARGE OF STUDENT DISCIPLINE WILL BE ARMED AND READY WITH SPRAY BOTTLES AND MAKEUP REMOVER...
I'M ONE TOO.
OH, BUT, ODAWARA-KUN, I THINK YOU CAN GET AWAY WITH CHANGING YOUR FACE.

SIGN: CLASS 2-3

PACKAGE: COSMETIC WIPES

TAMAO'S SHIRT: SOUSEKI NATSUME

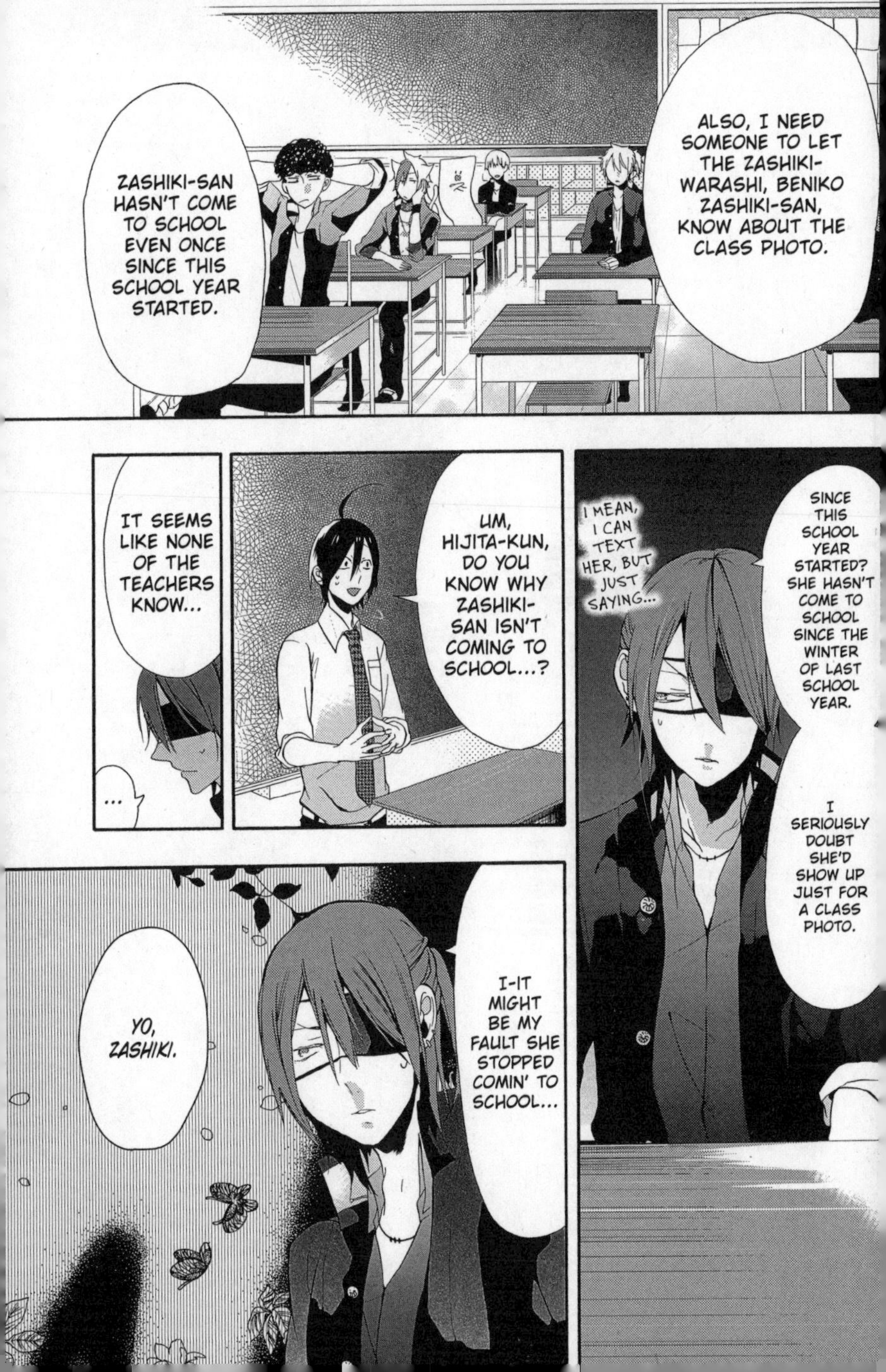
ALSO, I NEED SOMEONE TO LET THE ZASHIKI-WARASHI, BENIKO ZASHIKI-SAN, KNOW ABOUT THE CLASS PHOTO.
ZASHIKI-SAN HASN'T COME TO SCHOOL EVEN ONCE SINCE THIS SCHOOL YEAR STARTED.
SINCE THIS SCHOOL YEAR STARTED? SHE HASN'T COME TO SCHOOL SINCE THE WINTER OF LAST SCHOOL YEAR.
I MEAN, I CAN TEXT HER, BUT JUST SAYING...
I SERIOUSLY DOUBT SHE'D SHOW UP JUST FOR A CLASS PHOTO.
UM, HIJITA-KUN, DO YOU KNOW WHY ZASHIKI-SAN ISN'T COMING TO SCHOOL...?
IT SEEMS LIKE NONE OF THE TEACHERS KNOW...
...
I-IT MIGHT BE MY FAULT SHE STOPPED COMIN' TO SCHOOL...
YO, ZASHIKI.

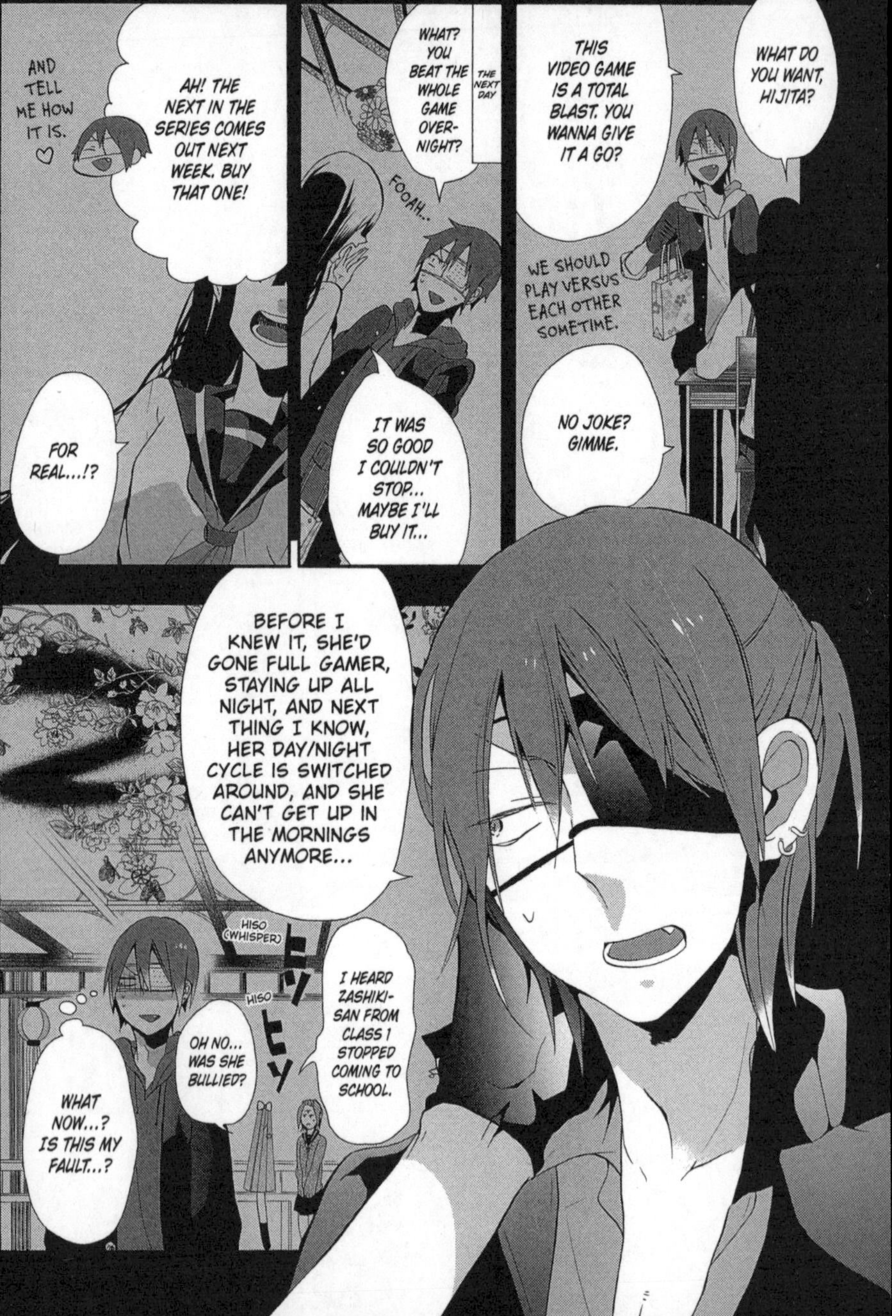
WHAT DO YOU WANT, HIJITA?
THIS VIDEO GAME IS A TOTAL BLAST. YOU WANNA GIVE IT A GO?
WE SHOULD PLAY VERSUS EACH OTHER SOMETIME.
NO JOKE? GIMME.
THE NEXT DAY
WHAT? YOU BEAT THE WHOLE GAME OVER-NIGHT?
FOOAH...
IT WAS SO GOOD I COULDN'T STOP... MAYBE I'LL BUY IT...
AH! THE NEXT IN THE SERIES COMES OUT NEXT WEEK. BUY THAT ONE!
AND TELL ME HOW IT IS. ♡
FOR REAL...!?
BEFORE I KNEW IT, SHE'D GONE FULL GAMER, STAYING UP ALL NIGHT, AND NEXT THING I KNOW, HER DAY/NIGHT CYCLE IS SWITCHED AROUND, AND SHE CAN'T GET UP IN THE MORNINGS ANYMORE...
HISO (WHISPER)
HISO
I HEARD ZASHIKI-SAN FROM CLASS 1 STOPPED COMING TO SCHOOL.
OH NO... WAS SHE BULLIED?
WHAT NOW...? IS THIS MY FAULT...?

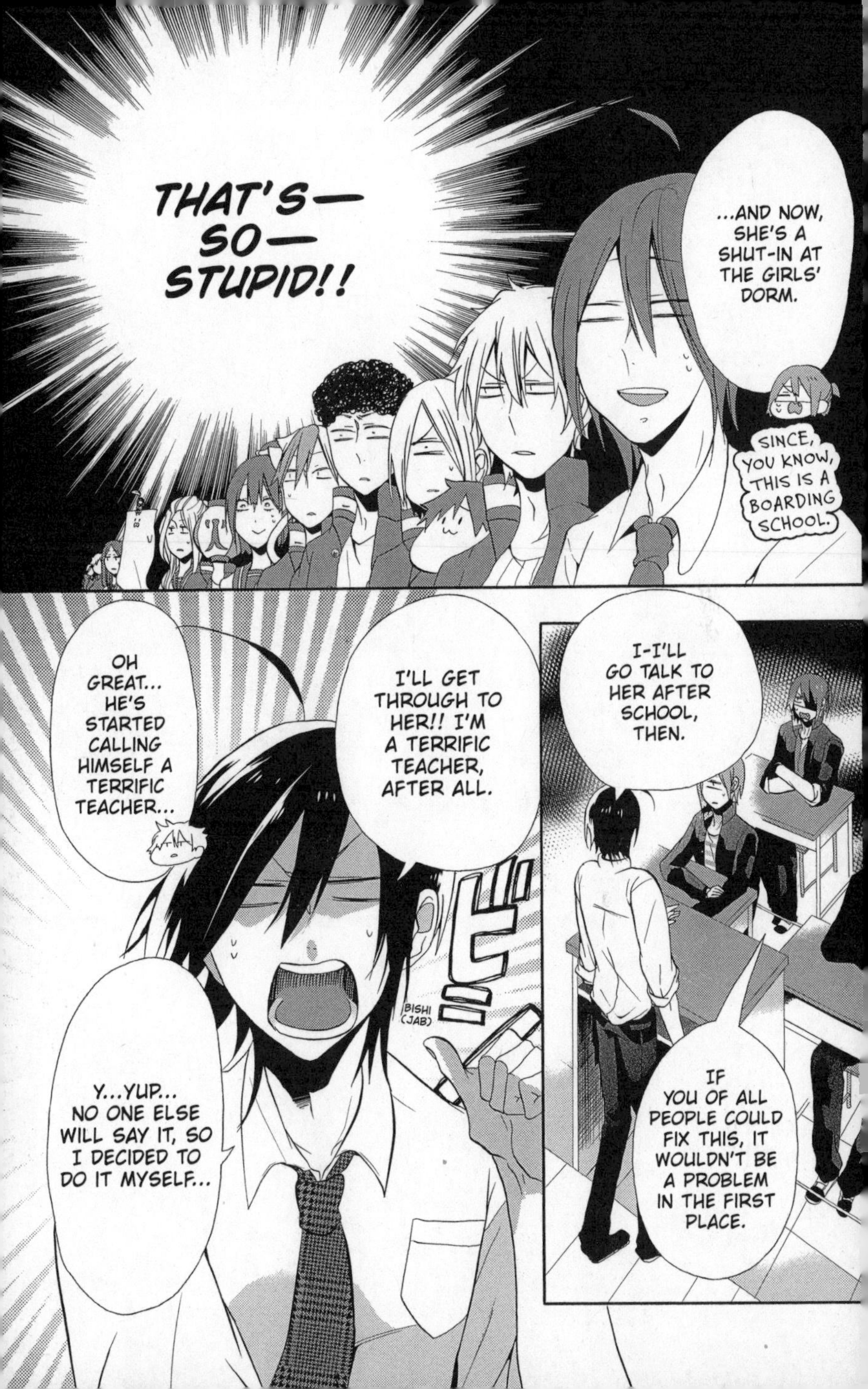
...AND NOW, SHE'S A SHUT-IN AT THE GIRLS' DORM.
SINCE, YOU KNOW, THIS IS A BOARDING SCHOOL.
THAT'S— SO— STUPID!!
I-I'LL GO TALK TO HER AFTER SCHOOL, THEN.
IF YOU OF ALL PEOPLE COULD FIX THIS, IT WOULDN'T BE A PROBLEM IN THE FIRST PLACE.
I'LL GET THROUGH TO HER!! I'M A TERRIFIC TEACHER, AFTER ALL.
OH GREAT... HE'S STARTED CALLING HIMSELF A TERRIFIC TEACHER...
BISHI (JAB)
Y...YUP... NO ONE ELSE WILL SAY IT, SO I DECIDED TO DO IT MYSELF...

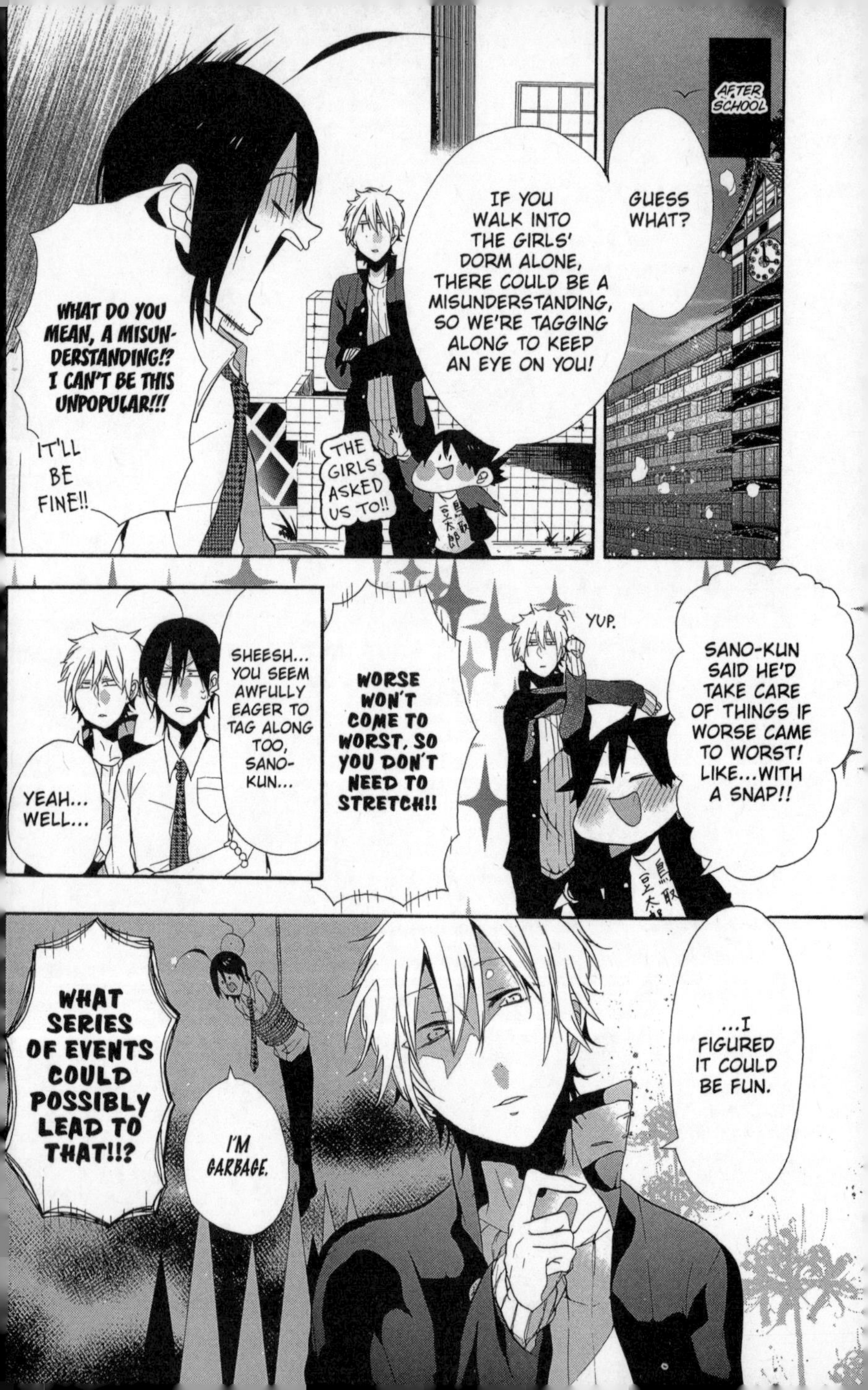
AFTER SCHOOL
GUESS WHAT?
IF YOU WALK INTO THE GIRLS' DORM ALONE, THERE COULD BE A MISUNDERSTANDING, SO WE'RE TAGGING ALONG TO KEEP AN EYE ON YOU!
THE GIRLS ASKED US TO!!
WHAT DO YOU MEAN, A MISUNDERSTANDING!? I CAN'T BE THIS UNPOPULAR!!!
IT'LL BE FINE!!
SANO-KUN SAID HE'D TAKE CARE OF THINGS IF WORSE CAME TO WORST! LIKE...WITH A SNAP!!
YUP.
WORSE WON'T COME TO WORST, SO YOU DON'T NEED TO STRETCH!!
SHEESH... YOU SEEM AWFULLY EAGER TO TAG ALONG TOO, SANO-KUN...
YEAH... WELL...
...I FIGURED IT COULD BE FUN.
I'M GARBAGE.
WHAT SERIES OF EVENTS COULD POSSIBLY LEAD TO THAT!!?

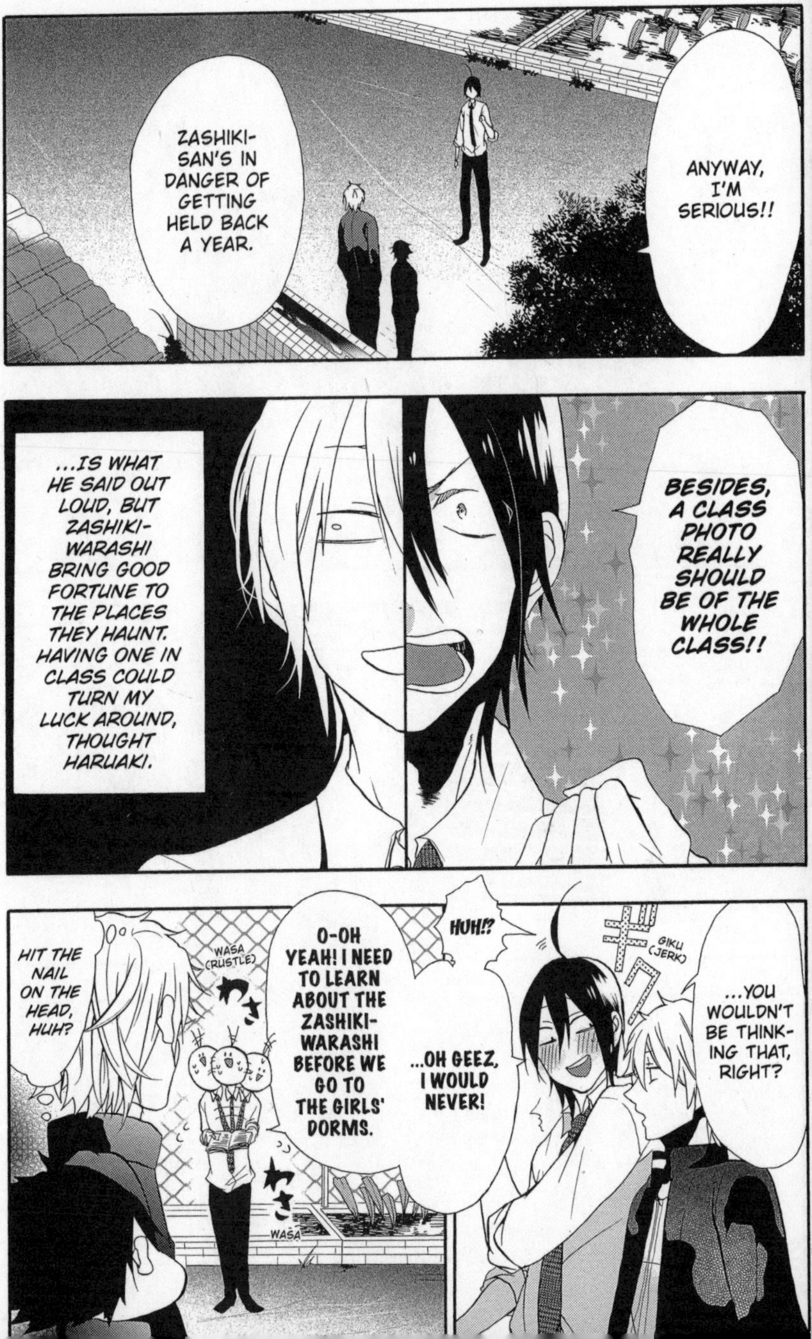
ANYWAY, I'M SERIOUS!!
ZASHIKI-SAN'S IN DANGER OF GETTING HELD BACK A YEAR.
BESIDES, A CLASS PHOTO REALLY SHOULD BE OF THE WHOLE CLASS!!
...IS WHAT HE SAID OUT LOUD, BUT ZASHIKI-WARASHI BRING GOOD FORTUNE TO THE PLACES THEY HAUNT. HAVING ONE IN CLASS COULD TURN MY LUCK AROUND, THOUGHT HARUAKI.
...YOU WOULDN'T BE THINKING THAT, RIGHT?
GIKU (JERK)
HUH!?
...OH GEEZ, I WOULD NEVER!
O-OH YEAH! I NEED TO LEARN ABOUT THE ZASHIKI-WARASHI BEFORE WE GO TO THE GIRLS' DORMS.
WASA (RUSTLE)
HIT THE NAIL ON THE HEAD, HUH?
WASA

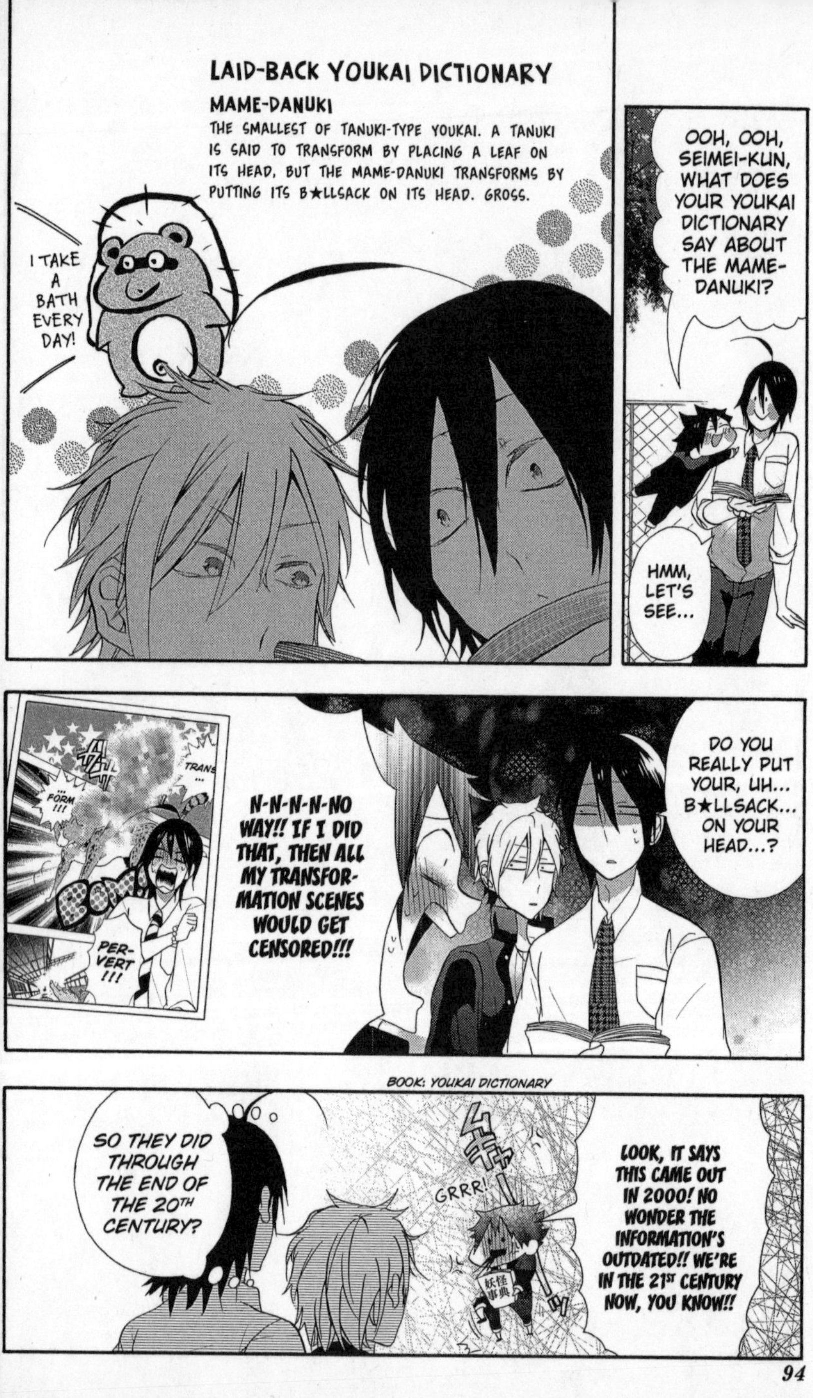
OOH, OOH, SEIMEI-KUN, WHAT DOES YOUR YOUKAI DICTIONARY SAY ABOUT THE MAME-DANUKI?
HMM, LET'S SEE...
LAID-BACK YOUKAI DICTIONARY
MAME-DANUKI
THE SMALLEST OF TANUKI-TYPE YOUKAI. A TANUKI IS SAID TO TRANSFORM BY PLACING A LEAF ON ITS HEAD, BUT THE MAME-DANUKI TRANSFORMS BY PUTTING ITS B★LLSACK ON ITS HEAD. GROSS.
I TAKE A BATH EVERY DAY!
DO YOU REALLY PUT YOUR, UH... B★LLSACK... ON YOUR HEAD...?
N-N-N-N-NO WAY!! IF I DID THAT, THEN ALL MY TRANSFORMATION SCENES WOULD GET CENSORED!!!
TRANS ...
... FORM !!!
PER-VERT !!!
BOOK: YOUKAI DICTIONARY
LOOK, IT SAYS THIS CAME OUT IN 2000! NO WONDER THE INFORMATION'S OUTDATED!! WE'RE IN THE 21ST CENTURY NOW, YOU KNOW!!
GRRR!
妖怪事典
SO THEY DID THROUGH THE END OF THE 20TH CENTURY?

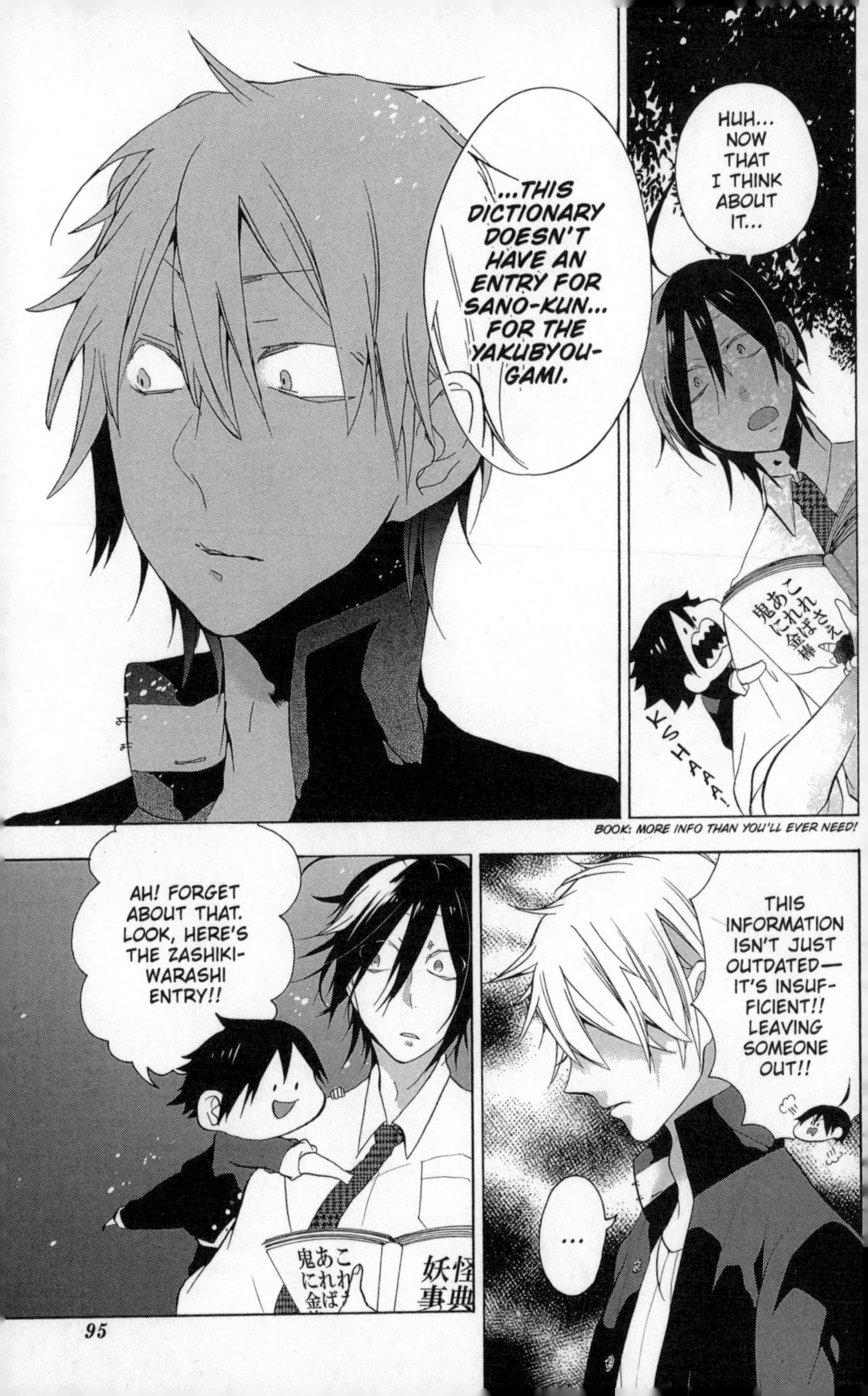
HUH... NOW THAT I THINK ABOUT IT...
KSHAAA!
...THIS DICTIONARY DOESN'T HAVE AN ENTRY FOR SANO-KUN... FOR THE YAKUBYOU-GAMI.
BOOK: MORE INFO THAN YOU'LL EVER NEED!
THIS INFORMATION ISN'T JUST OUTDATED—IT'S INSUF-FICIENT!! LEAVING SOMEONE OUT!!
...
AH! FORGET ABOUT THAT. LOOK, HERE'S THE ZASHIKI-WARASHI ENTRY!!
妖怪事典

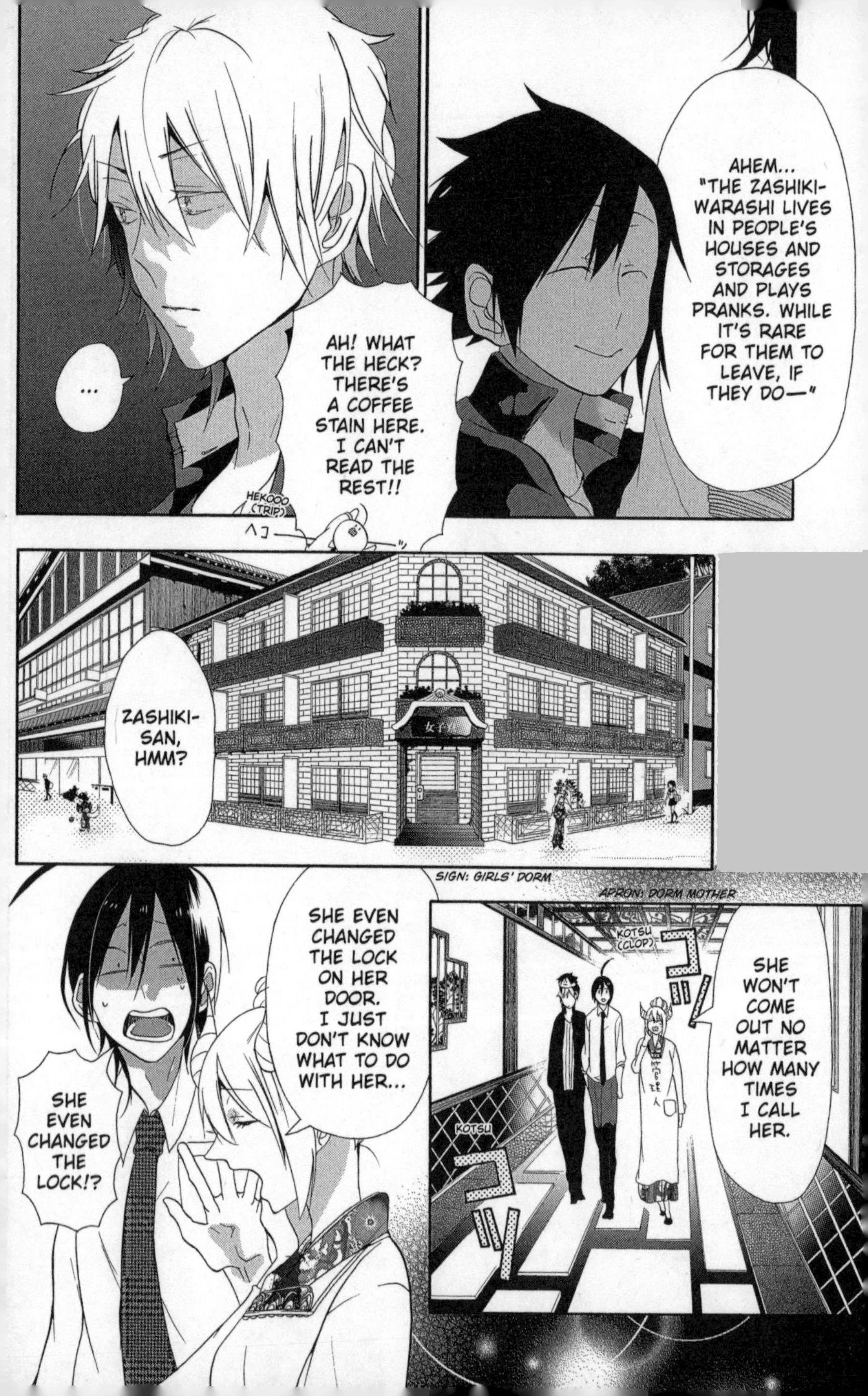
AHEM... "THE ZASHIKI-WARASHI LIVES IN PEOPLE'S HOUSES AND STORAGES AND PLAYS PRANKS. WHILE IT'S RARE FOR THEM TO LEAVE, IF THEY DO—"
AH! WHAT THE HECK? THERE'S A COFFEE STAIN HERE. I CAN'T READ THE REST!!
...
HEKOOO (TRIP)
ZASHIKI-SAN, HMM?
SIGN: GIRLS' DORM
APRON: DORM MOTHER
KOTSU (CLOP)
SHE WON'T COME OUT NO MATTER HOW MANY TIMES I CALL HER.
KOTSU
SHE EVEN CHANGED THE LOCK ON HER DOOR. I JUST DON'T KNOW WHAT TO DO WITH HER...
SHE EVEN CHANGED THE LOCK!?

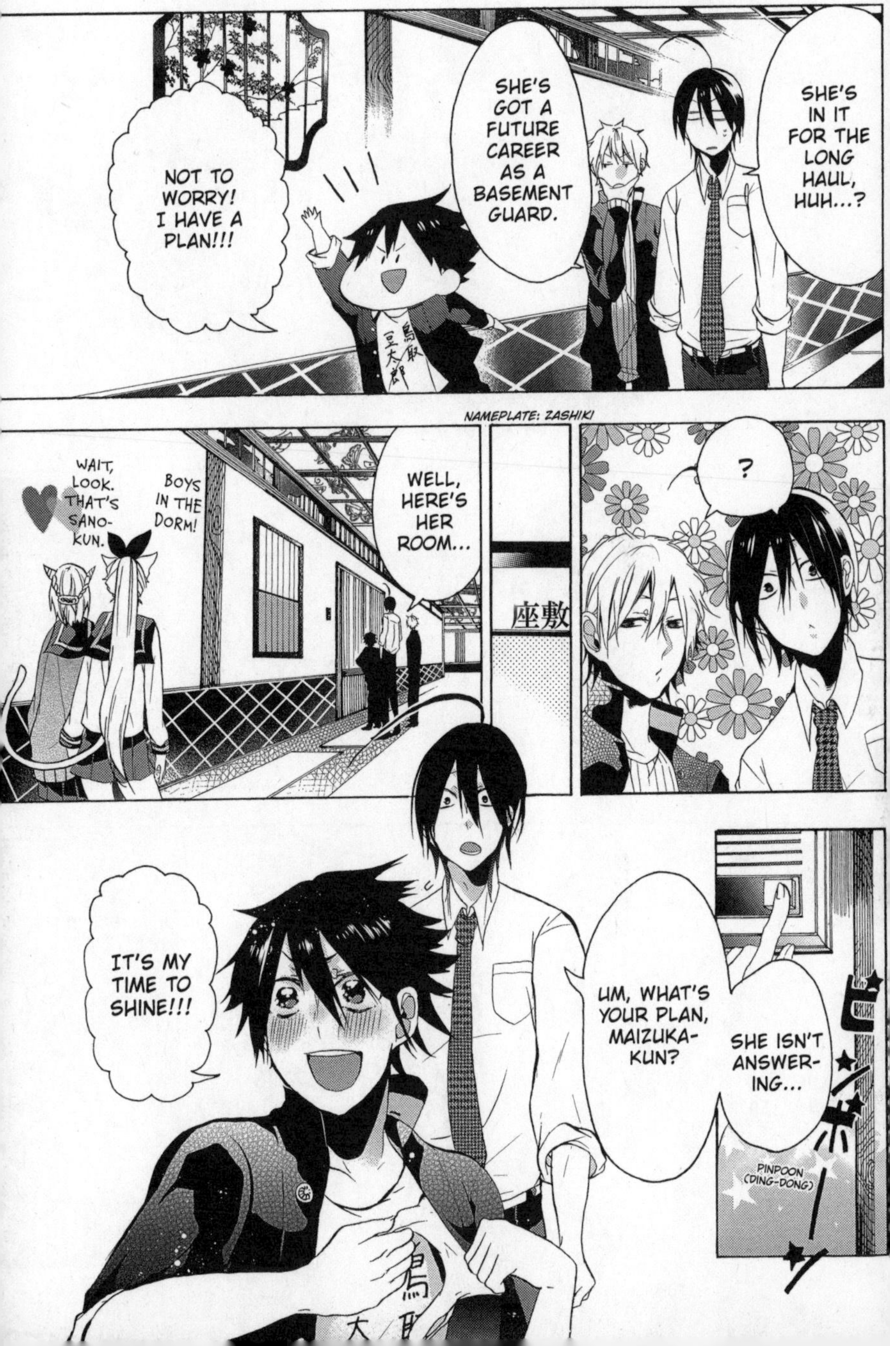
SHE'S IN IT FOR THE LONG HAUL, HUH...?
SHE'S GOT A FUTURE CAREER AS A BASEMENT GUARD.
NOT TO WORRY! I HAVE A PLAN!!!
NAMEPLATE: ZASHIKI
?
座敷
WELL, HERE'S HER ROOM...
BOYS IN THE DORM!
WAIT, LOOK. THAT'S SANO-KUN.
SHE ISN'T ANSWERING...
PINPOON (DING-DONG)
UM, WHAT'S YOUR PLAN, MAIZUKA-KUN?
IT'S MY TIME TO SHINE!!!

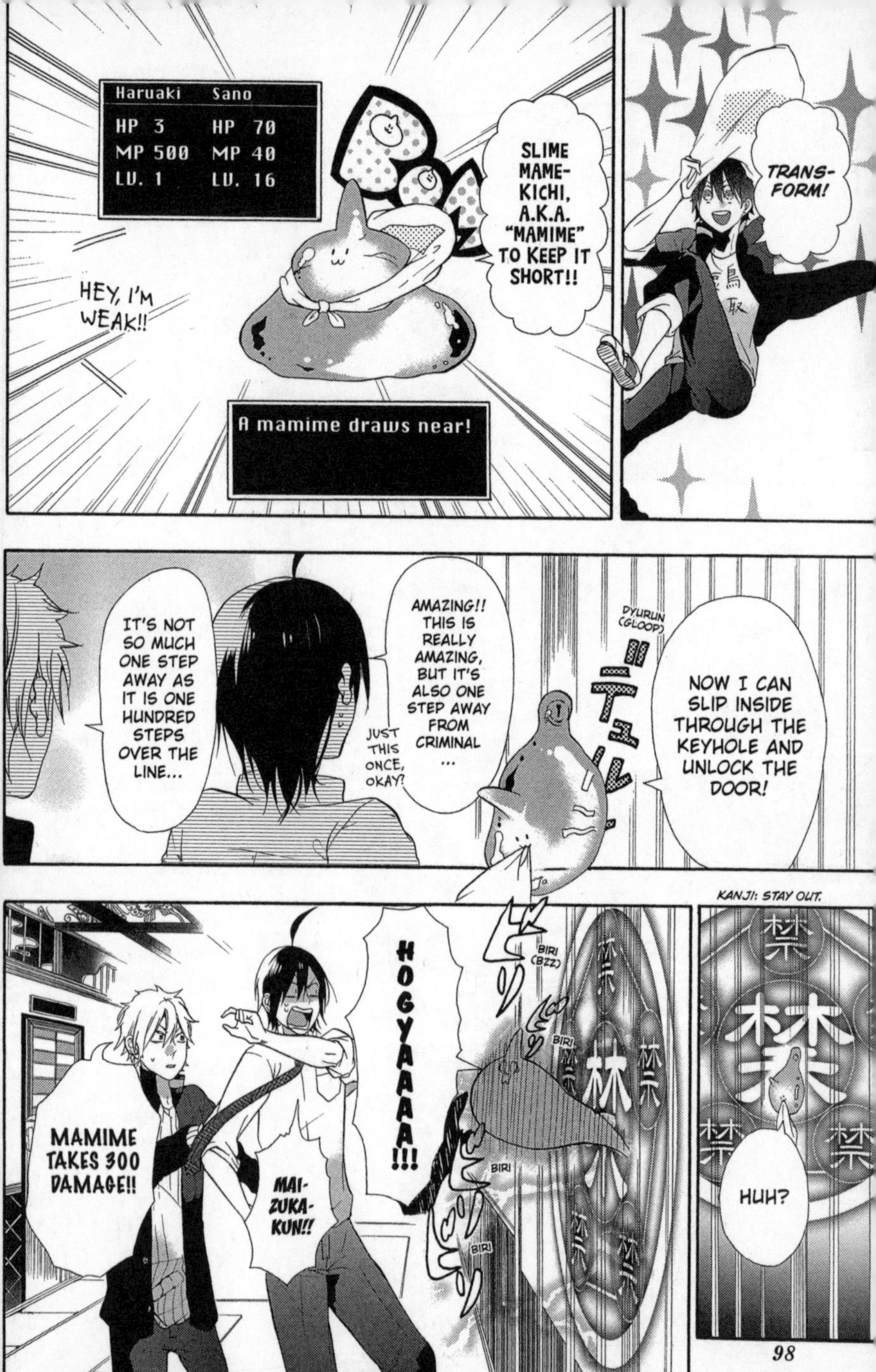
TRANS-FORM!
SLIME MAME-KICHI, A.K.A. "MAMIME" TO KEEP IT SHORT!!
Haruaki HP 3 MP 500 LV. 1
Sano HP 70 MP 40 LV. 16
HEY, I'M WEAK!!
A mamime draws near!
NOW I CAN SLIP INSIDE THROUGH THE KEYHOLE AND UNLOCK THE DOOR!
DYURUN (GLOOP)
AMAZING!! THIS IS REALLY AMAZING, BUT IT'S ALSO ONE STEP AWAY FROM CRIMINAL...
JUST THIS ONCE, OKAY?
IT'S NOT SO MUCH ONE STEP AWAY AS IT IS ONE HUNDRED STEPS OVER THE LINE...
KANJI: STAY OUT.
HUH?
BIRI (BZZ)
HOGYAAAA!!!
BIRI
BIRI
MAI-ZUKA-KUN!!
MAMIME TAKES 300 DAMAGE!!
BIRI

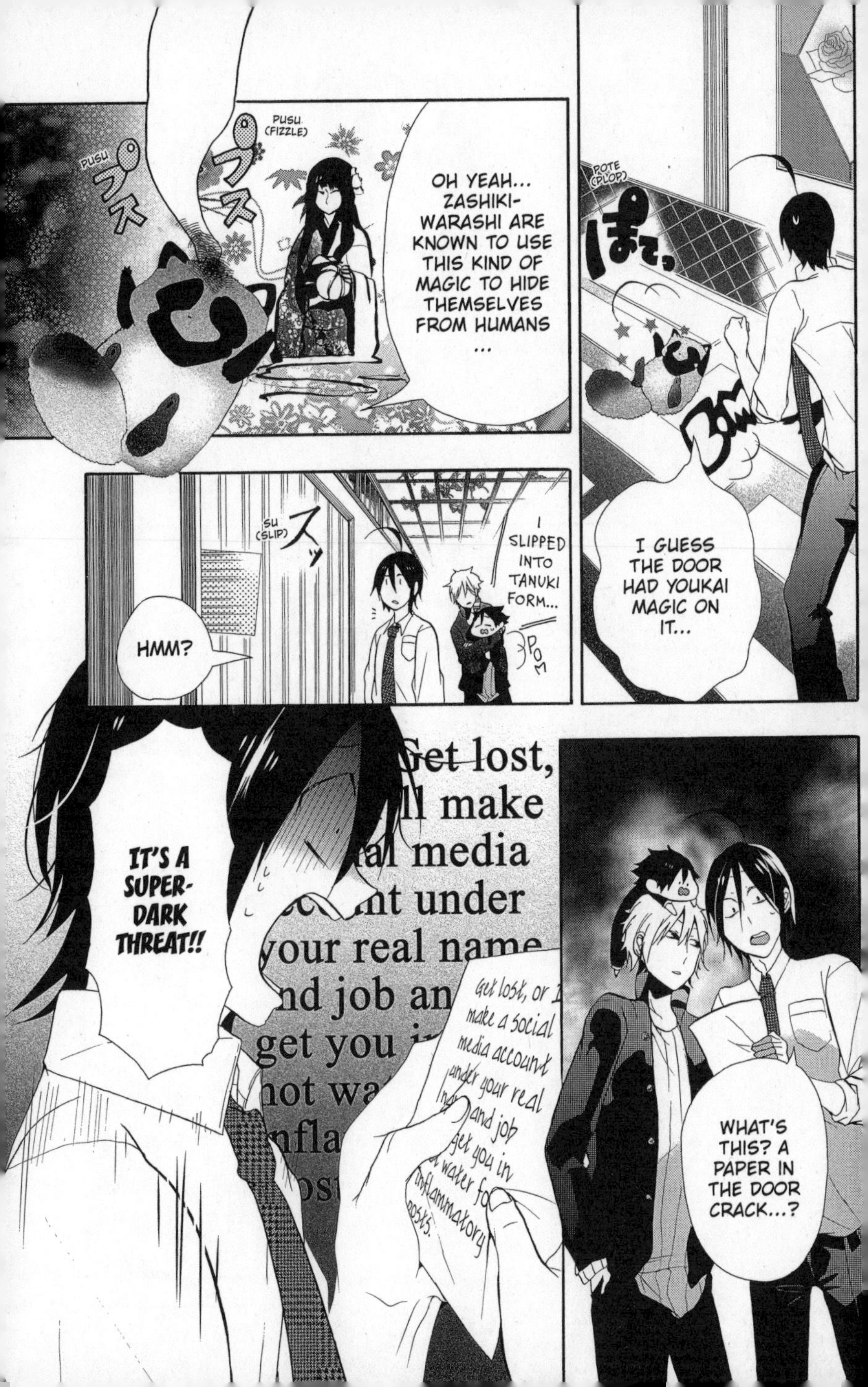
POTE (PLOP)
ぽてっ
I GUESS THE DOOR HAD YOUKAI MAGIC ON IT...
PUSU (FIZZLE)
プス
PUSU
プス
OH YEAH... ZASHIKI-WARASHI ARE KNOWN TO USE THIS KIND OF MAGIC TO HIDE THEMSELVES FROM HUMANS ...
SU (SLIP)
スッ
I SLIPPED INTO TANUKI FORM...
POM
HMM?
WHAT'S THIS? A PAPER IN THE DOOR CRACK...?
Get lost, or I
make a social
media account
under your real
and job
get you in
water fo
inflammatory
posts.
Get lost,
ll make
media
nt under
your real name
nd job an
get you i
IT'S A SUPER-DARK THREAT!!

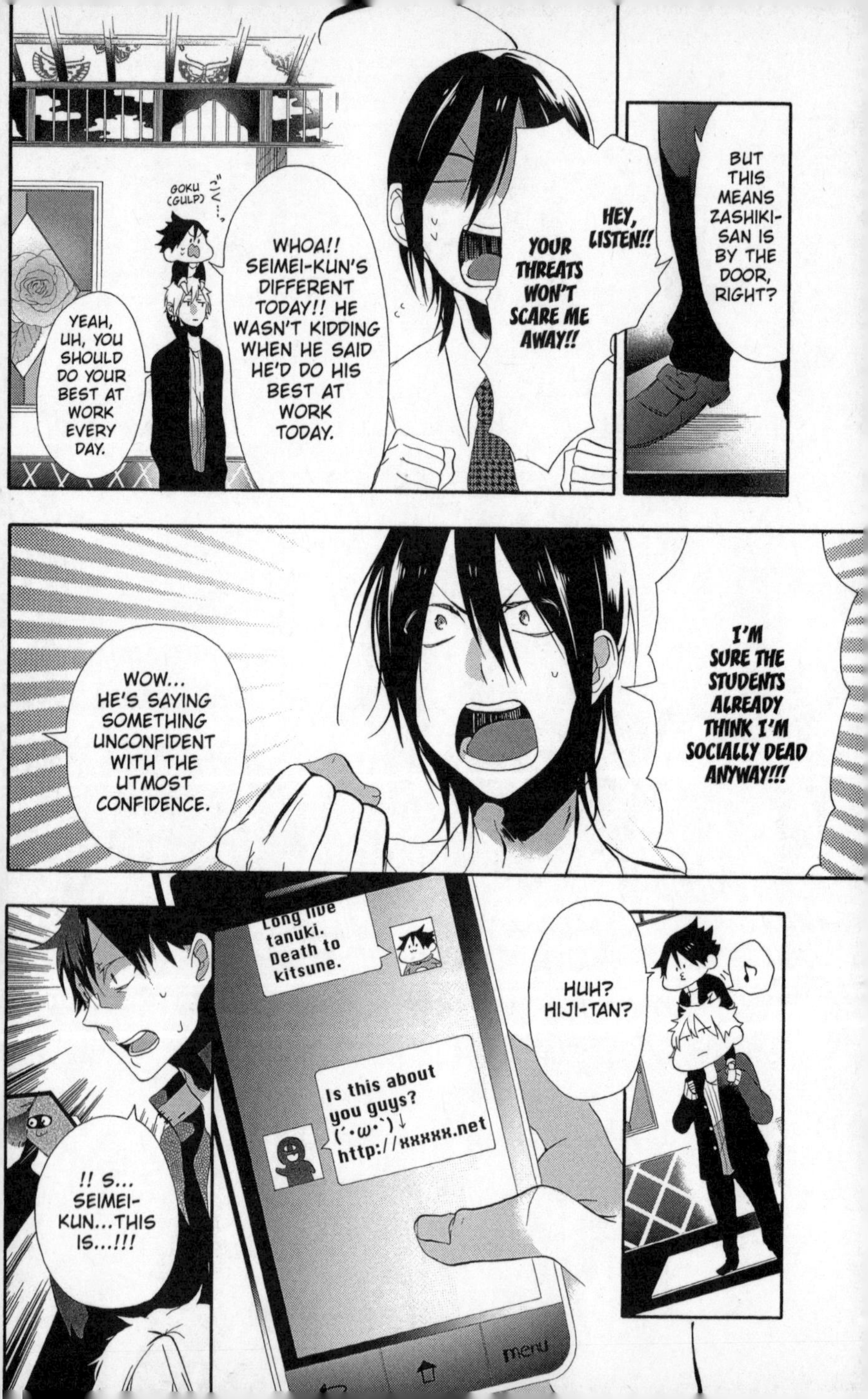
BUT THIS MEANS ZASHIKI-SAN IS BY THE DOOR, RIGHT?
HEY, LISTEN!!
YOUR THREATS WON'T SCARE ME AWAY!!
GOKU (GULP)
WHOA!! SEIMEI-KUN'S DIFFERENT TODAY!! HE WASN'T KIDDING WHEN HE SAID HE'D DO HIS BEST AT WORK TODAY.
YEAH, UH, YOU SHOULD DO YOUR BEST AT WORK EVERY DAY.
I'M SURE THE STUDENTS ALREADY THINK I'M SOCIALLY DEAD ANYWAY!!!
WOW... HE'S SAYING SOMETHING UNCONFIDENT WITH THE UTMOST CONFIDENCE.
HUH? HIJI-TAN?
Long live tanuki. Death to kitsune.
Is this about you guys? (´･ω･`)↓ http://xxxxx.net
menu
!! S... SEIMEI-KUN...THIS IS...!!!

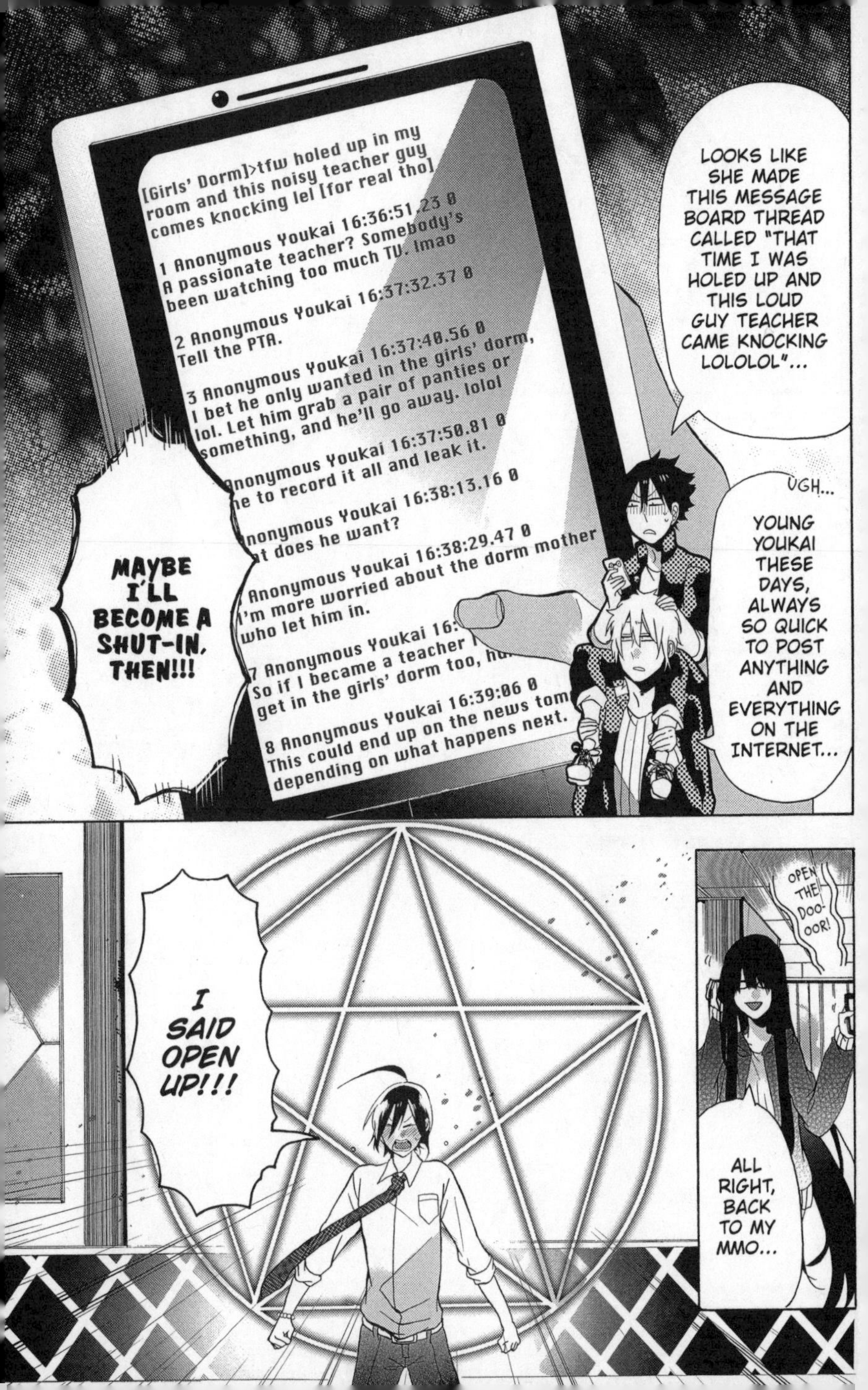
LOOKS LIKE SHE MADE THIS MESSAGE BOARD THREAD CALLED "THAT TIME I WAS HOLED UP AND THIS LOUD GUY TEACHER CAME KNOCKING LOLOLOL"...
UGH...
YOUNG YOUKAI THESE DAYS, ALWAYS SO QUICK TO POST ANYTHING AND EVERYTHING ON THE INTERNET...
[Girls' Dorm]>tfw holed up in my room and this noisy teacher guy comes knocking lel [for real tho]
comes knocking lel [for real tho] 16:36:51.23 0
1 Anonymous Youkai
A passionate teacher? Somebody's been watching too much TV. lmao
2 Anonymous Youkai 16:37:32.37 0
Tell the PTA.
3 Anonymous Youkai 16:37:40.56 0
I bet he only wanted in the girls' dorm, lol. Let him grab a pair of panties or something, and he'll go away. lolol
Anonymous Youkai 16:37:50.81 0
e to record it all and leak it.
nonymous Youkai 16:38:13.16 0
t does he want?
Anonymous Youkai 16:38:29.47 0
I'm more worried about the dorm mother who let him in.
7 Anonymous Youkai 16:
So if I became a teacher
get in the girls' dorm too,
8 Anonymous Youkai 16:39:06 0
This could end up on the news tom
depending on what happens next.
MAYBE I'LL BECOME A SHUT-IN, THEN!!!
OPEN THE DOOOOOR!
ALL RIGHT, BACK TO MY MMO...
I SAID OPEN UP!!!

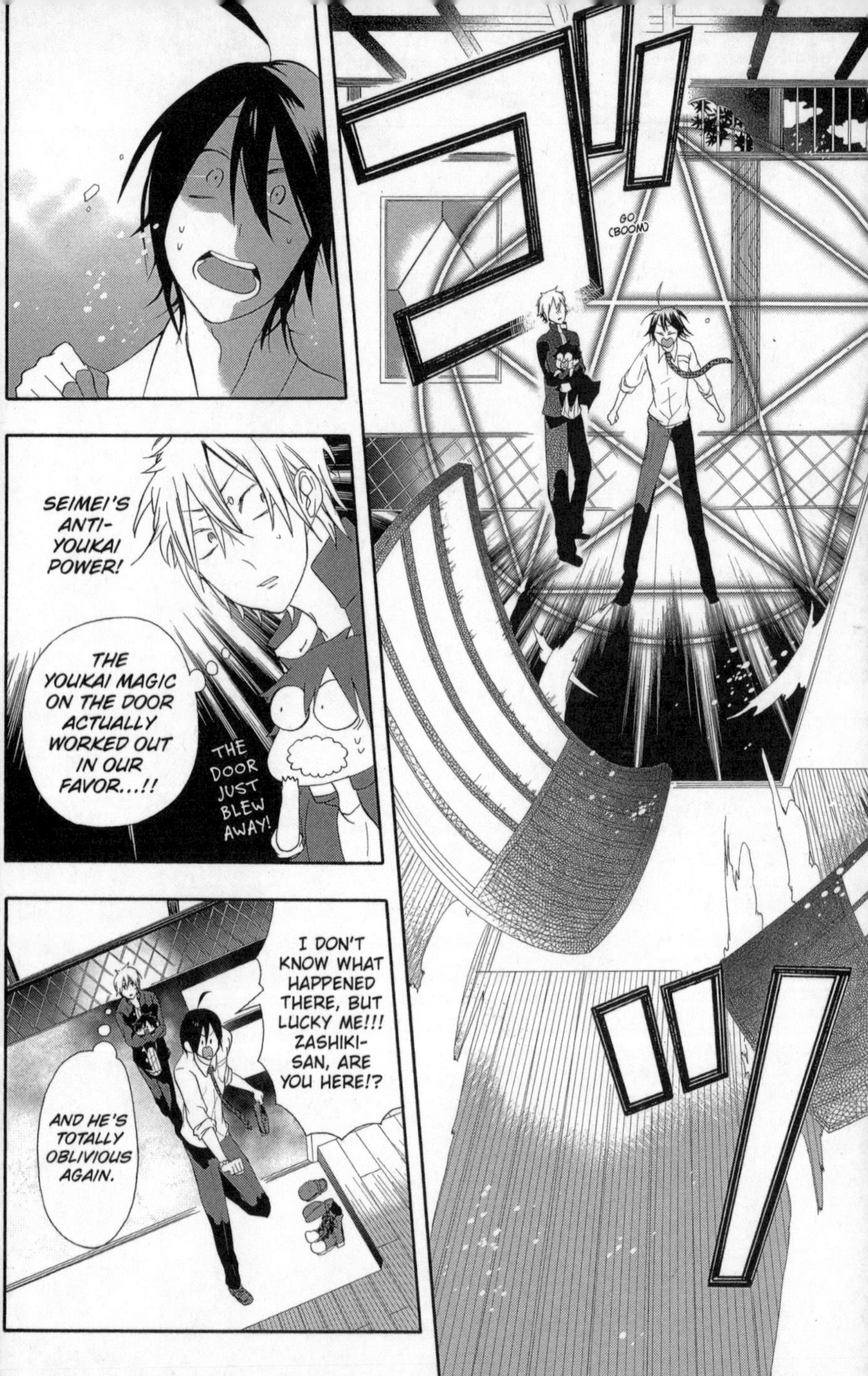
GO (BOOM)
SEIMEI'S ANTI-YOUKAI POWER!
THE YOUKAI MAGIC ON THE DOOR ACTUALLY WORKED OUT IN OUR FAVOR...!!
THE DOOR JUST BLEW AWAY!
I DON'T KNOW WHAT HAPPENED THERE, BUT LUCKY ME!!! ZASHIKI-SAN, ARE YOU HERE!?
AND HE'S TOTALLY OBLIVIOUS AGAIN.

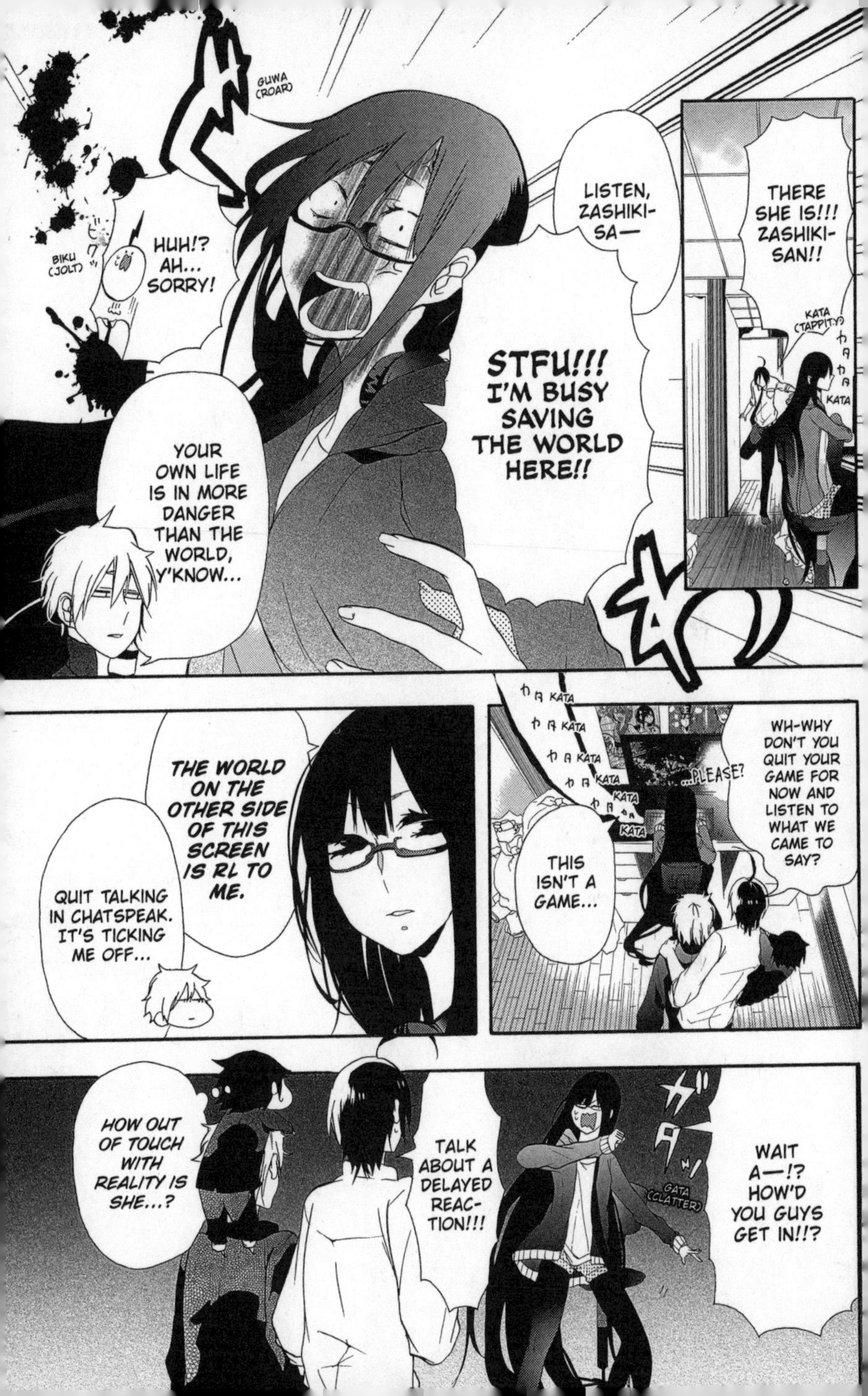
THERE SHE IS!!! ZASHIKI-SAN!!
KATA (TAPPITY)
KATA
LISTEN, ZASHIKI-SA—
STFU!!! I'M BUSY SAVING THE WORLD HERE!!
GUWA (ROAR)
HUH!? AH... SORRY!
BIKU (JOLT)
YOUR OWN LIFE IS IN MORE DANGER THAN THE WORLD, Y'KNOW...
WH-WHY DON'T YOU QUIT YOUR GAME FOR NOW AND LISTEN TO WHAT WE CAME TO SAY?
...PLEASE?
KATA
KATA
KATA
KATA
KATA
KATA
THIS ISN'T A GAME...
THE WORLD ON THE OTHER SIDE OF THIS SCREEN IS RL TO ME.
QUIT TALKING IN CHATSPEAK. IT'S TICKING ME OFF...
WAIT A—!? HOW'D YOU GUYS GET IN!!?
GATA (CLATTER)
TALK ABOUT A DELAYED REACTION!!!
HOW OUT OF TOUCH WITH REALITY IS SHE...?

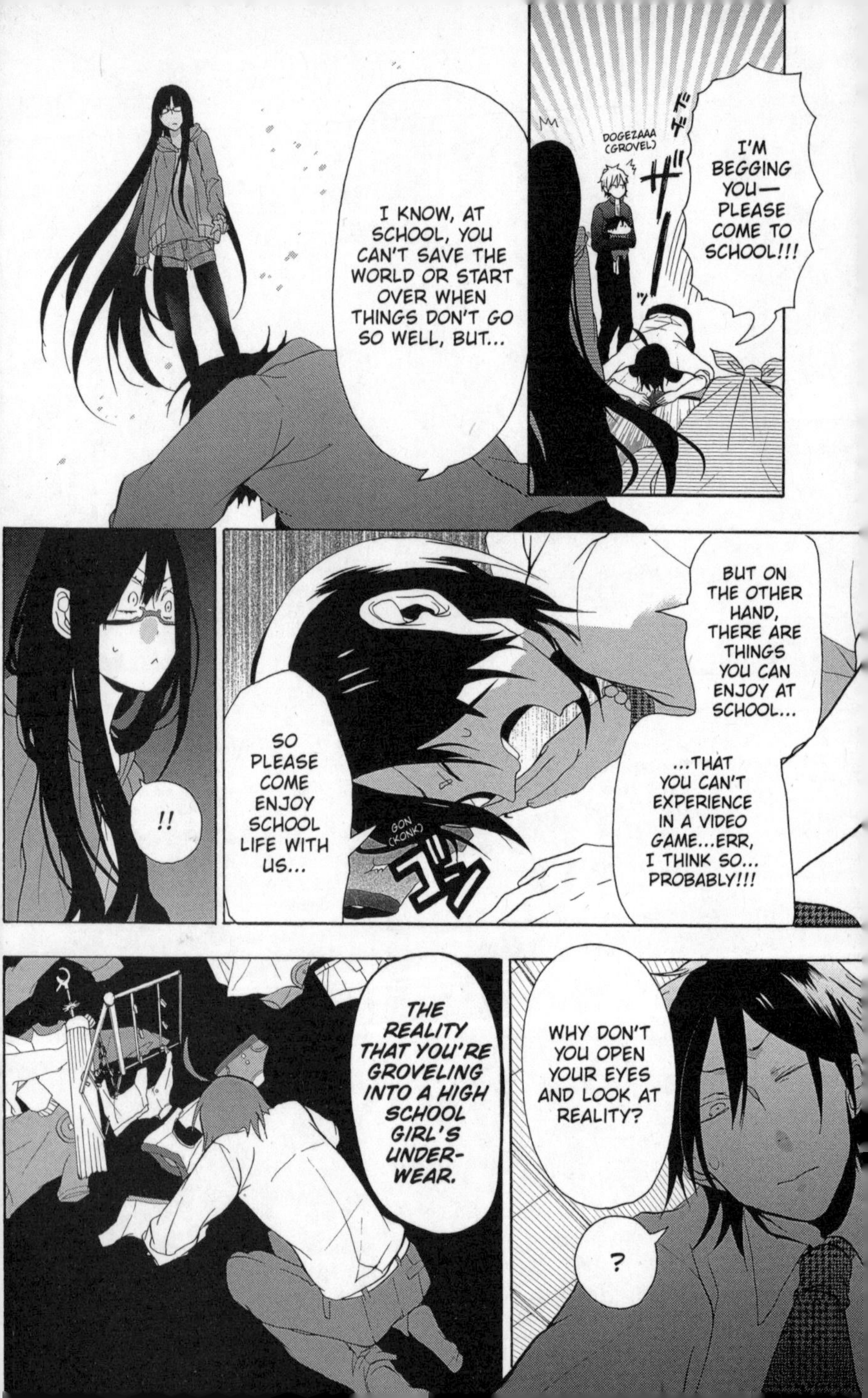
DOGEZAAA (GROVEL)
I'M BEGGING YOU—PLEASE COME TO SCHOOL!!!
I KNOW, AT SCHOOL, YOU CAN'T SAVE THE WORLD OR START OVER WHEN THINGS DON'T GO SO WELL, BUT...
BUT ON THE OTHER HAND, THERE ARE THINGS YOU CAN ENJOY AT SCHOOL...
...THAT YOU CAN'T EXPERIENCE IN A VIDEO GAME...ERR, I THINK SO... PROBABLY!!!
GON (KONK)
SO PLEASE COME ENJOY SCHOOL LIFE WITH US...
!!
WHY DON'T YOU OPEN YOUR EYES AND LOOK AT REALITY?
?
THE REALITY THAT YOU'RE GROVELING INTO A HIGH SCHOOL GIRL'S UNDER-WEAR.

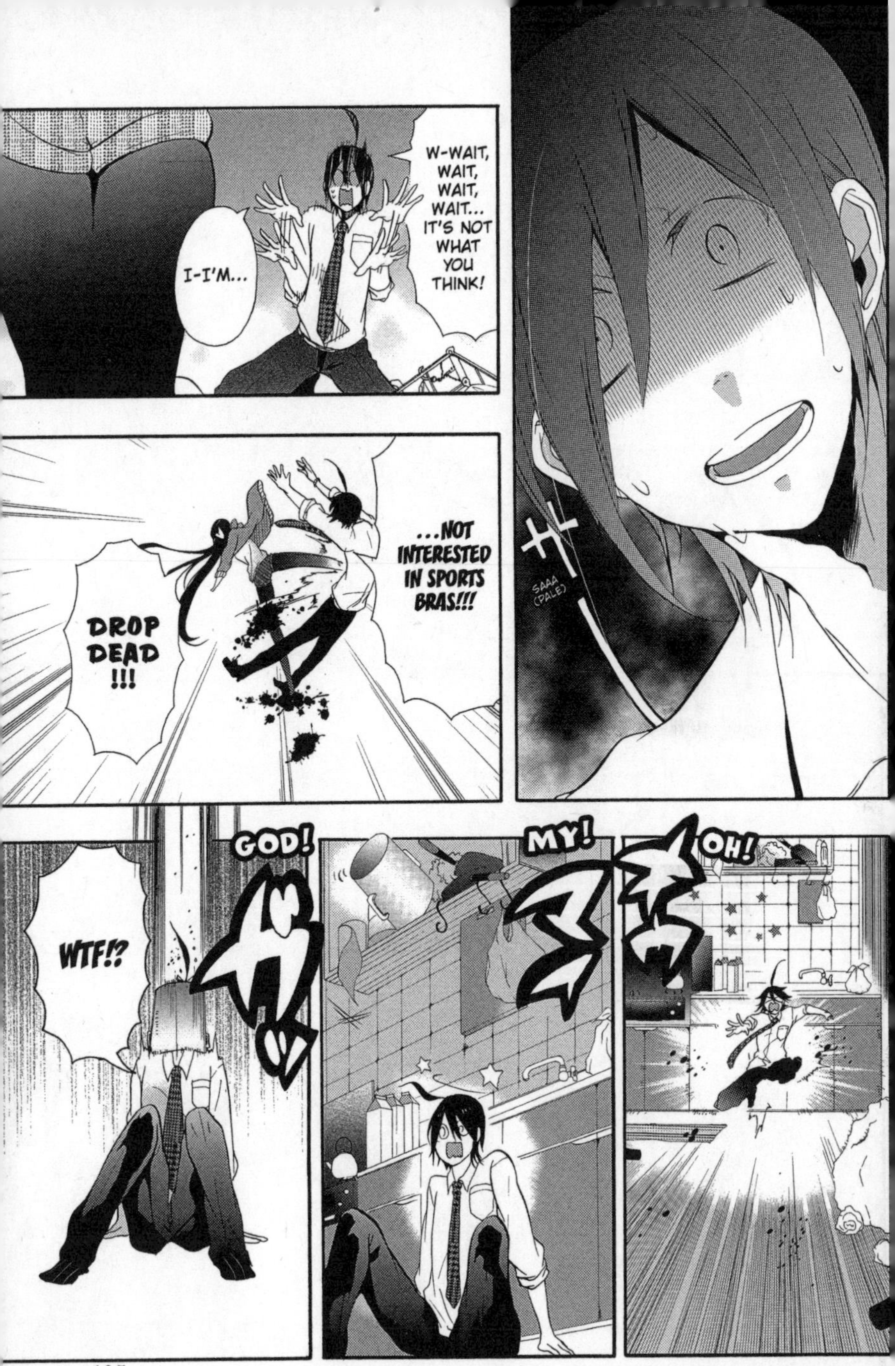
SAAA (PALE)
W-WAIT, WAIT, WAIT, WAIT... IT'S NOT WHAT YOU THINK!
I-I'M...
...NOT INTERESTED IN SPORTS BRAS!!!
DROP DEAD!!!
OH!
MY!
GOD!
WTF!?

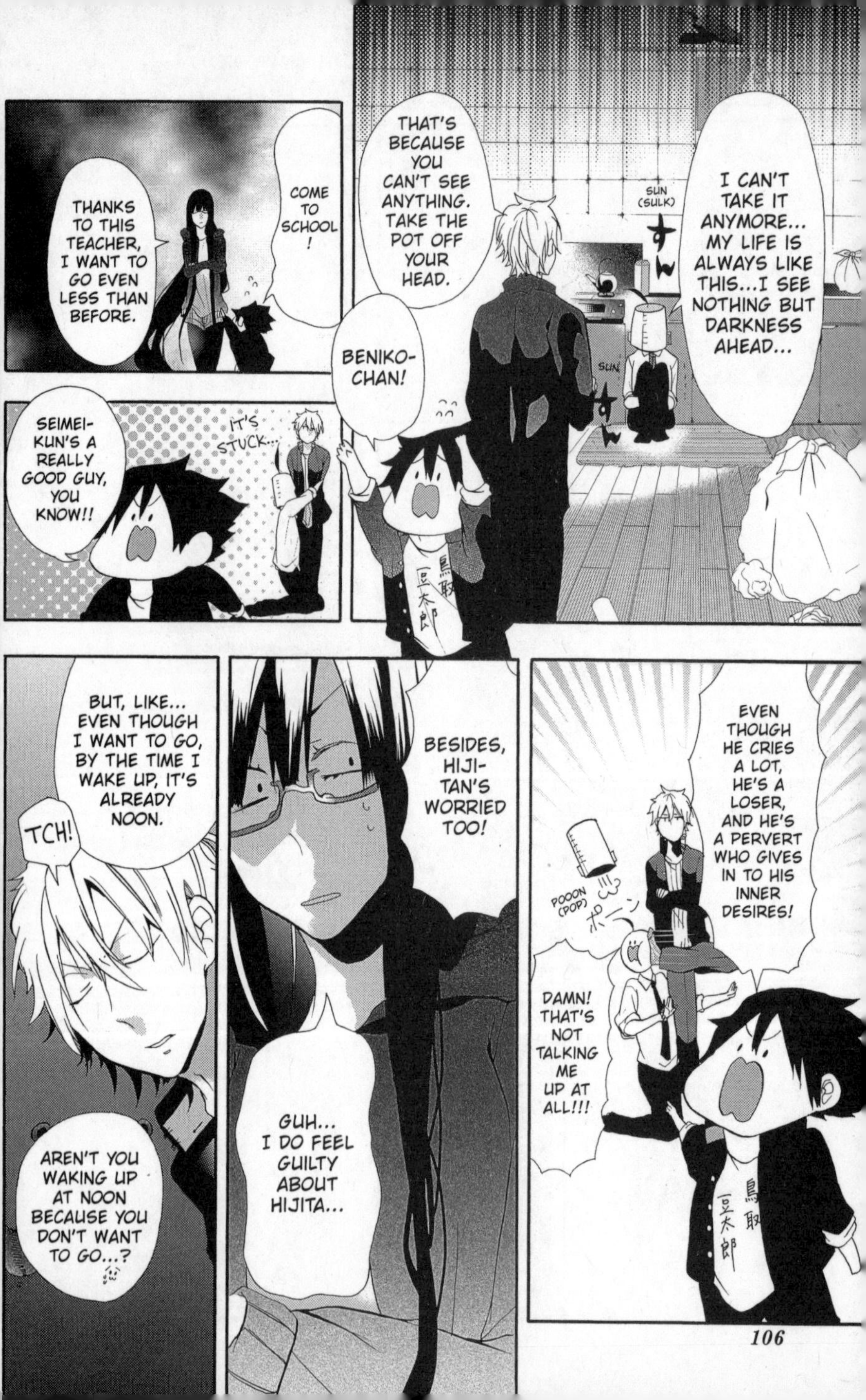

I CAN'T TAKE IT ANYMORE... MY LIFE IS ALWAYS LIKE THIS...I SEE NOTHING BUT DARKNESS AHEAD...
SUN (SULK)
THAT'S BECAUSE YOU CAN'T SEE ANYTHING. TAKE THE POT OFF YOUR HEAD.
SUN
BENIKO-CHAN!
COME TO SCHOOL!
THANKS TO THIS TEACHER, I WANT TO GO EVEN LESS THAN BEFORE.
IT'S STUCK...
SEIMEI-KUN'S A REALLY GOOD GUY, YOU KNOW!!
EVEN THOUGH HE CRIES A LOT, HE'S A LOSER, AND HE'S A PERVERT WHO GIVES IN TO HIS INNER DESIRES!
POOON (POP)
DAMN! THAT'S NOT TALKING ME UP AT ALL!!!
BESIDES, HIJI-TAN'S WORRIED TOO!
GUH... I DO FEEL GUILTY ABOUT HIJITA...
BUT, LIKE... EVEN THOUGH I WANT TO GO, BY THE TIME I WAKE UP, IT'S ALREADY NOON.
TCH!
AREN'T YOU WAKING UP AT NOON BECAUSE YOU DON'T WANT TO GO...?

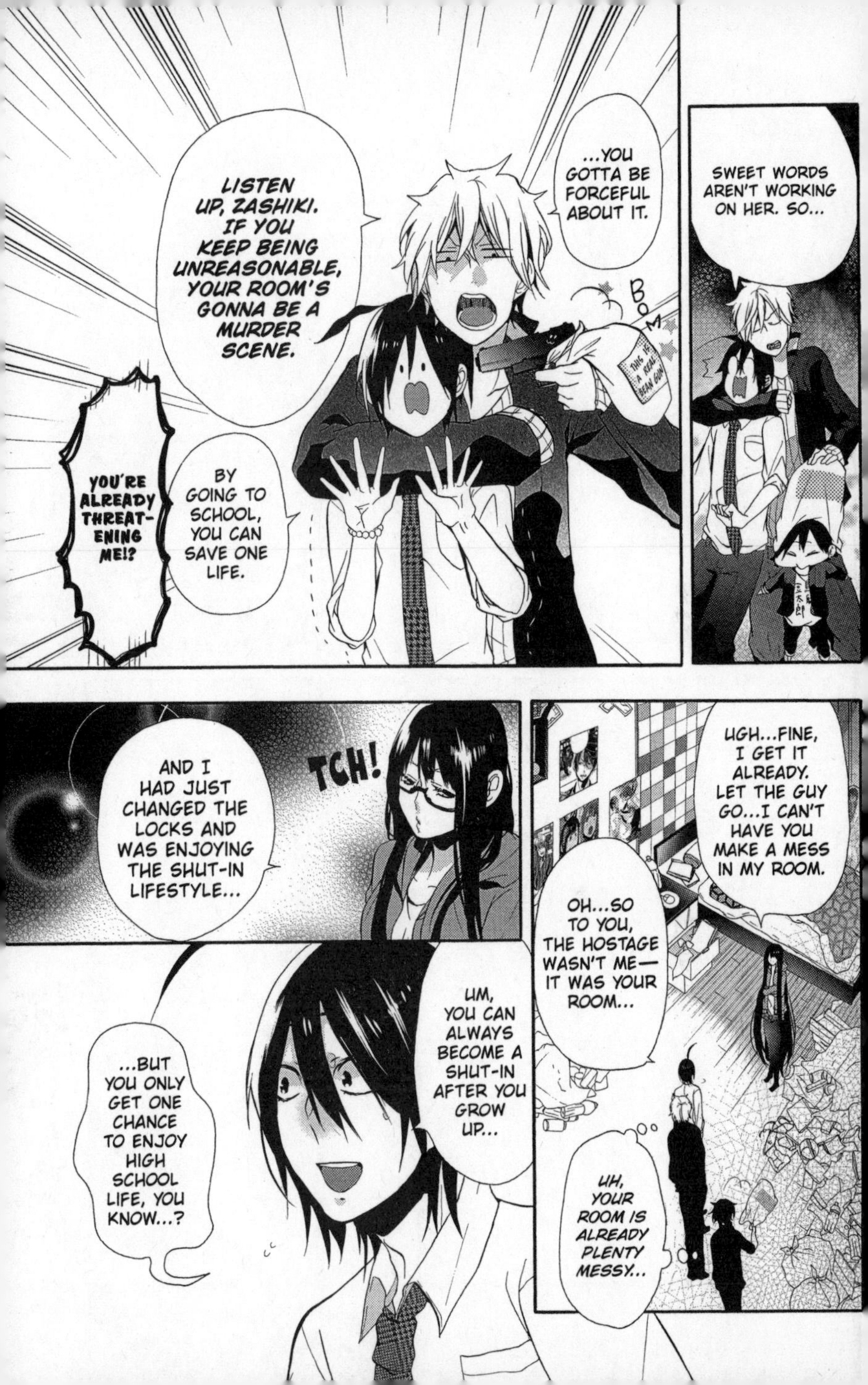
SWEET WORDS AREN'T WORKING ON HER. SO...
...YOU GOTTA BE FORCEFUL ABOUT IT.
BOM
LISTEN UP, ZASHIKI. IF YOU KEEP BEING UNREASONABLE, YOUR ROOM'S GONNA BE A MURDER SCENE.
THIS IS A REAL BEAN GUN
BY GOING TO SCHOOL, YOU CAN SAVE ONE LIFE.
YOU'RE ALREADY THREAT-ENING ME!?
UGH...FINE, I GET IT ALREADY. LET THE GUY GO...I CAN'T HAVE YOU MAKE A MESS IN MY ROOM.
OH...SO TO YOU, THE HOSTAGE WASN'T ME—IT WAS YOUR ROOM...
UH, YOUR ROOM IS ALREADY PLENTY MESSY...
TCH!
AND I HAD JUST CHANGED THE LOCKS AND WAS ENJOYING THE SHUT-IN LIFESTYLE...
UM, YOU CAN ALWAYS BECOME A SHUT-IN AFTER YOU GROW UP...
...BUT YOU ONLY GET ONE CHANCE TO ENJOY HIGH SCHOOL LIFE, YOU KNOW...?

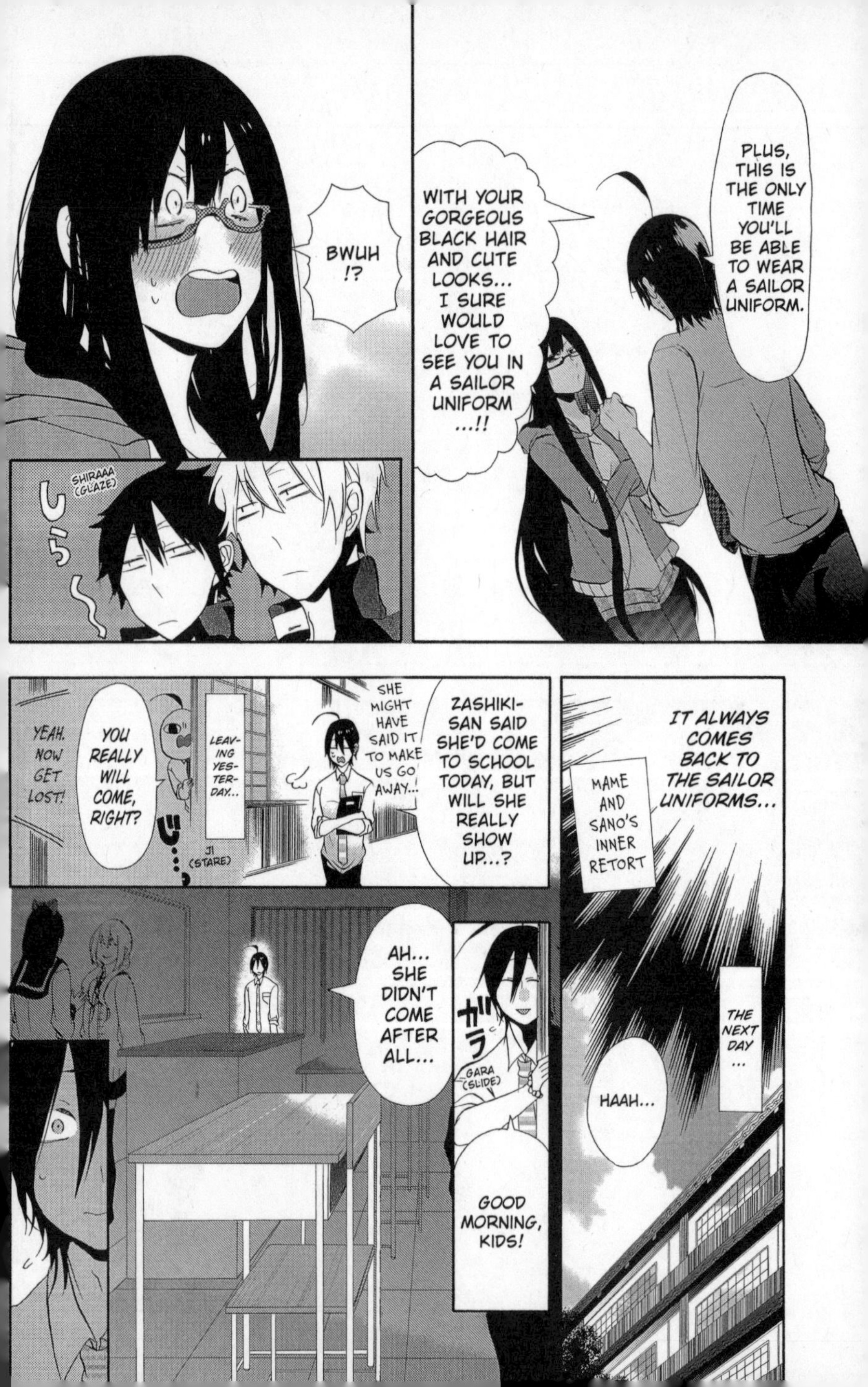
PLUS, THIS IS THE ONLY TIME YOU'LL BE ABLE TO WEAR A SAILOR UNIFORM.
WITH YOUR GORGEOUS BLACK HAIR AND CUTE LOOKS... I SURE WOULD LOVE TO SEE YOU IN A SAILOR UNIFORM ...!!
BWUH !?
しら〜
SHIRAAA (GLAZE)
IT ALWAYS COMES BACK TO THE SAILOR UNIFORMS...
MAME AND SANO'S INNER RETORT
ZASHIKI-SAN SAID SHE'D COME TO SCHOOL TODAY, BUT WILL SHE REALLY SHOW UP...?
SHE MIGHT HAVE SAID IT TO MAKE US GO AWAY...!
LEAVING YESTERDAY...
YOU REALLY WILL COME, RIGHT?
YEAH. NOW GET LOST!
じ…
JI (STARE)
THE NEXT DAY...
HAAH...
ガラ
GARA (SLIDE)
GOOD MORNING, KIDS!
AH... SHE DIDN'T COME AFTER ALL...

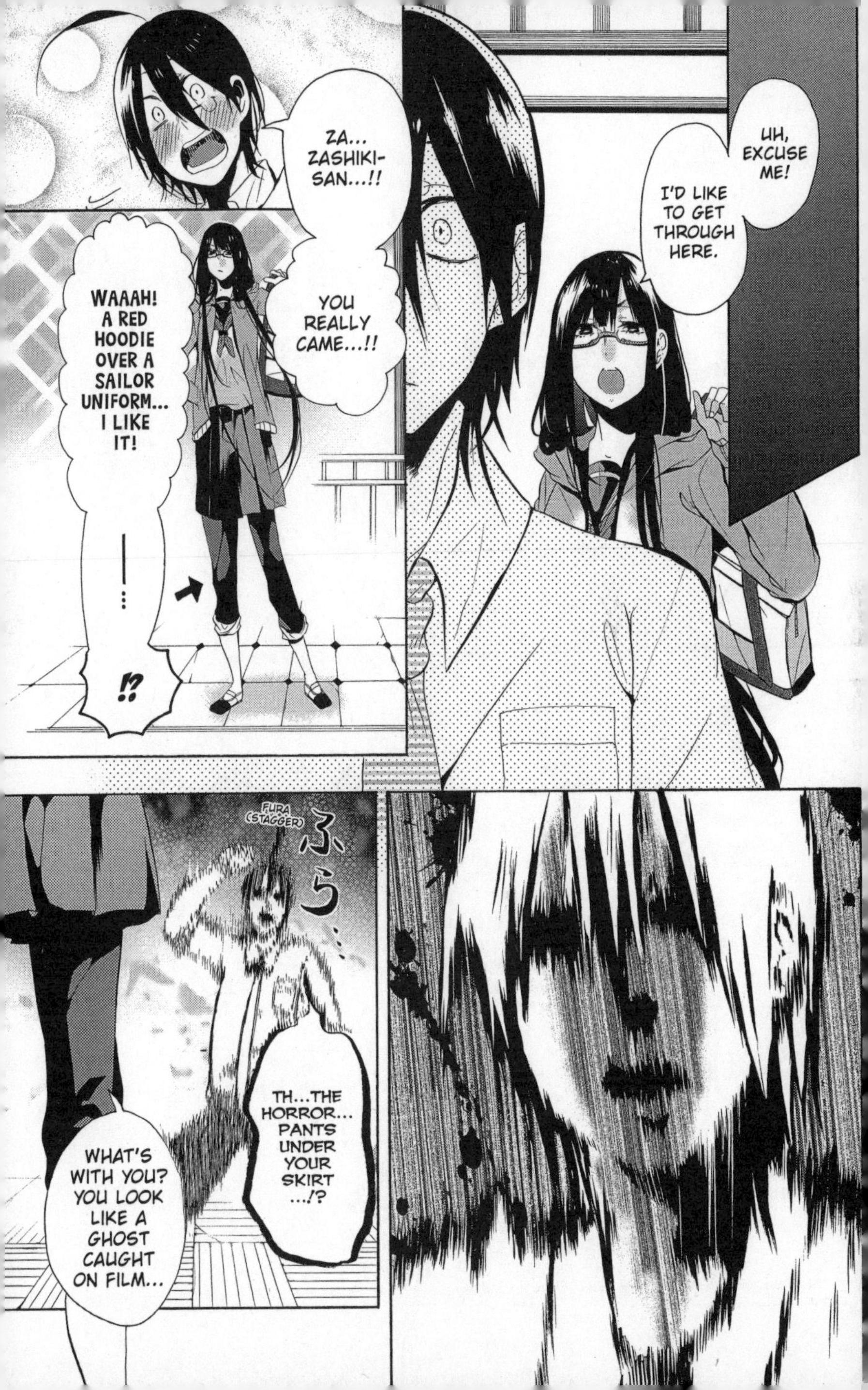
UH, EXCUSE ME!
I'D LIKE TO GET THROUGH HERE.
ZA... ZASHIKI-SAN...!!
YOU REALLY CAME...!!
WAAAH! A RED HOODIE OVER A SAILOR UNIFORM... I LIKE IT!
—...!?
ふら...
FURA (STAGGER)
TH...THE HORROR... PANTS UNDER YOUR SKIRT ...!?
WHAT'S WITH YOU? YOU LOOK LIKE A GHOST CAUGHT ON FILM...

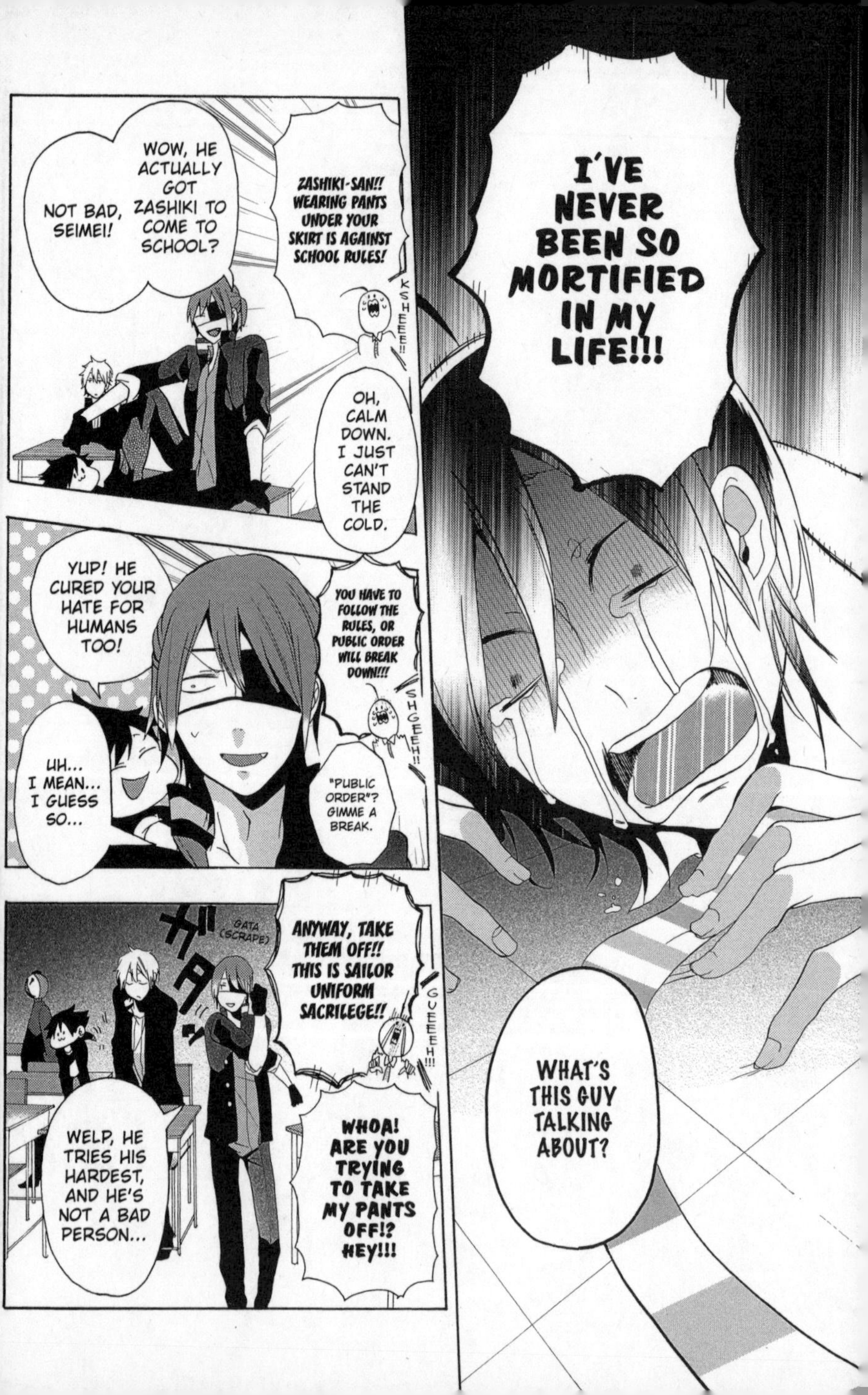
I'VE NEVER BEEN SO MORTIFIED IN MY LIFE!!!
WHAT'S THIS GUY TALKING ABOUT?
ZASHIKI-SAN!! WEARING PANTS UNDER YOUR SKIRT IS AGAINST SCHOOL RULES!
KSHEEEE!!
WOW, HE ACTUALLY GOT ZASHIKI TO COME TO SCHOOL?
NOT BAD, SEIMEI!
OH, CALM DOWN. I JUST CAN'T STAND THE COLD.
YOU HAVE TO FOLLOW THE RULES, OR PUBLIC ORDER WILL BREAK DOWN!!!
SHGEEEH!!
YUP! HE CURED YOUR HATE FOR HUMANS TOO!
"PUBLIC ORDER"? GIMME A BREAK.
UH... I MEAN... I GUESS SO...
ANYWAY, TAKE THEM OFF!! THIS IS SAILOR UNIFORM SACRILEGE!!
GUEEEEH!!!
GATA (SCRAPE)
WHOA! ARE YOU TRYING TO TAKE MY PANTS OFF!? HEY!!!
WELP, HE TRIES HIS HARDEST, AND HE'S NOT A BAD PERSON...

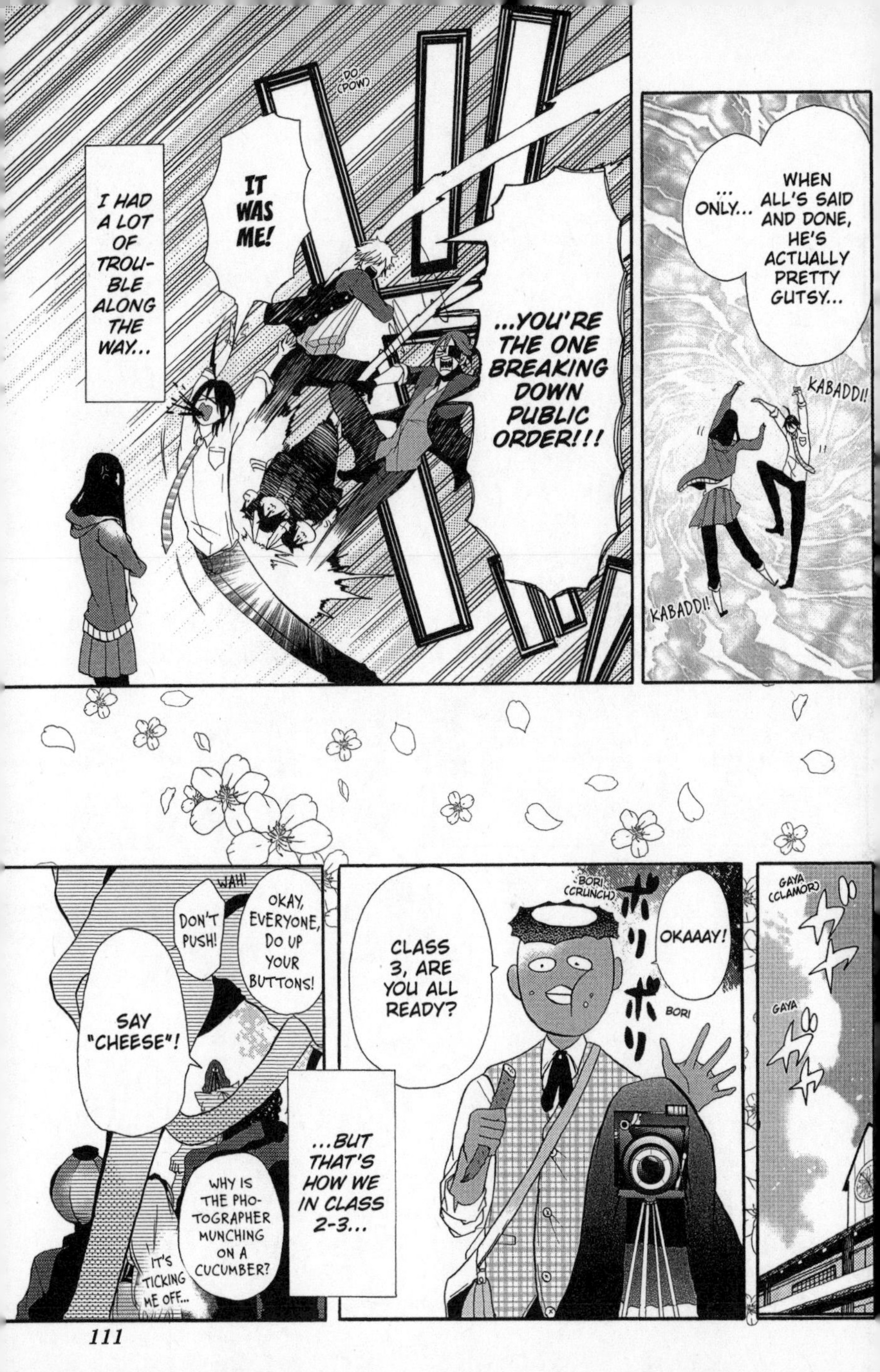
WHEN ALL'S SAID AND DONE, HE'S ACTUALLY PRETTY GUTSY...
...ONLY...
KABADDI!
KABADDI!
DO (POW)
IT WAS ME!
...YOU'RE THE ONE BREAKING DOWN PUBLIC ORDER!!!
I HAD A LOT OF TROUBLE ALONG THE WAY...
GAYA (CLAMOR)
GAYA
BORI (CRUNCH)
OKAAAY!
CLASS 3, ARE YOU ALL READY?
BORI
...BUT THAT'S HOW WE IN CLASS 2-3...
WAH!
OKAY, EVERYONE, DO UP YOUR BUTTONS!
DON'T PUSH!
SAY "CHEESE"!
WHY IS THE PHOTOGRAPHER MUNCHING ON A CUCUMBER?
IT'S TICKING ME OFF...

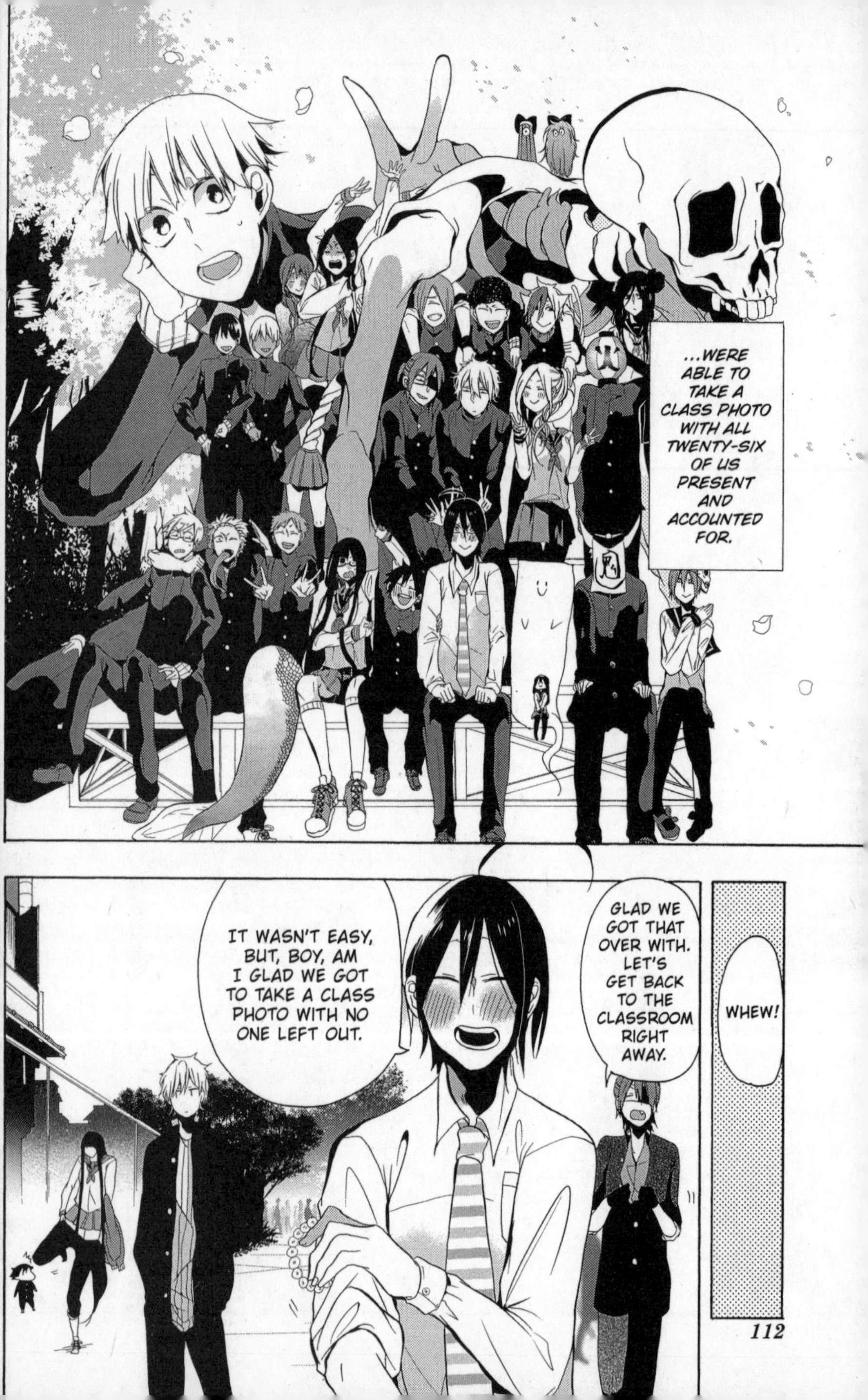
...WERE ABLE TO TAKE A CLASS PHOTO WITH ALL TWENTY-SIX OF US PRESENT AND ACCOUNTED FOR.
WHEW!
GLAD WE GOT THAT OVER WITH. LET'S GET BACK TO THE CLASSROOM RIGHT AWAY.
IT WASN'T EASY, BUT, BOY, AM I GLAD WE GOT TO TAKE A CLASS PHOTO WITH NO ONE LEFT OUT.

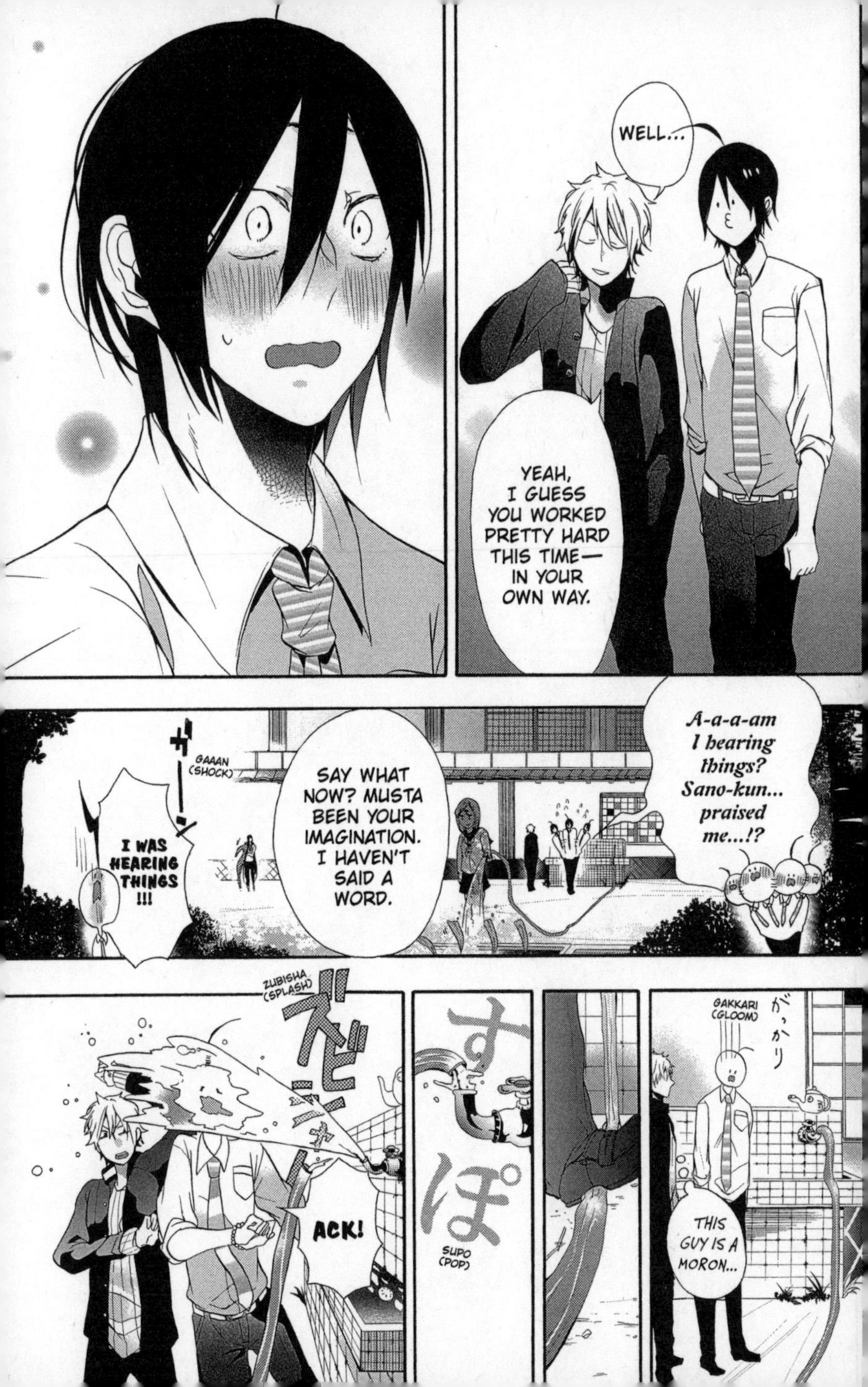
WELL...
YEAH, I GUESS YOU WORKED PRETTY HARD THIS TIME—IN YOUR OWN WAY.
A-a-a-am I hearing things? Sano-kun... praised me...!?
SAY WHAT NOW? MUSTA BEEN YOUR IMAGINATION. I HAVEN'T SAID A WORD.
GAAAN (SHOCK)
I WAS HEARING THINGS!!!
GAKKARI (GLOOM)
がっかり
THIS GUY IS A MORON...
すぽ
SUPO (POP)
ZUBISHA (SPLASH)
ACK!

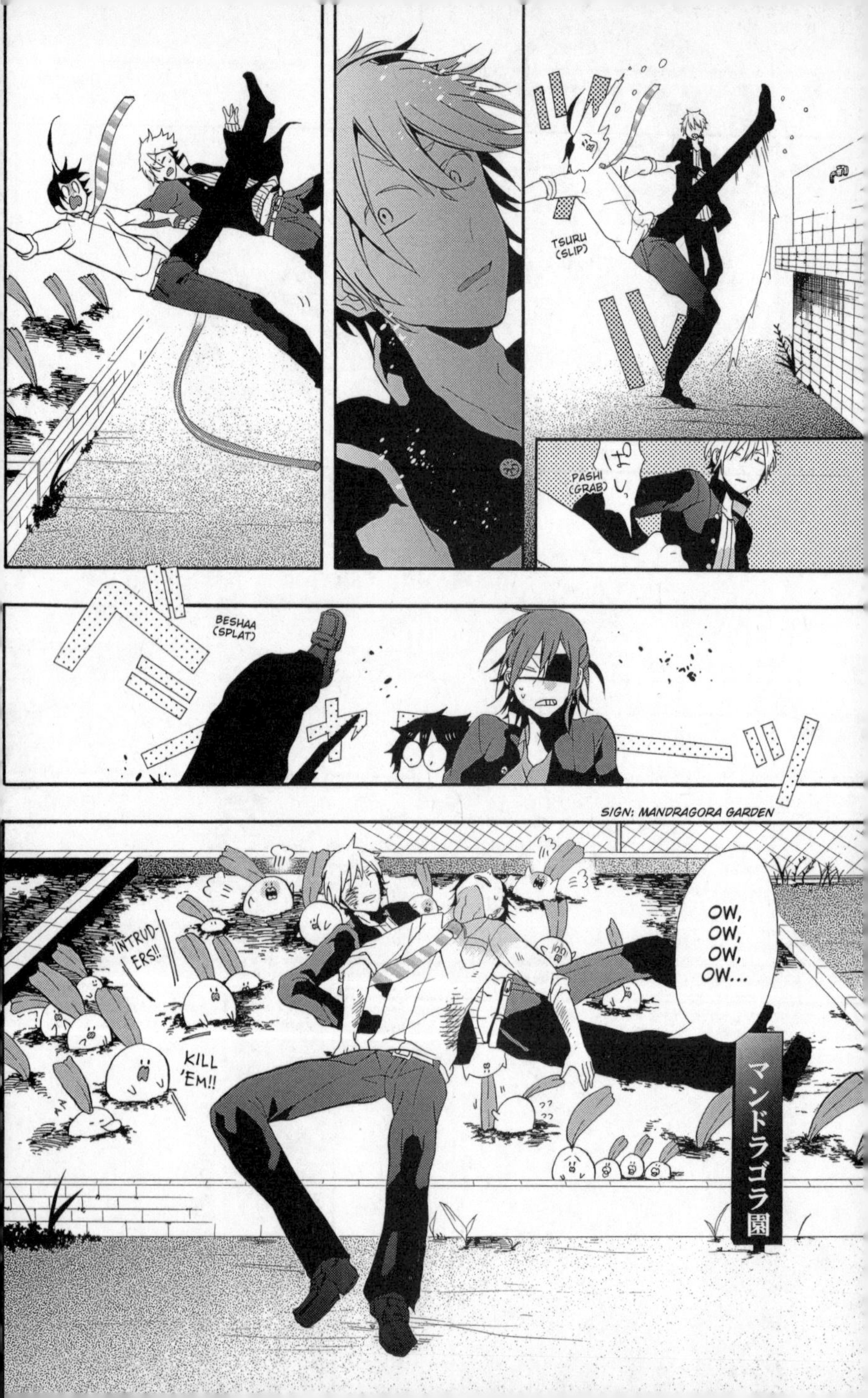
TSURU
(SLIP)
PASHI
(GRAB)
ぱしっ
BESHAA
(SPLAT)
SIGN: MANDRAGORA GARDEN
OW, OW, OW, OW...
INTRUDERS!!
KILL 'EM!!
マンドラゴラ園

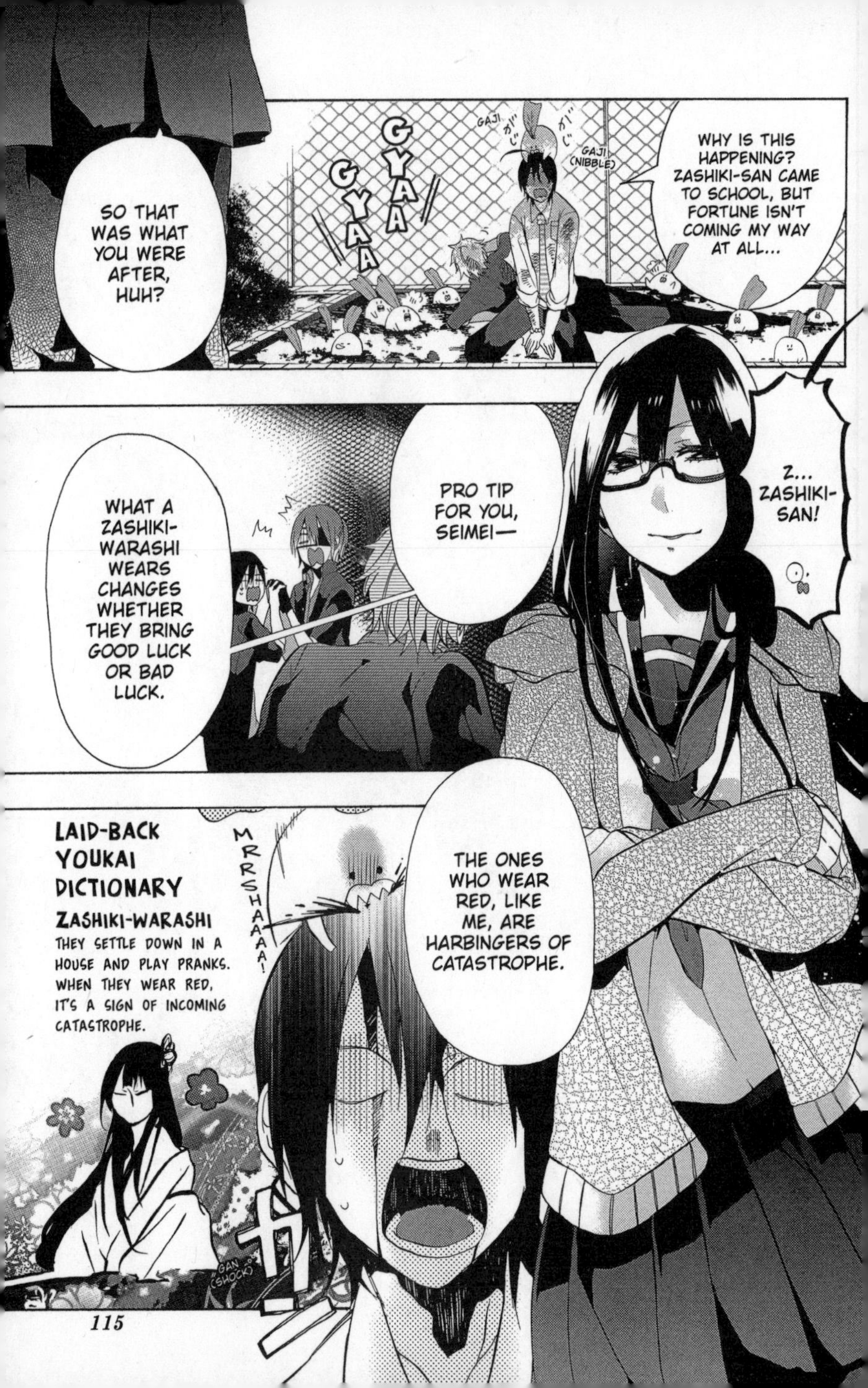
WHY IS THIS HAPPENING? ZASHIKI-SAN CAME TO SCHOOL, BUT FORTUNE ISN'T COMING MY WAY AT ALL...
GAJI
GAJI (NIBBLE)
GYAA
GYAA
SO THAT WAS WHAT YOU WERE AFTER, HUH?
Z... ZASHIKI-SAN!
PRO TIP FOR YOU, SEIMEI—
WHAT A ZASHIKI-WARASHI WEARS CHANGES WHETHER THEY BRING GOOD LUCK OR BAD LUCK.
THE ONES WHO WEAR RED, LIKE ME, ARE HARBINGERS OF CATASTROPHE.
MRRSHAAAAA!
GAN (SHOCK)
LAID-BACK YOUKAI DICTIONARY
ZASHIKI-WARASHI
THEY SETTLE DOWN IN A HOUSE AND PLAY PRANKS. WHEN THEY WEAR RED, IT'S A SIGN OF INCOMING CATASTROPHE.

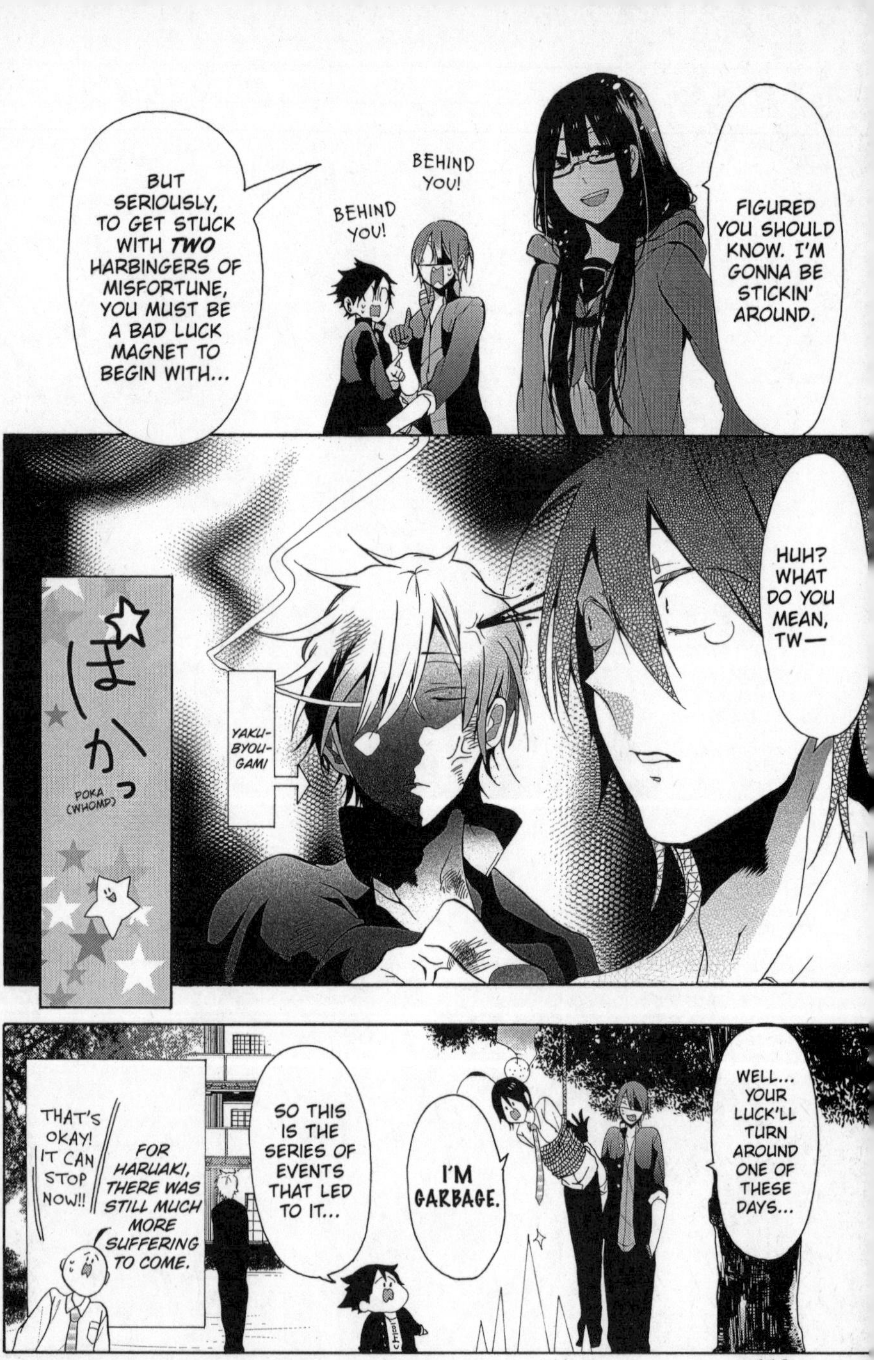

FIGURED YOU SHOULD KNOW. I'M GONNA BE STICKIN' AROUND.
BEHIND YOU!
BEHIND YOU!
BUT SERIOUSLY, TO GET STUCK WITH TWO HARBINGERS OF MISFORTUNE, YOU MUST BE A BAD LUCK MAGNET TO BEGIN WITH...
HUH? WHAT DO YOU MEAN, TW—
YAKU-BYOU-GAMI
ぽかっ
POKA (WHOMP)
WELL... YOUR LUCK'LL TURN AROUND ONE OF THESE DAYS...
I'M GARBAGE.
SO THIS IS THE SERIES OF EVENTS THAT LED TO IT...
FOR HARUAKI, THERE WAS STILL MUCH MORE SUFFERING TO COME.
THAT'S OKAY! IT CAN STOP NOW!!

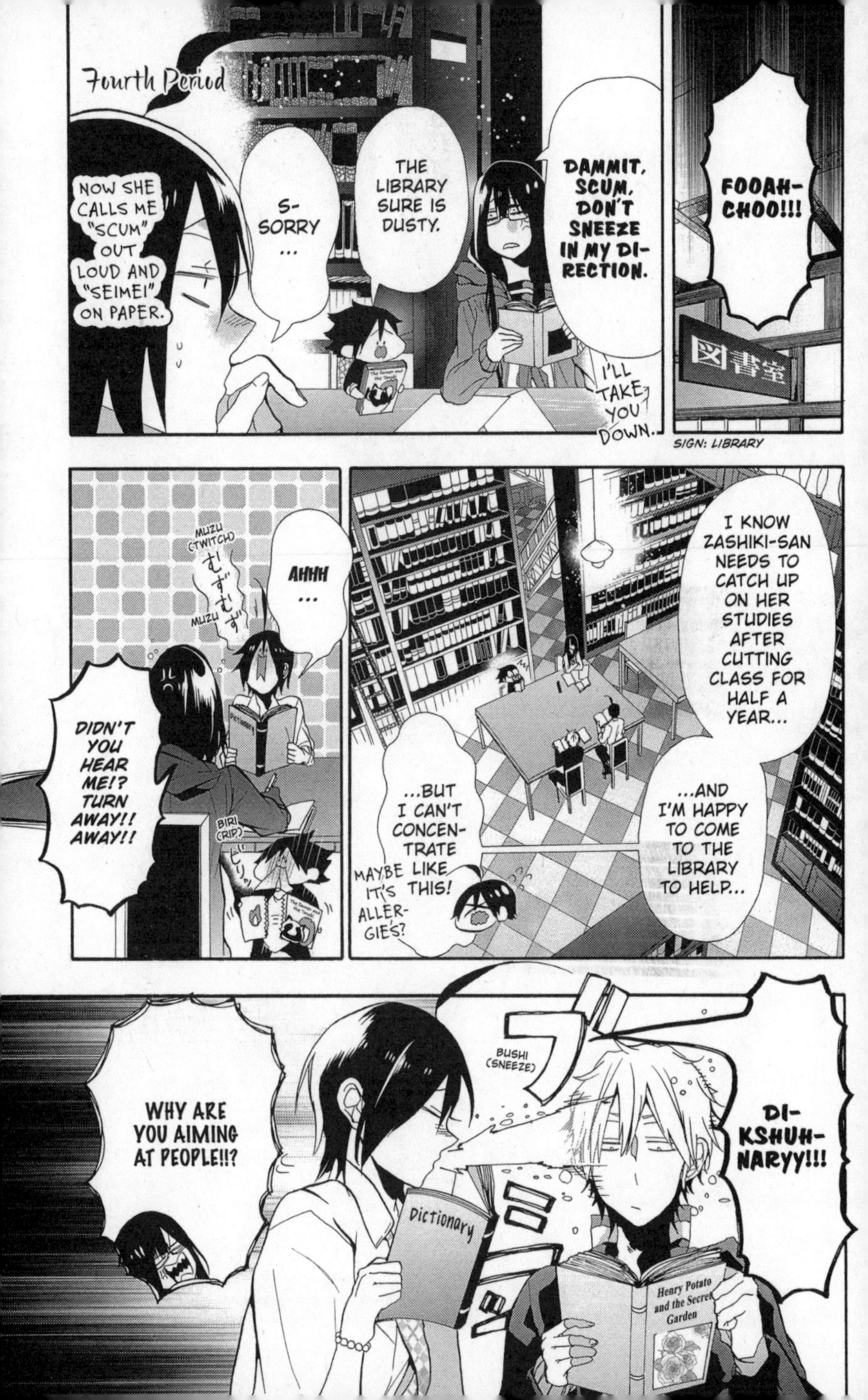
FOOAH-CHOO!!!
図書室
SIGN: LIBRARY
Fourth Period
DAMMIT, SCUM, DON'T SNEEZE IN MY DIRECTION.
I'LL TAKE YOU DOWN.
THE LIBRARY SURE IS DUSTY.
S-SORRY ...
NOW SHE CALLS ME "SCUM" OUT LOUD AND "SEIMEI" ON PAPER.
I KNOW ZASHIKI-SAN NEEDS TO CATCH UP ON HER STUDIES AFTER CUTTING CLASS FOR HALF A YEAR...
...AND I'M HAPPY TO COME TO THE LIBRARY TO HELP...
...BUT I CAN'T CONCENTRATE
MAYBE IT'S LIKE THIS! ALLERGIES?
AHHH ...
MUZU (TWITCH) むずむず MUZU
DIDN'T YOU HEAR ME!? TURN AWAY!! AWAY!!
BIRI (RIP)
DI-KSHUH-NARYY!!!
BUSHI (SNEEZE)
WHY ARE YOU AIMING AT PEOPLE!!?
Dictionary
Henry Potato and the Secret Garden

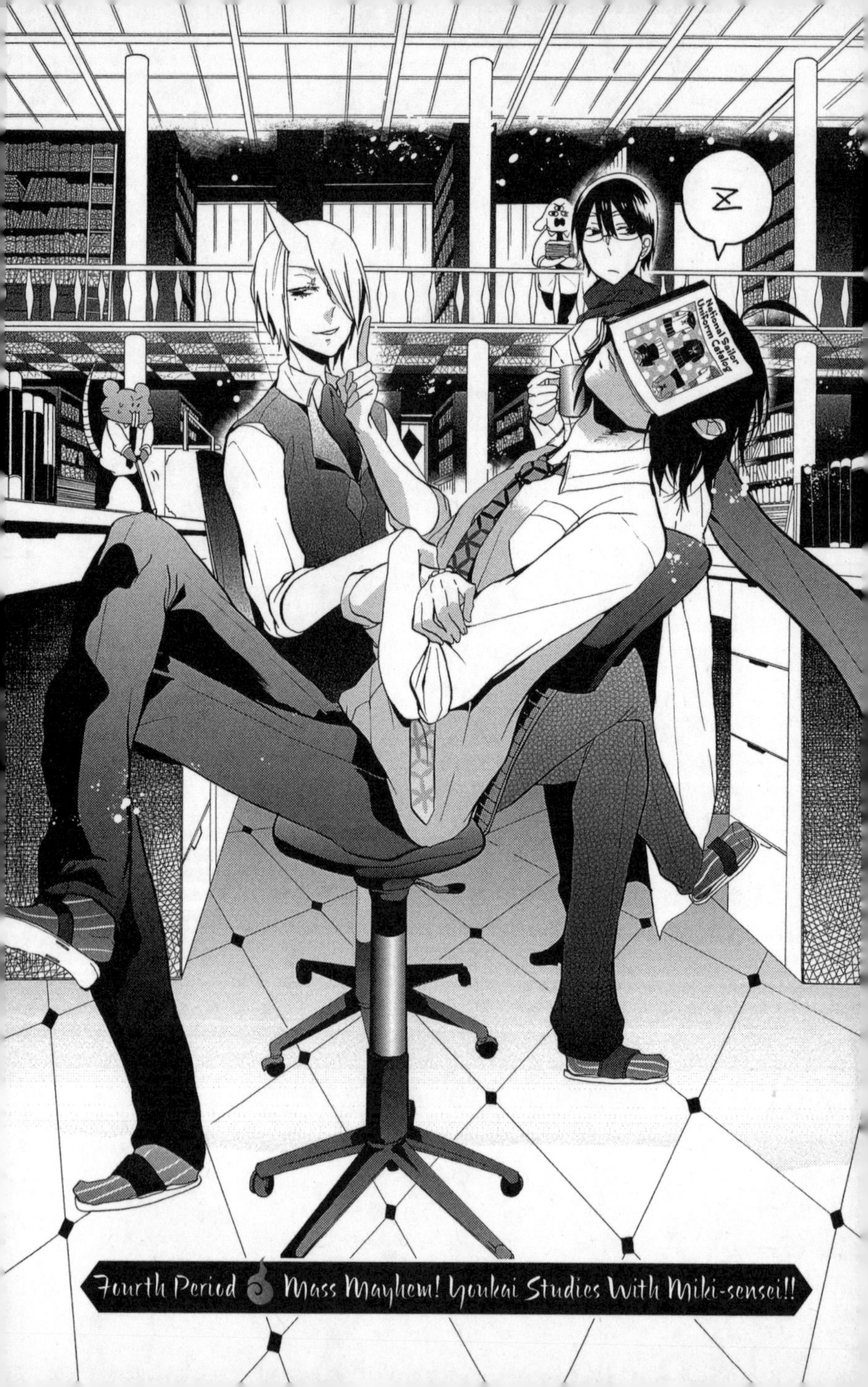
Z
National Sailor Uniform Catalog

Fourth Period Mass Mayhem! Youkai Studies With Miki-sensei!!

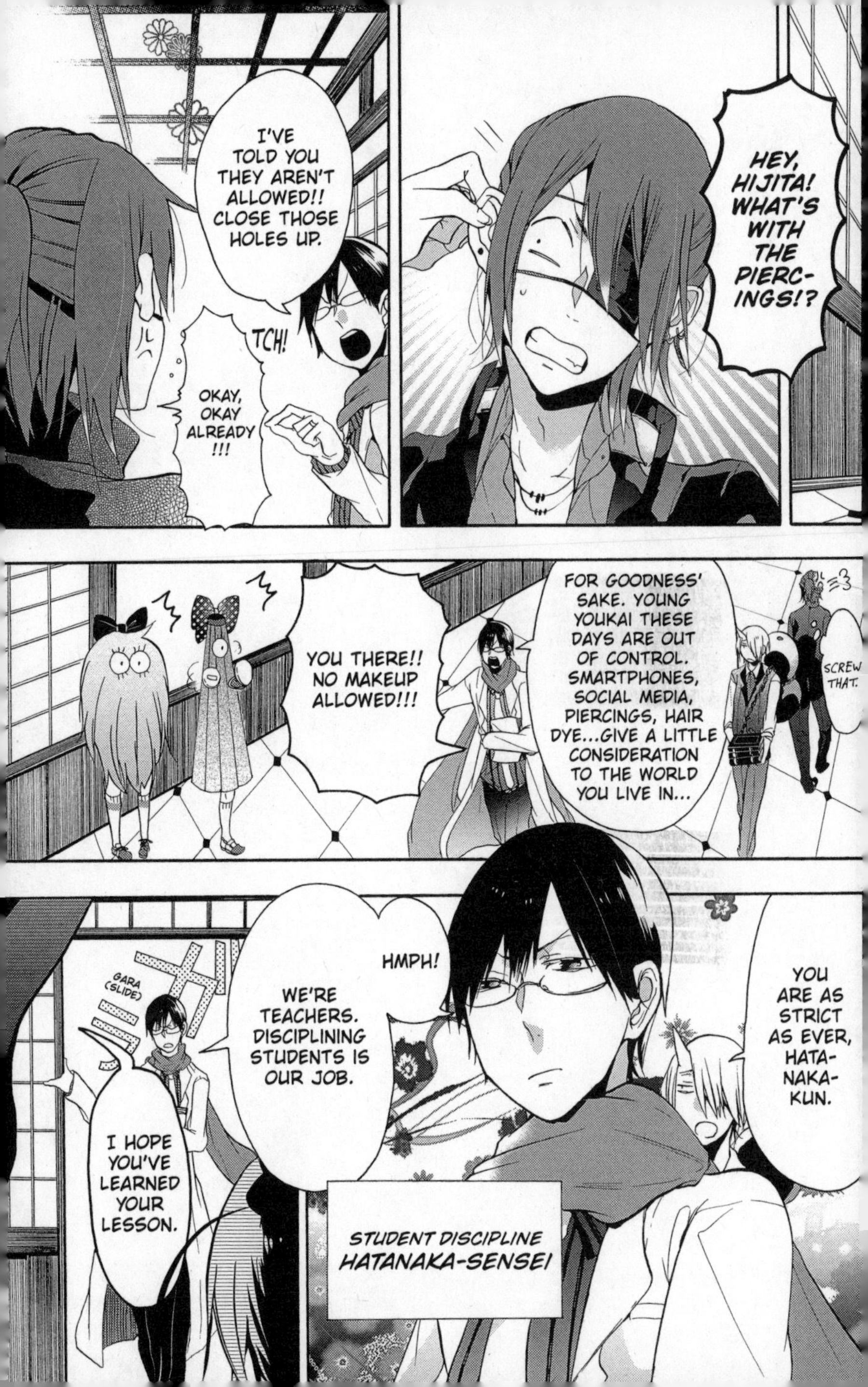
HEY, HIJITA! WHAT'S WITH THE PIERCINGS!?
I'VE TOLD YOU THEY AREN'T ALLOWED!! CLOSE THOSE HOLES UP.
TCH!
OKAY, OKAY ALREADY!!!
SCREW THAT.
FOR GOODNESS' SAKE. YOUNG YOUKAI THESE DAYS ARE OUT OF CONTROL. SMARTPHONES, SOCIAL MEDIA, PIERCINGS, HAIR DYE...GIVE A LITTLE CONSIDERATION TO THE WORLD YOU LIVE IN...
YOU THERE!! NO MAKEUP ALLOWED!!!
YOU ARE AS STRICT AS EVER, HATA-NAKA-KUN.
HMPH!
WE'RE TEACHERS. DISCIPLINING STUDENTS IS OUR JOB.
STUDENT DISCIPLINE HATANAKA-SENSEI
GARA (SLIDE)
I HOPE YOU'VE LEARNED YOUR LESSON.

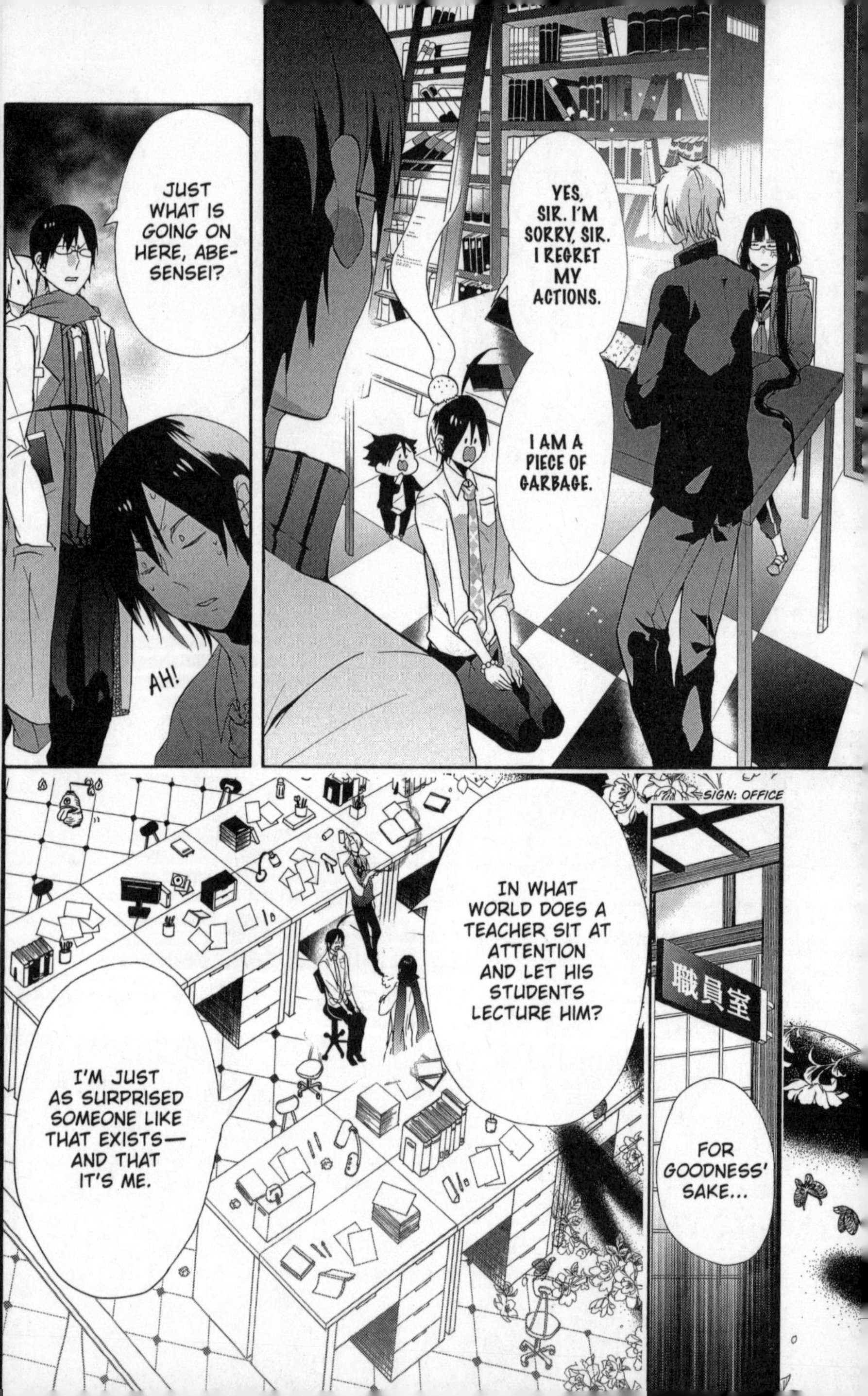
YES, SIR. I'M SORRY, SIR. I REGRET MY ACTIONS.
I AM A PIECE OF GARBAGE.
JUST WHAT IS GOING ON HERE, ABE-SENSEI?
AH!
SIGN: OFFICE
職員室
FOR GOODNESS' SAKE...
IN WHAT WORLD DOES A TEACHER SIT AT ATTENTION AND LET HIS STUDENTS LECTURE HIM?
I'M JUST AS SURPRISED SOMEONE LIKE THAT EXISTS—AND THAT IT'S ME.

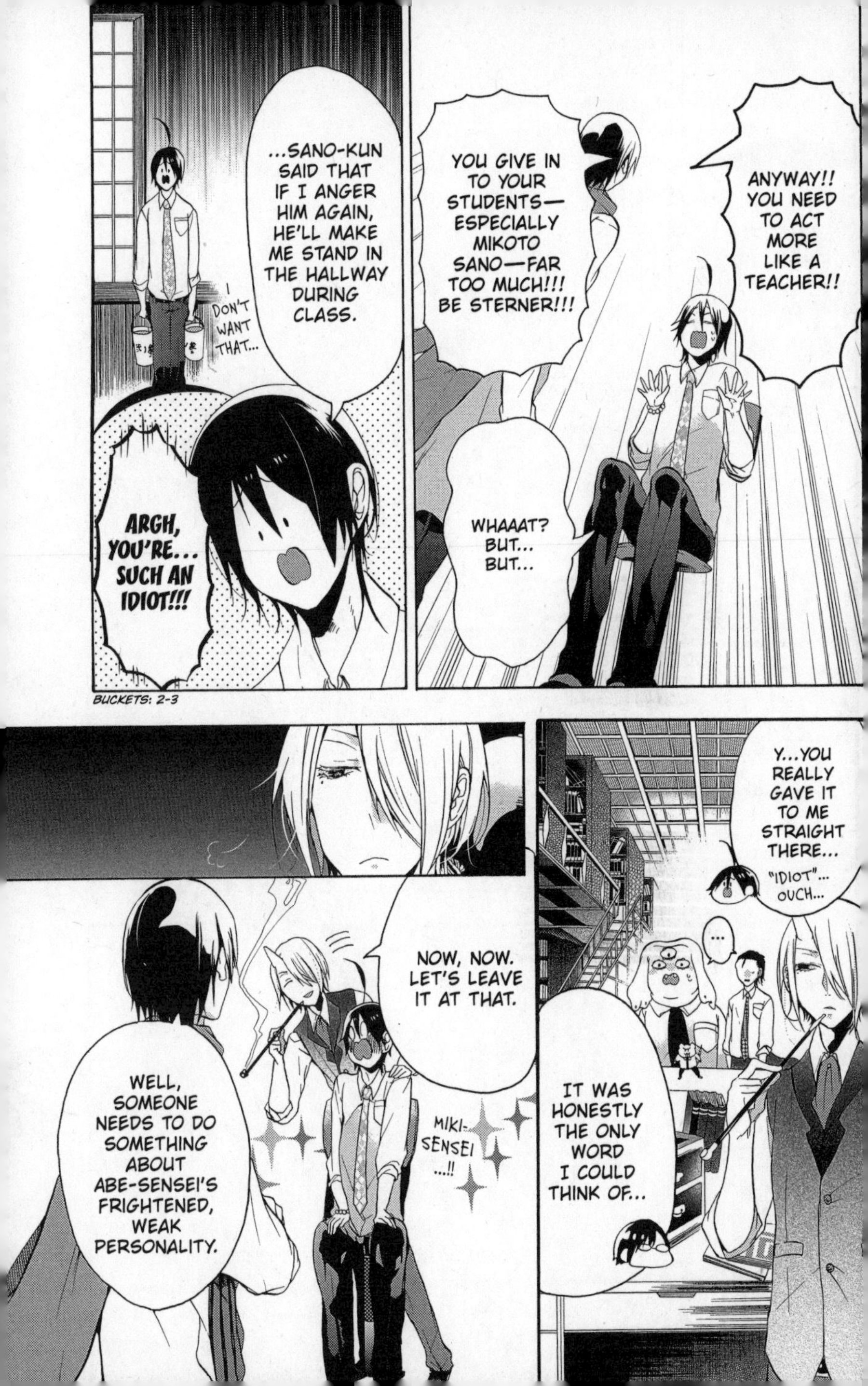
ANYWAY!! YOU NEED TO ACT MORE LIKE A TEACHER!!
YOU GIVE IN TO YOUR STUDENTS—ESPECIALLY MIKOTO SANO—FAR TOO MUCH!!! BE STERNER!!!
WHAAAT? BUT... BUT...
...SANO-KUN SAID THAT IF I ANGER HIM AGAIN, HE'LL MAKE ME STAND IN THE HALLWAY DURING CLASS.
I DON'T WANT THAT...
ARGH, YOU'RE... SUCH AN IDIOT!!!
BUCKETS: 2-3
Y...YOU REALLY GAVE IT TO ME STRAIGHT THERE...
"IDIOT"... OUCH...
...
IT WAS HONESTLY THE ONLY WORD I COULD THINK OF...
NOW, NOW. LET'S LEAVE IT AT THAT.
WELL, SOMEONE NEEDS TO DO SOMETHING ABOUT ABE-SENSEI'S FRIGHTENED, WEAK PERSONALITY.
MIKI-SENSEI...!!

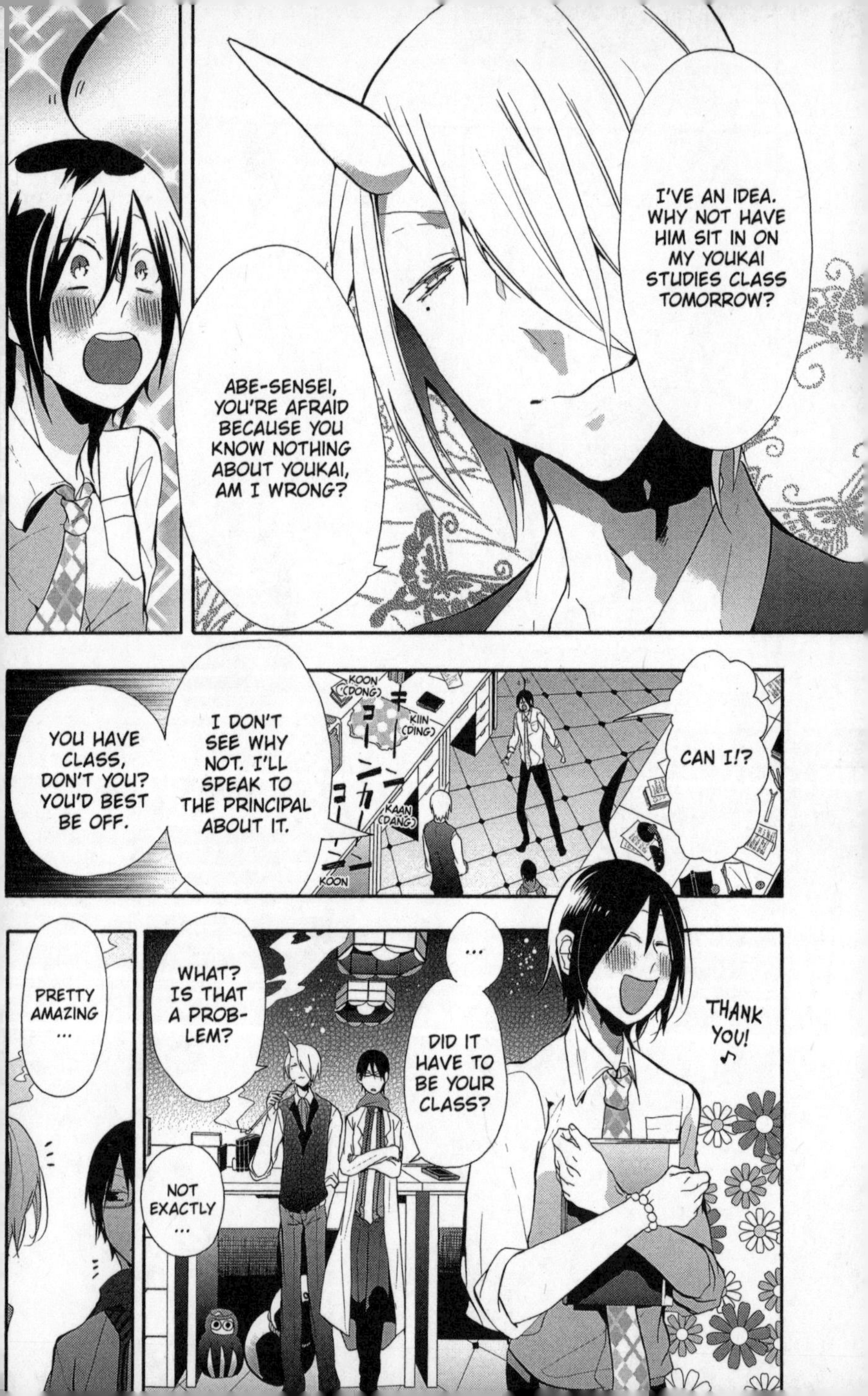
I'VE AN IDEA. WHY NOT HAVE HIM SIT IN ON MY YOUKAI STUDIES CLASS TOMORROW?
ABE-SENSEI, YOU'RE AFRAID BECAUSE YOU KNOW NOTHING ABOUT YOUKAI, AM I WRONG?
CAN I!?
KOON (DONG)
KIIN (DING)
I DON'T SEE WHY NOT. I'LL SPEAK TO THE PRINCIPAL ABOUT IT.
KAAN (DANG)
KOON
YOU HAVE CLASS, DON'T YOU? YOU'D BEST BE OFF.
THANK YOU! ♪
...
DID IT HAVE TO BE YOUR CLASS?
WHAT? IS THAT A PROB-LEM?
NOT EXACTLY ...
PRETTY AMAZING ...

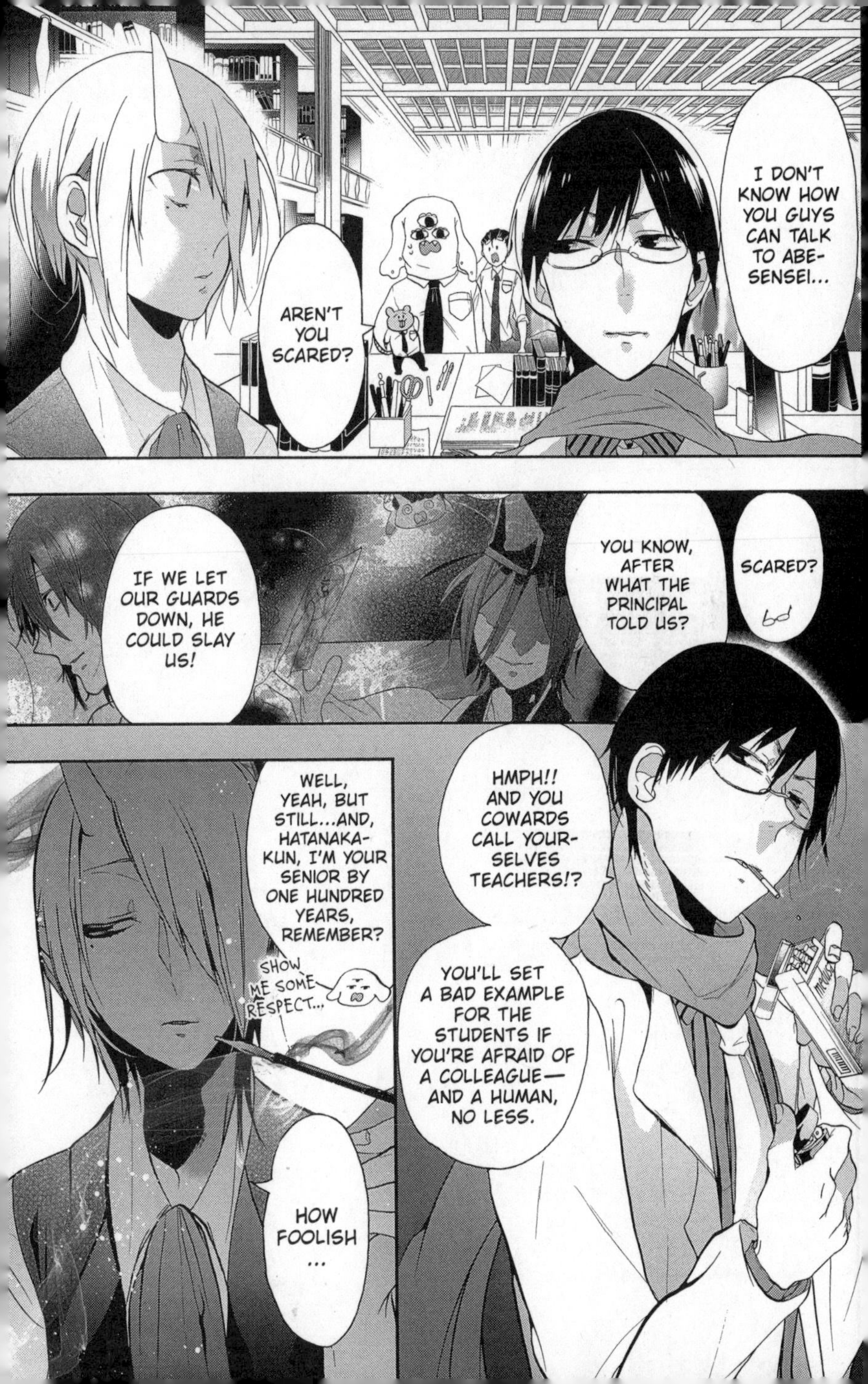
I DON'T KNOW HOW YOU GUYS CAN TALK TO ABE-SENSEI...
AREN'T YOU SCARED?
SCARED?
YOU KNOW, AFTER WHAT THE PRINCIPAL TOLD US?
IF WE LET OUR GUARDS DOWN, HE COULD SLAY US!
HMPH!! AND YOU COWARDS CALL YOUR-SELVES TEACHERS!?
YOU'LL SET A BAD EXAMPLE FOR THE STUDENTS IF YOU'RE AFRAID OF A COLLEAGUE—AND A HUMAN, NO LESS.
WELL, YEAH, BUT STILL...AND, HATANAKA-KUN, I'M YOUR SENIOR BY ONE HUNDRED YEARS, REMEMBER?
SHOW ME SOME RESPECT...
HOW FOOLISH ...

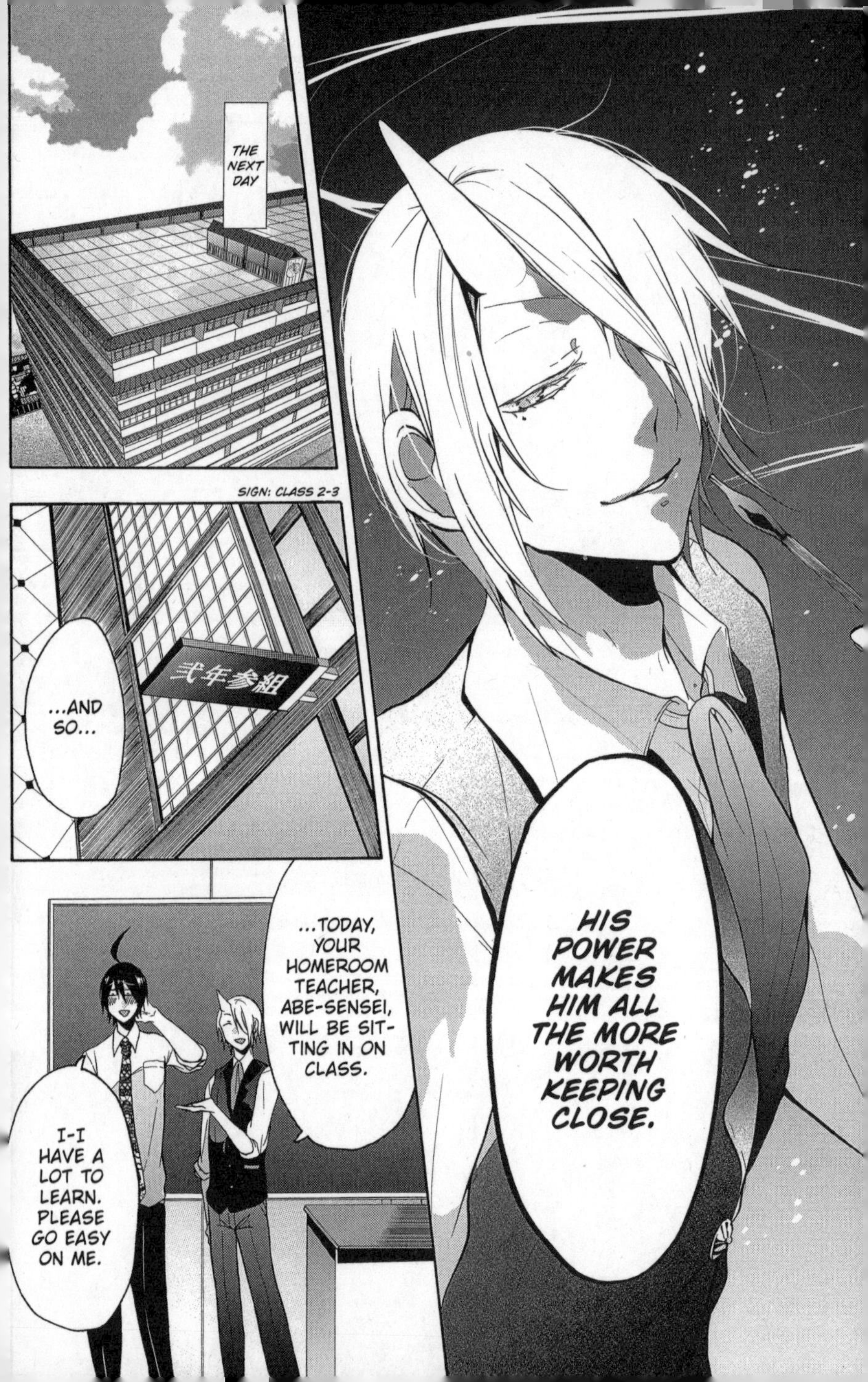
HIS POWER MAKES HIM ALL THE MORE WORTH KEEPING CLOSE.
THE NEXT DAY
SIGN: CLASS 2-3
弐年参組
...AND SO...
...TODAY, YOUR HOMEROOM TEACHER, ABE-SENSEI, WILL BE SIT-TING IN ON CLASS.
I-I HAVE A LOT TO LEARN. PLEASE GO EASY ON ME.

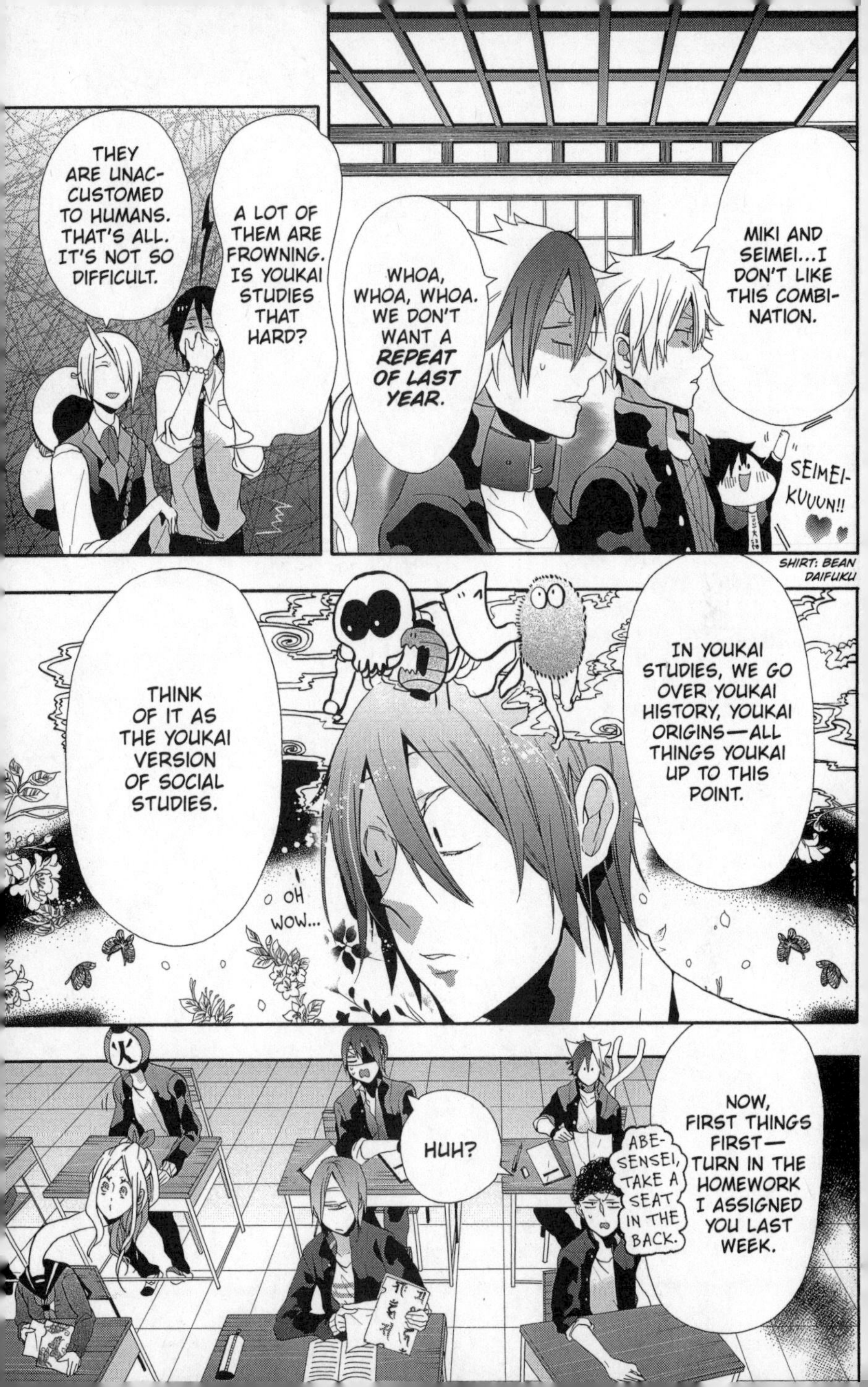
MIKI AND SEIMEI...I DON'T LIKE THIS COMBINATION.
WHOA, WHOA, WHOA. WE DON'T WANT A *REPEAT OF LAST YEAR.*
SEIMEI-KUUUN!!
SHIRT: BEAN DAIFUKU
A LOT OF THEM ARE FROWNING. IS YOUKAI STUDIES THAT HARD?
THEY ARE UNACCUSTOMED TO HUMANS. THAT'S ALL. IT'S NOT SO DIFFICULT.
IN YOUKAI STUDIES, WE GO OVER YOUKAI HISTORY, YOUKAI ORIGINS—ALL THINGS YOUKAI UP TO THIS POINT.
THINK OF IT AS THE YOUKAI VERSION OF SOCIAL STUDIES.
OH WOW...
NOW, FIRST THINGS FIRST—TURN IN THE HOMEWORK I ASSIGNED YOU LAST WEEK.
ABE-SENSEI, TAKE A SEAT IN THE BACK.
HUH?

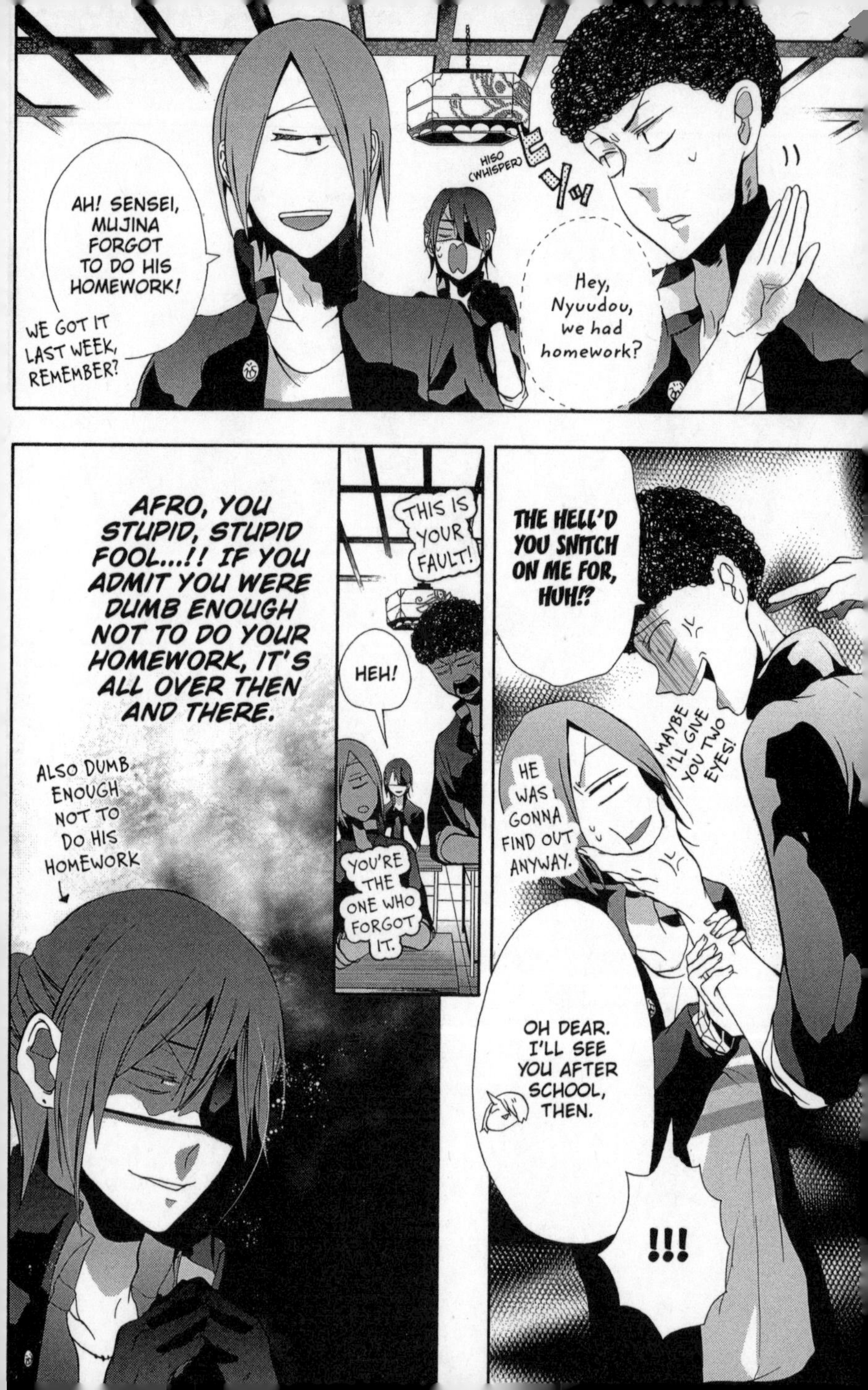
HISO (WHISPER)
Hey, Nyuudou, we had homework?
AH! SENSEI, MUJINA FORGOT TO DO HIS HOMEWORK!
WE GOT IT LAST WEEK, REMEMBER?
THE HELL'D YOU SNITCH ON ME FOR, HUH!?
MAYBE I'LL GIVE YOU TWO EYES!
HE WAS GONNA FIND OUT ANYWAY.
OH DEAR. I'LL SEE YOU AFTER SCHOOL, THEN.
!!!
THIS IS YOUR FAULT!
HEH!
YOU'RE THE ONE WHO FORGOT IT.
AFRO, YOU STUPID, STUPID FOOL...!! IF YOU ADMIT YOU WERE DUMB ENOUGH NOT TO DO YOUR HOMEWORK, IT'S ALL OVER THEN AND THERE.
ALSO DUMB ENOUGH NOT TO DO HIS HOMEWORK ↓

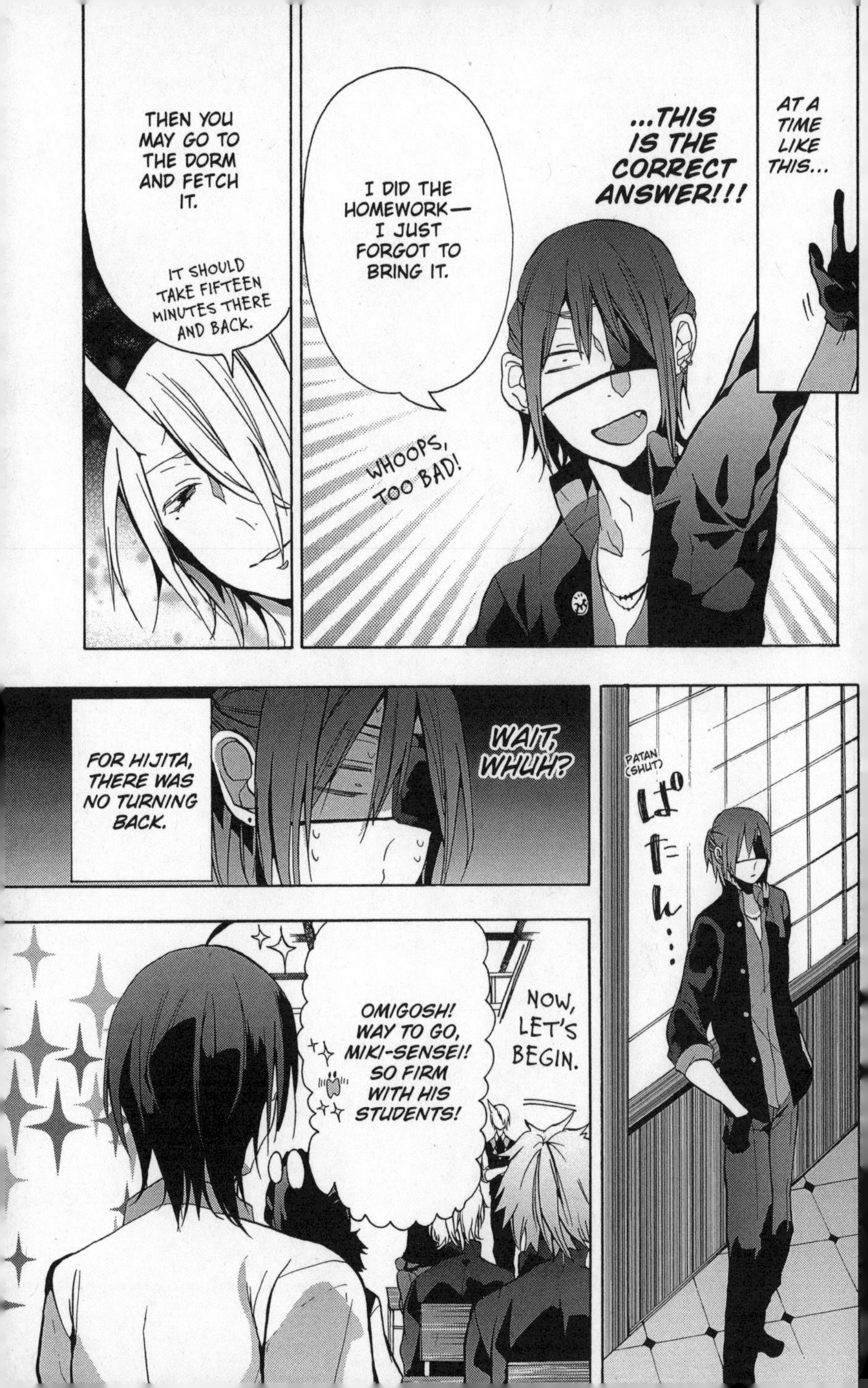
AT A TIME LIKE THIS...
...THIS IS THE CORRECT ANSWER!!!
I DID THE HOMEWORK— I JUST FORGOT TO BRING IT.
WHOOPS, TOO BAD!
THEN YOU MAY GO TO THE DORM AND FETCH IT.
IT SHOULD TAKE FIFTEEN MINUTES THERE AND BACK.
PATAN (SHUT)
ぱたん…
WAIT, WHUH?
FOR HIJITA, THERE WAS NO TURNING BACK.
NOW, LET'S BEGIN.
OMIGOSH! WAY TO GO, MIKI-SENSEI! SO FIRM WITH HIS STUDENTS!

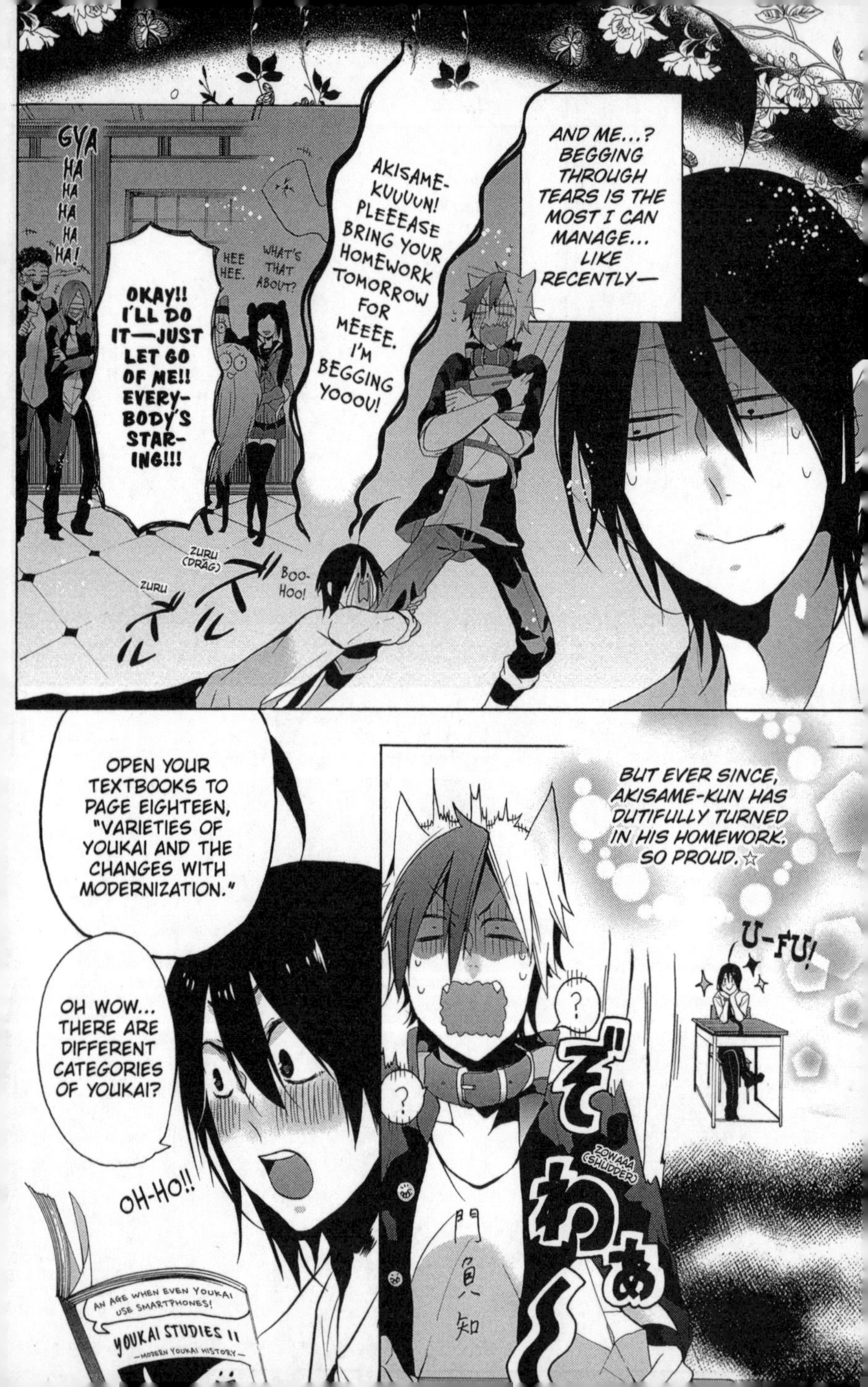
AND ME...? BEGGING THROUGH TEARS IS THE MOST I CAN MANAGE... LIKE RECENTLY—
AKISAME-KUUUUN! PLEEEEASE BRING YOUR HOMEWORK TOMORROW FOR MEEEE. I'M BEGGING YOOOU!
WHAT'S THAT ABOUT?
HEE HEE.
OKAY!! I'LL DO IT—JUST LET GO OF ME!! EVERYBODY'S STARING!!!
GYA HA HA HA HA HA!
BOO-HOO!
ZURU (DRAG)
ZURU
BUT EVER SINCE, AKISAME-KUN HAS DUTIFULLY TURNED IN HIS HOMEWORK. SO PROUD. ☆
U-FU!
?
?
ぞわぁ〜
ZOWAAA (SHUDDER)
OPEN YOUR TEXTBOOKS TO PAGE EIGHTEEN, "VARIETIES OF YOUKAI AND THE CHANGES WITH MODERNIZATION."
OH WOW... THERE ARE DIFFERENT CATEGORIES OF YOUKAI?
OH-HO!!
AN AGE WHEN EVEN YOUKAI USE SMARTPHONES!
YOUKAI STUDIES II
—MODERN YOUKAI HISTORY—

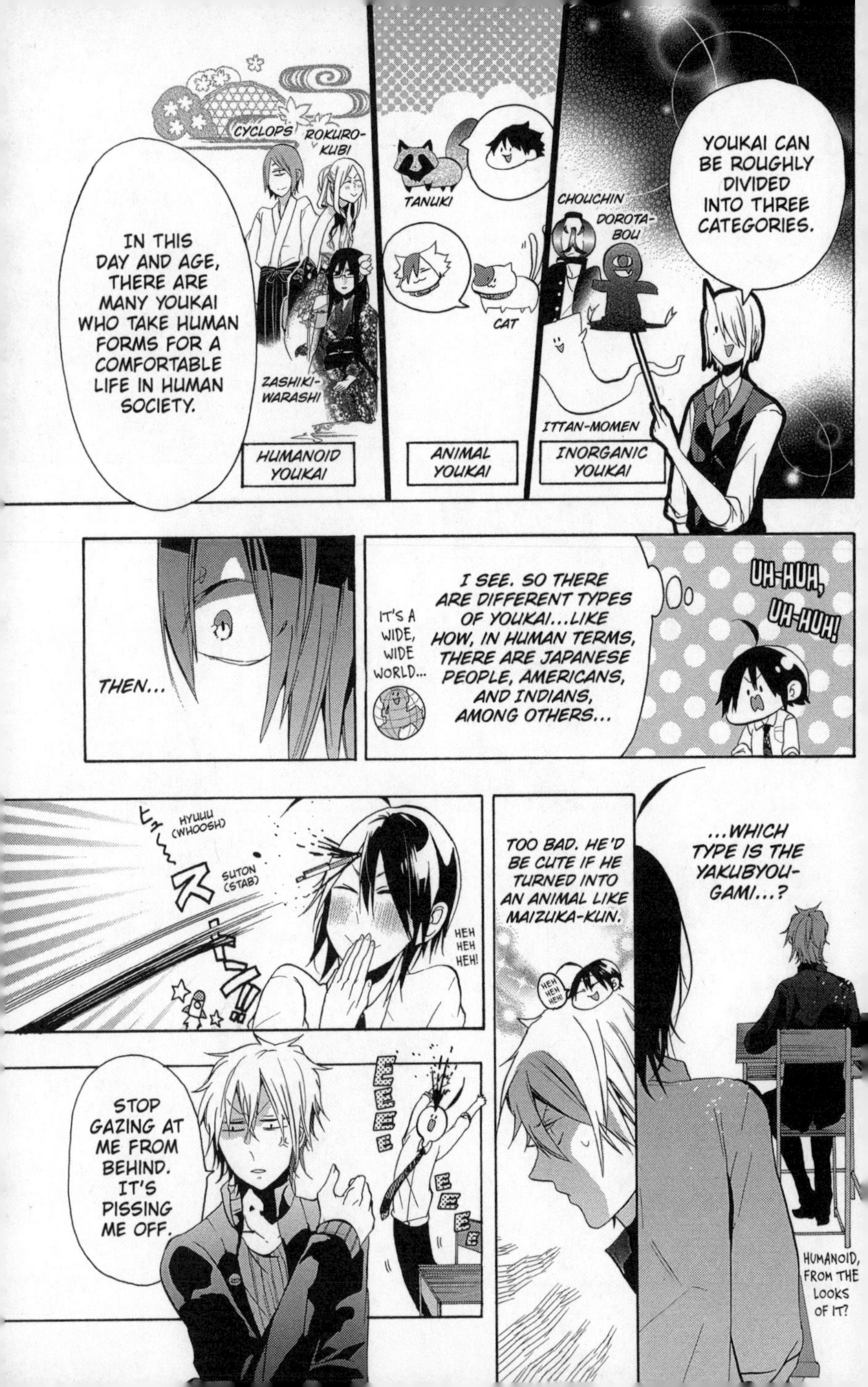

YOUKAI CAN BE ROUGHLY DIVIDED INTO THREE CATEGORIES.
CHOUCHIN
DOROTA-BOU
ITTAN-MOMEN
INORGANIC YOUKAI
TANUKI
CAT
ANIMAL YOUKAI
CYCLOPS
ROKURO-KUBI
ZASHIKI-WARASHI
HUMANOID YOUKAI
IN THIS DAY AND AGE, THERE ARE MANY YOUKAI WHO TAKE HUMAN FORMS FOR A COMFORTABLE LIFE IN HUMAN SOCIETY.
UH-HUH, UH-HUH!
I SEE. SO THERE ARE DIFFERENT TYPES OF YOUKAI...LIKE HOW, IN HUMAN TERMS, THERE ARE JAPANESE PEOPLE, AMERICANS, AND INDIANS, AMONG OTHERS...
IT'S A WIDE, WIDE WORLD...
THEN...
...WHICH TYPE IS THE YAKUBYOU-GAMI...?
TOO BAD. HE'D BE CUTE IF HE TURNED INTO AN ANIMAL LIKE MAIZUKA-KUN.
HEH HEH HEH!
HUMANOID, FROM THE LOOKS OF IT?
HYUUU (WHOOSH)
SUTON (STAB)
HEH HEH HEH!
STOP GAZING AT ME FROM BEHIND. IT'S PISSING ME OFF.

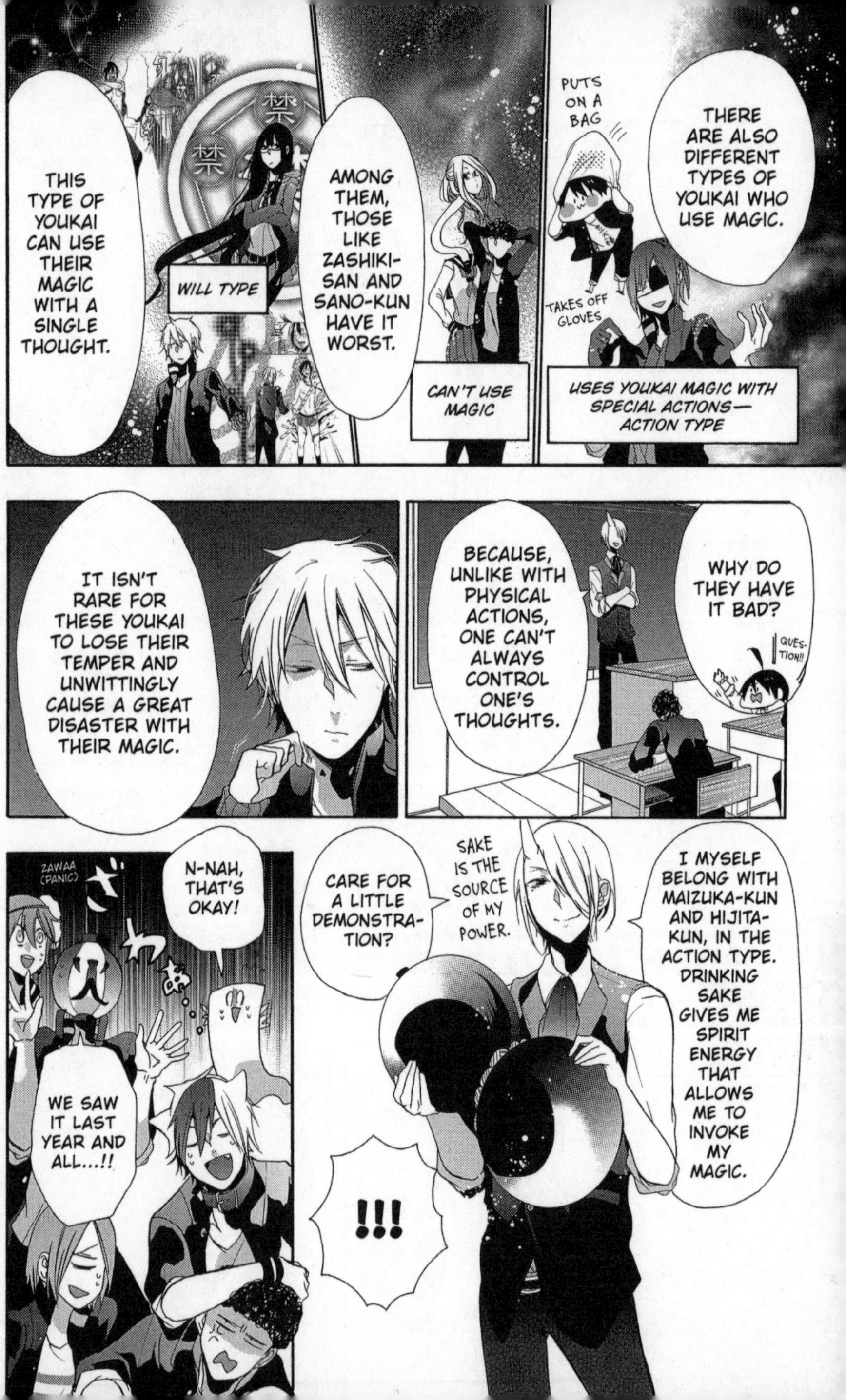
THERE ARE ALSO DIFFERENT TYPES OF YOUKAI WHO USE MAGIC.
PUTS ON A BAG
TAKES OFF GLOVES
USES YOUKAI MAGIC WITH SPECIAL ACTIONS— ACTION TYPE
CAN'T USE MAGIC
WILL TYPE
THIS TYPE OF YOUKAI CAN USE THEIR MAGIC WITH A SINGLE THOUGHT.
AMONG THEM, THOSE LIKE ZASHIKI-SAN AND SANO-KUN HAVE IT WORST.
WHY DO THEY HAVE IT BAD?
QUES-TION!!
BECAUSE, UNLIKE WITH PHYSICAL ACTIONS, ONE CAN'T ALWAYS CONTROL ONE'S THOUGHTS.
IT ISN'T RARE FOR THESE YOUKAI TO LOSE THEIR TEMPER AND UNWITTINGLY CAUSE A GREAT DISASTER WITH THEIR MAGIC.
I MYSELF BELONG WITH MAIZUKA-KUN AND HIJITA-KUN, IN THE ACTION TYPE. DRINKING SAKE GIVES ME SPIRIT ENERGY THAT ALLOWS ME TO INVOKE MY MAGIC.
SAKE IS THE SOURCE OF MY POWER.
CARE FOR A LITTLE DEMONSTRA-TION?
!!!
ZAWAA (PANIC)
N-NAH, THAT'S OKAY!
WE SAW IT LAST YEAR AND ALL...!!

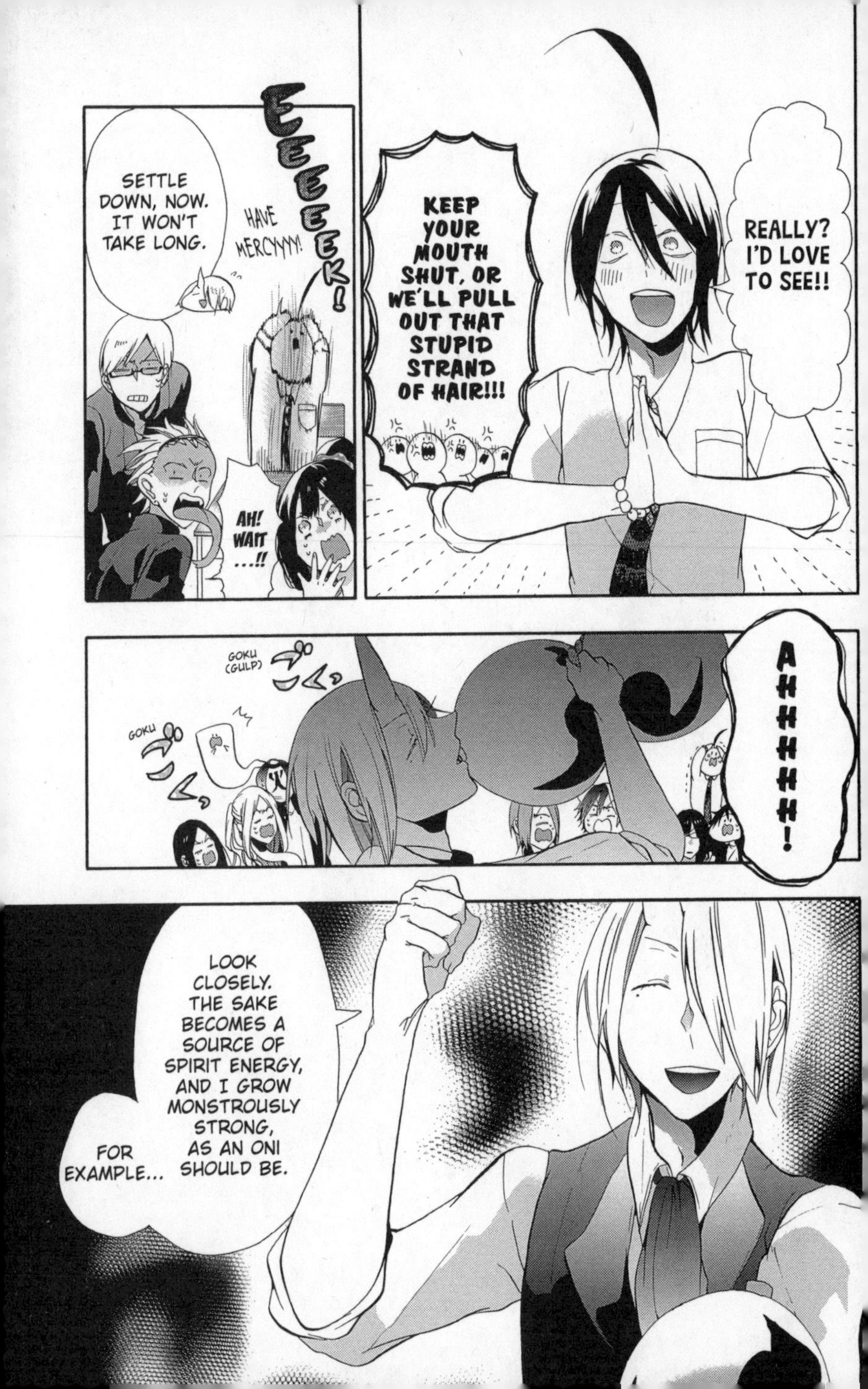
REALLY? I'D LOVE TO SEE!!
KEEP YOUR MOUTH SHUT, OR WE'LL PULL OUT THAT STUPID STRAND OF HAIR!!!
EEEEEEK!
HAVE MERCYYYY!
SETTLE DOWN, NOW. IT WON'T TAKE LONG.
AH! WAIT ...!!
AHHHHHH!
GOKU (GULP)
GOKU
LOOK CLOSELY. THE SAKE BECOMES A SOURCE OF SPIRIT ENERGY, AND I GROW MONSTROUSLY STRONG, AS AN ONI SHOULD BE.
FOR EXAMPLE...

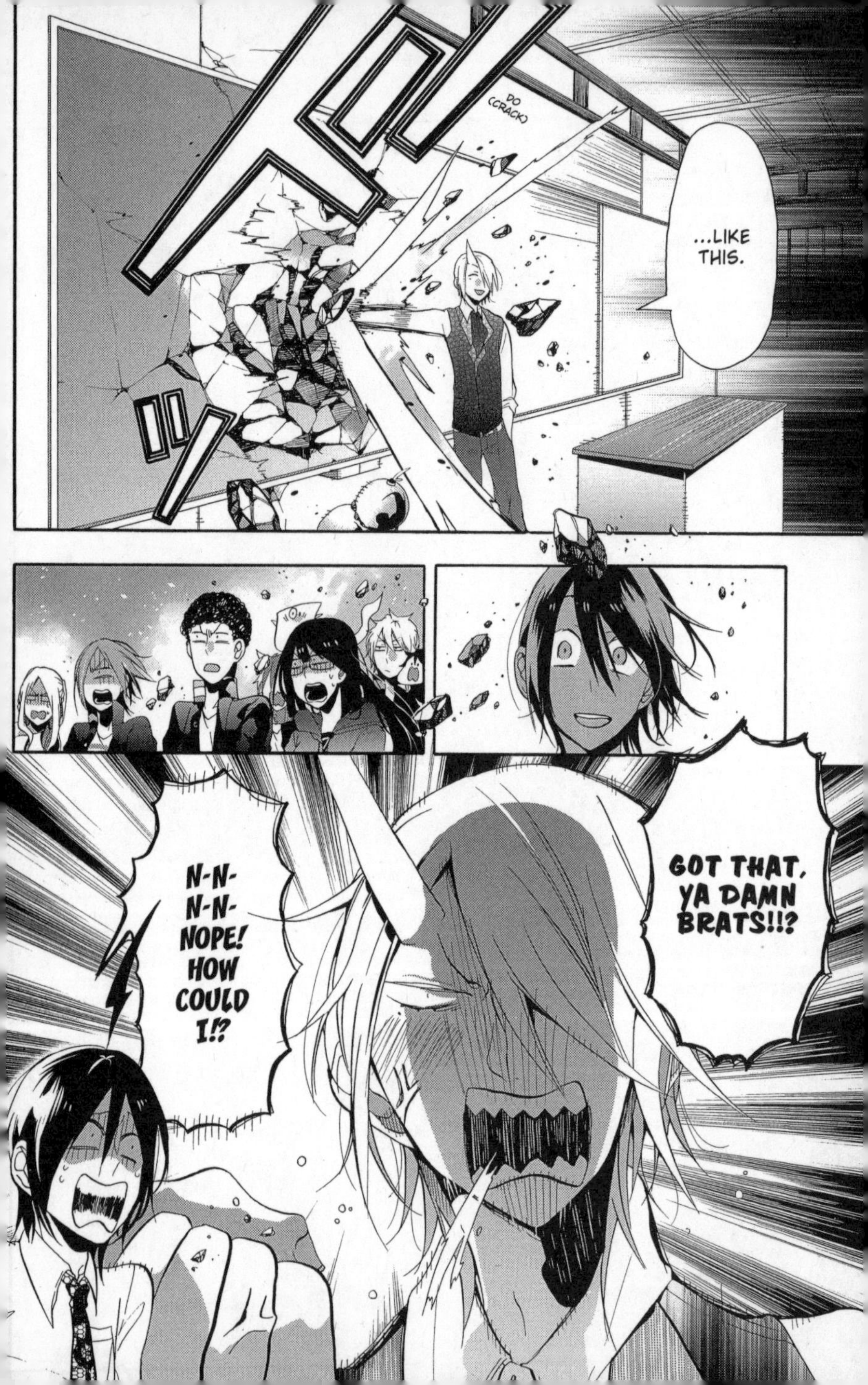
DO
(CRACK)
...LIKE THIS.
GOT THAT, YA DAMN BRATS!!?
N-N-N-N-NOPE! HOW COULD I!?

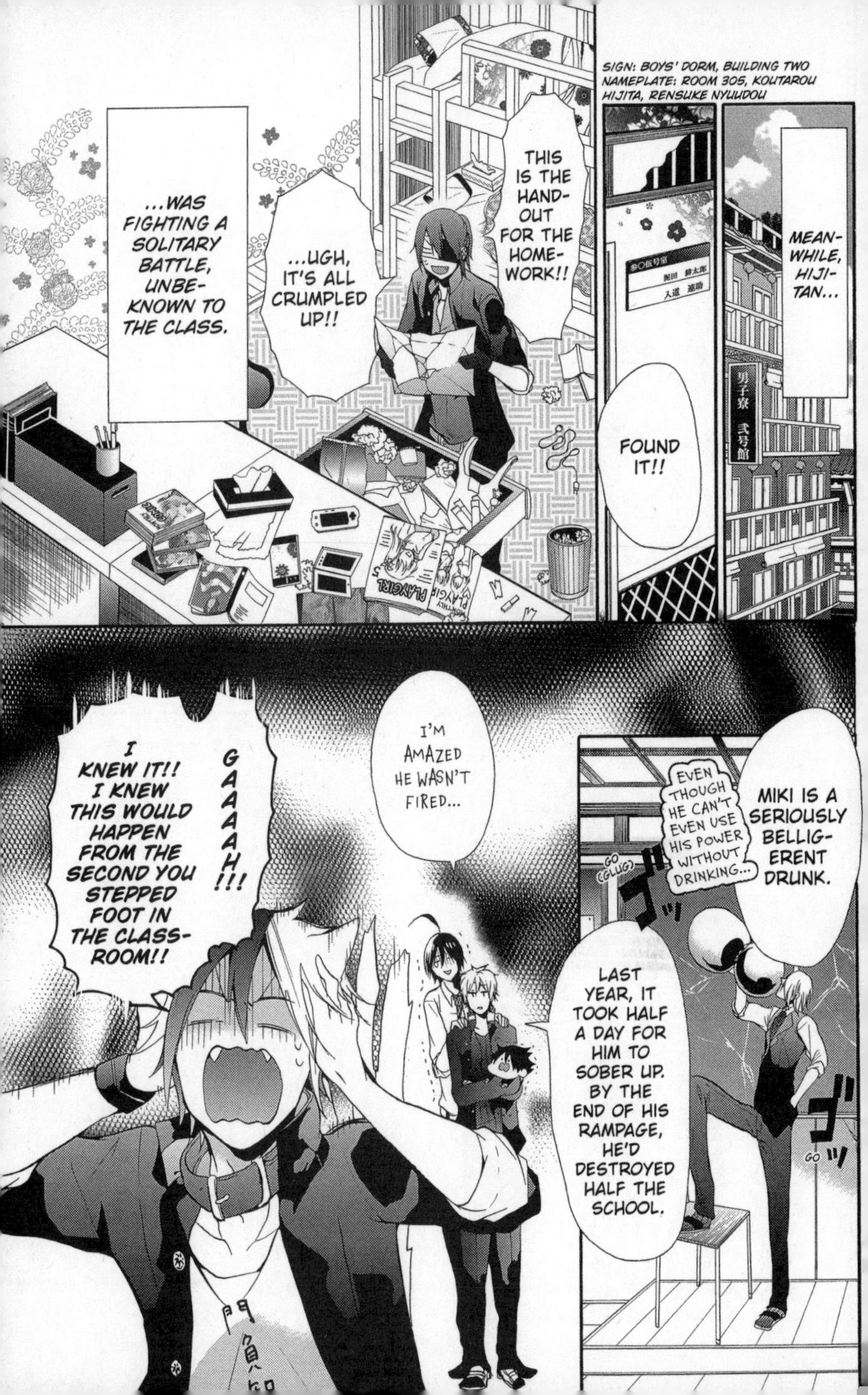
SIGN: BOYS' DORM, BUILDING TWO
NAMEPLATE: ROOM 305, KOUTAROU HIJITA, RENSUKE NYUUDOU
MEAN-WHILE, HIJI-TAN...
男子寮 弐号館
FOUND IT!!
THIS IS THE HAND-OUT FOR THE HOME-WORK!!
...UGH, IT'S ALL CRUMPLED UP!!
...WAS FIGHTING A SOLITARY BATTLE, UNBE-KNOWN TO THE CLASS.
MIKI IS A SERIOUSLY BELLIG-ERENT DRUNK.
EVEN THOUGH HE CAN'T EVEN USE HIS POWER WITHOUT DRINKING...
GO (GLUG)
ゴッ
LAST YEAR, IT TOOK HALF A DAY FOR HIM TO SOBER UP. BY THE END OF HIS RAMPAGE, HE'D DESTROYED HALF THE SCHOOL.
GO
ゴッ
I'M AMAZED HE WASN'T FIRED...
GAAAAAH!!!
I KNEW IT!! I KNEW THIS WOULD HAPPEN FROM THE SECOND YOU STEPPED FOOT IN THE CLASS-ROOM!!

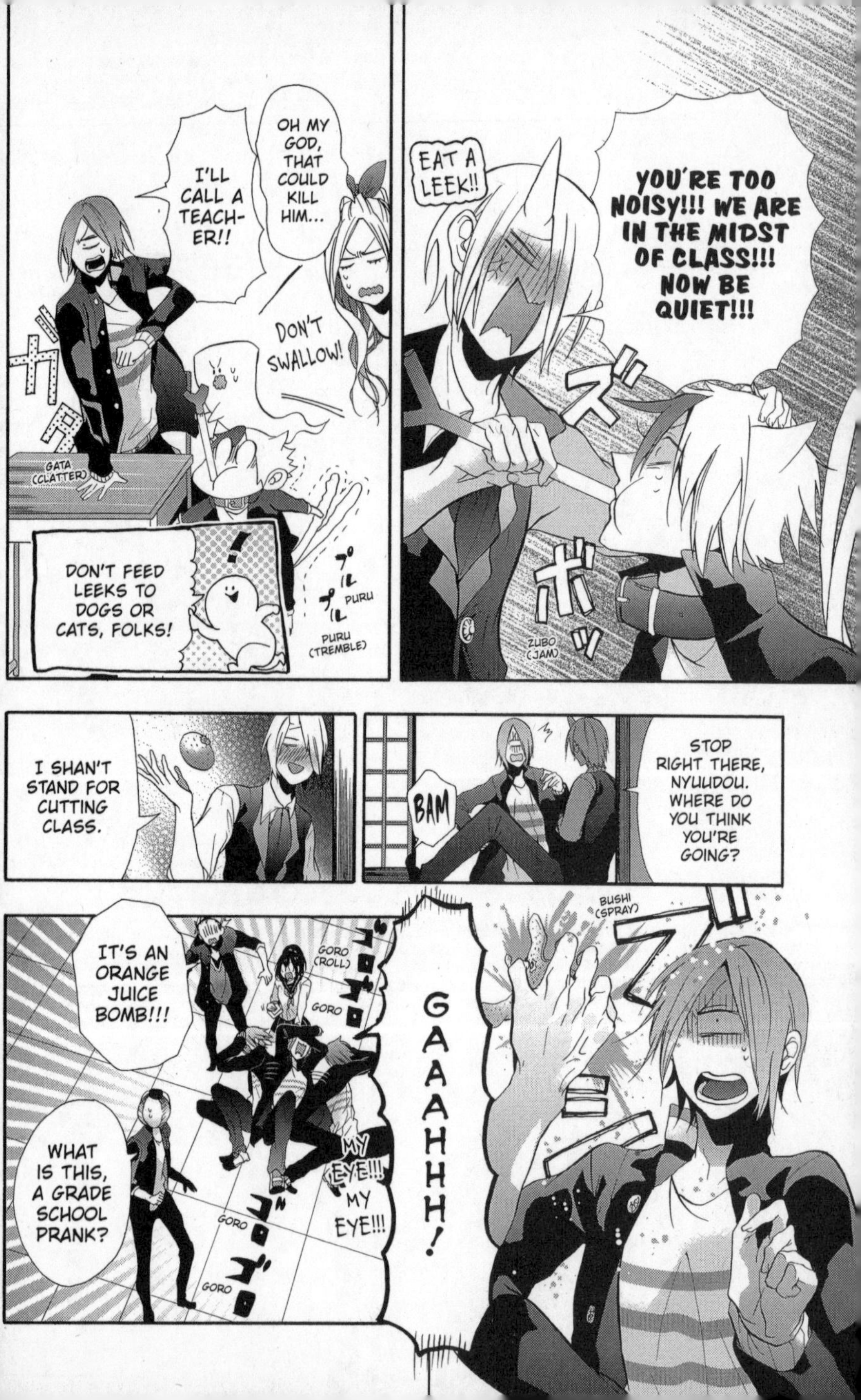
YOU'RE TOO NOISY!!! WE ARE IN THE MIDST OF CLASS!!! NOW BE QUIET!!!
EAT A LEEK!!
ZUBO (JAM)
OH MY GOD, THAT COULD KILL HIM...
I'LL CALL A TEACHER!!
DON'T SWALLOW!
GATA (CLATTER)
PURU
PURU (TREMBLE)
DON'T FEED LEEKS TO DOGS OR CATS, FOLKS!
STOP RIGHT THERE, NYUUDOU. WHERE DO YOU THINK YOU'RE GOING?
BAM
I SHAN'T STAND FOR CUTTING CLASS.
BUSHI (SPRAY)
GAAAHHH!
MY EYE!!! MY EYE!!!
GORO (ROLL)
GORO
IT'S AN ORANGE JUICE BOMB!!!
WHAT IS THIS, A GRADE SCHOOL PRANK?
GORO
GORO

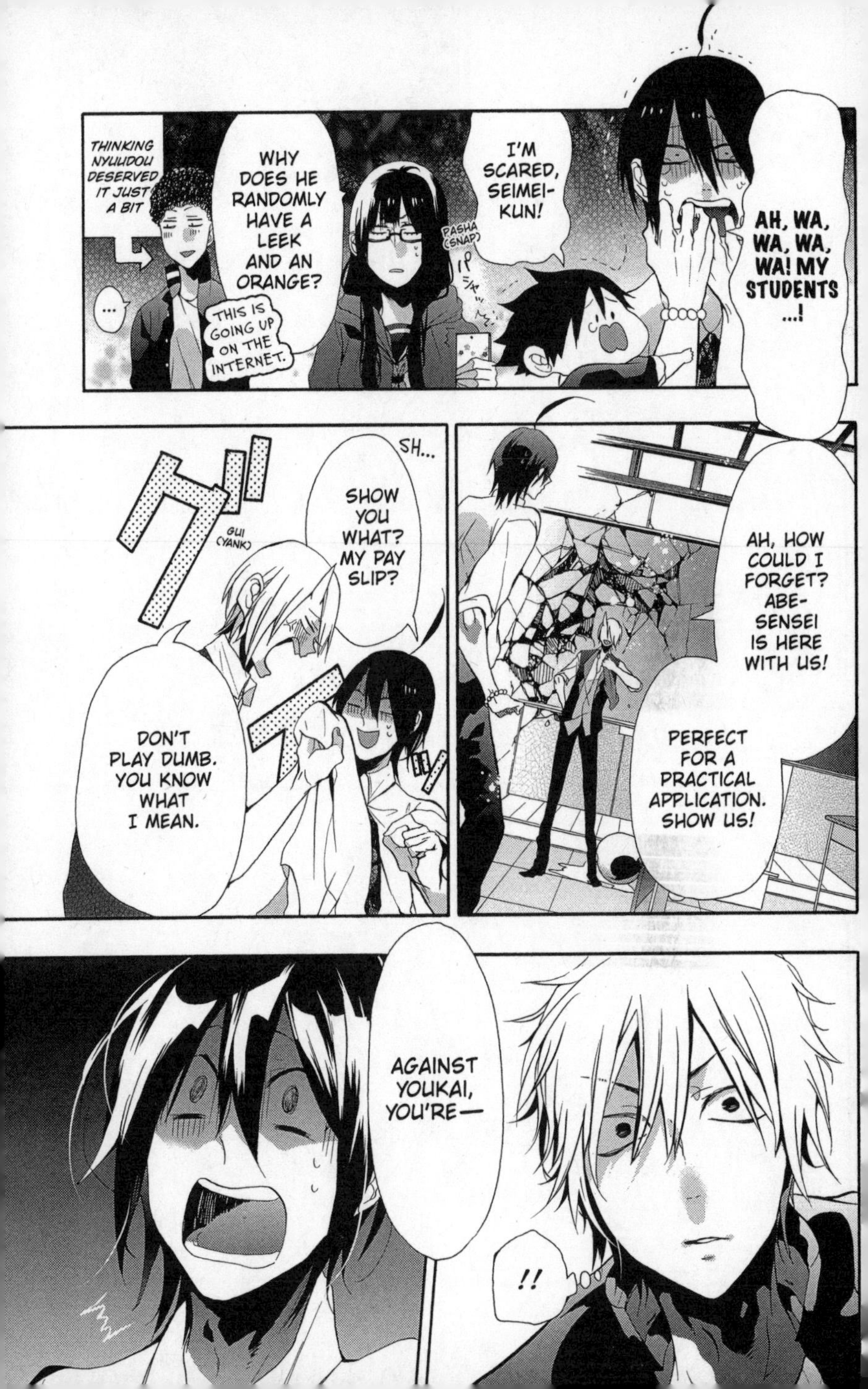
AH, WA, WA, WA, WA! MY STUDENTS ...!
I'M SCARED, SEIMEI-KUN!
PASHA (SNAP)
WHY DOES HE RANDOMLY HAVE A LEEK AND AN ORANGE?
THIS IS GOING UP ON THE INTERNET.
THINKING NYUUDOU DESERVED IT JUST A BIT
...
AH, HOW COULD I FORGET? ABE-SENSEI IS HERE WITH US!
PERFECT FOR A PRACTICAL APPLICATION. SHOW US!
SH...
SHOW YOU WHAT? MY PAY SLIP?
GUI (YANK)
DON'T PLAY DUMB. YOU KNOW WHAT I MEAN.
AGAINST YOUKAI, YOU'RE—
!!

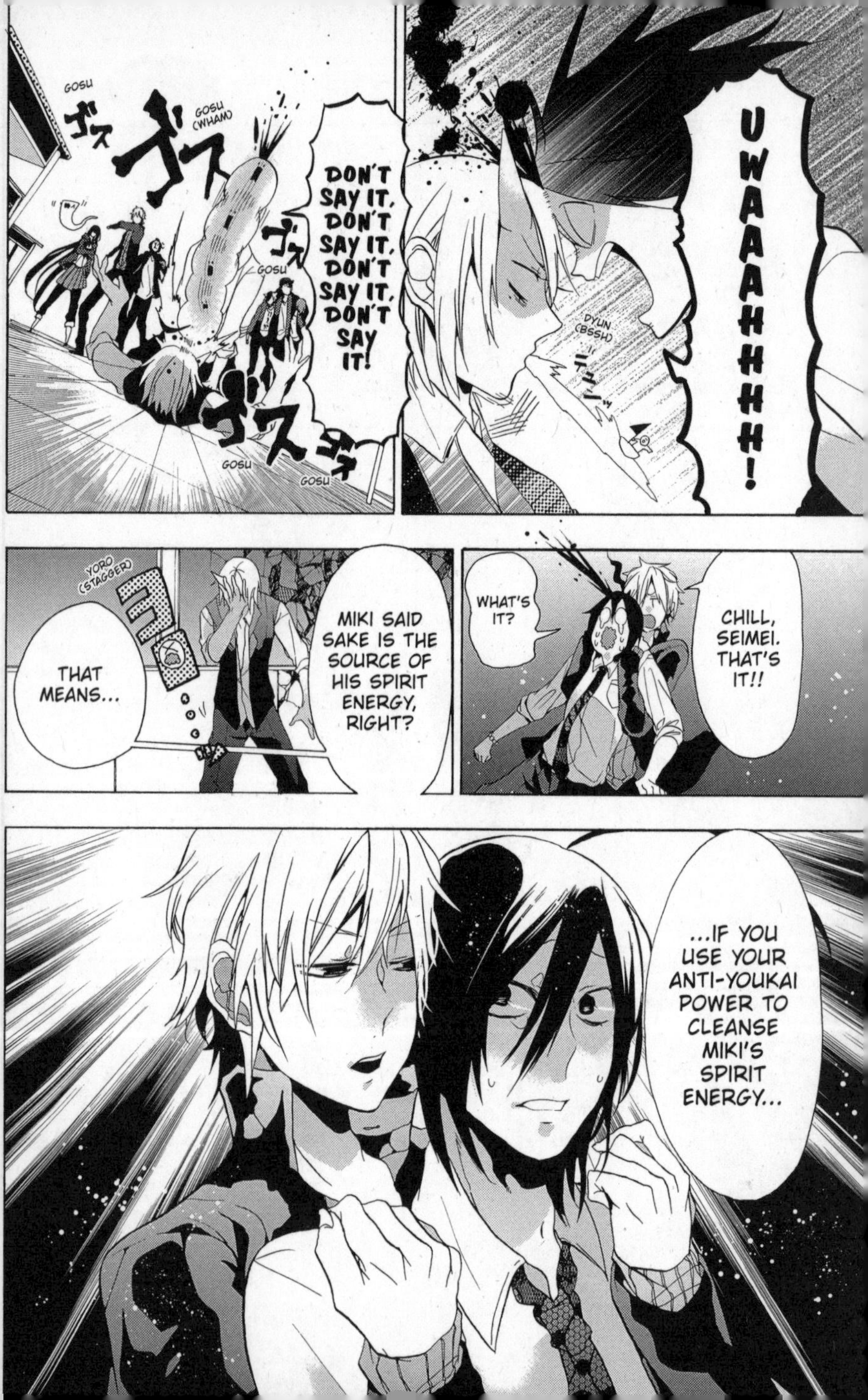
UWAAAHHHH!
DYUN (BSSH)
GOSU (WHAM)
GOSU
DON'T SAY IT, DON'T SAY IT, DON'T SAY IT, DON'T SAY IT!
GOSU
GOSU
GOSU
CHILL, SEIMEI. THAT'S IT!!
WHAT'S IT?
MIKI SAID SAKE IS THE SOURCE OF HIS SPIRIT ENERGY, RIGHT?
YORO (STAGGER)
THAT MEANS...
...IF YOU USE YOUR ANTI-YOUKAI POWER TO CLEANSE MIKI'S SPIRIT ENERGY...

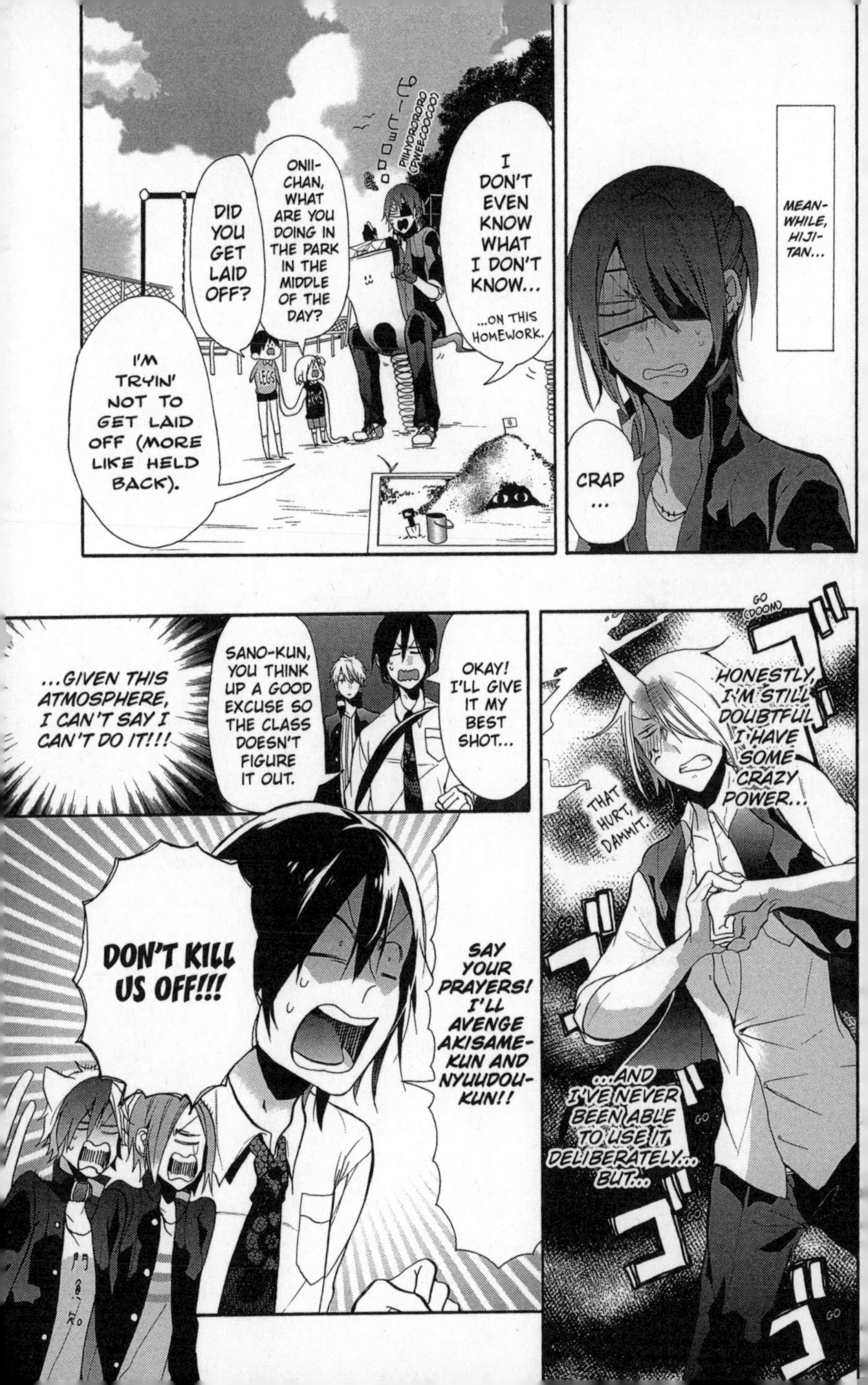
MEAN-WHILE, HIJI-TAN...
CRAP...
I DON'T EVEN KNOW WHAT I DON'T KNOW...
...ON THIS HOMEWORK.
PIIHYORORORO (PWEEOOOOOO)
ONII-CHAN, WHAT ARE YOU DOING IN THE PARK IN THE MIDDLE OF THE DAY?
DID YOU GET LAID OFF?
I'M TRYIN' NOT TO GET LAID OFF (MORE LIKE HELD BACK).
LEGS
ARMS
GO (DOOM)
HONESTLY, I'M STILL DOUBTFUL I HAVE SOME CRAZY POWER...
THAT HURT, DAMMIT.
GO
...AND I'VE NEVER BEEN ABLE TO USE IT DELIBERATELY... BUT...
GO
GO
GO
OKAY! I'LL GIVE IT MY BEST SHOT...
SANO-KUN, YOU THINK UP A GOOD EXCUSE SO THE CLASS DOESN'T FIGURE IT OUT.
...GIVEN THIS ATMOSPHERE, I CAN'T SAY I CAN'T DO IT!!!
SAY YOUR PRAYERS! I'LL AVENGE AKISAME-KUN AND NYUUDOU-KUN!!
DON'T KILL US OFF!!!

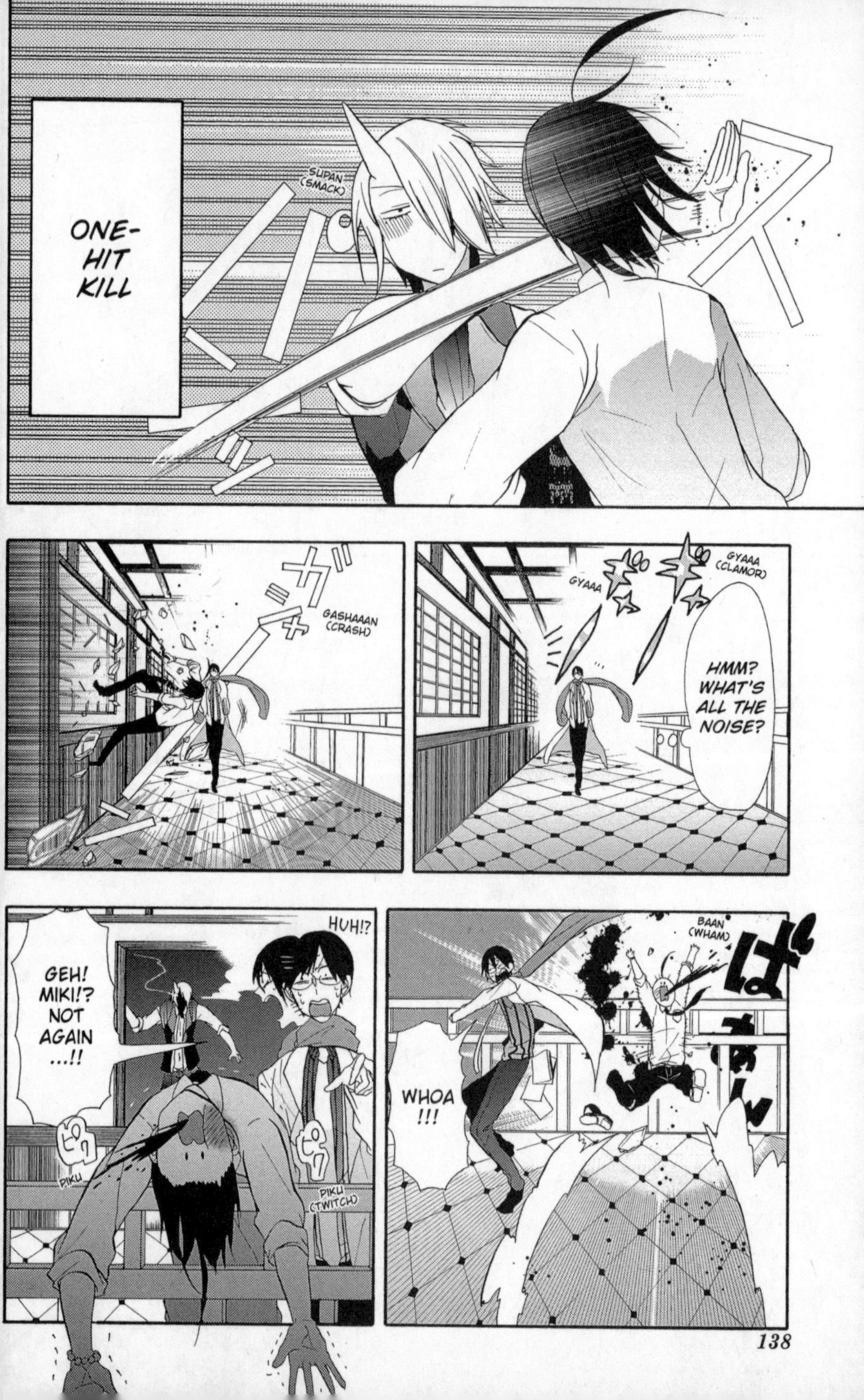
SUPAN (SMACK)
ONE-HIT KILL
GYAAA (CLAMOR)
GYAAA
HMM? WHAT'S ALL THE NOISE?
GASHAAAN (CRASH)
BAAN (WHAM)
WHOA!!!
HUH!?
GEH! MIKI!? NOT AGAIN...!!
PIKU (TWITCH)
PIKU

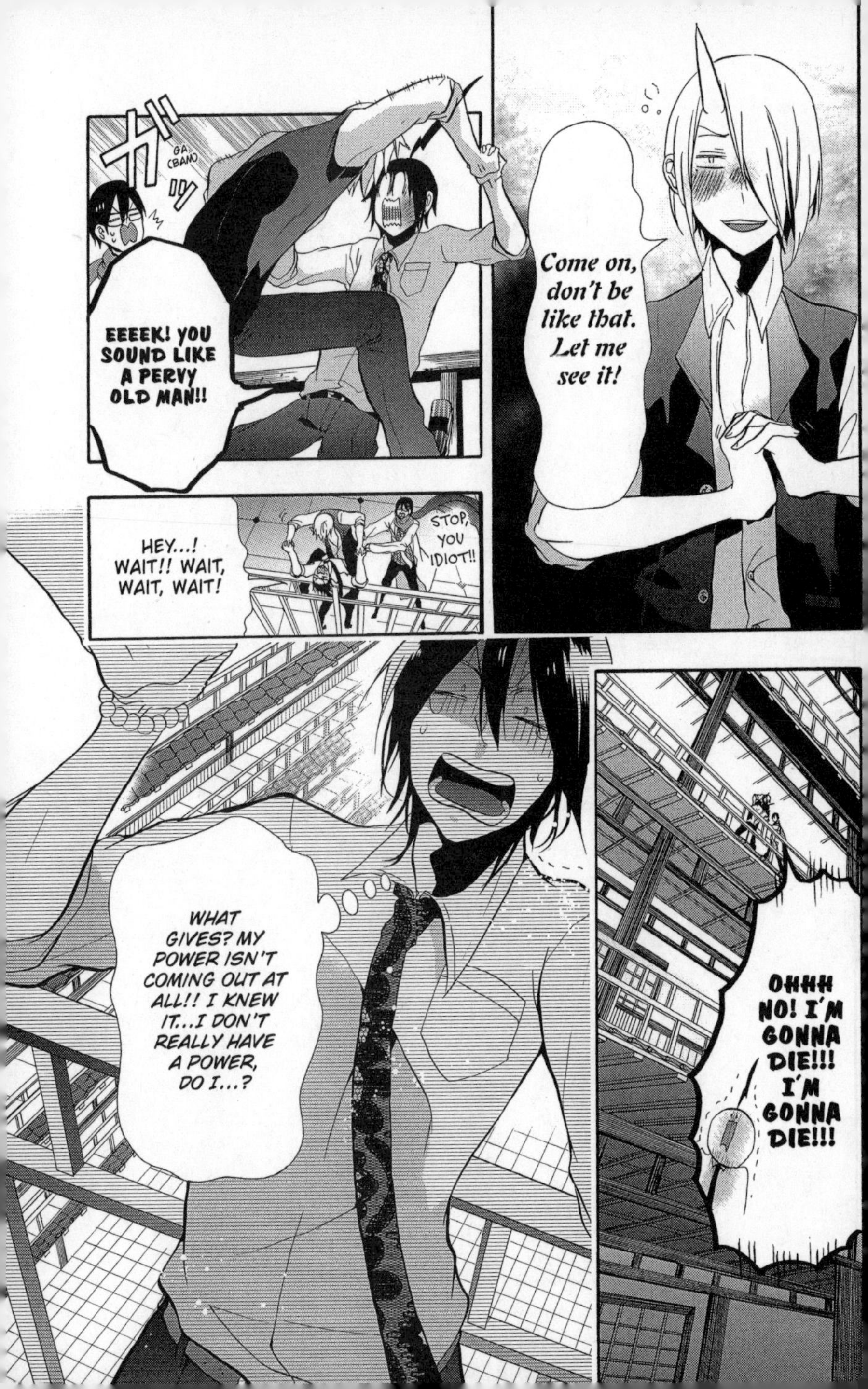
Come on, don't be like that. Let me see it!
GA (BAM)
EEEEK! YOU SOUND LIKE A PERVY OLD MAN!!
STOP, YOU IDIOT!!
HEY...! WAIT!! WAIT, WAIT, WAIT!
OHHHH NO! I'M GONNA DIE!!! I'M GONNA DIE!!!
WHAT GIVES? MY POWER ISN'T COMING OUT AT ALL!! I KNEW IT...I DON'T REALLY HAVE A POWER, DO I...?

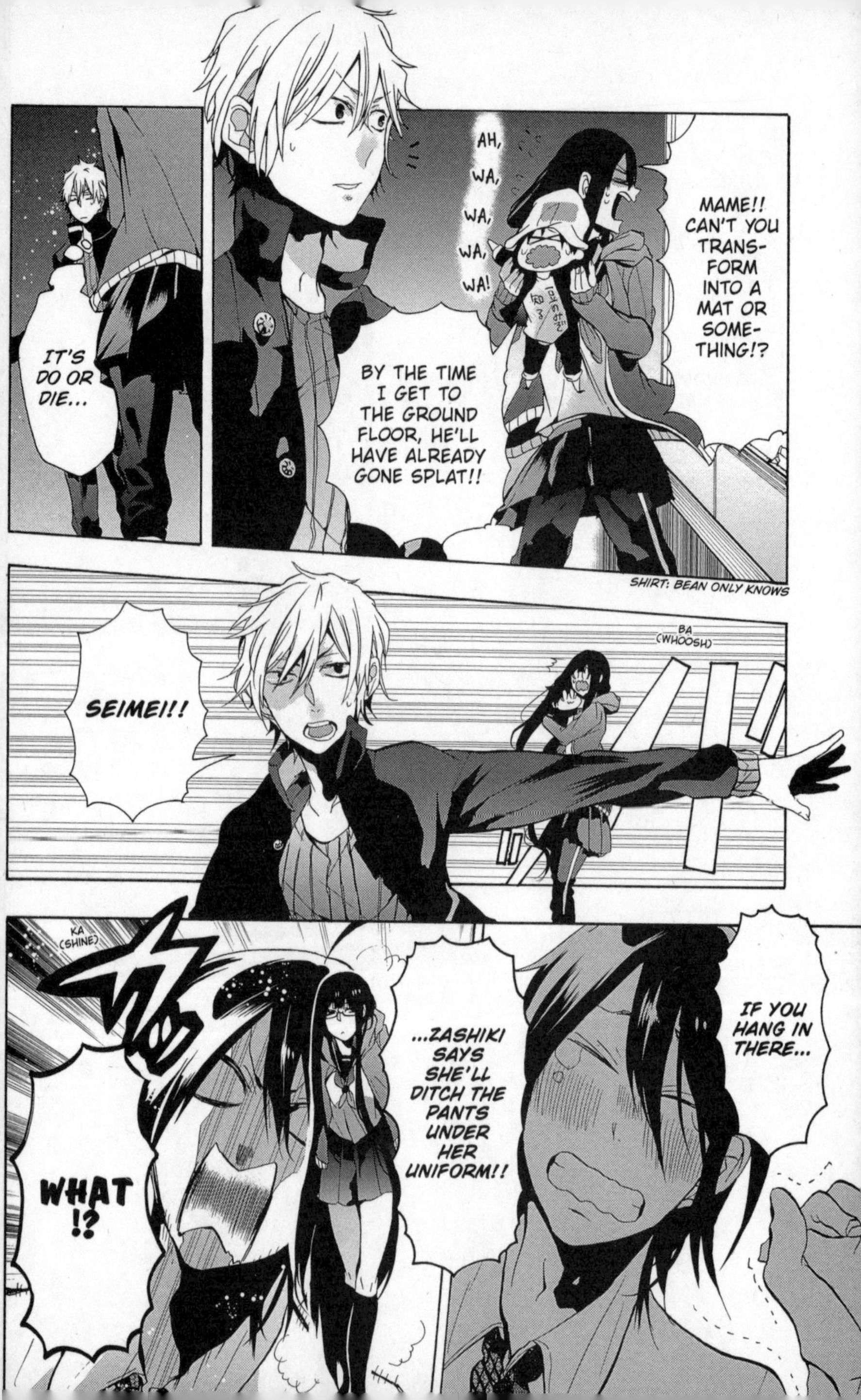
AH, WA, WA, WA, WA!
MAME!! CAN'T YOU TRANSFORM INTO A MAT OR SOMETHING!?
BY THE TIME I GET TO THE GROUND FLOOR, HE'LL HAVE ALREADY GONE SPLAT!!
SHIRT: BEAN ONLY KNOWS
IT'S DO OR DIE...
BA (WHOOSH)
SEIMEI!!
IF YOU HANG IN THERE...
...ZASHIKI SAYS SHE'LL DITCH THE PANTS UNDER HER UNIFORM!!
KA (SHINE)
WHAT!?

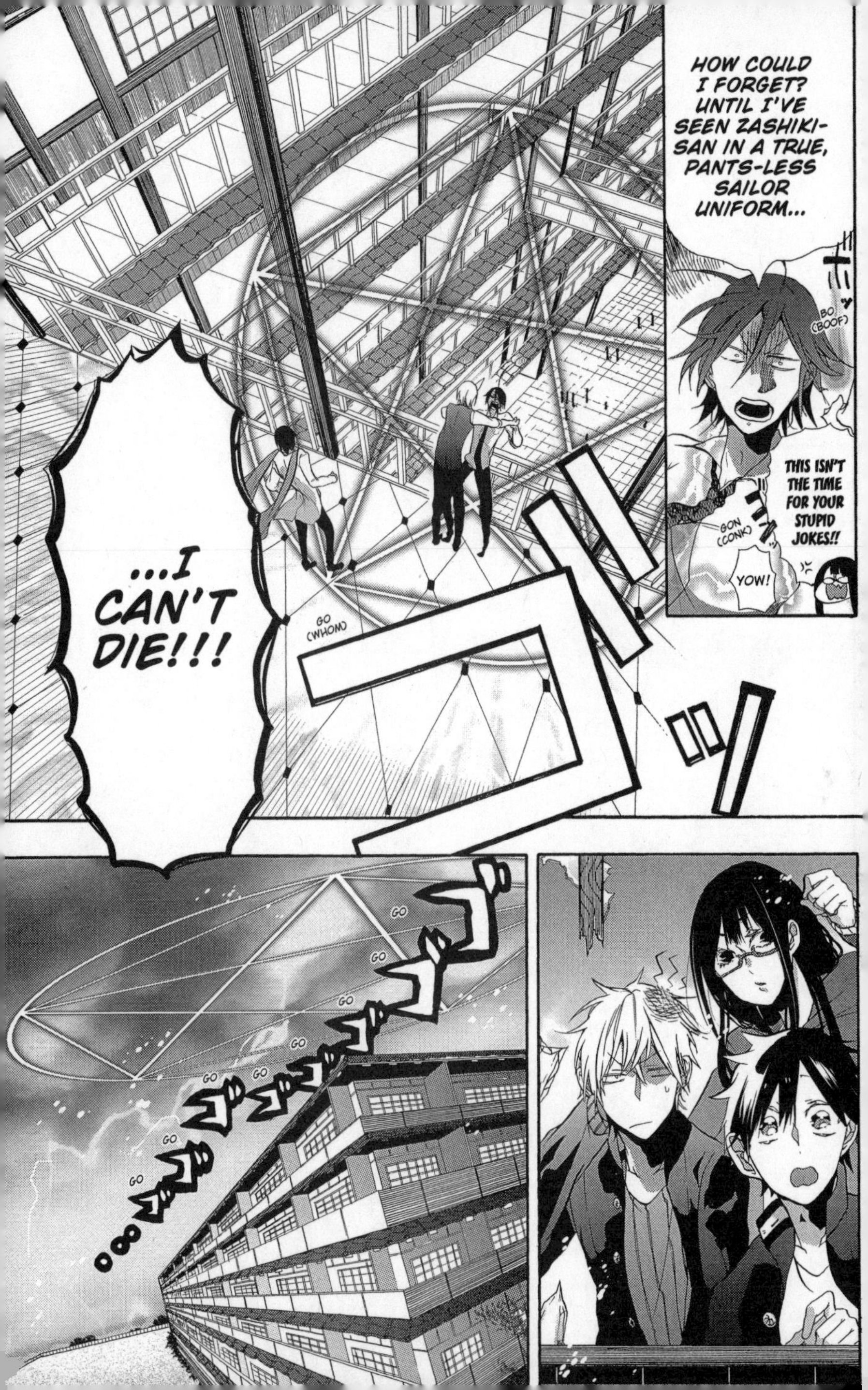
HOW COULD I FORGET? UNTIL I'VE SEEN ZASHIKI-SAN IN A TRUE, PANTS-LESS SAILOR UNIFORM...
BO (BOOF)
THIS ISN'T THE TIME FOR YOUR STUPID JOKES!!
GON (CONK)
YOW!
...I CAN'T DIE!!!
GO (WHOMP)
GO
GO
GO
GO
GO
GO
GO
GO

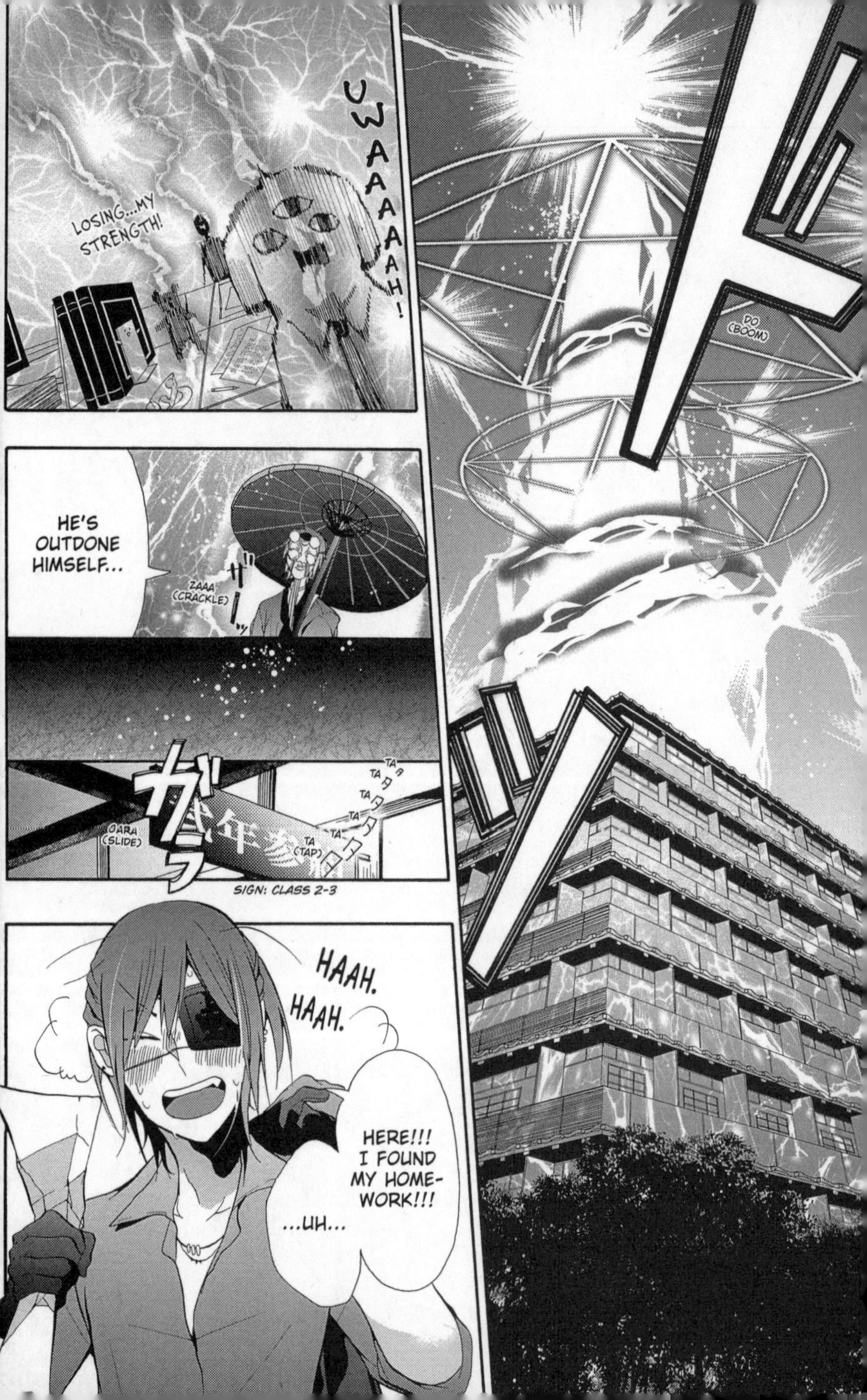
DO (BOOM)
UWAAAAAAH!
LOSING...MY STRENGTH!
HE'S OUTDONE HIMSELF...
ZAAA (CRACKLE)
TA TA TA TA TA TA (TAP)
GARA (SLIDE)
SIGN: CLASS 2-3
HAAH. HAAH.
HERE!!! I FOUND MY HOME-WORK!!!
...UH...

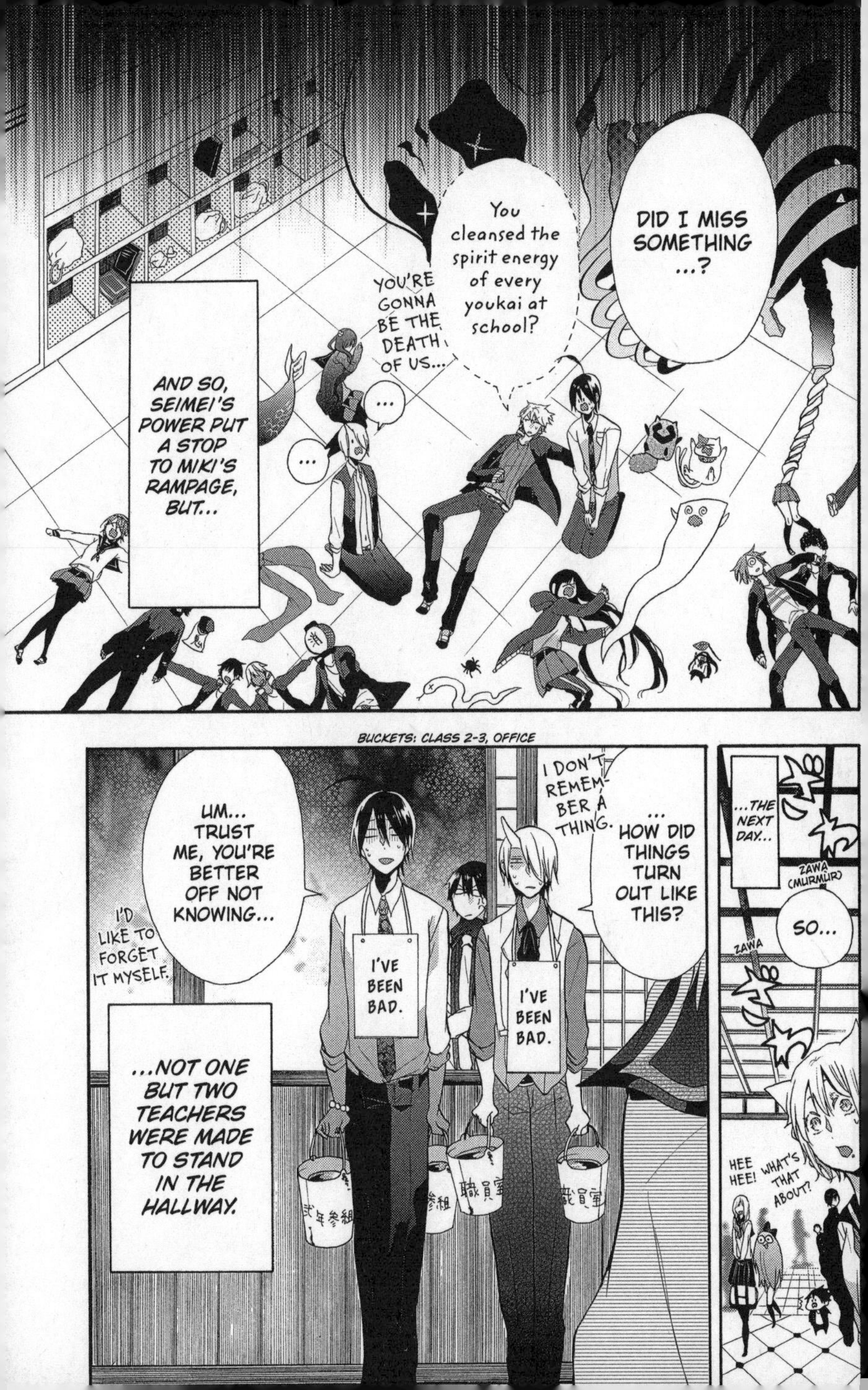

DID I MISS SOMETHING ...?
You cleansed the spirit energy of every youkai at school?
YOU'RE GONNA BE THE DEATH OF US...
...
...
AND SO, SEIMEI'S POWER PUT A STOP TO MIKI'S RAMPAGE, BUT...
BUCKETS: CLASS 2-3, OFFICE
...THE NEXT DAY...
ZAWA (MURMUR)
SO...
ZAWA
WHAT'S THAT ABOUT?
HEE HEE!
I DON'T REMEMBER A THING.
... HOW DID THINGS TURN OUT LIKE THIS?
UM... TRUST ME, YOU'RE BETTER OFF NOT KNOWING...
I'D LIKE TO FORGET IT MYSELF.
I'VE BEEN BAD.
I'VE BEEN BAD.
...NOT ONE BUT TWO TEACHERS WERE MADE TO STAND IN THE HALLWAY.

A TERRiFieD Teacher
at GHOUL School!

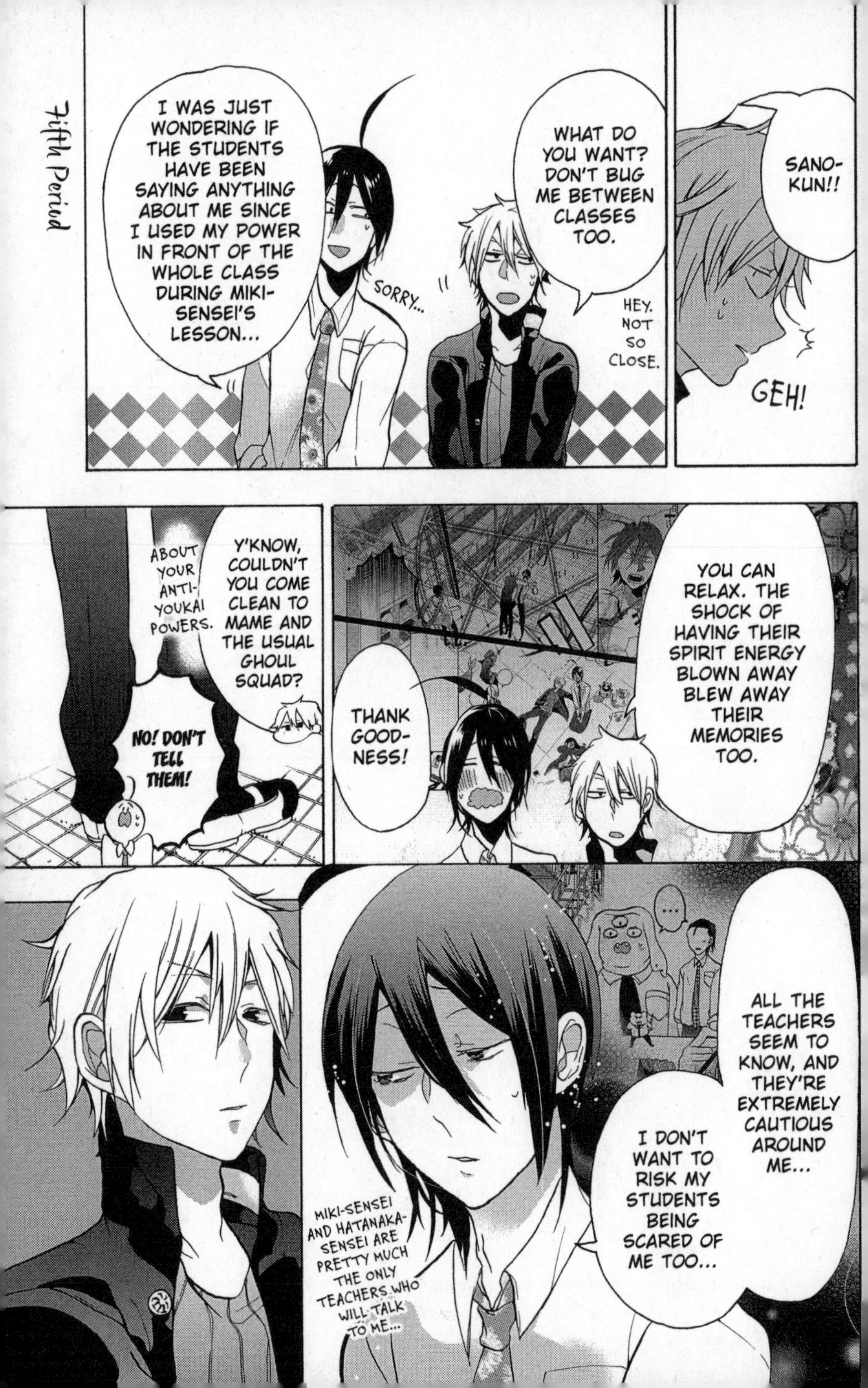
SANO-KUN!!
GEH!
WHAT DO YOU WANT? DON'T BUG ME BETWEEN CLASSES TOO.
I WAS JUST WONDERING IF THE STUDENTS HAVE BEEN SAYING ANYTHING ABOUT ME SINCE I USED MY POWER IN FRONT OF THE WHOLE CLASS DURING MIKI-SENSEI'S LESSON...
HEY. NOT SO CLOSE.
SORRY...
YOU CAN RELAX. THE SHOCK OF HAVING THEIR SPIRIT ENERGY BLOWN AWAY BLEW AWAY THEIR MEMORIES TOO.
THANK GOODNESS!
Y'KNOW, COULDN'T YOU COME CLEAN TO MAME AND THE USUAL GHOUL SQUAD?
ABOUT YOUR ANTI-YOUKAI POWERS.
NO! DON'T TELL THEM!
...
ALL THE TEACHERS SEEM TO KNOW, AND THEY'RE EXTREMELY CAUTIOUS AROUND ME...
I DON'T WANT TO RISK MY STUDENTS BEING SCARED OF ME TOO...
MIKI-SENSEI AND HATANAKA-SENSEI ARE PRETTY MUCH THE ONLY TEACHERS WHO WILL TALK TO ME...

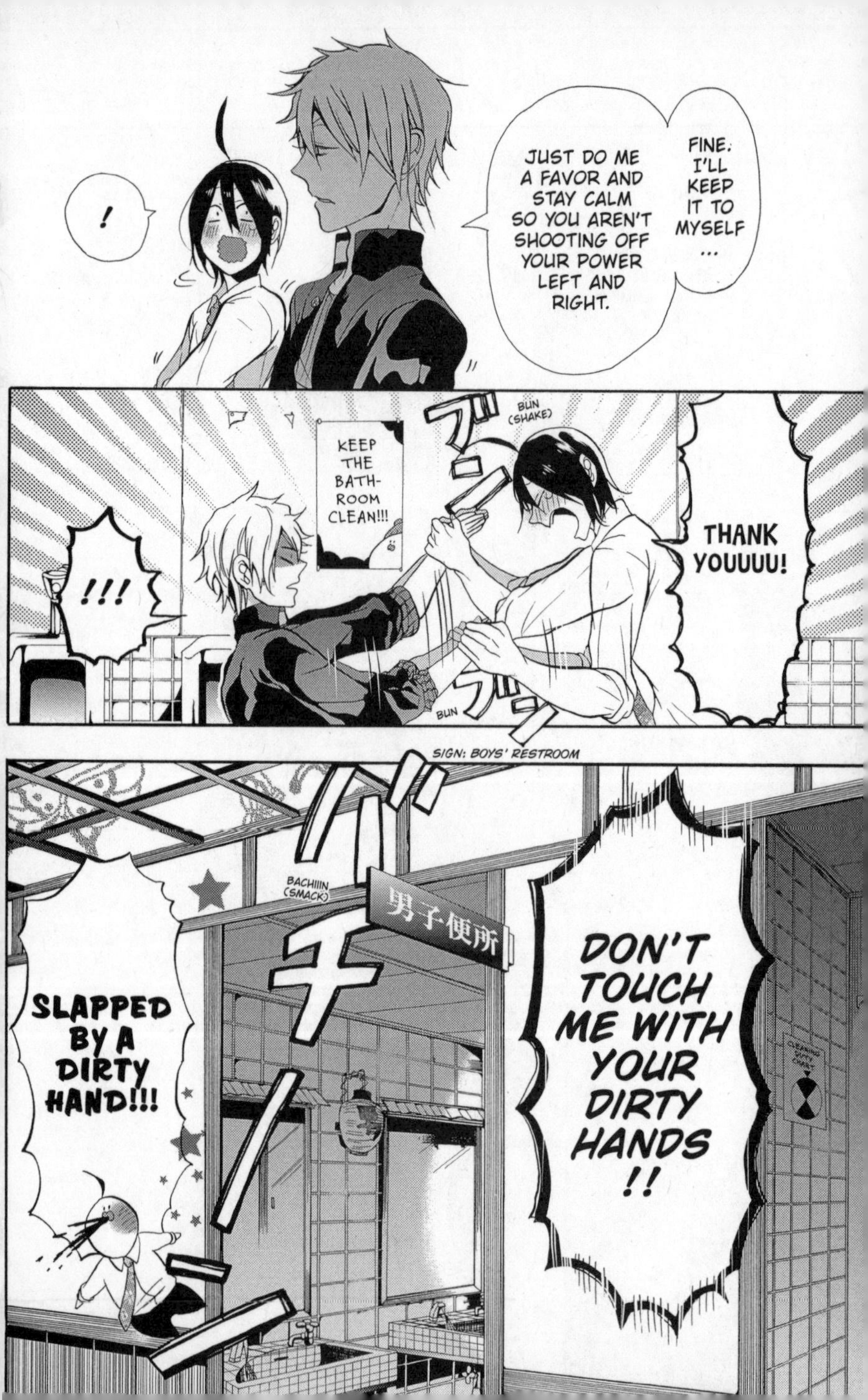
FINE. I'LL KEEP IT TO MYSELF...
JUST DO ME A FAVOR AND STAY CALM SO YOU AREN'T SHOOTING OFF YOUR POWER LEFT AND RIGHT.
!
THANK YOUUUU!
BUN (SHAKE)
KEEP THE BATH-ROOM CLEAN!!!
BUN
!!!
SIGN: BOYS' RESTROOM
DON'T TOUCH ME WITH YOUR DIRTY HANDS!!
男子便所
BACHIIIN (SMACK)
SLAPPED BY A DIRTY HAND!!!

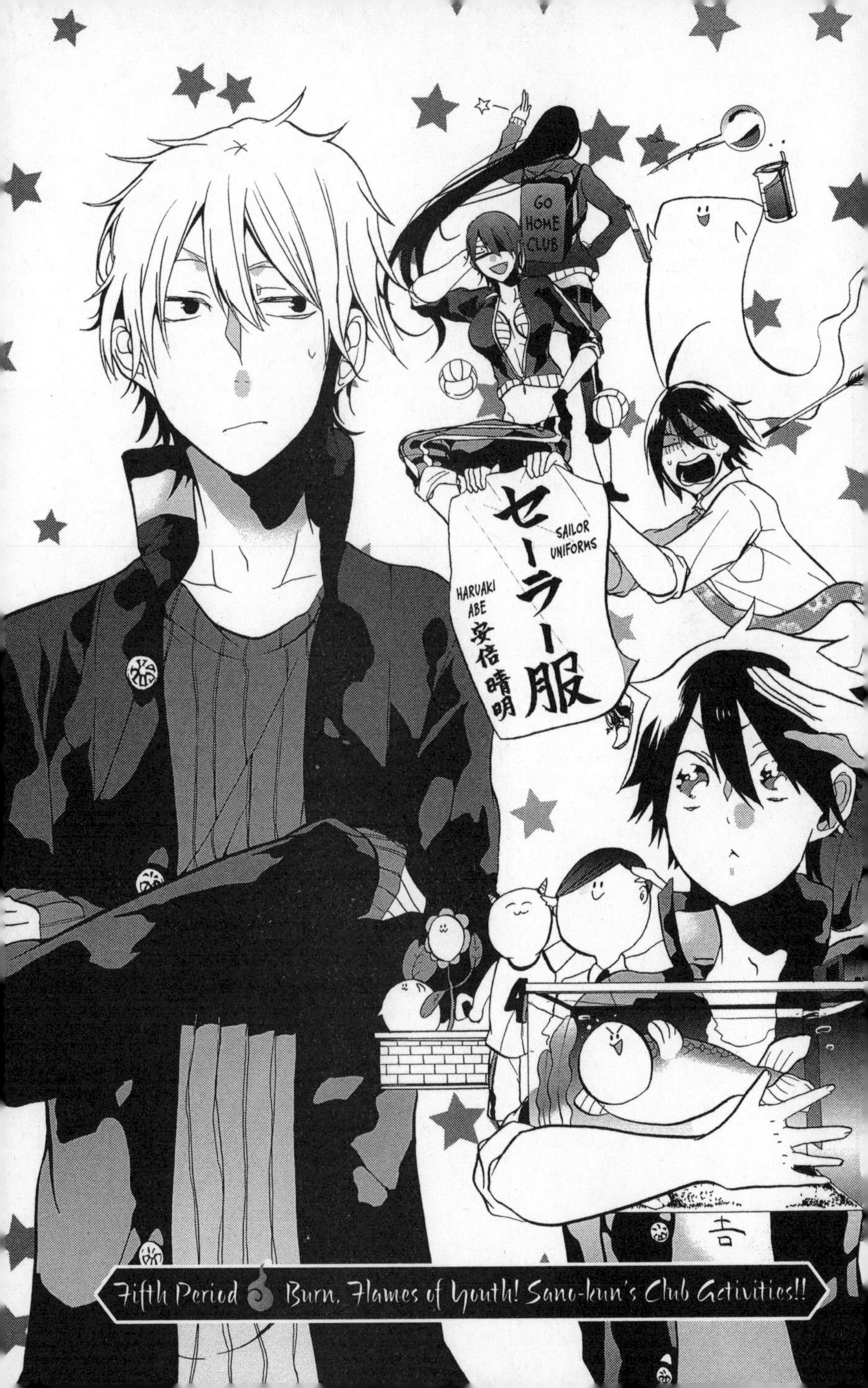
GO HOME CLUB
セーラー服
SAILOR UNIFORMS
HARUAKI ABE
安倍晴明
吉
Fifth Period Burn, Flames of Youth! Sano-kun's Club Activities!!

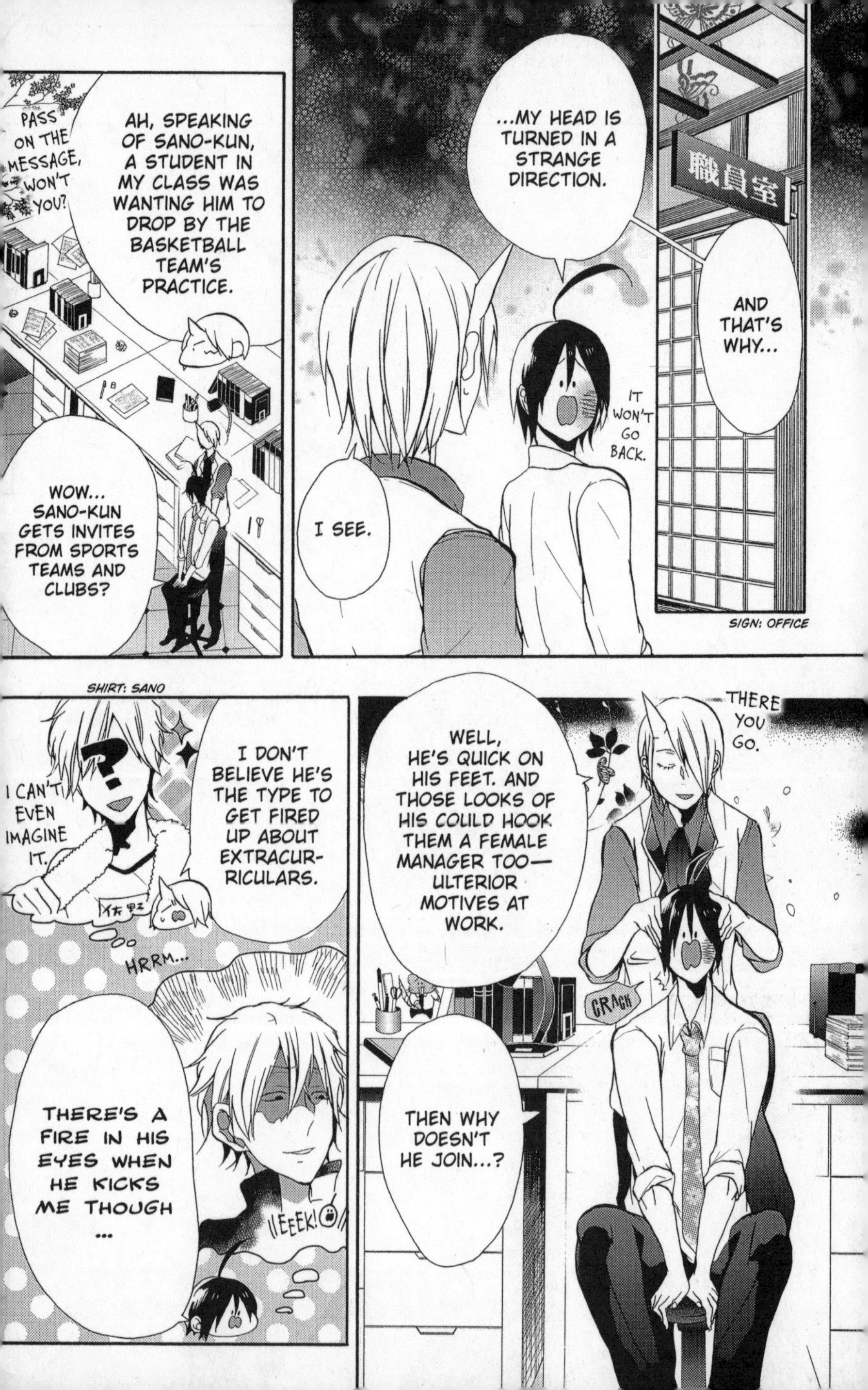
職員室
AND THAT'S WHY...
...MY HEAD IS TURNED IN A STRANGE DIRECTION.
IT WON'T GO BACK.
I SEE.
SIGN: OFFICE
AH, SPEAKING OF SANO-KUN, A STUDENT IN MY CLASS WAS WANTING HIM TO DROP BY THE BASKETBALL TEAM'S PRACTICE.
PASS ON THE MESSAGE, WON'T YOU?
WOW... SANO-KUN GETS INVITES FROM SPORTS TEAMS AND CLUBS?
THERE YOU GO.
WELL, HE'S QUICK ON HIS FEET. AND THOSE LOOKS OF HIS COULD HOOK THEM A FEMALE MANAGER TOO—ULTERIOR MOTIVES AT WORK.
CRACK
THEN WHY DOESN'T HE JOIN...?
SHIRT: SANO
I DON'T BELIEVE HE'S THE TYPE TO GET FIRED UP ABOUT EXTRACUR-RICULARS.
I CAN'T EVEN IMAGINE IT.
佐野
HRRM...
THERE'S A FIRE IN HIS EYES WHEN HE KICKS ME THOUGH ...
EEEK!

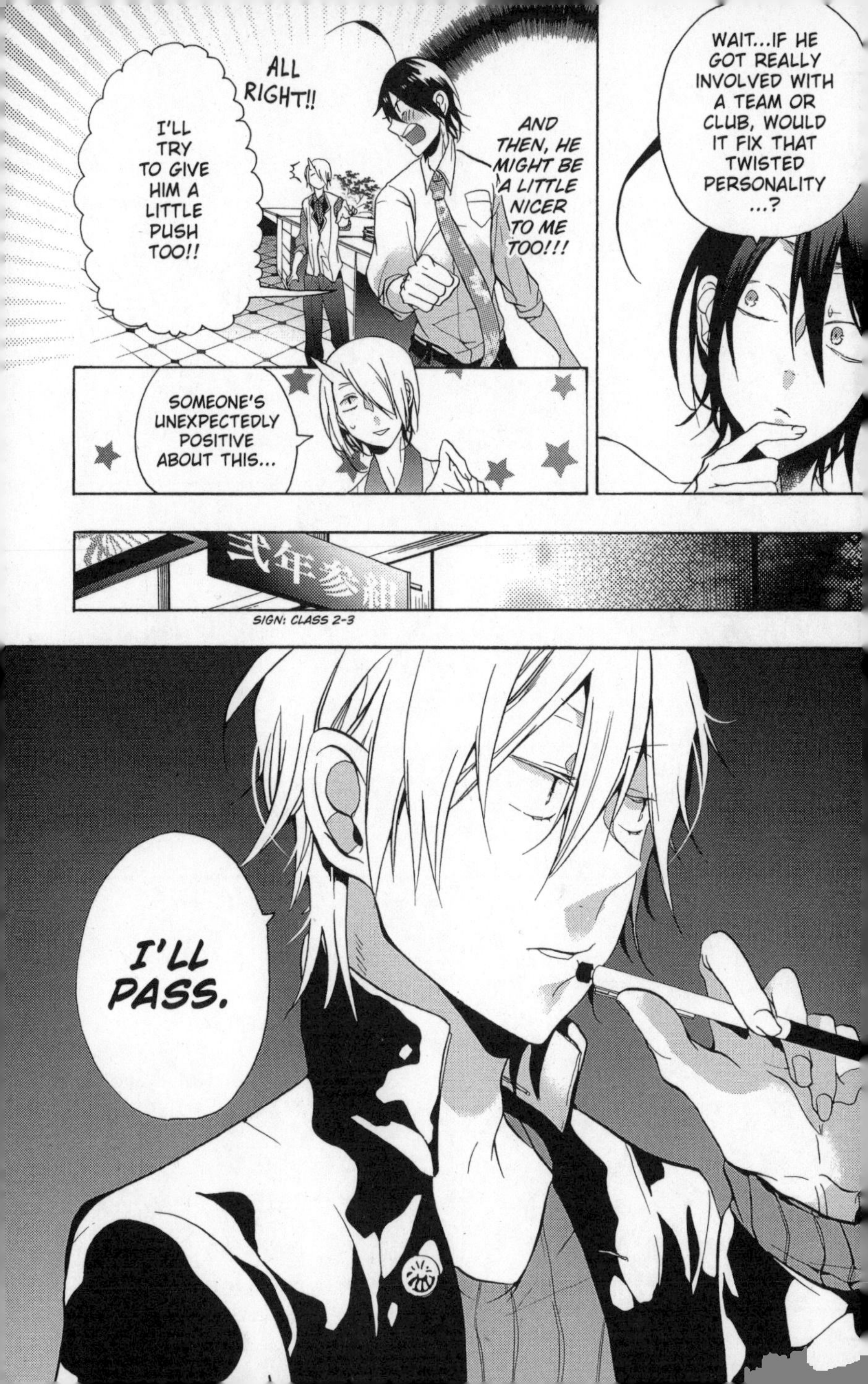
WAIT...IF HE GOT REALLY INVOLVED WITH A TEAM OR CLUB, WOULD IT FIX THAT TWISTED PERSONALITY ...?
ALL RIGHT!!
I'LL TRY TO GIVE HIM A LITTLE PUSH TOO!!
AND THEN, HE MIGHT BE A LITTLE NICER TO ME TOO!!!
SOMEONE'S UNEXPECTEDLY POSITIVE ABOUT THIS...
SIGN: CLASS 2-3
I'LL PASS.

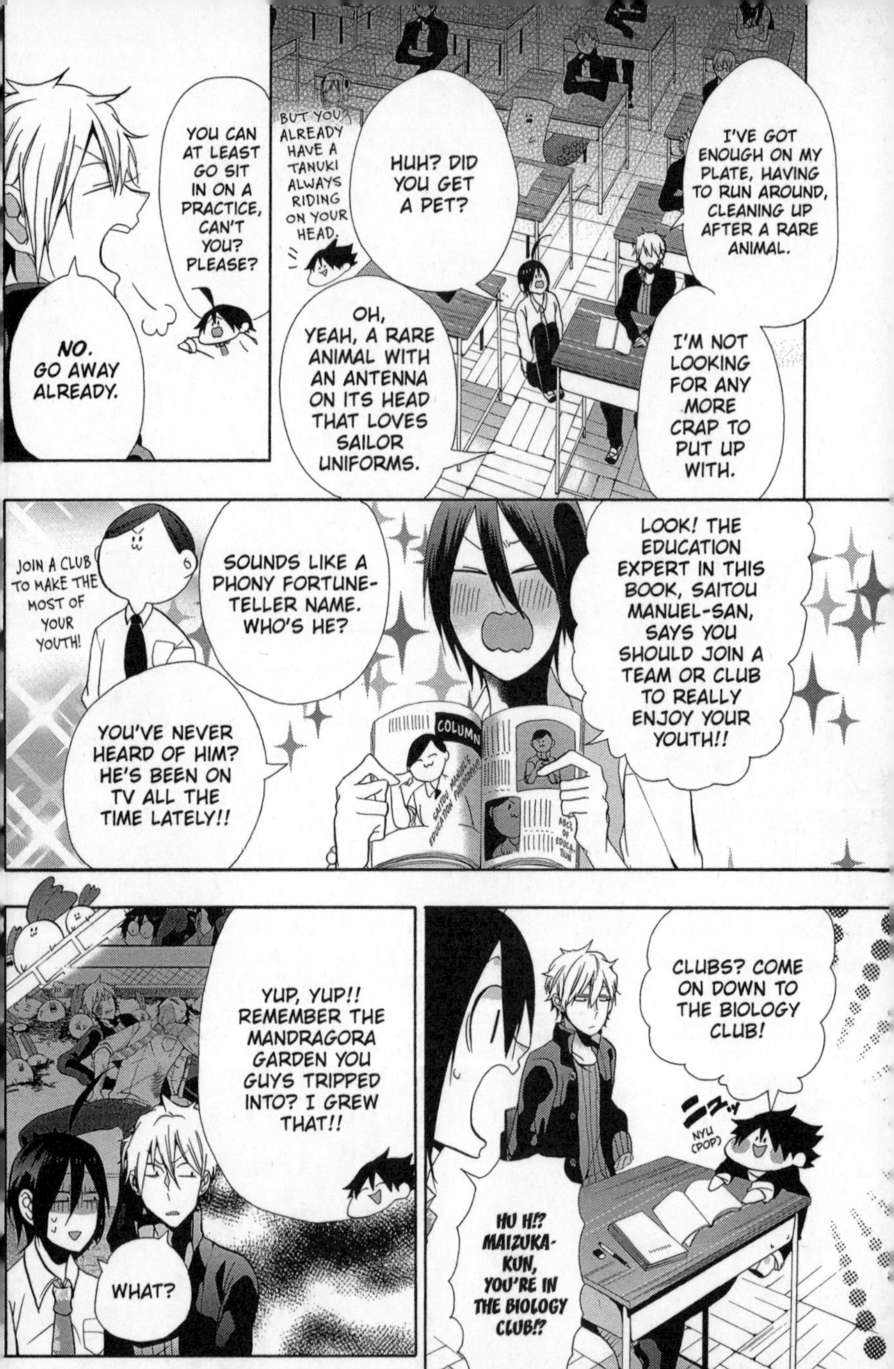

I'VE GOT ENOUGH ON MY PLATE, HAVING TO RUN AROUND, CLEANING UP AFTER A RARE ANIMAL.
HUH? DID YOU GET A PET?
BUT YOU ALREADY HAVE A TANUKI ALWAYS RIDING ON YOUR HEAD.
OH, YEAH, A RARE ANIMAL WITH AN ANTENNA ON ITS HEAD THAT LOVES SAILOR UNIFORMS.
I'M NOT LOOKING FOR ANY MORE CRAP TO PUT UP WITH.
YOU CAN AT LEAST GO SIT IN ON A PRACTICE, CAN'T YOU? PLEASE?
NO. GO AWAY ALREADY.
LOOK! THE EDUCATION EXPERT IN THIS BOOK, SAITOU MANUEL-SAN, SAYS YOU SHOULD JOIN A TEAM OR CLUB TO REALLY ENJOY YOUR YOUTH!!
COLUMN
SOUNDS LIKE A PHONY FORTUNE-TELLER NAME. WHO'S HE?
JOIN A CLUB TO MAKE THE MOST OF YOUR YOUTH!
YOU'VE NEVER HEARD OF HIM? HE'S BEEN ON TV ALL THE TIME LATELY!!
CLUBS? COME ON DOWN TO THE BIOLOGY CLUB!
NYU (POP)
HU H!? MAIZUKA-KUN, YOU'RE IN THE BIOLOGY CLUB!?
YUP, YUP!! REMEMBER THE MANDRAGORA GARDEN YOU GUYS TRIPPED INTO? I GREW THAT!!
WHAT?

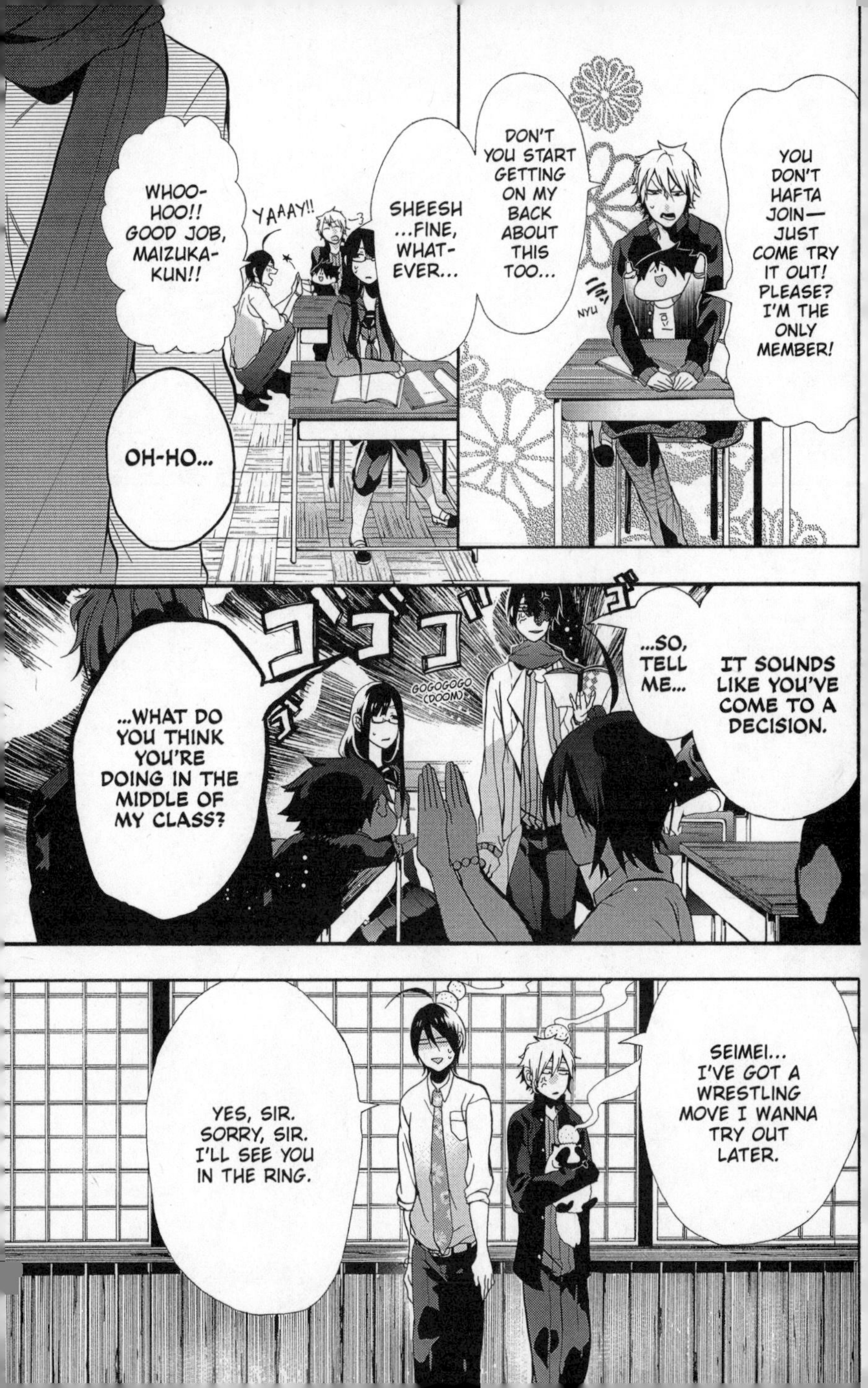
YOU DON'T HAFTA JOIN—JUST COME TRY IT OUT! PLEASE? I'M THE ONLY MEMBER!
DON'T YOU START GETTING ON MY BACK ABOUT THIS TOO...
NYU
SHEESH ...FINE, WHAT-EVER...
YAAAY!!
WHOO-HOO!! GOOD JOB, MAIZUKA-KUN!!
OH-HO...
IT SOUNDS LIKE YOU'VE COME TO A DECISION.
...SO, TELL ME...
GOGOGOGO (DOOM)
...WHAT DO YOU THINK YOU'RE DOING IN THE MIDDLE OF MY CLASS?
SEIMEI... I'VE GOT A WRESTLING MOVE I WANNA TRY OUT LATER.
YES, SIR. SORRY, SIR. I'LL SEE YOU IN THE RING.

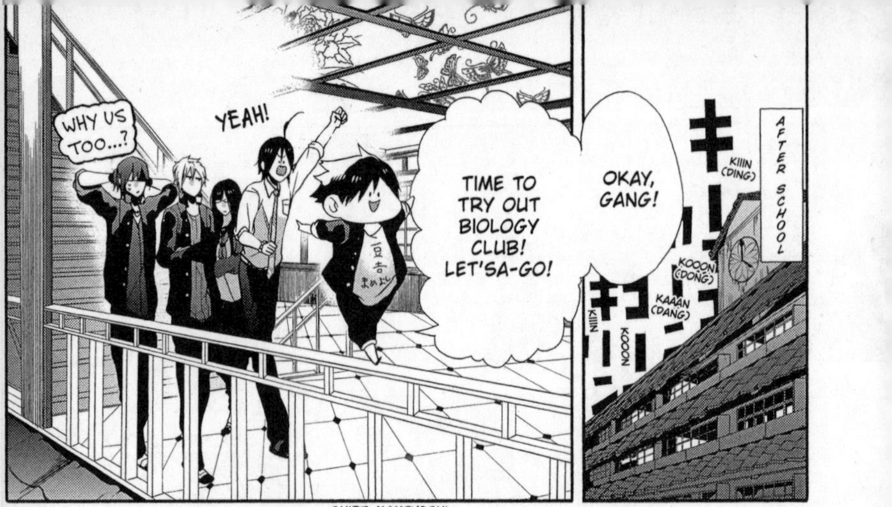
AFTER SCHOOL
KIIIN (DING)
KOOON (DONG)
KAAAN (DANG)
KIIIN
KOOON
OKAY, GANG!
TIME TO TRY OUT BIOLOGY CLUB! LET'SA-GO!
YEAH!
WHY US TOO...?

SHIRT: MAMEYOSHI

CALLIGRAPHY: SAILOR UNIFORMS, HARUAKI ABE

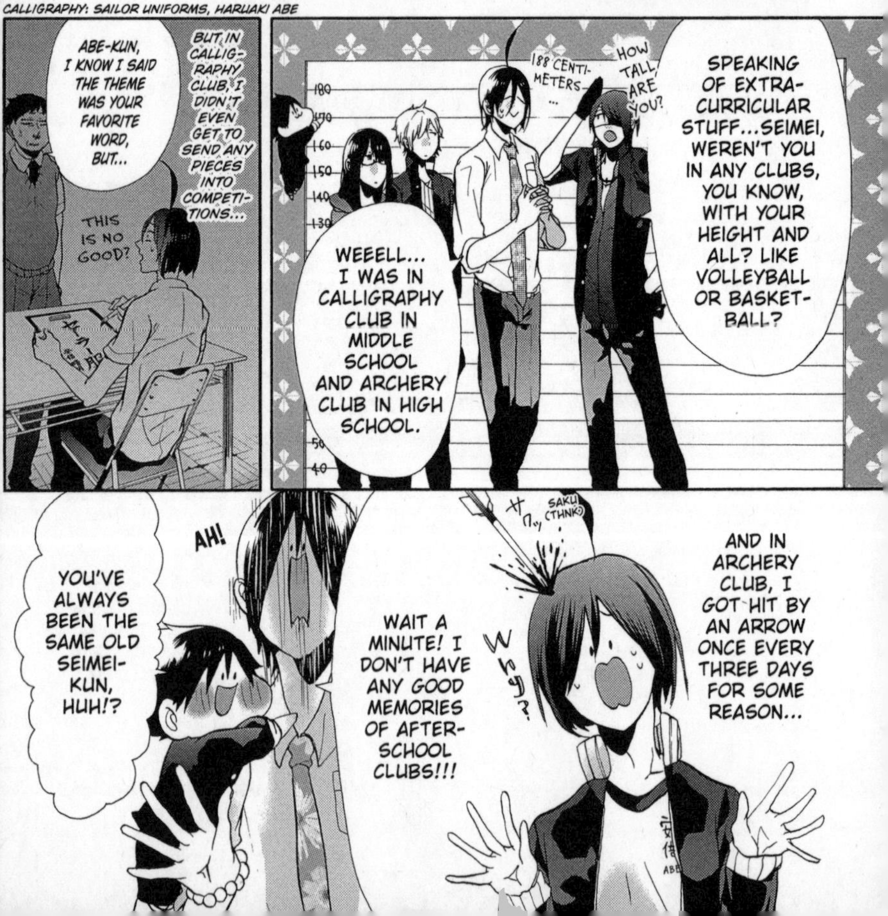
SPEAKING OF EXTRA-CURRICULAR STUFF...SEIMEI, WEREN'T YOU IN ANY CLUBS, YOU KNOW, WITH YOUR HEIGHT AND ALL? LIKE VOLLEYBALL OR BASKET-BALL?
HOW TALL ARE YOU?
188 CENTI-METERS-...
180
170
160
150
140
130
50
40
WEEELL... I WAS IN CALLIGRAPHY CLUB IN MIDDLE SCHOOL AND ARCHERY CLUB IN HIGH SCHOOL.
BUT IN CALLIG-RAPHY CLUB, I DIDN'T EVEN GET TO SEND ANY PIECES INTO COMPETI-TIONS...
ABE-KUN, I KNOW I SAID THE THEME WAS YOUR FAVORITE WORD, BUT...
THIS IS NO GOOD?
AND IN ARCHERY CLUB, I GOT HIT BY AN ARROW ONCE EVERY THREE DAYS FOR SOME REASON...
SAKU (THNK)
ABE
WAIT A MINUTE! I DON'T HAVE ANY GOOD MEMORIES OF AFTER-SCHOOL CLUBS!!!
AH!
YOU'VE ALWAYS BEEN THE SAME OLD SEIMEI-KUN, HUH!?

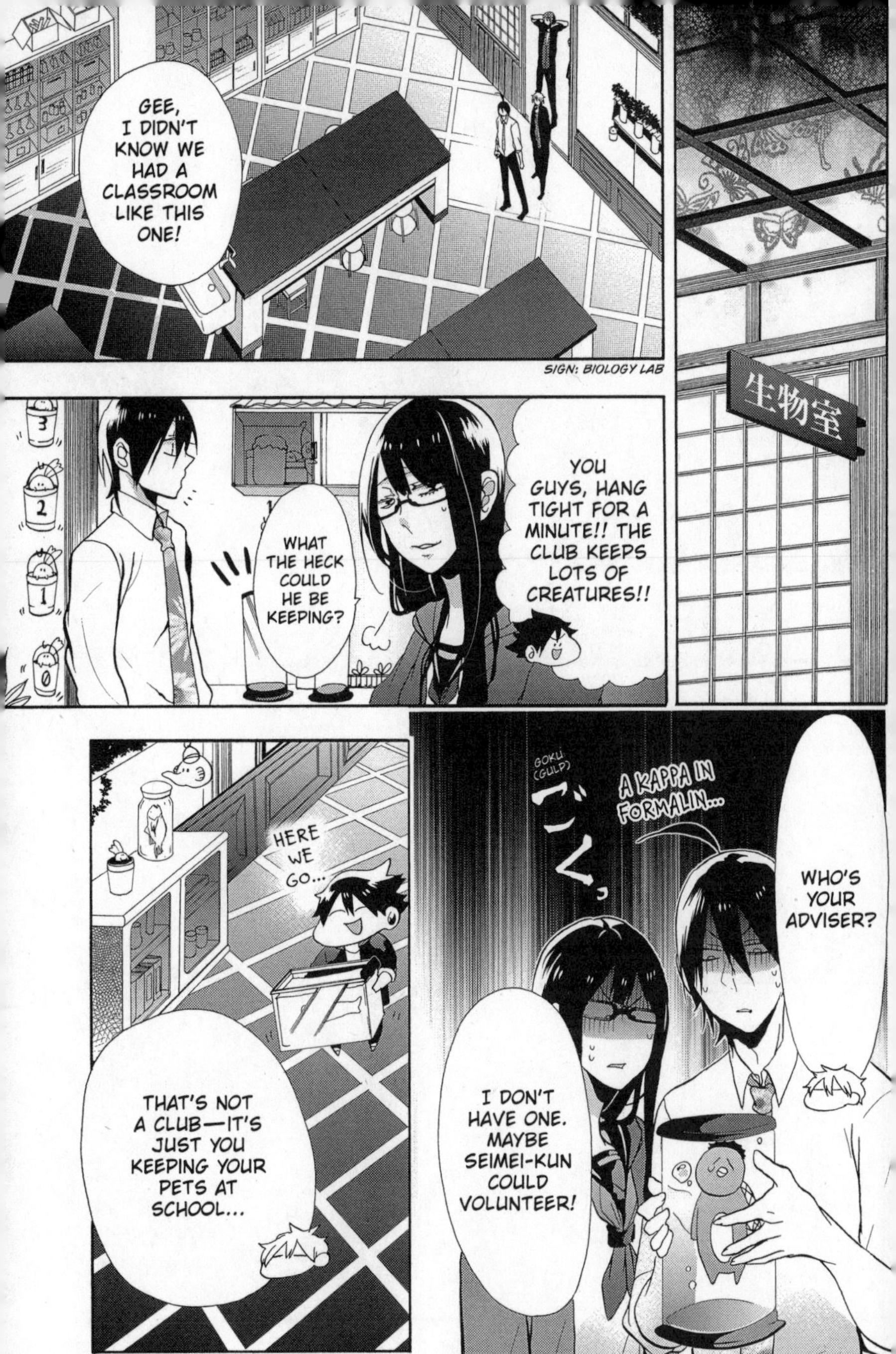
生物室
SIGN: BIOLOGY LAB
GEE, I DIDN'T KNOW WE HAD A CLASSROOM LIKE THIS ONE!
YOU GUYS, HANG TIGHT FOR A MINUTE!! THE CLUB KEEPS LOTS OF CREATURES!!
WHAT THE HECK COULD HE BE KEEPING?
GOKU (GULP)
A KAPPA IN FORMALIN...
WHO'S YOUR ADVISER?
I DON'T HAVE ONE. MAYBE SEIMEI-KUN COULD VOLUNTEER!
HERE WE GO...
THAT'S NOT A CLUB—IT'S JUST YOU KEEPING YOUR PETS AT SCHOOL...

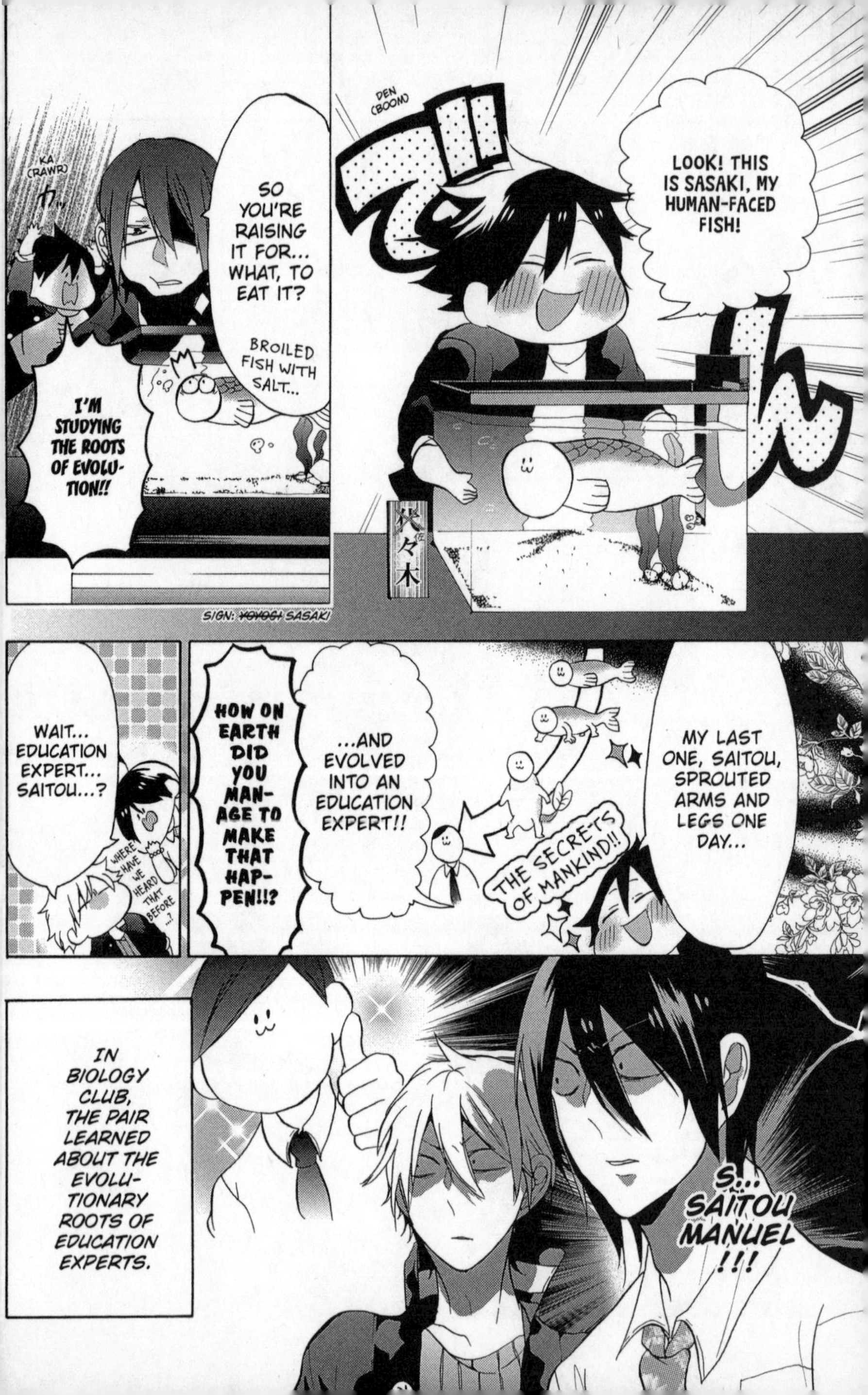
DEN (BOOM)
LOOK! THIS IS SASAKI, MY HUMAN-FACED FISH!
KA (RAWR)
SO YOU'RE RAISING IT FOR... WHAT, TO EAT IT?
BROILED FISH WITH SALT...
I'M STUDYING THE ROOTS OF EVOLUTION!!
SIGN: ~~YOYOGI~~ SASAKI
MY LAST ONE, SAITOU, SPROUTED ARMS AND LEGS ONE DAY...
THE SECRETS OF MANKIND!!
...AND EVOLVED INTO AN EDUCATION EXPERT!!
HOW ON EARTH DID YOU MANAGE TO MAKE THAT HAPPEN!!?
WAIT... EDUCATION EXPERT... SAITOU...?
WHERE HAVE WE HEARD THAT BEFORE...?
S... SAITOU MANUEL!!!
IN BIOLOGY CLUB, THE PAIR LEARNED ABOUT THE EVOLUTIONARY ROOTS OF EDUCATION EXPERTS.

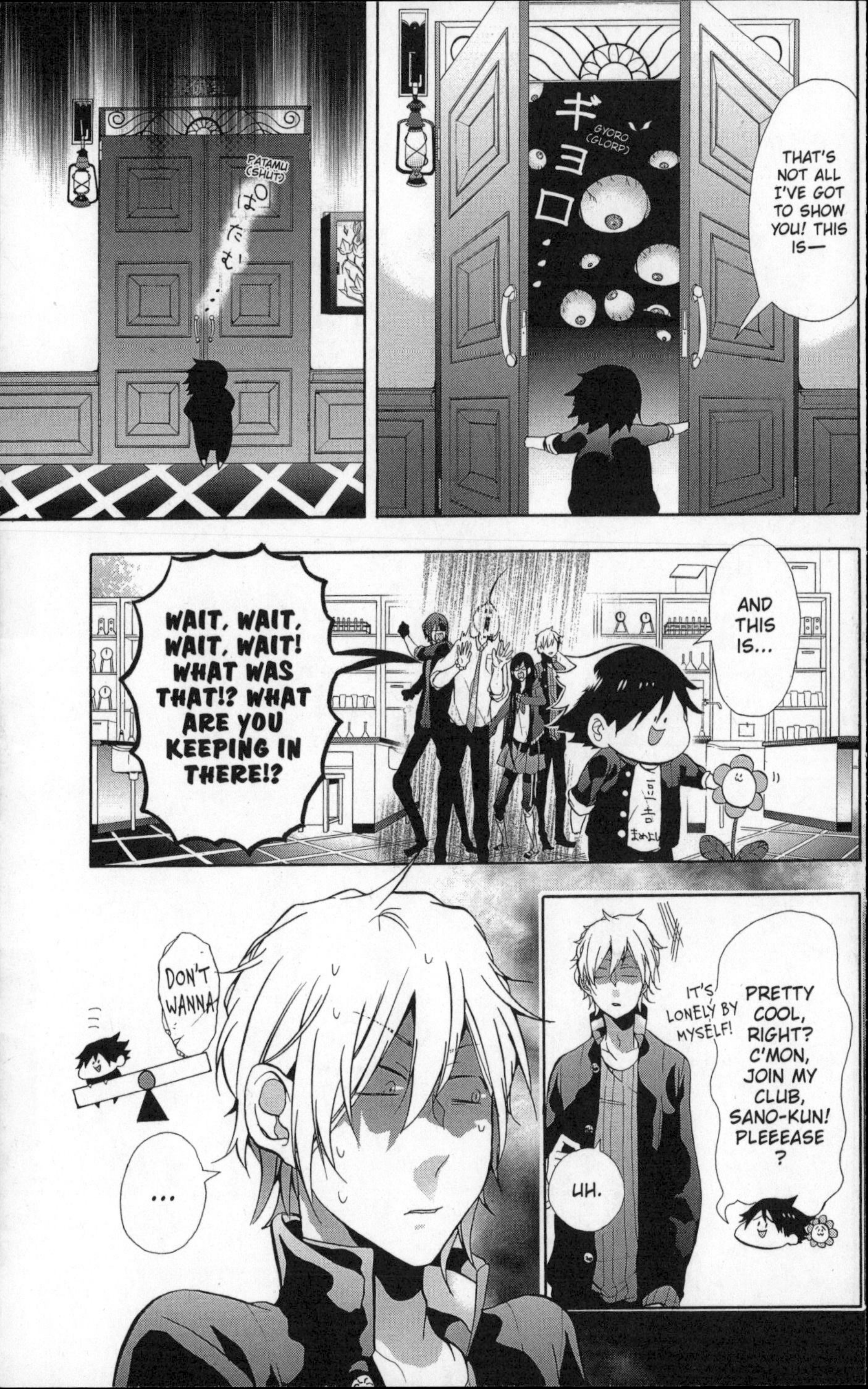
THAT'S NOT ALL I'VE GOT TO SHOW YOU! THIS IS—
ギョロ
GYORO (GLORP)
ぱたむ!…
PATAMU (SHUT)
AND THIS IS...
WAIT, WAIT, WAIT, WAIT! WHAT WAS THAT!? WHAT ARE YOU KEEPING IN THERE!?
PRETTY COOL, RIGHT? C'MON, JOIN MY CLUB, SANO-KUN! PLEEEASE?
IT'S LONELY BY MYSELF!
UH.
DON'T WANNA
...

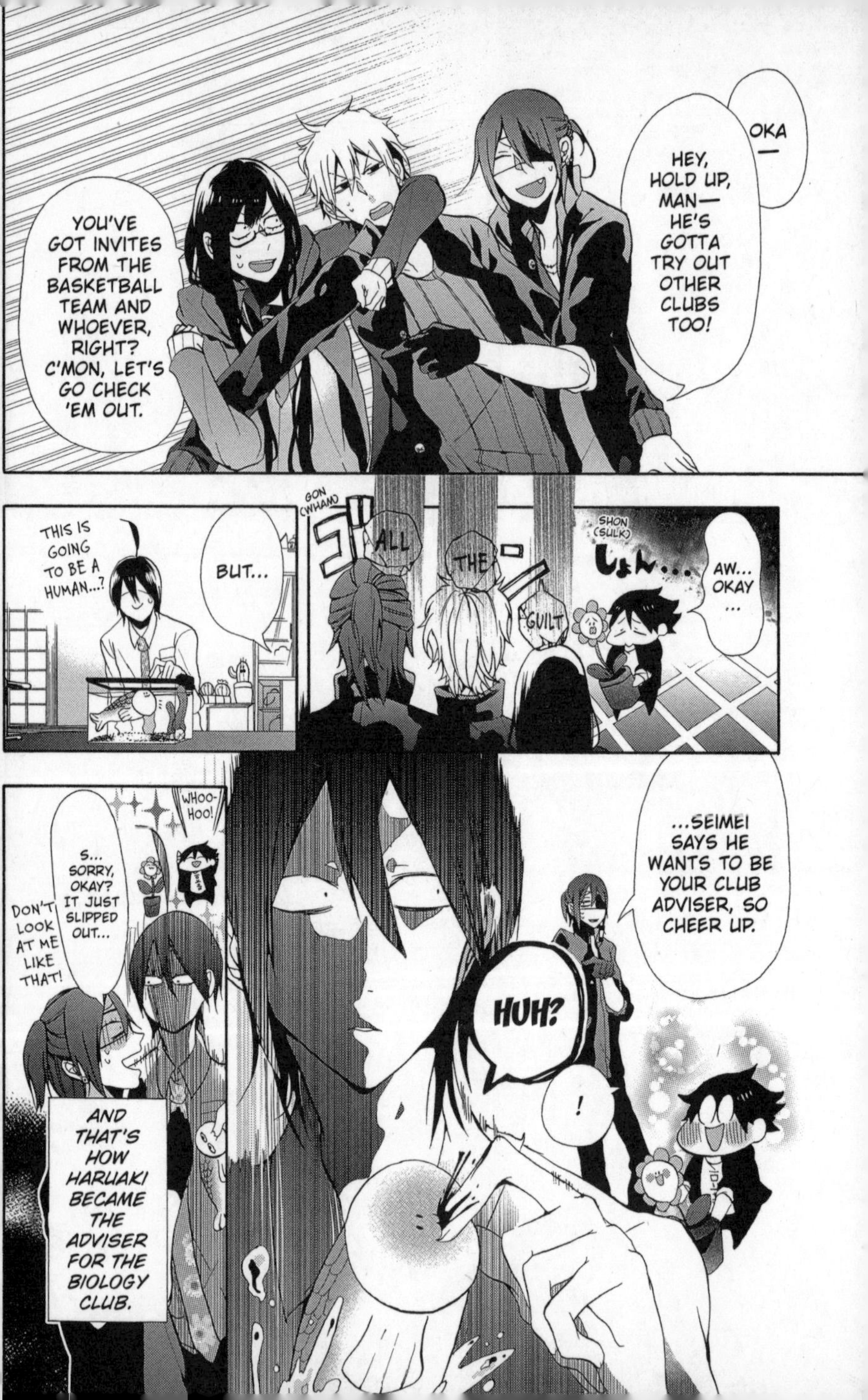
OKA—
HEY, HOLD UP, MAN—HE'S GOTTA TRY OUT OTHER CLUBS TOO!
YOU'VE GOT INVITES FROM THE BASKETBALL TEAM AND WHOEVER, RIGHT? C'MON, LET'S GO CHECK 'EM OUT.
SHON (SULK)
しょん…
AW... OKAY ...
GON (WHAM)
ALL THE GUILT
BUT...
THIS IS GOING TO BE A HUMAN...?
...SEIMEI SAYS HE WANTS TO BE YOUR CLUB ADVISER, SO CHEER UP.
HUH?
!
WHOO-HOO!
S... SORRY, OKAY? IT JUST SLIPPED OUT...
DON'T LOOK AT ME LIKE THAT!
AND THAT'S HOW HARUAKI BECAME THE ADVISER FOR THE BIOLOGY CLUB.

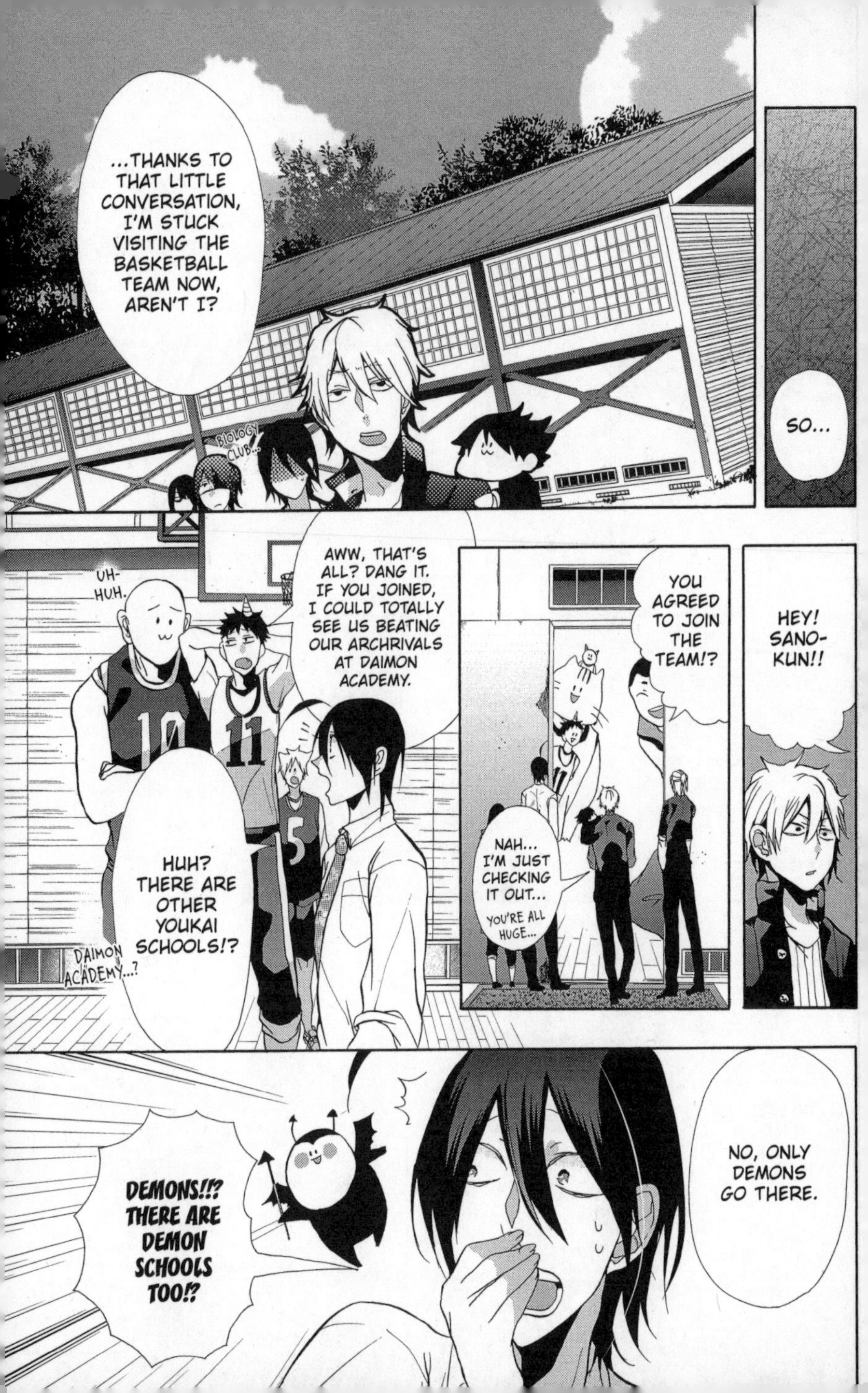
SO...
...THANKS TO THAT LITTLE CONVERSATION, I'M STUCK VISITING THE BASKETBALL TEAM NOW, AREN'T I?
BIOLOGY CLUB...
HEY! SANO-KUN!!
YOU AGREED TO JOIN THE TEAM!?
NAH... I'M JUST CHECKING IT OUT...
YOU'RE ALL HUGE...
AWW, THAT'S ALL? DANG IT. IF YOU JOINED, I COULD TOTALLY SEE US BEATING OUR ARCHRIVALS AT DAIMON ACADEMY.
UH-HUH.
HUH? THERE ARE OTHER YOUKAI SCHOOLS!?
DAIMON ACADEMY...?
NO, ONLY DEMONS GO THERE.
DEMONS!!? THERE ARE DEMON SCHOOLS TOO!?

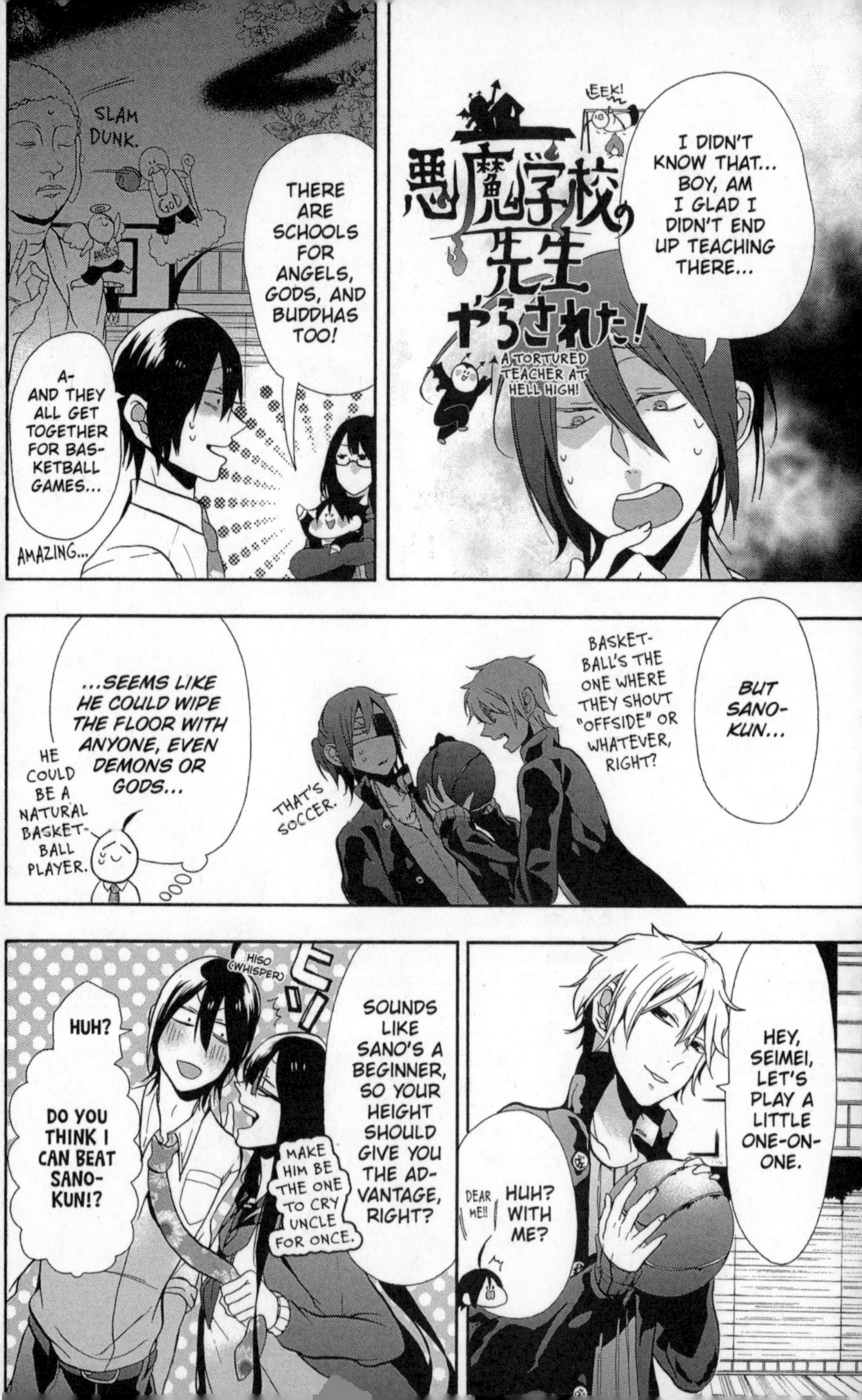
悪魔学校の先生やらされた!
A TORTURED TEACHER AT HELL HIGH!
EEK!
I DIDN'T KNOW THAT... BOY, AM I GLAD I DIDN'T END UP TEACHING THERE...
THERE ARE SCHOOLS FOR ANGELS, GODS, AND BUDDHAS TOO!
SLAM DUNK.
GOD
ANGELS
A- AND THEY ALL GET TOGETHER FOR BASKETBALL GAMES...
AMAZING...
BUT SANO-KUN...
BASKETBALL'S THE ONE WHERE THEY SHOUT "OFFSIDE" OR WHATEVER, RIGHT?
THAT'S SOCCER.
...SEEMS LIKE HE COULD WIPE THE FLOOR WITH ANYONE, EVEN DEMONS OR GODS...
HE COULD BE A NATURAL BASKETBALL PLAYER.
HEY, SEIMEI, LET'S PLAY A LITTLE ONE-ON-ONE.
HUH? WITH ME?
DEAR ME!!
SOUNDS LIKE SANO'S A BEGINNER, SO YOUR HEIGHT SHOULD GIVE YOU THE ADVANTAGE, RIGHT?
HISO (WHISPER)
MAKE HIM BE THE ONE TO CRY UNCLE FOR ONCE.
HUH?
DO YOU THINK I CAN BEAT SANO-KUN!?

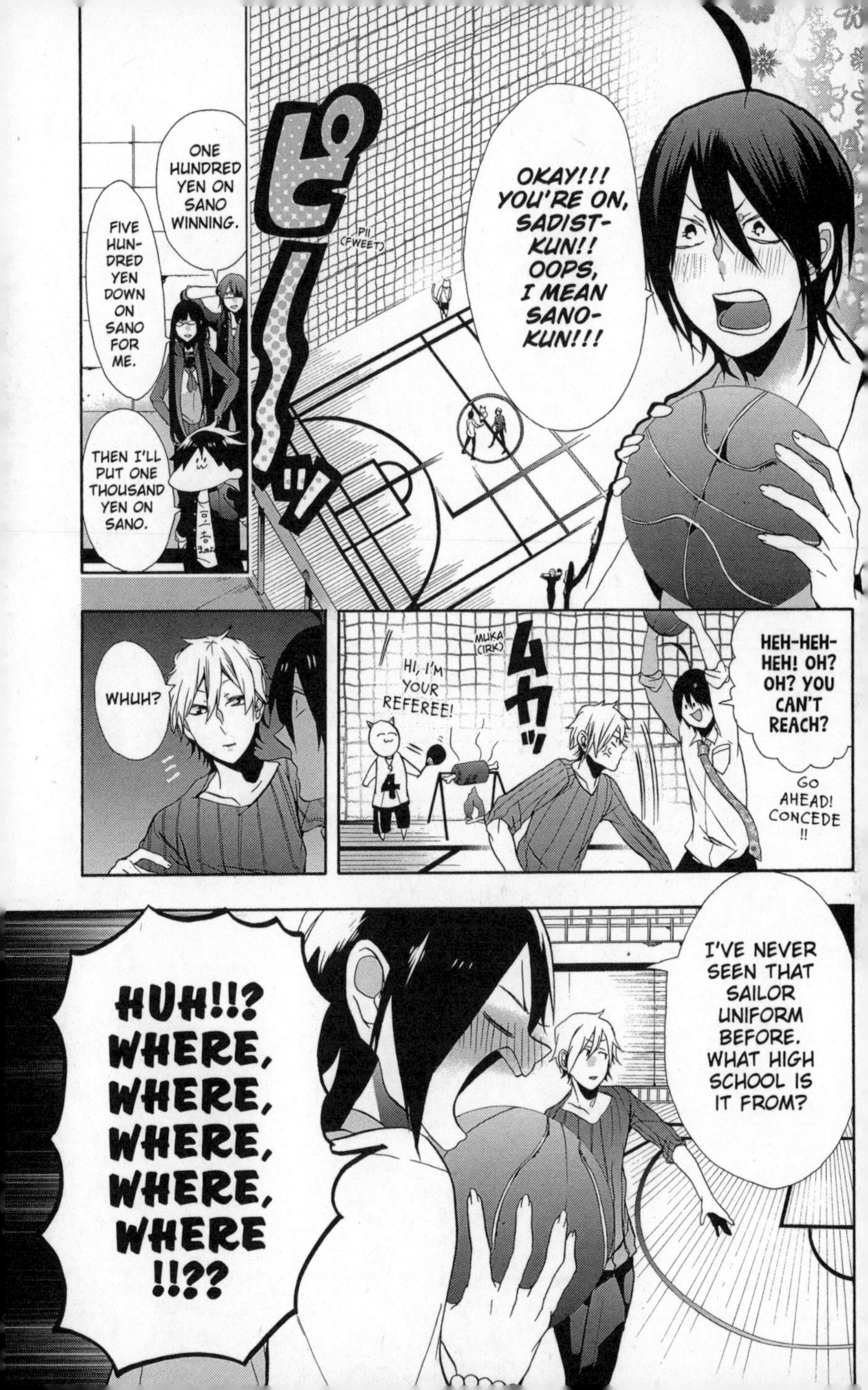
OKAY!!! YOU'RE ON, SADIST-KUN!! OOPS, I MEAN SANO-KUN!!!
PII (FWEET)
ONE HUNDRED YEN ON SANO WINNING.
FIVE HUNDRED YEN DOWN ON SANO FOR ME.
THEN I'LL PUT ONE THOUSAND YEN ON SANO.
HEH-HEH-HEH! OH? OH? YOU CAN'T REACH?
GO AHEAD! CONCEDE !!
MUKA (IRK)
HI, I'M YOUR REFEREE!
WHUH?
I'VE NEVER SEEN THAT SAILOR UNIFORM BEFORE. WHAT HIGH SCHOOL IS IT FROM?
HUH!!? WHERE, WHERE, WHERE, WHERE, WHERE !!??

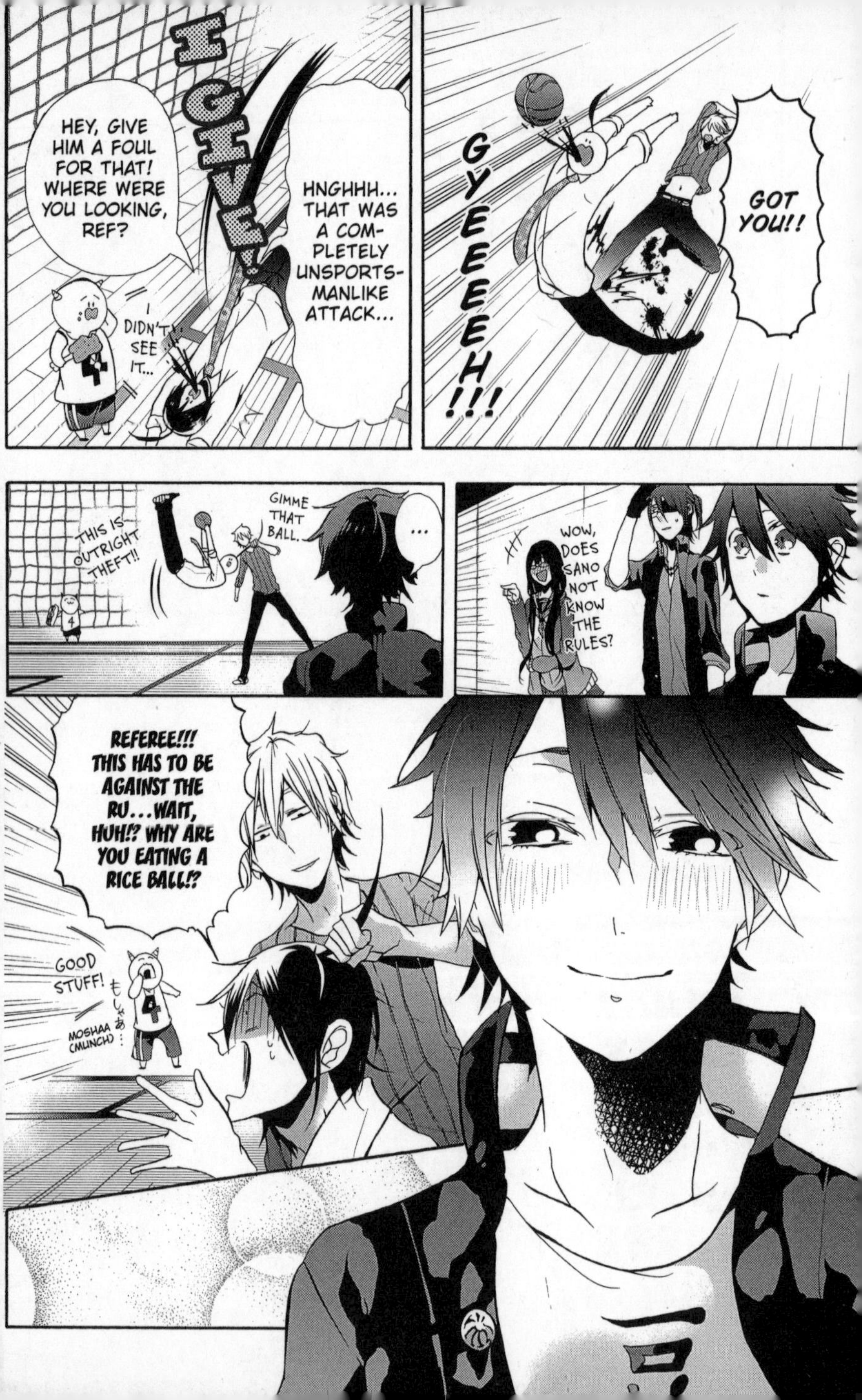
GOT YOU!!
GYEEEEEH!!!
HNGHHH... THAT WAS A COMPLETELY UNSPORTSMANLIKE ATTACK...
I GIVE!
HEY, GIVE HIM A FOUL FOR THAT! WHERE WERE YOU LOOKING, REF?
I DIDN'T SEE IT...
WOW, DOES SANO NOT KNOW THE RULES?
...
GIMME THAT BALL.
THIS IS OUTRIGHT THEFT!!
REFEREE!!! THIS HAS TO BE AGAINST THE RU...WAIT, HUH!? WHY ARE YOU EATING A RICE BALL!?
GOOD STUFF!
もしゃあ…
MOSHAA (MUNCH)

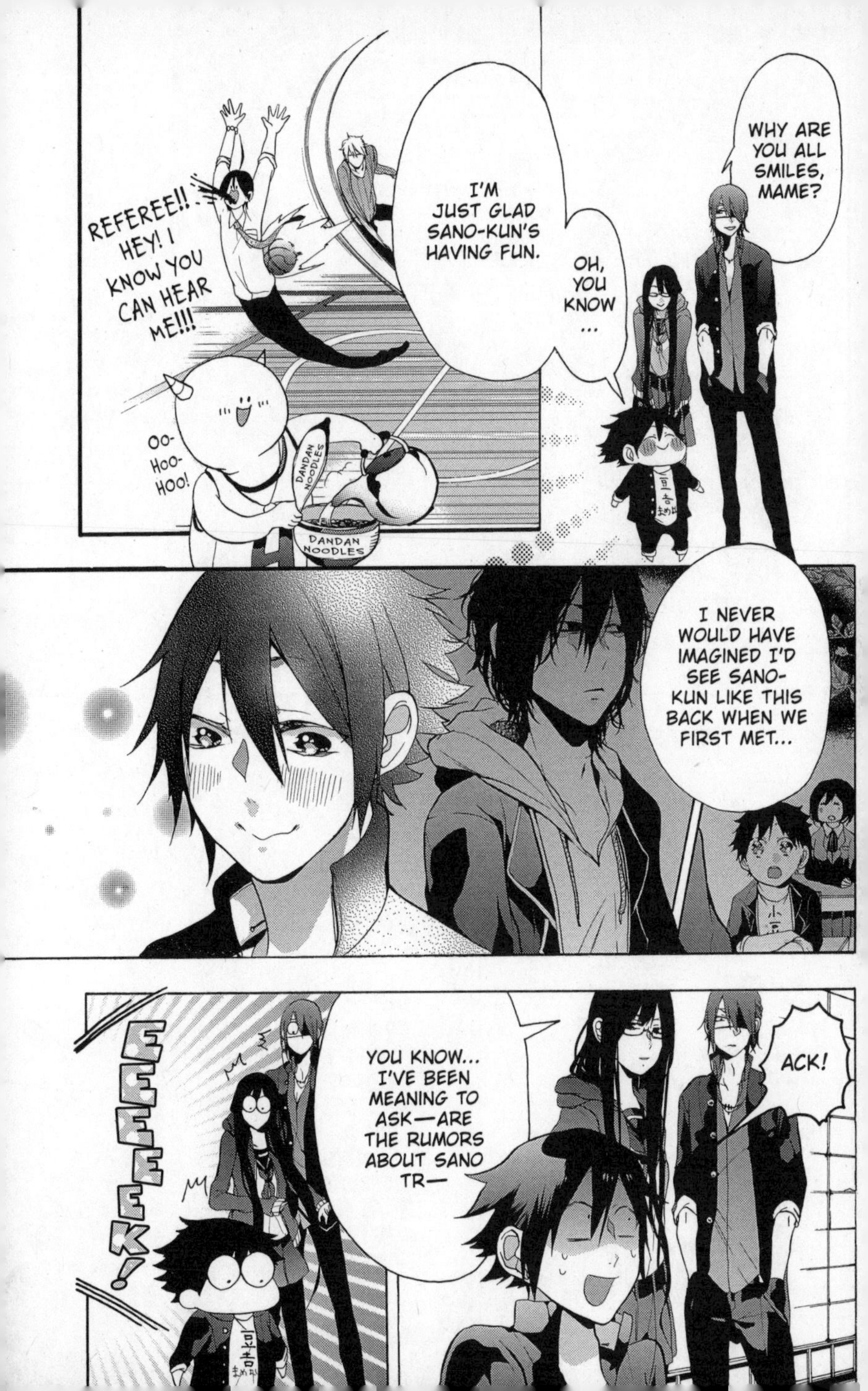
WHY ARE YOU ALL SMILES, MAME?
OH, YOU KNOW ...
I'M JUST GLAD SANO-KUN'S HAVING FUN.
REFEREE!! HEY! I KNOW YOU CAN HEAR ME!!!
OO-HOO-HOO!
DANDAN NOODLES
DANDAN NOODLES
I NEVER WOULD HAVE IMAGINED I'D SEE SANO-KUN LIKE THIS BACK WHEN WE FIRST MET...
ACK!
YOU KNOW... I'VE BEEN MEANING TO ASK—ARE THE RUMORS ABOUT SANO TR—
EEEEEK!

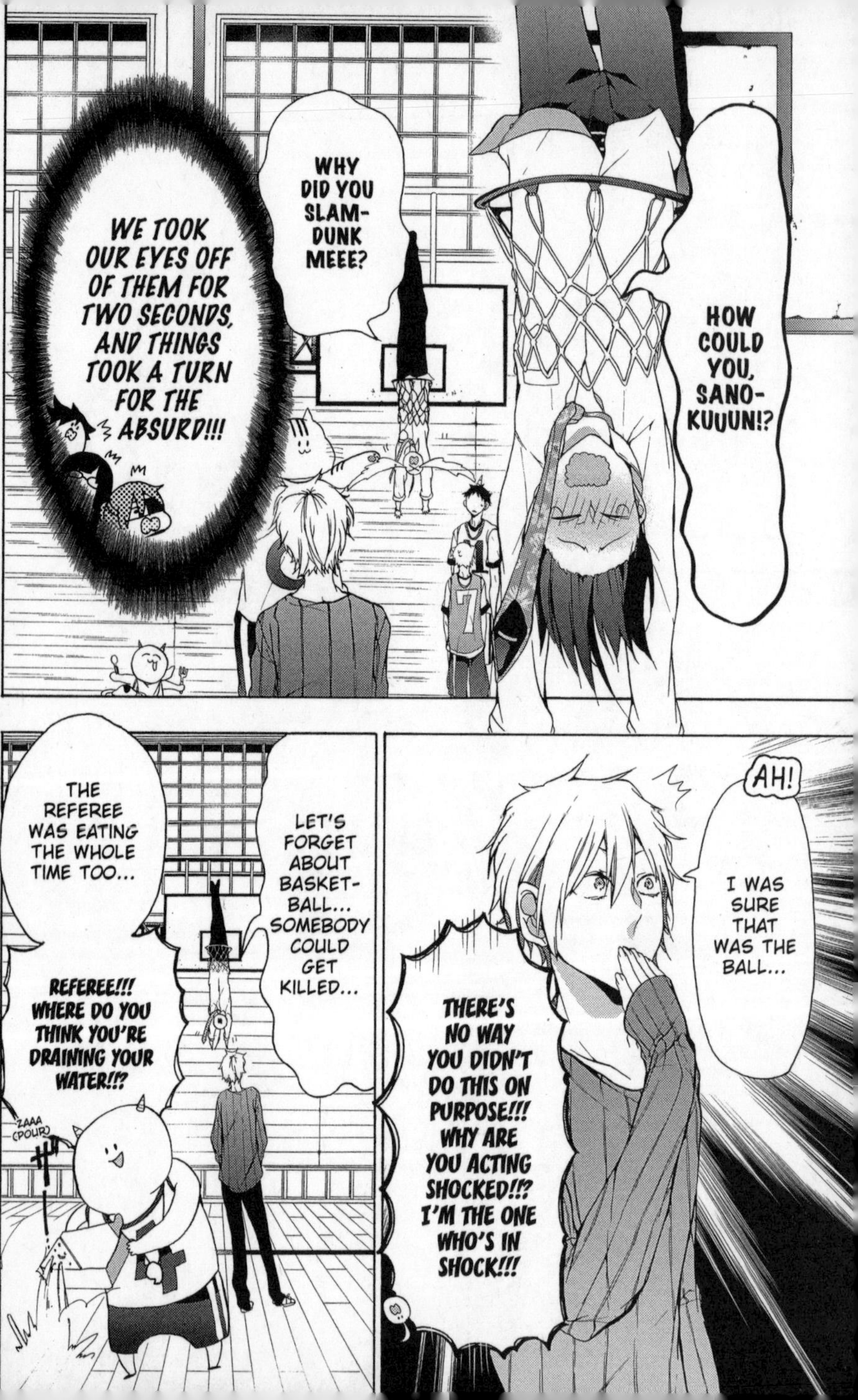
HOW COULD YOU, SANO-KUUUN!?
WHY DID YOU SLAM-DUNK MEEE?
WE TOOK OUR EYES OFF OF THEM FOR TWO SECONDS, AND THINGS TOOK A TURN FOR THE ABSURD!!!
AH!
I WAS SURE THAT WAS THE BALL...
THERE'S NO WAY YOU DIDN'T DO THIS ON PURPOSE!!! WHY ARE YOU ACTING SHOCKED!!? I'M THE ONE WHO'S IN SHOCK!!!
LET'S FORGET ABOUT BASKET-BALL... SOMEBODY COULD GET KILLED...
THE REFEREE WAS EATING THE WHOLE TIME TOO...
REFEREE!!! WHERE DO YOU THINK YOU'RE DRAINING YOUR WATER!!?
ZAAA
(POUR)

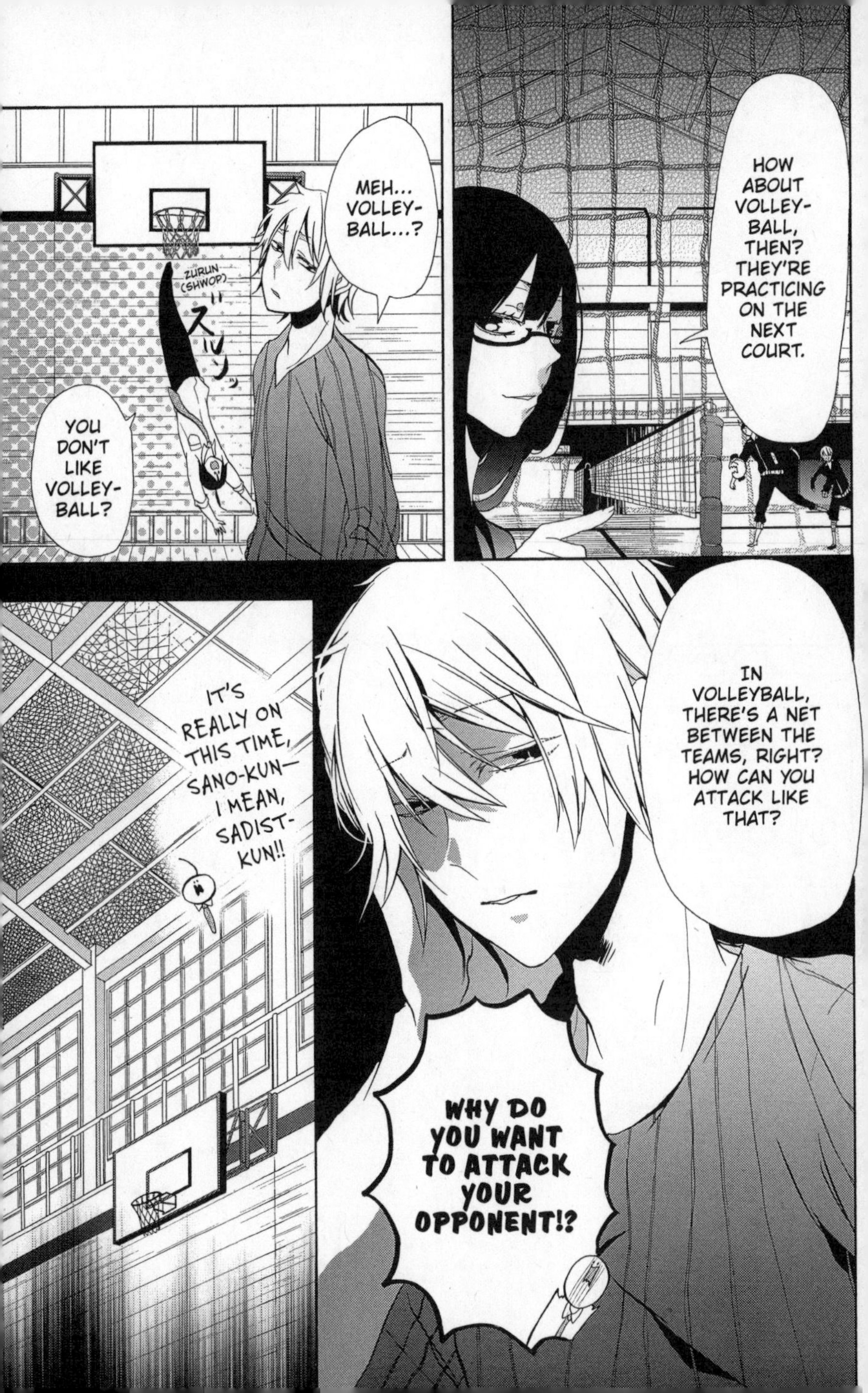
HOW ABOUT VOLLEY-BALL, THEN? THEY'RE PRACTICING ON THE NEXT COURT.
MEH... VOLLEY-BALL...?
ZURUN (SHWOP)
YOU DON'T LIKE VOLLEY-BALL?
IN VOLLEYBALL, THERE'S A NET BETWEEN THE TEAMS, RIGHT? HOW CAN YOU ATTACK LIKE THAT?
WHY DO YOU WANT TO ATTACK YOUR OPPONENT!?
IT'S REALLY ON THIS TIME, SANO-KUN— I MEAN, SADIST-KUN!!

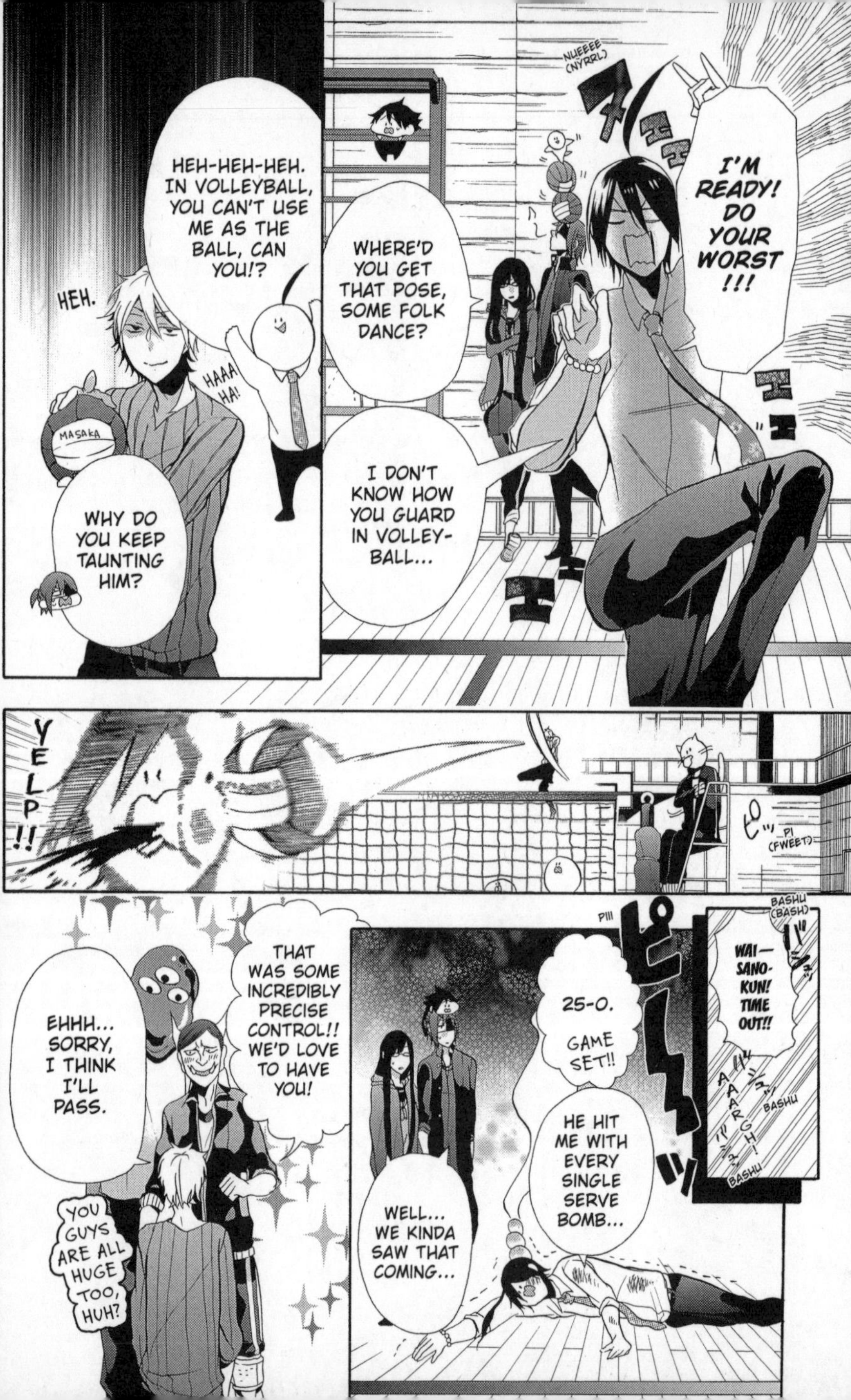
NUEEEE (NYRRL)
I'M READY! DO YOUR WORST!!!
WHERE'D YOU GET THAT POSE, SOME FOLK DANCE?
I DON'T KNOW HOW YOU GUARD IN VOLLEY-BALL...
HEH-HEH-HEH. IN VOLLEYBALL, YOU CAN'T USE ME AS THE BALL, CAN YOU!?
HEH.
HAAAHA!
MASAKA
WHY DO YOU KEEP TAUNTING HIM?
PI (FWEET)
YELP!!
BASHU (BASH)
WAI— SANO-KUN! TIME OUT!!
AAARGH!
BASHU
BASHU
PIII
25-0. GAME SET!!
HE HIT ME WITH EVERY SINGLE SERVE BOMB...
WELL... WE KINDA SAW THAT COMING...
THAT WAS SOME INCREDIBLY PRECISE CONTROL!! WE'D LOVE TO HAVE YOU!
EHHH... SORRY, I THINK I'LL PASS.
YOU GUYS ARE ALL HUGE TOO, HUH?

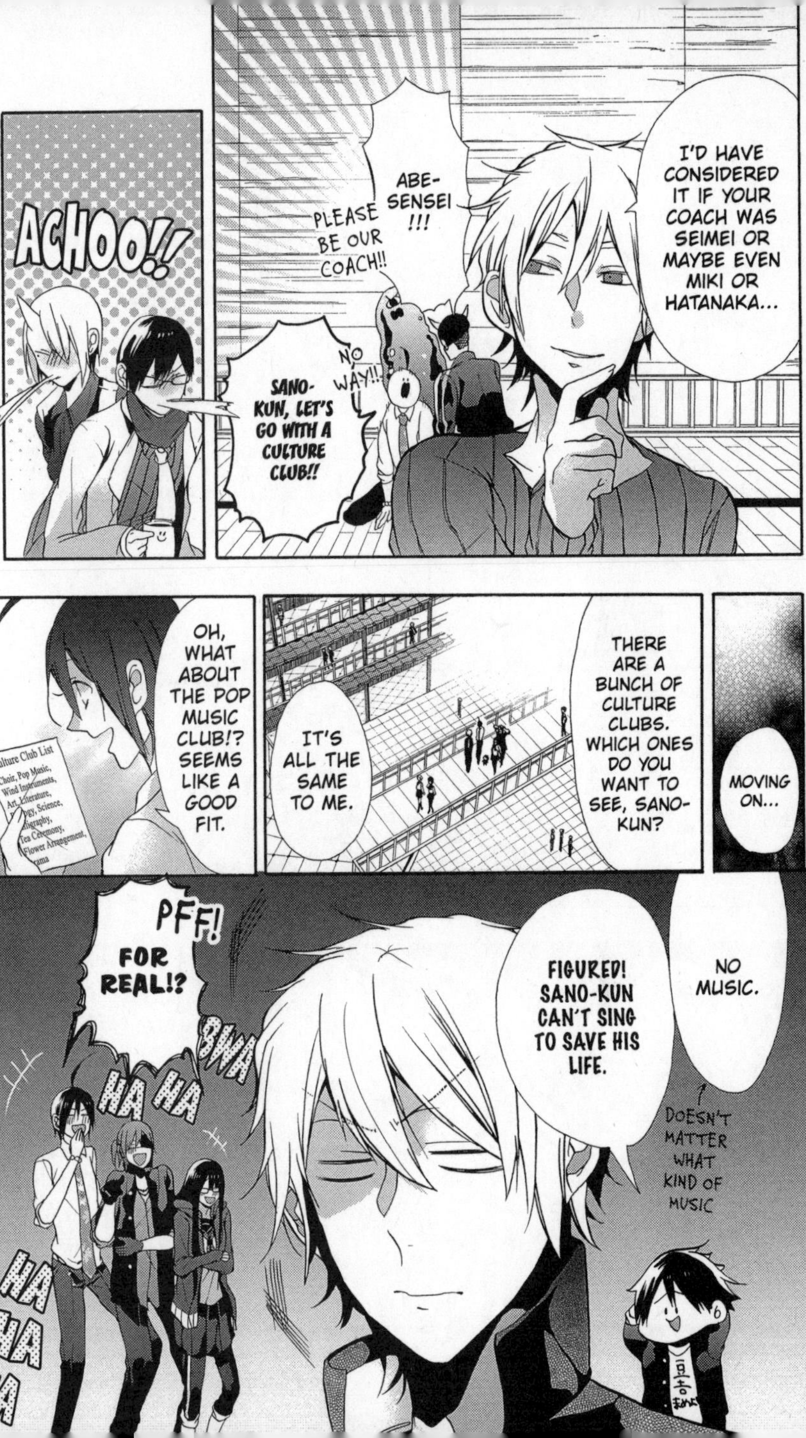

I'D HAVE CONSIDERED IT IF YOUR COACH WAS SEIMEI OR MAYBE EVEN MIKI OR HATANAKA…
ABE-SENSEI!!!
PLEASE BE OUR COACH!!
NO WAY!!
SANO-KUN, LET'S GO WITH A CULTURE CLUB!!
ACHOO!!
MOVING ON…
THERE ARE A BUNCH OF CULTURE CLUBS. WHICH ONES DO YOU WANT TO SEE, SANO-KUN?
IT'S ALL THE SAME TO ME.
OH, WHAT ABOUT THE POP MUSIC CLUB!? SEEMS LIKE A GOOD FIT.
Culture Club List
Choir, Pop Music,
Wind Instruments,
Art, Literature,
Tea Ceremony,
Flower Arrangement,
NO MUSIC.
DOESN'T MATTER WHAT KIND OF MUSIC
FIGURED! SANO-KUN CAN'T SING TO SAVE HIS LIFE.
PFF!
FOR REAL!?
BWA HA HA
HA HA HA HA

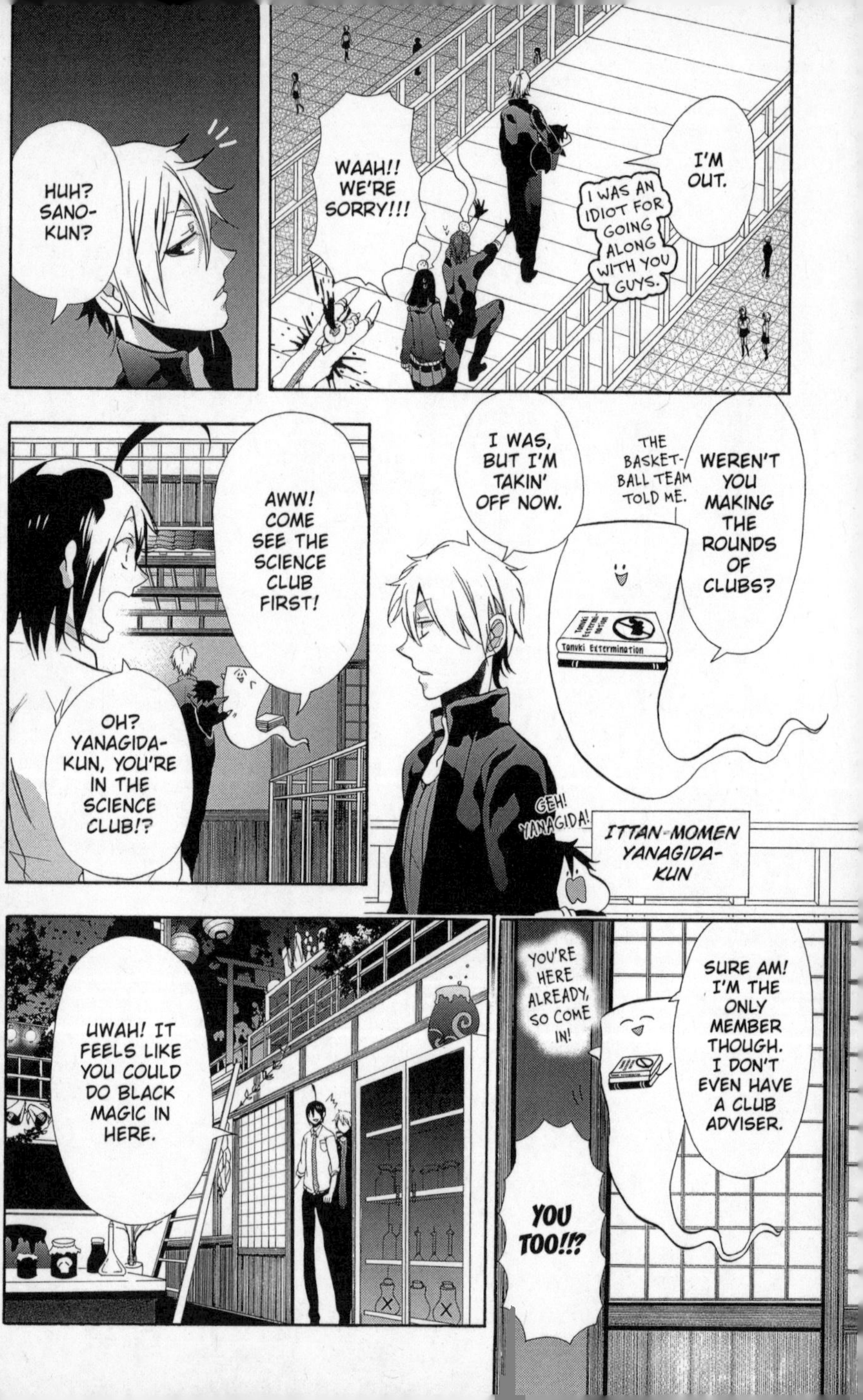
I'M OUT.
I WAS AN IDIOT FOR GOING ALONG WITH YOU GUYS.
WAAH!! WE'RE SORRY!!!
HUH? SANO-KUN?
WEREN'T YOU MAKING THE ROUNDS OF CLUBS?
THE BASKET-BALL TEAM TOLD ME.
Tanuki Extermination
I WAS, BUT I'M TAKIN' OFF NOW.
GEH! YANAGIDA!
ITTAN-MOMEN YANAGIDA-KUN
AWW! COME SEE THE SCIENCE CLUB FIRST!
OH? YANAGIDA-KUN, YOU'RE IN THE SCIENCE CLUB!?
SURE AM! I'M THE ONLY MEMBER THOUGH. I DON'T EVEN HAVE A CLUB ADVISER.
YOU'RE HERE ALREADY, SO COME IN!
YOU TOO!!?
UWAH! IT FEELS LIKE YOU COULD DO BLACK MAGIC IN HERE.

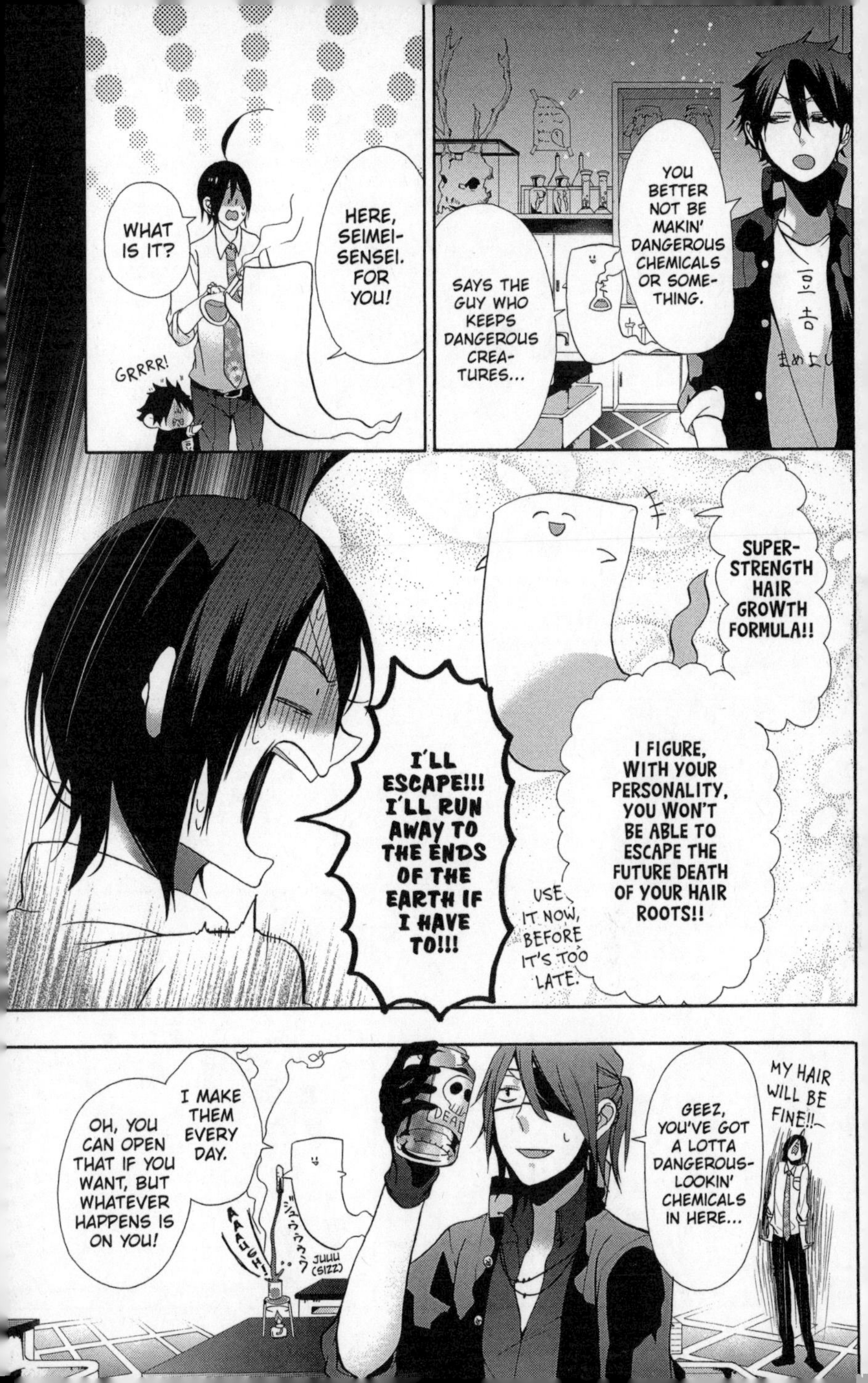
YOU BETTER NOT BE MAKIN' DANGEROUS CHEMICALS OR SOME-THING.
SAYS THE GUY WHO KEEPS DANGEROUS CREA-TURES...
HERE, SEIMEI-SENSEI. FOR YOU!
WHAT IS IT?
GRRRR!
SUPER-STRENGTH HAIR GROWTH FORMULA!!
I FIGURE, WITH YOUR PERSONALITY, YOU WON'T BE ABLE TO ESCAPE THE FUTURE DEATH OF YOUR HAIR ROOTS!!
USE IT NOW, BEFORE IT'S TOO LATE.
I'LL ESCAPE!!! I'LL RUN AWAY TO THE ENDS OF THE EARTH IF I HAVE TO!!!
MY HAIR WILL BE FINE!!
GEEZ, YOU'VE GOT A LOTTA DANGEROUS-LOOKIN' CHEMICALS IN HERE...
I MAKE THEM EVERY DAY.
OH, YOU CAN OPEN THAT IF YOU WANT, BUT WHATEVER HAPPENS IS ON YOU!
JUUU (SIZZ)
AAAUGH!!

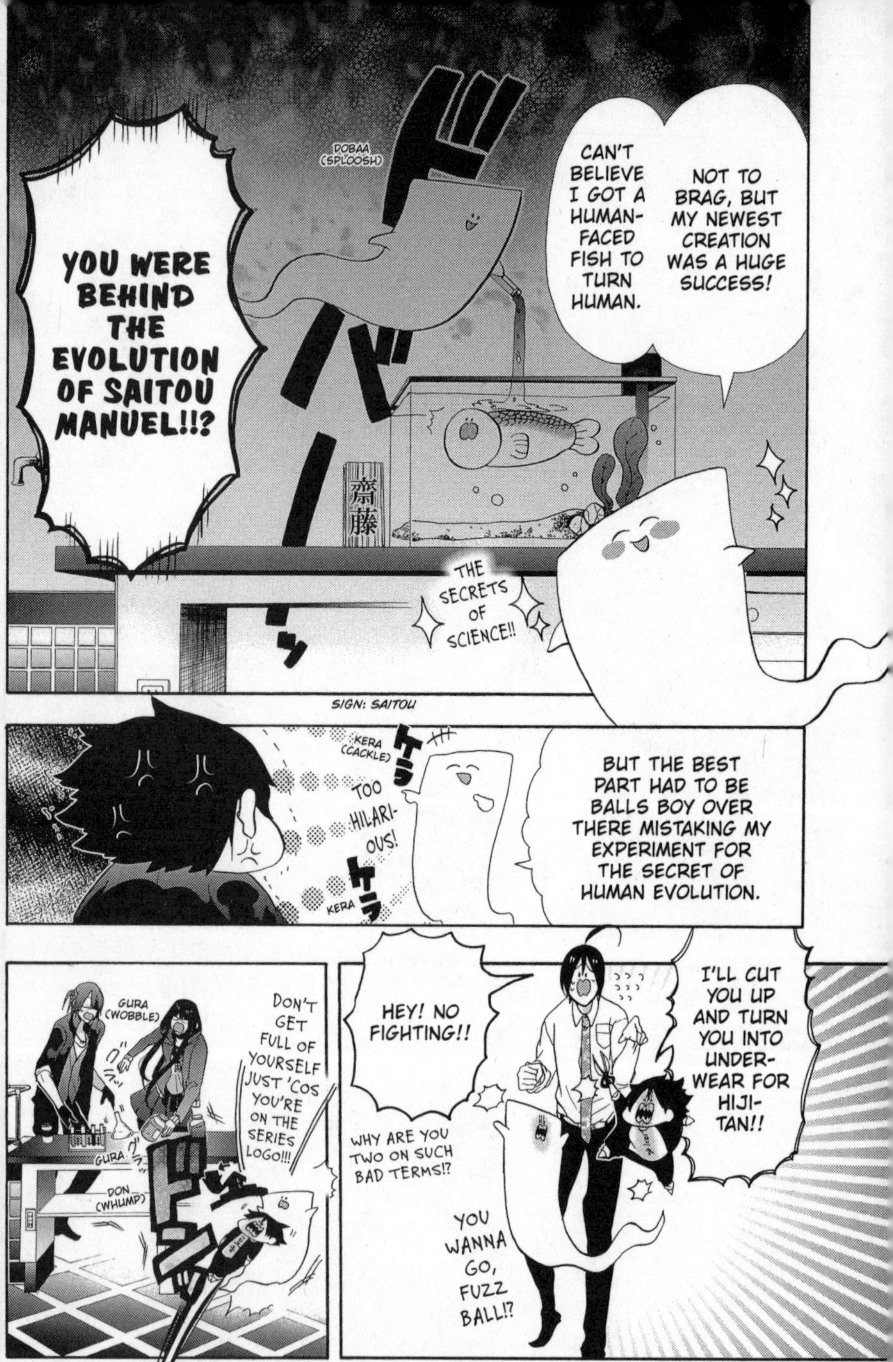
NOT TO BRAG, BUT MY NEWEST CREATION WAS A HUGE SUCCESS!
CAN'T BELIEVE I GOT A HUMAN-FACED FISH TO TURN HUMAN.
DOBAA (SPLOOSH)
YOU WERE BEHIND THE EVOLUTION OF SAITOU MANUEL!!?
THE SECRETS OF SCIENCE!!
SIGN: SAITOU
BUT THE BEST PART HAD TO BE BALLS BOY OVER THERE MISTAKING MY EXPERIMENT FOR THE SECRET OF HUMAN EVOLUTION.
KERA (CACKLE)
TOO HILARIOUS!
KERA
I'LL CUT YOU UP AND TURN YOU INTO UNDERWEAR FOR HIJI-TAN!!
HEY! NO FIGHTING!!
WHY ARE YOU TWO ON SUCH BAD TERMS!?
YOU WANNA GO, FUZZ BALL!?
DON'T GET FULL OF YOURSELF JUST 'COS YOU'RE ON THE SERIES LOGO!!!
GURA (WOBBLE)
GURA
DON (WHUMP)

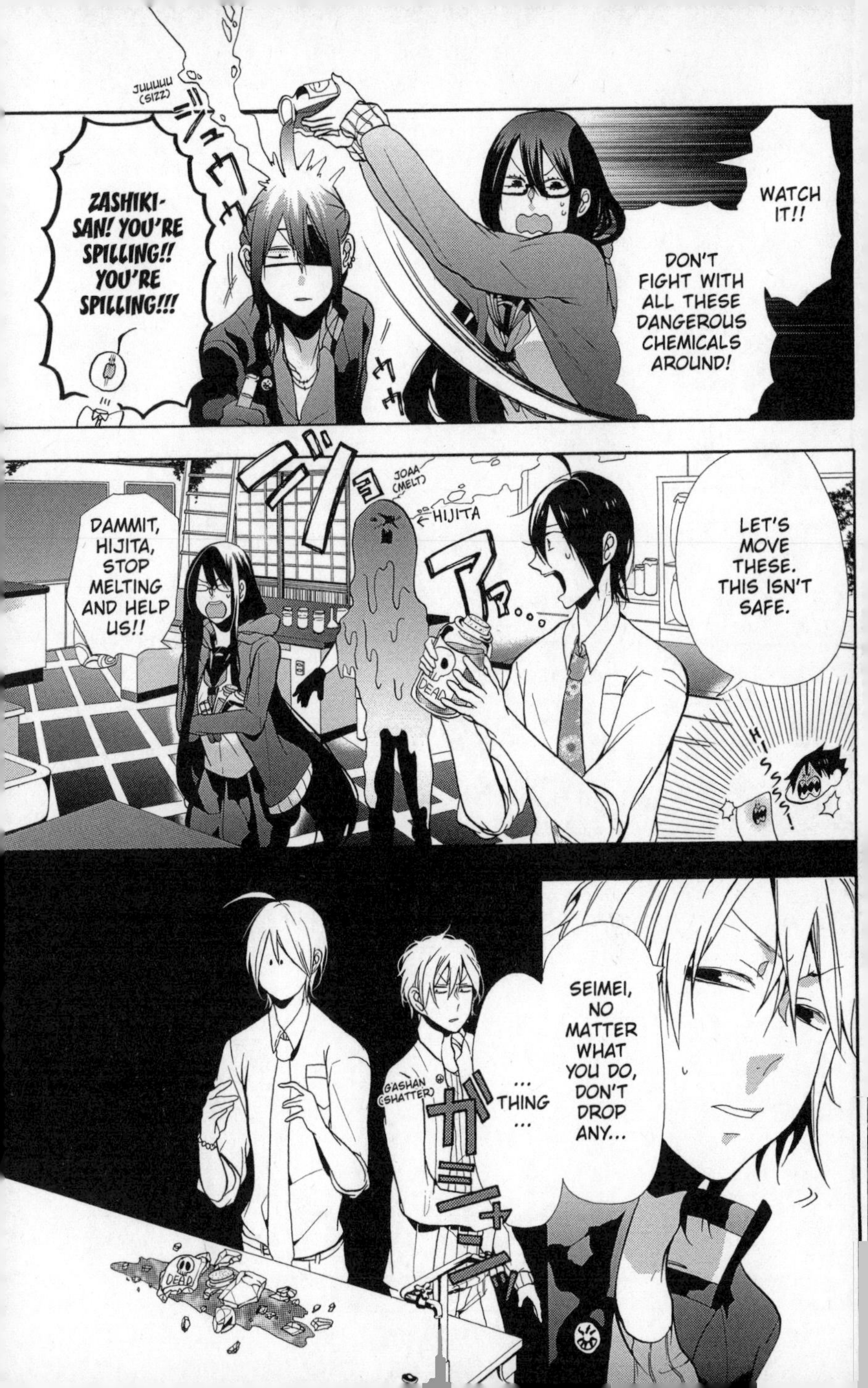
WATCH IT!!
DON'T FIGHT WITH ALL THESE DANGEROUS CHEMICALS AROUND!
JUUUUU (SIZZ)
ZASHIKI-SAN! YOU'RE SPILLING!! YOU'RE SPILLING!!!
LET'S MOVE THESE. THIS ISN'T SAFE.
HISSSS!
JOAA (MELT)
← HIJITA
DAMMIT, HIJITA, STOP MELTING AND HELP US!!
SEIMEI, NO MATTER WHAT YOU DO, DON'T DROP ANY...
...THING...
GASHAN (SHATTER)

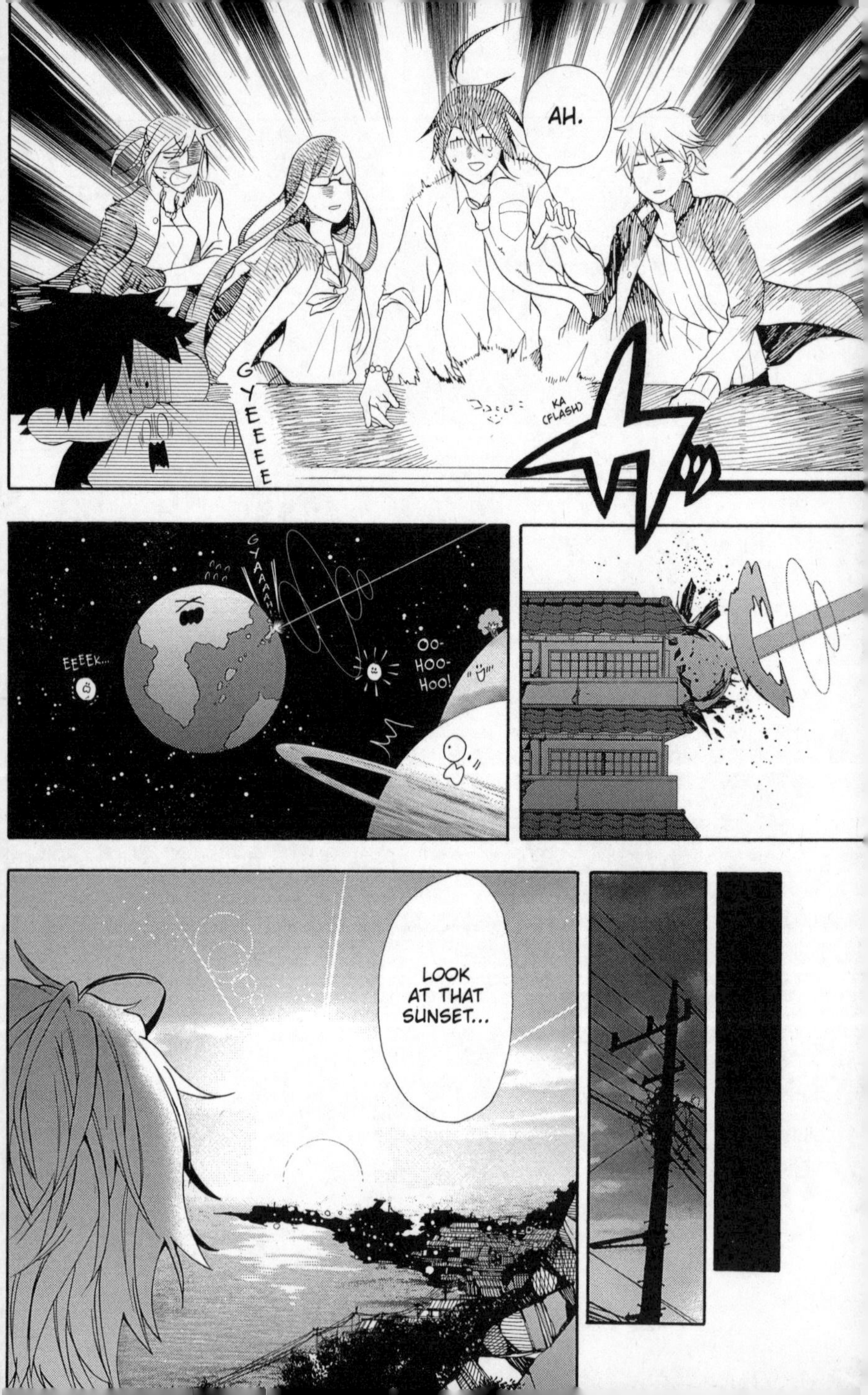
AH.
KA (FLASH)
GYEEEEE
OO-HOO-HOO!
GYAAAAH!
EEEEK...
LOOK AT THAT SUNSET...

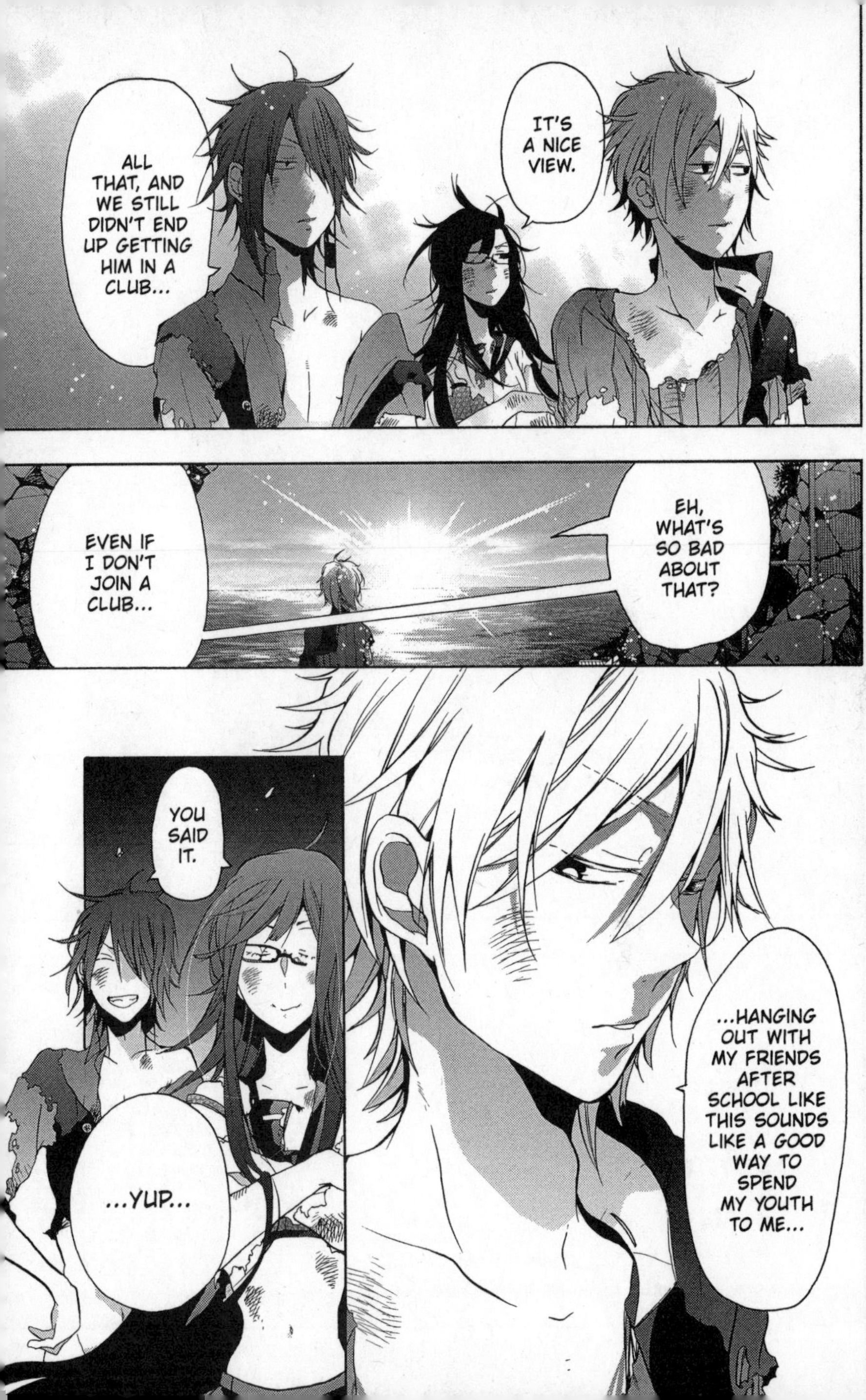
IT'S A NICE VIEW.
ALL THAT, AND WE STILL DIDN'T END UP GETTING HIM IN A CLUB...
EH, WHAT'S SO BAD ABOUT THAT?
EVEN IF I DON'T JOIN A CLUB...
...HANGING OUT WITH MY FRIENDS AFTER SCHOOL LIKE THIS SOUNDS LIKE A GOOD WAY TO SPEND MY YOUTH TO ME...
YOU SAID IT.
...YUP...

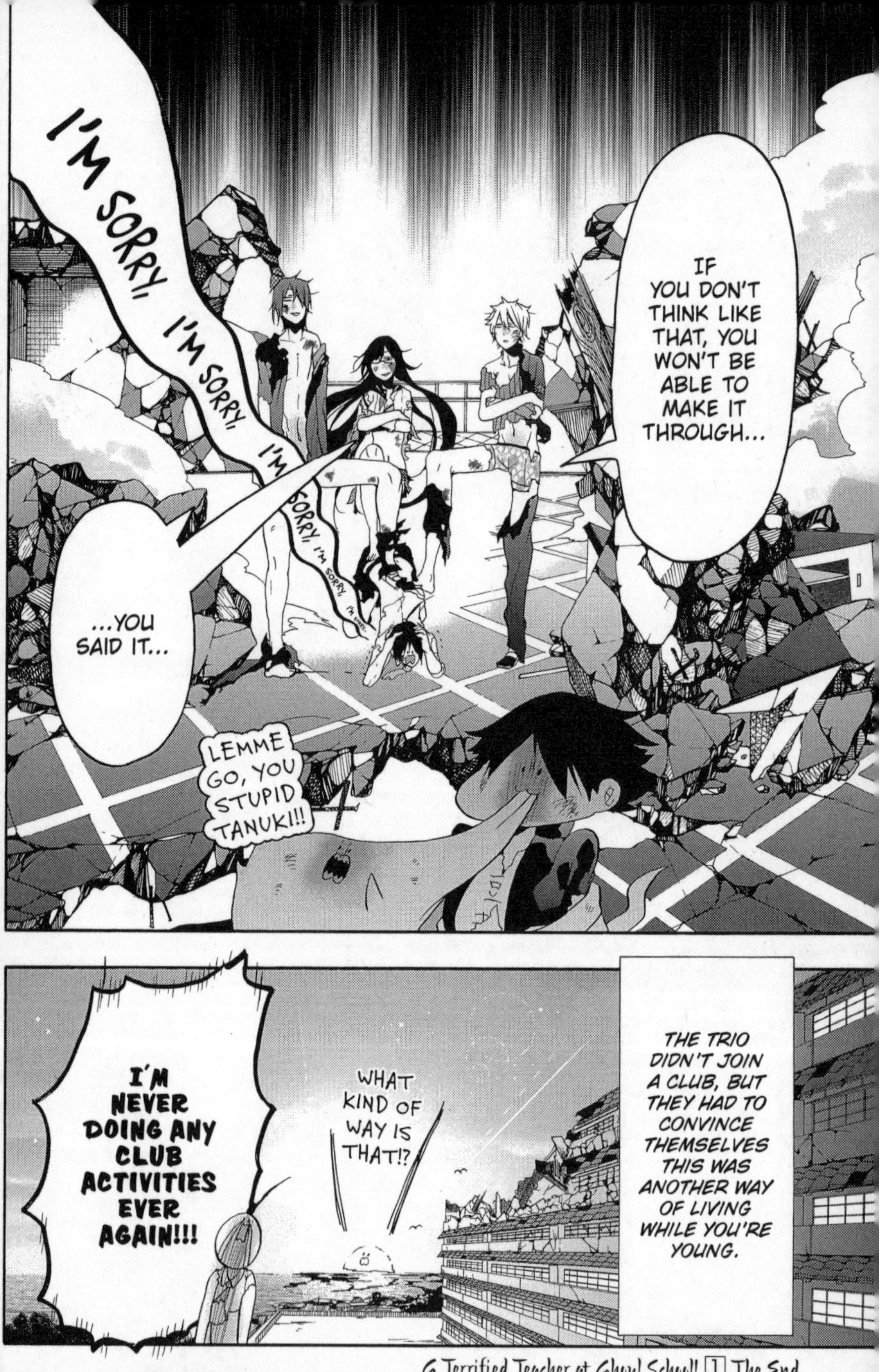
IF YOU DON'T THINK LIKE THAT, YOU WON'T BE ABLE TO MAKE IT THROUGH...
I'M SORRY. I'M SORRY. I'M SORRY. I'M SORRY. I'M SORRY. I'M SORRY.
...YOU SAID IT...
LEMME GO, YOU STUPID TANUKI!!!
THE TRIO DIDN'T JOIN A CLUB, BUT THEY HAD TO CONVINCE THEMSELVES THIS WAS ANOTHER WAY OF LIVING WHILE YOU'RE YOUNG.
WHAT KIND OF WAY IS THAT!?
I'M NEVER DOING ANY CLUB ACTIVITIES EVER AGAIN!!!

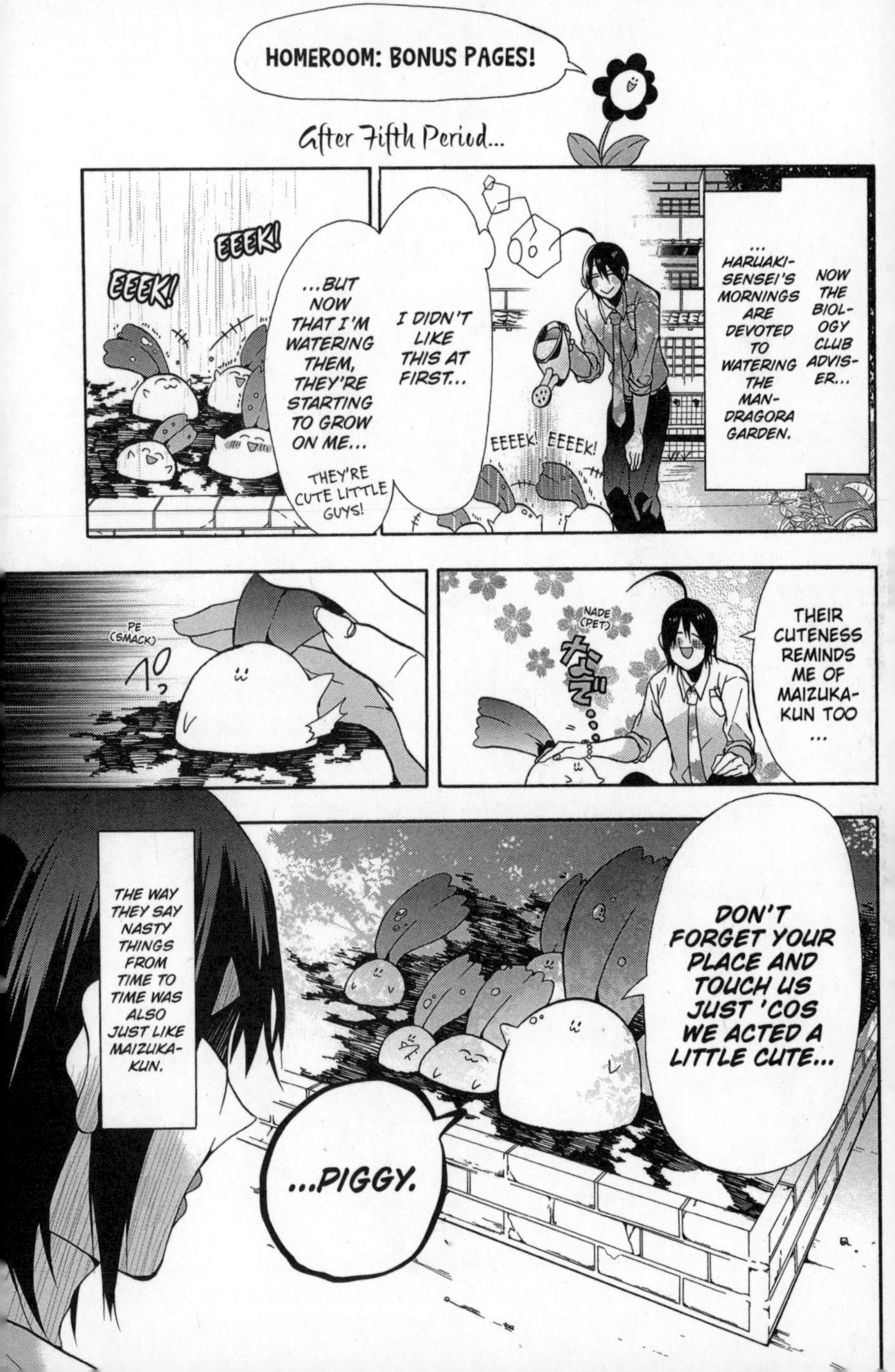
HOMEROOM: BONUS PAGES!
After Fifth Period...
NOW THE BIOLOGY CLUB ADVISER...
...HARUAKI-SENSEI'S MORNINGS ARE DEVOTED TO WATERING THE MANDRAGORA GARDEN.
I DIDN'T LIKE THIS AT FIRST...
...BUT NOW THAT I'M WATERING THEM, THEY'RE STARTING TO GROW ON ME...
EEEEK! EEEEK!
THEY'RE CUTE LITTLE GUYS!
EEEK!
EEEK!
THEIR CUTENESS REMINDS ME OF MAIZUKA-KUN TOO ...
NADE (PET)
PE (SMACK)
DON'T FORGET YOUR PLACE AND TOUCH US JUST 'COS WE ACTED A LITTLE CUTE...
THE WAY THEY SAY NASTY THINGS FROM TIME TO TIME WAS ALSO JUST LIKE MAIZUKA-KUN.
...PIGGY.

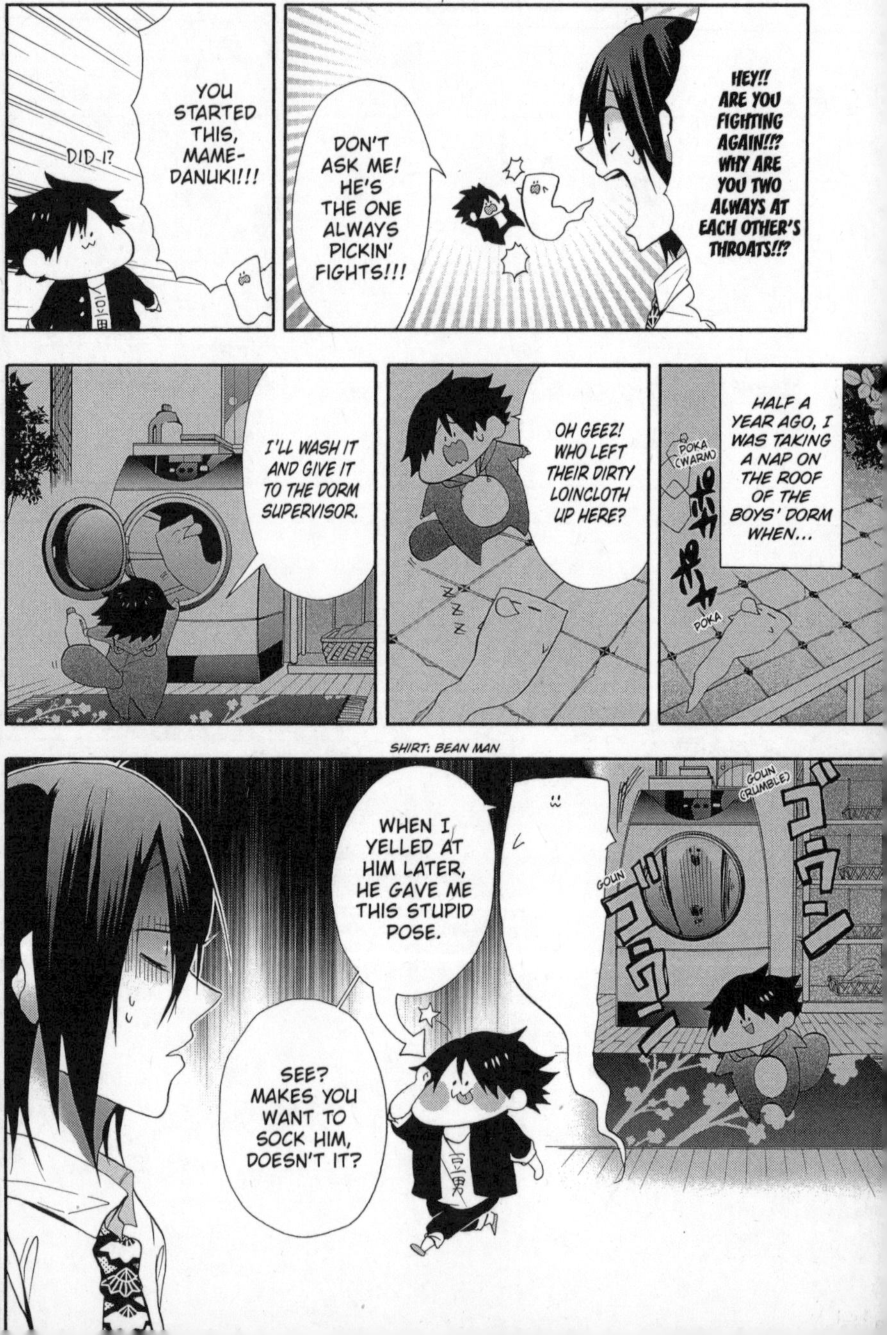
HEY!! ARE YOU FIGHTING AGAIN!!? WHY ARE YOU TWO ALWAYS AT EACH OTHER'S THROATS!!?
DON'T ASK ME! HE'S THE ONE ALWAYS PICKIN' FIGHTS!!!
YOU STARTED THIS, MAME-DANUKI!!!
DID-I?
HALF A YEAR AGO, I WAS TAKING A NAP ON THE ROOF OF THE BOYS' DORM WHEN...
POKA (WARM)
POKA
OH GEEZ! WHO LEFT THEIR DIRTY LOINCLOTH UP HERE?
I'LL WASH IT AND GIVE IT TO THE DORM SUPERVISOR.
SHIRT: BEAN MAN
GOUN (RUMBLE)
GOUN
WHEN I YELLED AT HIM LATER, HE GAVE ME THIS STUPID POSE.
SEE? MAKES YOU WANT TO SOCK HIM, DOESN'T IT?

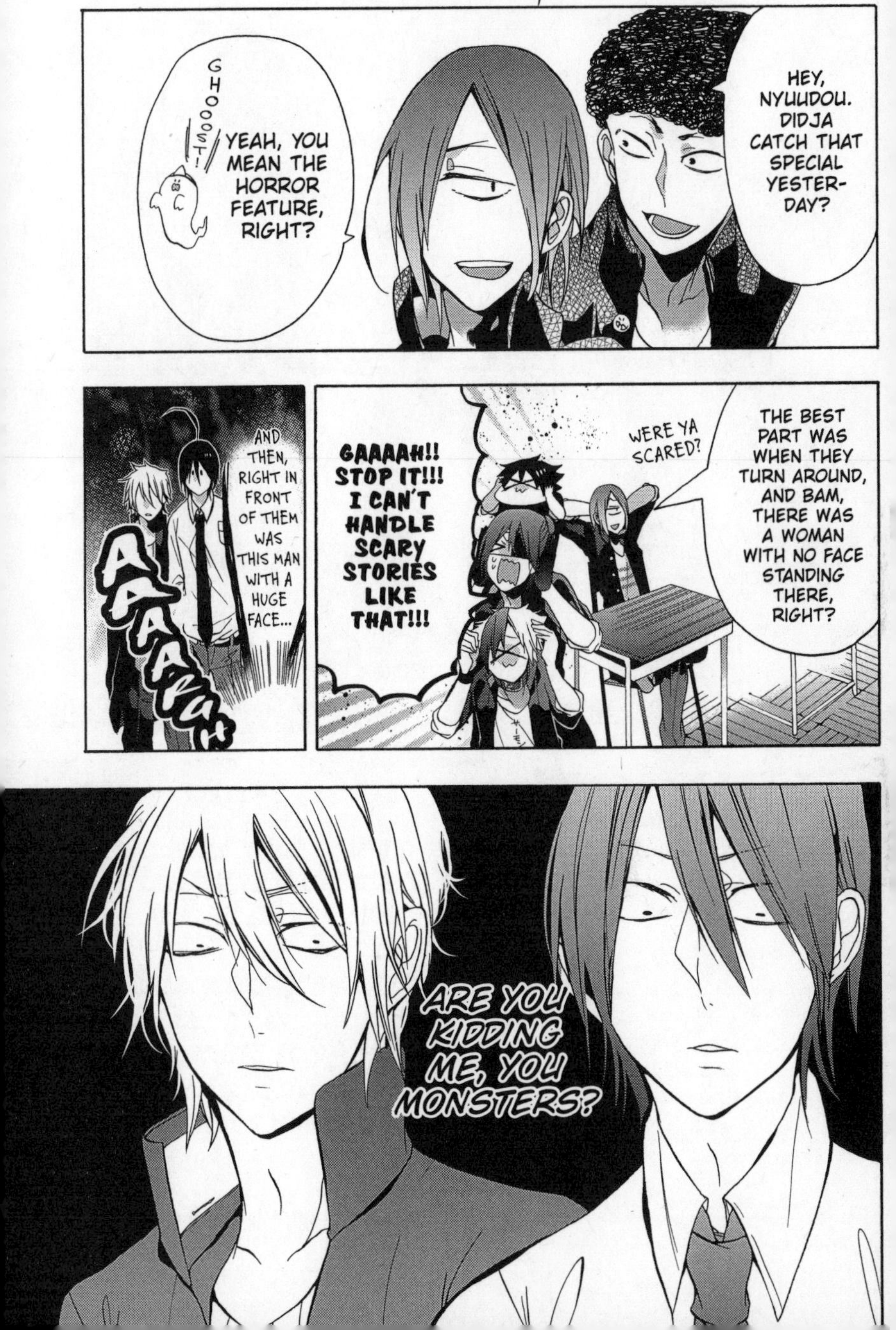
HEY, NYUUDOU. DIDJA CATCH THAT SPECIAL YESTER-DAY?
YEAH, YOU MEAN THE HORROR FEATURE, RIGHT?
GHOOOST!
THE BEST PART WAS WHEN THEY TURN AROUND, AND BAM, THERE WAS A WOMAN WITH NO FACE STANDING THERE, RIGHT?
WERE YA SCARED?
GAAAAH!! STOP IT!!! I CAN'T HANDLE SCARY STORIES LIKE THAT!!!
AND THEN, RIGHT IN FRONT OF THEM WAS THIS MAN WITH A HUGE FACE...
AAAAAAH
ARE YOU KIDDING ME, YOU MONSTERS?

I Am a (Two-Tailed) Cat

1 AKI-SAME-KUN, THE NEKO-MATA.

2 AT LUNCH, HE EATS CAT FOOD.

TIME TO DIG IN!!

MEOW MEOW PURR-ING.

3 HE HATES BATHS.

WHY DO I GOTTA GIVE YOU BATHS!!?

RRROWR!

4 HE CATCHES COCKROACHES.

SCUTTLE SCUTTLE

AND SHOWS THEM TO YOU.

SPECIAL THANKS!

 My assistant: Hiromi Suito-sama

My editor: Katou-sama

My friend Min, who wrote Haruaki's calligraphy for Chapter 5

The designer and the editorial department

My family, relatives, and friends

 And everyone who read this far!

So lovely to meet you. I'm Mai Tanaka. Thank you so much for picking up *A Terrified Teacher at Ghoul School!!* This is my first real serialization, my first paperback volume, my first youkai story, my first jam-packed-with-jokes comedy, and my first so many other things that I'm quivering more than a newborn fawn. Shaking in my boots! My most humble thanks for your continued support!

Mai Tanaka

 SEE YOU IN CLASS FOR VOLUME 2!

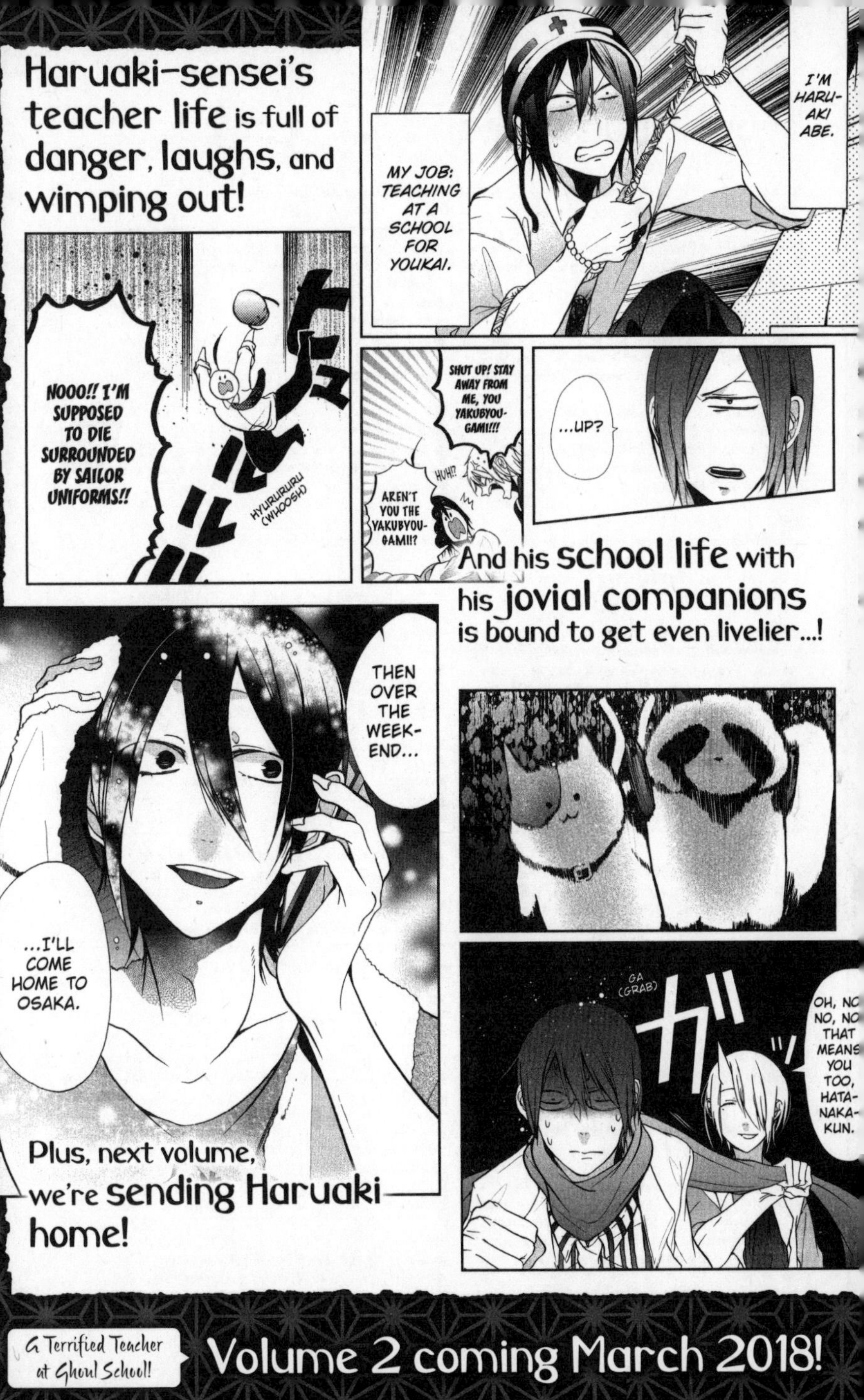
Haruaki-sensei's teacher life is full of danger, laughs, and wimping out!
I'M HARU-AKI ABE.
MY JOB: TEACHING AT A SCHOOL FOR YOUKAI.
...UP?
SHUT UP! STAY AWAY FROM ME, YOU YAKUBYOU-GAMI!!!
HUH!?
AREN'T YOU THE YAKUBYOU-GAMI!?
NOOO!! I'M SUPPOSED TO DIE SURROUNDED BY SAILOR UNIFORMS!!
HYURURURU (WHOOSH)
And his school life with his jovial companions is bound to get even livelier...!
GA (GRAB)
OH, NO NO, NO THAT MEANS YOU TOO, HATA-NAKA-KUN.
THEN OVER THE WEEK-END...
...I'LL COME HOME TO OSAKA.
Plus, next volume, we're sending Haruaki home!

G Terrified Teacher at Ghoul School!

Volume 2 coming March 2018!

Translation Notes

PAGE 3

"Youkai" is a term used to refer to supernatural creatures, haunted objects, ghosts, and more from Japanese folklore.

A Terrified Teacher at Ghoul School! uses older number kanji on the classroom signs and elsewhere, in keeping with the classical-inspired architecture on the island.

PAGE 5

Haruaki's name is written with the same kanji as historical figure and legend **Abe no Seimei** (921 to 1005). Abe no Seimei was a diviner for the imperial court said to have all kinds of supernatural powers.

Hyakki Academy's name comes from the **hyakki yagyou** ("night parade of one hundred demons"). It's said that every year, Nurarihyon, king of the *youkai*, leads his ghoulish subjects on a parade through the streets on summer nights, and if you happen to run into it, you'll be spirited away.

PAGE 8

Similar to the use of old-fashioned number kanji, sometimes signs and so on in *Ghoul School* are also written in an old-fashioned way, like this "convenience" sign being written in hiragana, even though it would normally be written in katakana, since it's a loanword.

PAGE 11

The *nurari* sound effect that accompanies the principal's appearance is an obvious clue for Japanese readers as to what kind of *youkai* he is: **Nurarihyon**. Nurarihyon is the leader of the *youkai*. This large-headed *youkai* is said to invite itself into homes and sit down for tea. It's skilled at catching people unaware, and only the most cautious people will notice it. It usually appears dressed in the fine clothes of a merchant and walks with the calm confidence of the master of a distinguished family. The name sounds like an onomatopoeia, with the "nurari" part probably coming from its slippery, sneaky nature and the "hyon" from how it seems to pop up out of nowhere.

PAGE 22

Yakubyougami (gods of pestilence) wander around town alone or in groups of five, spreading disease and misfortune. In olden times, Japanese villagers would hang big dolls or sandals at the village entrance or practice other customs like making azuki bean gruel on the third day of every month to keep them away. As for Sano, his first name is written with the "life" character, and the *sa* character in his family name can mean "to help," which might run counter to his *youkai* type...

PAGE 26

The *nopperabou* looks just like an ordinary person, until you see they have no face. They might appear with a face at first, then wipe it away to terrify unwitting humans. They're really only after giving people a good scare. Mujina's family name comes from a transforming badger *youkai* of the same name that can transform into nopperabou.

The *gashadokuro* is a giant, skeletal *youkai* formed by the resentment of people who died a dog's death (like soldiers in the battlefield, people who weren't buried, or people who starved to death). It only appears at night, walking along with its chattering bones to attack people when it finds them. A very powerful and very dangerous *youkai*.

There are several kinds of cyclops *youkai*; Nyuudou is a **hitotsume-kozou** (one-eyed boy), which are relatively harmless and like to suddenly appear and surprise people. Nyuudou's family name might come from a type of two-meter (six-and-a-half-foot) tall cyclops *youkai* called hitotsume-nyuudou (one-eyed priest).

The **dorotabou** (muddy rice-field monk) appears as a one-eyed figure rising out of the mud. Once upon a time, it was a poor man who toiled hard on his field to raise rice, and his hard work paid off, with his harvest growing over the years. When he died, his child inherited the field, but the child was a lazy drunkard who neglected it and eventually sold it off to a stranger. This *youkai* then appeared in the field, saying "Give me back my field!" Hijita's name is also related to his *youkai* type: the kanji in his family name are "mud" + "field," and the *kou* kanji in his given name is for tilling. (The *-tarou* is just an ordinary name ending for boys.)

PAGE 27

The *mame-danuki* is the smallest type of transforming tanuki (raccoon dog). It covers itself with its massive scrotum to transform or it might even use it as an umbrella. They also like to haunt people and cause trouble for them. Mame's given name is the *mame* (bean) from "mame-danuki" plus *kichi* (luck), and the first kanji in his family name is the character for "tanuki."

PAGE 28

The "one, two, three" being used by Mame here is actually "sashi, suse, so," referring to the five fundamental seasonings used in Japanese cooking: sugar, salt, vinegar, soy sauce, and miso.

PAGE 32

The *binbougami* (poverty god), true to its name, is a god that brings poverty with it. Often appears as a man in dirty, tattered clothing.

PAGE 40

The "*pom*" sound effect is used as a "poof" here, but the sound is also associated with tanuki drumming on their bellies. Pom, poko, pom...

PAGE 58

The faculty dorm supervisor is a **kuchisake onna** (slit-mouth woman). This urban legend appears at dusk as a woman with a mask over her mouth. She'll turn to passersby and ask them if she is pretty—once they answer, she takes off her mask, revealing that her mouth is ripped from ear to ear, and asks again. She'll kill her victim outright for a "no" and slit her mouth like hers for a "yes." There are various local customs to save yourself from her.

PAGE 62

The **shutendouji** (little drunkard) is the commander of the oni (ogres). He takes his subordinates into towns and raises hell, stealing noblemen's daughters to keep or to eat. He loves to drink, and he was also beautiful when he was young. The kanji characters in Miki's name are "god" + "sake/alcohol," relating to his *youkai* ability.

PAGE 65

The "**koban**" on Akisame's shirt refers to an oval-shaped gold coin from the Edo period of Japan. The Japanese idiom *neko ni koban* ("gold coins for cats") has the same meaning as "casting pearls before swine."

PAGE 68

In Japanese, the back cover of Haruaki's dictionary uses the idiom *oni ni kanabou* ("giving an iron club to an ogre"), which means to make something very certain. The ogre was strong enough without a club—giving him one would be overkill. Likewise, the dictionary is claiming to inspire a similar level of confidence in one's knowledge of *youkai*.

PAGE 72
One Hundred Poems by One Hundred Poets (*Hyakunin Isshu*) is a classical Japanese anthology of waka poems. It is commonly taught in school and also used for the card game karuta (thus, the cards on the chapter cover).

PAGE 74
The first kanji in *Hyakunin Isshu* #89 are actually the same as the kanji in Akisame's first name, Tamao, so it's fitting that he's the one reading this poem.

PAGE 85
Tottori is a prefecture in Japan with a capital city of the same name.

PAGE 86
The lines on the bottom right are a reference to a line spoken by the character Pazu near the beginning of the Ghibli film *Castle in the Sky* ("*Oyakata! Sora kara onna no ko ga!*" — "Boss! A girl [came down] from the sky!"). The line has achieved something of a meme status.

PAGE 88
Odawara is a *chouchin* (paper lantern) *youkai*. The paper lantern ghost is usually something of a stock monster that flies around and scares people.

The girl with the long neck is a *rokurokubi*. This *youkai*, usually a woman, looks and acts like a normal human in the day, but after going to bed at night, their neck stretches and looks for prey. In the morning, their body goes back to normal. They might have red marks or similar evidence of their true nature on their neck.

Akisame is a *nekomata*, a two-tailed cat that can stand on its hind legs. This *youkai* is associated with poltergeist-like phenomena, strange fire, and death—mischievous nekomata might reanimate a dead body and make it dance, for example.

Natsume Souseki (1867 to 1916) was a Japanese novelist best known for *Kokoro*, *Bocchan*, and, of course (since it's Akisame wearing this shirt), *I Am a Cat*.

PAGE 89
The *zashiki-warashi* is a mischievous *youkai* that haunts houses or storehouses. The zashiki-warashi might cause poltergeist-like phenomena with their pranks, but they bring prosperity to the house they possess.

PAGE 111
Kabaddi is a team sport that is popular in India and South Asia. Two teams occupy halves of a court, taking turns sending a player into the opposing team's territory. The player's goal is to touch an opponent and retreat to safety, while the other team has to tackle him to prevent him from escaping and earning a point for his team.

The photographer is a *kappa*—a water imp. Sometimes, they're blamed for drownings, but often, they're just mischievous. And they love cucumber.

PAGE 115
Not only does Beniko's family name relate to her *youkai* type, so do the characters for her given name ("crimson/red" + "child"), now that we know that her color matters.

PAGE 117
Mame is reading *Kachi-Kachi Yama* (Crackling Mountain), a tanuki-themed folktale. In the story, a farmer catches a tanuki that was tearing up his fields and asks his wife to make them some tanuki soup. While the farmer is away, the tanuki tricks the farmer's wife into freeing it and makes the wife into soup instead. The tanuki disguises itself as the farmer's wife, feeds the soup to the farmer, and then reveals the truth and runs away. As the man grieves, a rabbit approaches and vows to avenge the farmer's wife's death. The rabbit proceeds to trick the tanuki, acting friendly but actually torturing it. One of its tricks is to set fire to kindling the tanuki is carrying. The tanuki asks what the crackling sound of the fire is, but the rabbit reassures him, saying it's just the sound of Crackling Mountain, and so the tanuki gets badly burned. The story ends with the rabbit tricking the tanuki into taking a boat made of dirt far out into a lake, and the boat falls apart and sinks in the water, along with the tanuki. It's no wonder Mame rips the book up...

PAGE 119
Hatanaka-sensei chastises a *karakasa obake* (a paper umbrella ghost that hops around on one leg) and an *asaoke no ke* (a hair *youkai*).

PAGE 125
Daifuku is a Japanese confection that typically consists of azuki bean paste filling wrapped in a mochi (chewy, sticky rice cake) shell.

PAGE 129
The *ittan-momen* (a bolt of cloth) looks like a flying sheet of cloth, and people who don't pay it much attention might think it's a piece of laundry that was blown away by the wind—but don't be fooled by its appearance! This dangerous *youkai* attacks people by wrapping around their necks or covering their faces and suffocating them.

PAGE 152
"Mameyoshi" is an alternate pronunciation of the kanji for Mamekichi's name.

188 centimeters is about six feet and two inches.

PAGE 154
The human-faced fish, or *jinmengyo*, is basically just a fish that looks like it has a human face. Usually a koi fish.

PAGE 176
The title for this bonus page is another reference to Natsume Souseki's *I Am a Cat*.

FRONT INSIDE COVER
Several national holidays happen in the first week of May, or **Golden Week**, so many people in Japan get the week off.

Mame wrote his book report on **Bunbuku Chagama**, a folktale about a poor man who saved a tanuki caught in a trap. The tanuki transforms itself into a teakettle and tells the man to sell it for money, as a reward for his help. After being sold, unable to handle the heat of the fire, the tanuki teakettle sprouts legs and runs back to the poor man. The poor man and the tanuki end up charging admission for people to see a tightrope-walking teakettle, and bo live happily ever after. Seems like Mame read a picture book for his report...

BACK INSIDE COVER
In the Japanese, when Sano confronts Hijita over stealing Mame book report, he replaces the first kanji character in Hijita's name ("mud") with the character for "ditch."

A Terrified Teacher at Ghoul School! Vol. 1

Mai Tanaka

◊ Translation: **AMANDA HALEY**

◊ Lettering: **LYS BLAKESLEE**

YOKAI GAKKO NO SENSEI HAJIMEMASHITA! Vol. 1 © 2015 Mai Tanaka/ SQUARE ENIX CO., LTD. First published in Japan in 2015 by SQUARE ENIX CO., LTD. English translation rights arranged with SQUARE ENIX CO., LTD. and Yen Press, LLC through Tuttle-Mori Agency, Inc., Tokyo.

English translation © 2017 by SQUARE ENIX CO., LTD.

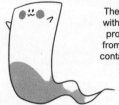

Yen Press
1290 Avenue of the Americas
New York, NY 10104

Visit us at yenpress.com
facebook.com/yenpress
twitter.com/yenpress
yenpress.tumblr.com
instagram.com/yenpress

First Yen Press Edition:
December 2017

Yen Press is an imprint of Yen Press, LLC.
The Yen Press name and logo are trademarks of Yen Press, LLC.

The publisher is not responsible for websites (or their content) that are not owned by the publisher.

Library of Congress Control Number: 2017954141

ISBNs: 978-0-316-41417-3 (paperback)
978-0-316-44720-1 (ebook)

10 9 8 7 6 5 4 3 2 1

BVG

Printed in the United States of America